About the

USA Today bestselling author Natalie Anderson writes emotional contemporary romance full of sparkling banter, sizzling heat, and uplifting endings – perfect for readers who love to escape with empowered heroines and arrogant alphas who are too sexy for their own good. When not writing, you'll find her wrangling her four children, three cats, two goldish, and one dog...and snuggled in a heap on the sofa with her husband at the end of the day. Follow her at natalie-anderson.com

USA Today bestselling author **Olivia Gates** has published over thirty books in contemporary, action/adventure, and paranormal romance. And whether in today's world or the others she creates, she writes larger than life heroes and heroines worthy of them, the only ones who'll bring those sheikhs, princes, billionaires, or gods to their knees. She loves to hear from readers at oliviagates@gmail.com or on facebook.com/oliviagatesauthor, Twitter @Oliviagates. For her latest news visit oliviagates.com

Kelly Hunter has always had a weakness for fairytales, fantasy worlds, and losing herself in a good book. She is married with two children, avoids cooking and cleaning and, despite the best efforts of her family, is no sports fan! Kelly is, however, a keen gardener and has a fondness for roses. Kelly was born in Australia and has travelled extensively. Although she enjoys living and working in different parts of the world, she still calls Australia home.

Royal Temptation

Royal Temptation:

A Convenient Crown

NATALIE ANDERSON

OLIVIA GATES

KELLY HUNTER

MILLS & BOON

First Published in Great Britain 2023
by Mills & Boon, an imprint of HarperCollins*Publishers* Ltd,
1 London Bridge Street, London, SE1 9GF

www.harpercollins.co.uk

HarperCollins*Publishers*
Macken House, 39/40 Mayor Street Upper,
Dublin 1, D01 C9W8, Ireland

ISBN: 978-0-263-31894-4

This book is produced from independently certified FSC™ paper
to ensure responsible forest management.

For more information visit: www.harpercollins.co.uk/green

Printed and Bound in the UK using 100% Renewable Electricity
at CPI Group (UK) Ltd, Croydon, CR0 4YY

SHY QUEEN IN THE ROYAL SPOTLIGHT

NATALIE ANDERSON

For my own Prince Charming and the four delightful
sprites we've been blessed with.

I love you.

CHAPTER ONE

'Fı?'

Hester Moss heard the front door slam and froze.

'Fifi? Damn it, where the hell are you?'

Fifi?

Hester gaped as it dawned on her just who the owner of that voice was. As Princess Fiorella's assistant while she was studying in Boston, Hester had met a few of the important people the Princess consorted with, but she'd been in the Princess's *brother's* presence only once. That one time there'd been many present and she certainly hadn't spoken to him. But, like everyone, she knew he was outrageous, arrogant and entitled. Not surprising given he ruled the stunning Mediterranean island kingdom that was the world's favourite playground.

She'd had no idea he was coming to visit his sister. It wasn't in the immaculate schedule she kept for the Princess, nor in any correspondence. Surely it would have been all in caps, bold, underlined *and* highlighted if it had been planned? Perhaps he was trying to fly beneath the radar—after all, he attracted huge publicity wherever he went. But if that were the case, why was he *shouting*?

'Fifi?'

No one spoke with such familiarity to the Princess, or with such audible impatience. For a split second Hester considered staying silent and hiding, but she suspected it was only a matter of seconds before he stormed into her bedroom. With a cautious glance at the corner Hester sped to the door and quickly stepped out into their living room.

And there he was. Prince Alek Salustri of Triscari, currently turning the lounge she and the Princess shared into a Lilliputian-sized container—one that was far too small to hold a man like him. Not just a prince. Not just powerful. He was lithe, honed perfection and for a moment all Hester could do was stare—inhaling the way his jet-black suit covered his lean muscled frame. The black shirt beneath the superbly tailored jacket was teamed with a sleek, matte-black tie and he held his dark-lensed aviator sunglasses in his hand, totally exuding impatience and danger. It was more than the bespoke clothing and luxurious style. He was so at ease in his place in the world—monstrously self-assured and confident because he just owned it. Everything. Except right now?

He was angry. The moment his coal-black gaze landed on her, he grew angrier still.

'Oh.' His frown slipped from surly all the way down to thunderous. 'You're the secretary.'

Not for the first time Hester found herself in the position of not being who or what had been hoped for. But she was too practised at masking emotion to flinch. No matter what, she never let anyone see they'd struck a nerve. And being the source of irritation for a spoilt playboy prince? Didn't bother her in the least.

'Your Highness.' She nodded, but her knees had locked too tight to perform a curtsey. 'Unfortunately Princess Fiorella isn't here.'

'I can see that.' He ground his teeth. 'Where is she?'

She kept her hands at her sides, refusing to curl them into fists and reveal any anxiety. It was her job to protect Princess Fiorella from unwanted interruption, only Prince

Alek wasn't just higher up the ladder than most of the people she shielded the Princess from, he was at the very top. The apex predator himself.

'At a bio lab,' Hester drew breath and answered. 'She should be back in about half an hour unless she decides to go for a coffee instead of coming back here right away.'

'Damn.' Another stormy emotion flashed across his face and he turned to pace across the room. 'She's with people?'

Hester nodded.

'And no phone?'

'Her bodyguard has one but the Princess prefers to be able to concentrate in class without interruption. Would you like me to message—?'

'No,' he snapped. 'I need to see her alone. I'll wait for her here.'

He still looked so fierce that Hester was tempted to send a quick message regardless. Except blatantly disobeying his order didn't seem wise.

She watched warily as he paced, brusquely sidestepping Hester's scrupulously clean desk.

'Is there anything I can help you with?' She was annoyed with how nervous her query sounded. She was never nervous dealing with Princess Fiorella. But she wasn't quite sure how to handle this man. Any man, actually.

He paused and regarded her, seeming to see her properly for the first time. She stared back, acutely aware of his coal-black bottomless gaze. Whether those beautiful eyes were soulful or soul*less*, she wasn't sure. She only knew she couldn't tear her own away.

With slow-dawning horror she realised the inanity of her question. As if she could ever help him? He was Prince Alek—the Prince of Night, of Sin…of *Scandal*.

His phone buzzed and he answered it impatiently. 'I've already said no,' he snapped after a moment.

Even from across the room Hester heard the pleading tones of someone remonstrating.

'I will not do that,' the Prince said firmly. 'I've already stated there will be no damn marriage. I have no desire to—' He broke off and looked grim as he listened. 'Then we will find another way. I will not—' He broke off again with a smothered curse and then launched into a volley of Italian.

Hester stared at the top of her desk and wished she could disappear. Clearly he wasn't concerned enough by her presence to bother remaining polite or care that she could hear him berating the ancient laws of his own lands.

The world had been waiting for him to be crowned since his father's death ten months ago, but he hadn't because 'Playboy Prince Alek' had so far shown little interest in acquiring the wife necessary for his coronation to occur. None of those billion *Ten Best Possible Brides* lists scattered across the world's media had apparently inspired him. Nor had the growing impatience of his people.

Perhaps he'd been taking time to get over his father's passing. Hester had seen Princess Fiorella's bereft grief and had tried to alleviate any stresses on the younger woman as best she could because she knew how devastating and how incredibly isolating it was to become an orphan. She'd been pleased to see the Princess had begun spending more time with friends recently. But Prince Alek hadn't retreated from his social life—in fact he'd accelerated it. In the last month he'd been photographed with a different woman every other night as if he were flaunting his refusal to do as that old law decreed and settle down.

Now the Prince growled and shoved his phone back into his pocket, turning to face her. As she desperately tried to think of something innocuous to say a muffled thud echoed from the bedroom she'd stepped out of. Hester maintained her dispassionate expression but it was too much to hope he hadn't heard it.

'What was that?' He cocked his head, looking just like that predator whose acute hearing had picked up the unmistakable sounds of nearby prey. 'Why won't you let me into her room?'

'Nothing—'

'I'm her *brother*. What are you hiding? Is she in there with a man or something?'

Before she could move, the Prince strode past her and opened the door as if he owned the place.

'Of course you would think that,' she muttered crossly, running after him.

He'd halted just inside the doorway. 'What the hell is that?'

'A terrified cat, no thanks to you.' She pushed past him and carefully crept forward so as not to frighten the hissing half-wild thing any more than it already was.

'What's it doing in here?'

'Having dinner.' She gingerly picked it up and opened the window. 'Or at least, it was.'

'I can't believe Fi owns that cat.' He stared at the creature with curling cynicism. 'Not exactly a thoroughbred Prussian Blue, is she?'

Hester's anger smoked. Of course he wouldn't see past the exterior of the grey and greyer, mangled-eared, all but feral cat. '*He* might not be handsome, but he's lonely and vulnerable. He eats in here every day.' She set him down on the narrow ledge.

'How on earth does he get down?' He walked to the window and watched beside her as the cat carefully climbed down to the last available fire escape rung before practically flying the last ten feet to the ground. 'Impressive.'

'He knows how to survive.' But as Hester glared at the

Prince her nose tingled. She blinked rapidly but couldn't hold back her usual reaction.

'Did you just sneeze?' Prince Alek turned that unfathomable stare on her. 'Are you *allergic* to cats?'

'Well, why should he starve just because I'm a bad fit for him?' She plucked a tissue from the packet on the bedside table and blew her nose pointedly.

But apparently the Prince had lost interest already, because he was now studying the narrow bedroom with a scowl.

'I'd no idea Fi read so many thrillers.' He picked up the tome next to the tissues. 'I thought she was all animals. And how does she even move in this space?'

Hester awkwardly watched, trying to see the room through his eyes. A narrow white box with a narrow white bed. A neat pile of books. An occasional cat. A complete cliché.

'Where's she put all her stuff?' He frowned, running a finger over the small wooden box that was the only decorative item in the room.

Hester stilled and faced the wretched moment. 'This isn't Princess Fiorella's bedroom.' She gritted her teeth for a second and then continued. 'It's mine.'

He froze then shot her a look of fury and chagrin combined, snatching his finger from tracing the carved grooves in the lid of the box. 'Why didn't you say so sooner?'

'You stormed in here before I had the chance. I guess you're used to doing anything you want,' she snapped, embarrassed by the invasion of privacy and her own failure to speak up sooner.

But then she realised what she'd said and she couldn't suck it back. She clasped her hands in front of her but kept her head high and her features calm.

Never show them you're afraid.

She'd learned long ago how to act around people with

power over her, how to behave in the hope bullies would get bored and leave her alone. With stillness and calm—on the outside at least.

Prince Alek stared at her for a long moment in stunned silence. But then his expression transformed, a low rumble of laughter sounded and suddenly Hester was the one stunned.

Dimples. On a grown man. And they were gorgeous.

Her jaw dropped as his mood flipped from frustrated to good-humoured in a lightning flash.

'You think I'm spoilt?' he asked as his laughter ebbed.

'Aren't you?' she answered before thinking.

His smile was everything. A wide slash across that perfect face that somehow elevated it beyond angelically beautiful, to warm and human. Even with those perfectly straight white teeth he looked roguish. That twist of his full lips was a touch lopsided and the cute creases in his cheeks appearing and disappearing like a playful cupid's wink.

'I wouldn't think that being forced to find a bride is in the definition of being spoiled,' he said lazily.

'You mean for your coronation?' She could hardly pretend not to know about it when she'd overheard half that phone call.

'Yes. My coronation,' he echoed dryly, leaving her room with that leisurely, relaxed manner that belied the speed and strength of him. 'They won't change that stupid law.'

'Are you finding the democratic process a bitter pill to swallow?' she asked, oddly pleased that the man didn't get everything his own way. 'Won't all the old boys do what you want them to?'

He turned to stare at her coolly, the dimples dispelled, but she gazed back limpidly.

'It's an archaic law,' he said quietly. 'It ought to have been changed years ago.'

'It's tradition,' she replied, walking past him into the

centre of the too-small living room. 'Perhaps there's something appealing about stability.'

'Stability?'

There was something impish in his echo that caused her to swiftly glance back. She caught him eyeing her rear end. A startling wave of heat rose within—exasperating her. She knew he wasn't interested, he was just so highly sexed he couldn't help himself assessing any passing woman. Her just-smoking anger sizzled.

'Of having a monarch who's not distracted and chasing skirt all the time,' she said pointedly.

His lips curled. 'Not *all* the time. I like to rest on Thursdays.' He leaned against the doorframe to her bedroom.

'So it's a rest day today?'

'Of course.' His gaze glanced down her body in a swift assessment but then returned to her face and all trace of humour was gone. 'Do you truly think it's okay to force someone to get *married* before they can do the job they've spent their life training for?'

There was a throb of tension despite the light way he asked the question. He cocked his head, daring her to answer honestly. 'You think I should sacrifice my personal life for my country?'

Actually she thought nothing of the sort but she'd backed herself into a corner by arguing with him. 'I think there could be benefits in an arranged union.'

'Benefits?' His eyebrows lifted, scepticism oozing from his perfect pores. 'What possible benefits could there be?'

Oh, he really didn't want his continuous smorgasbord of women curtailed in any way, did he?

'What if you have the right contract with the right bride?' she argued emotionlessly. 'You both know what you're heading into. It's a cool, logical decision for the betterment of your nation.'

'Cool and logical?' His eyebrows arched. 'What are you, an android?'

Right now, she rather wished she were. It was maddening that she found him attractive—especially when she knew what a player he was. Doubtless this was how every woman who came within a hundred feet of him felt, which was exactly why he was able to play as hard and as frequently as he did. When a man was that blessed by the good-looks gods, mere mortals like her had little defence against him.

'Perhaps when you're King you can lobby for the change.' She shrugged, wanting to close the conversation she never should have started.

'Indeed. But apparently in order to become King I must marry.'

'It's quite the conundrum for you,' she said lightly.

'It has no bearing on my ability to do my job. It's an anachronism.'

'Then why not just make an arrangement with one of your many "friends"?' she muttered with frustration. 'I'm sure they'd all be willing to bear the burden of being your bride.'

He laughed and a gleam flickered in his eyes. 'Don't think I haven't thought about it. Problem is they'd all take it too seriously and assume it was going to be happily ever after.'

'Yes, I imagine that would be a problem.' She nodded, primly sarcastic.

He straightened from the doorway and stepped closer. 'Not for someone like you, though.'

'Pardon?'

'You'd understand the arrangement perfectly well and I get the impression the last thing you'd want is happily ever after with me.'

Too stunned—and somehow hurt—to stop, she answered back sharply. 'I just don't imagine it would be possible.'

Those eyebrows arched again. 'With anyone or only with me?'

She suddenly remembered who it was she'd just insulted. 'Sorry.' She clamped her lips together.

'Don't be, you're quite right,' he said with another low laugh. 'The difficulty I have is finding someone who understands the situation, its limitations, and who has the discretion to pull it off.'

'Quite a tall order.' She wished he'd leave. Or let her leave. Because somehow this was dangerous. *He* was dangerous.

He eyed her for another long moment before glancing to survey the neat desk she'd retreated behind. 'You're the epitome of discretion.'

'Because my desk is tidy?'

'Because you're smart enough to understand such an arrangement.' He lifted his chin and arrogantly speared her with his mesmerising gaze. 'And we have no romantic history to get tangled in,' he drawled. 'In fact, I think you might be my perfect bride.'

There was a look on his face—a mischievous delight tempting her to smile and join the joke. But this wasn't funny.

So she sent him a dismissive glance before turning to stare at her desk. 'No.'

'Why not?' The humour dropped from his voice and left only cool calculation.

Definitely dangerous. Definitely more ruthless than his careless façade suggested.

'You're not serious,' she said.

'Actually, I rather think I am.'

'No,' she repeated, but her voice faded. She forced her arms across her waist to stop herself moving restlessly, to stop that insidious heat from rising, to stop temptation escaping her control.

She *never* felt temptation. She never *felt*. She'd been too busy trying to simply survive for so long…but now?

His gaze didn't leave her face. 'Why not take a moment to think about it?'

'What is there to think about?' she asked with exaggerated disbelief. 'It's preposterous.'

And it was. He'd walked in less than five minutes ago and was now proposing. He was certifiable.

'I don't think so,' he countered calmly. 'I think it could work very well.'

He made it seem easy, as if it were nothing.

'You don't think you should take this a little more seriously instead of proposing to the first woman you see today?'

'Why shouldn't I propose to you?'

Hester breathed slowly, struggling to slow her building anger. 'No one would ever believe you'd want to marry me.'

'Why?'

She mentally begged for mercy. 'Because I'm nothing like the women you normally date.'

His gaze skidded down her in that cool and yet hot assessing way again. 'I disagree.'

She gritted her teeth. She didn't need him to start telling her she was attractive in a false show of charm.

'It's just clothes and make-up.' He stole the wind from her sails. 'Fancy packaging.'

'Smoke and mirrors?' She swallowed the bitterness that rose within her because she just knew how little the world thought of her 'packaging'. 'I meant I'm not from your level of society. I'm not a *princess*.'

'So? These "levels" shouldn't matter.' He shrugged carelessly.

'I'm not even from your country,' she continued, ignoring his interruption. 'It's not what's expected of you.'

He glanced beyond her, seeming to study some speck on the wall behind her. 'I'll do as they dictate, but they don't get to dictate *everything*. I don't want to marry anyone, certainly not a princess. I'll choose who I want.' His gaze flicked back to her, that arrogant amusement gleaming again. 'It would be quite the fairy tale.'

'It would be quite unbelievable,' she countered acerbically. She couldn't believe he was even continuing this conversation.

'Why would it, though?' he pondered. 'You've been working for Fi for how long?'

'Twelve months.'

'But you knew her before that.'

'For three months before, yes.'

Hester had been assigned as Princess Fiorella's roommate when the Princess came to America to study. Hester was four years older and already into her graduate studies so it had been more of a study support role. It turned out that Fiorella was smart as, and hadn't needed much tutoring, but it hadn't been long before Hester had begun helping her with her mountains of correspondence, to the point that Fiorella had asked her to work for her on a formal basis. It had enabled Hester to reduce her other varsity tutoring, she'd finished her thesis and now focused on her voluntary work at the drop-in centre in the city.

She scheduled Fiorella's diaries, replied to messages and emails and organised almost everything without leaving their on-campus apartment. It was perfect.

'Then you've passed all our security checks and proven your ability to meet our family's specific demands.' Prince Alek took another step closer towards her.

Hester stared at him, unable to believe he was still going with this.

'Furthermore it's perfectly believable that we would know each other behind palace walls,' he added. 'No one knows what might have been going on within the privacy of the palace.'

'Sorry to poke holes in your narrative, but I've never actually *been* to the palace,' she pointed out tartly. She'd never been to Triscari. In fact, she'd never been out of the country at all. 'In addition, we've been in the same airspace only once before.'

Prince Alek had escorted Fiorella to the university in lieu of the King all those months ago.

'And this is the first time we've actually spoken,' she finished, proving the impossibility of his proposal with a tilt of her chin.

'I'm flattered you've kept count.' His wolfish smile flashed. 'No one else needs know that though. For all anyone else knows, the times I've called or visited Fi might've been a cover to see you.' He nodded slowly and that thoughtful look deepened as he stepped closer still. 'It could work very well.'

Hester's low-burning anger lifted. How could he assume this would work so easily? Did he think she'd be instantly compliant? Or flattered even? He really was a prince—used to people bowing and scraping and catering to his every whim. Had he ever been told no? If not, his response was going to be interesting.

'Well, thank you all the same, Your Highness.' She cleared her throat. 'But my answer is no. Why don't I tell your sister you'll be waiting for her at your usual hotel?'

She wished Princess Fiorella would hurry up and get home and take her insane brother away.

'Because I'm not there, I'm here and you're not getting rid of me...' He suddenly frowned. 'Forgive me, I've forgotten your name.'

Seriously? He'd just suggested they get married and he didn't even know her name?

'I don't think you ever knew it,' she said wryly. 'Hester Moss.'

'Hester.' He repeated her name a couple more times softly, turning it over in his mouth as if taking the time to decide on the flavour and then savouring it. 'That's very good.' Another smile curved his mouth. 'I'm Alek.'

'I'm aware of who you are, Your Highness.' And she was not going to let him try to seduce her into complying with his crazy scheme.

Except deep inside her something flipped. A miniscule seed long crushed by the weight of loss and bullying now sparked into a tiny wistful ache for adventure.

Prince Alek was studying her as if he were assessing a new filly for his famous stables. That damned smile flickered around his mouth again and the dimples danced— all teasing temptation. 'I think this could work very well, *Hester.*'

His soft emphasis of her name whispered over her skin. He was so used to getting his way—so handsome, so charming, he was utterly spoilt. Had he not actually heard her say the word no or did he just not believe it was possible that she meant it?

'I think you like a joke,' she said almost hoarsely. 'But I don't want to be a joke.'

His expression tightened. 'You wouldn't be. But this could be fun.'

'I don't need fun.'

'Don't you? Then what do you need?' He glanced back into her bedroom. 'You need money.'

'Do I?' she asked idly.

'Everyone normal needs money.'

Everyone normal? Did he mean not royal? 'I don't, I have sufficient,' she lied.

He watched her unwaveringly and she saw the scepticism clearly in his eyes.

'Besides,' she added shakily, 'I have a job.'

'Working for my sister.'

'Yes.' She cocked her head, perceiving danger in his silken tones. 'Or are you going to have me fired if I keep saying no to you?'

His smile vanished. 'First thing to learn—and there will be a lot to learn—I'm not a total jerk. Why not listen to my proposition in full before jumping to conclusions?'

'It didn't cross my mind you were really serious about this.'

'I really am,' he said slowly, as if he didn't quite believe it of himself either. 'I want you to marry me. I'll be crowned King. You'll live a life of luxury in the palace.' He glanced toward her room before turning back to her. 'You'll want for nothing.'

Did he think her sparse little bedroom was miserable? How dared he assume what she might *want*? She wanted for nothing now—not people or things. Not for herself. Except that wasn't *quite* true—and that little seed stirred again, growing bigger already.

'You don't want to stop and think things through?' she asked.

'I've already thought all the things. This is a good plan.'

'For you, perhaps. But *I* don't like being told what to do,' she said calmly. And she didn't like vapid promises of luxury, or the prospect of being part of something that would involve being around so many *people*.

But the Prince just laughed. 'My sister tells you what to do all the time.'

'That's different. She pays me.'

'And I will pay you more. I will pay you very, *very* well.'

Somehow that just made this 'proposal' so much worse.

But, of course, it was the only way this proposal would have ever happened. As a repellent job offer.

He looked amused as he studied her. 'I am talking about a marriage *in name only*, Hester. We don't need to have sex. I'm not asking you to prostitute yourself.'

His brutal honesty shocked her. So did the flood of heat that suddenly stormed along her veins—a torrent of confusion and…other things she didn't wish to examine. She braced, struggling to stay her customary calm self. 'An heir isn't part of the expectation?'

He stiffened. 'Thankfully that is not another onerous legal requirement. We can divorce after a period. I'll then change the stupid law and marry again if I'm ever actually willing. I've years to figure that one out once I'm crowned.'

Hester swallowed. He was clearly not interested in having kids. Nor ever marrying anyone for real. He didn't even try to hide the distaste in his eyes. Too bad for him because providing an heir was going to be part of his job at some point. But not hers.

'We'll marry for no more than a year,' he said decisively. 'Think of it as a secondment. Just a year and then back to normal.'

Back to normal? As the ex-wife of a king? There'd be nothing normal after that. Or of spending a year in his presence as his pretend wife. She was hardly coping with these last ten minutes.

He hadn't even thought to ask if she was single. He'd taken one look at her and assumed everything. And he was right. Which made it worse. Another wave of bitterness swept over her even though she knew it was pathetic. Hester Moss, inconsequential nobody.

'Can you use your country's money to buy yourself a bride?' she blurted bitterly.

'This will be from my personal purse,' he answered

crisply. 'Perhaps you aren't aware I'm a successful man in my own right?'

She didn't want to consider all that she knew about him. But it was there, in a blinding neon lights, the harsh reality of Prince Alek's *reputation*. She couldn't think past it—couldn't believe he could either.

'There's a bigger problem,' she said baldly.

'And that is?'

'You've a very active social life.' She glanced down, unable to hold his gaze as she raised this. 'Am I supposed to have just accepted that?'

'I didn't realise you've been reading my personal diary.'

'I didn't need to,' she said acidly. 'It's all over the newspapers.'

'And you believe everything you read?'

'Are you saying it's not true?'

There was a moment and she knew. It was all *so* true.

'I've not been a monk,' he admitted through gritted teeth. 'But I didn't take advantage of any woman any more than she took advantage of me.' He gazed at her for a long moment and drew in an audible breath. 'Perhaps you've held me at bay. Perhaps I've been hiding my broken heart.'

'By sleeping with anyone willing?' she asked softly, that anger burgeoning again.

'Not *all* of them.' He actually had the audacity to laugh. 'Not even my stamina is that strong.'

Just most of them, then? 'And can you go without that… intimacy for a whole year?'

He stilled completely and stared fixedly at her. 'Plenty of people can and do,' he said eventually. 'Why assume I'm unable to control myself?'

That heat burned her cheeks even hotter. 'It's not the lifestyle you're accustomed to.'

'You'd be amazed what hardships I can handle,' he retorted. 'Will *you* be able to handle it?'

He was well within his rights to question her when she'd done the same to him. But she didn't have to speak the truth. Provoked, she brazenly flung up her chin and snapped, 'Never.'

But he suddenly laughed. 'You're so serene even when you lie.' He laughed again. 'Marry me. Make me the happiest man on earth.'

'If I said yes, it would serve you right,' she muttered.

'Go on, then, Ms Moss,' he dared her softly. 'Put me in my place.'

A truly terrible temptation swirled within her and with it came a terribly seductive image. She shook her head to clear it. She couldn't get mesmerised into madness just because he was unbearably handsome and had humour to boot. 'It's impossible.'

'I think you could do it.' His eyes gleamed and she grew wary of what he was plotting. 'If you don't need money...' he trailed off, his voice lifting with imperceptible disbelief '...then give it to someone who does.'

Hester froze.

His gaze narrowed instantly. 'What's your favourite charity?' He sounded smoothly practical, but she sensed he was circling like a shark, in ever-decreasing circles, having sensed weakness he was about to make his killer move.

'I'll make a massive donation,' he offered. 'Millions. Think of all those worthy causes you could help. All those people. Or is it animals—cats, of course. Perhaps the planet? Your pick. Divide it amongst them all, I don't care.'

'Because you're cynical.' But her heart thudded. Because she'd give the money to people who she knew desperately needed help.

'Actually, I'm not at all,' he denied with quiet conviction. 'If we find ourselves in the position to be able to help others in any way, or to leave the place in a better condition than which we found it, then we should, shouldn't we? It's called being decent.'

He pinned her with that intense gaze of his. Soulful or soul*less*? Her heart beat with painfully strong thuds.

'You can't say no to that, can you?' he challenged her.

He was questioning her humanity? Her compassion? She stared back at him—he had no idea of her history, and yet he'd struck her with this.

'If you don't need it,' he pressed her, 'isn't there someone in your life who does?'

There were very, very few people in her life. But he'd seen. He knew this was the chink in her armour. And while she really wanted to say no again, just to have it enforced for once in his precious life, how could she not say yes?

At the drop-in centre she'd been trying to help a teen mother and her toddler for the past three weeks. Lucia and her daughter, Zoe, were alone and unsupported having been rejected by family and on the move ever since. If someone didn't step in and help them, Lucia was at risk of having Zoe taken and put into care. Hester had given Lucia what spare cash she could and tried to arrange emergency accommodation. She knew too well what it was to be scared and without security or safety or a loving home.

'You're emotionally blackmailing me,' she said lowly, struggling to stop those thoughts from overwhelming her.

'Am I?' He barely breathed. 'Is it working?'

He watched her for another long moment as she inwardly wrestled with the possibilities. She knew how much it mattered for Lucia and Zoe to stay together. Her parents had fought to stay together and to keep her with them and when they'd died she'd discovered how horrible it was to be foisted upon unwilling family. With money came resources and power and freedom.

Prince Alek sent her a surprisingly tentative smile.

'Come on, Hester.' He paused. 'Wouldn't it be a little bit fun?'

Did she look as if she needed 'fun'? Of course she did. She knew what she looked like. Most of the time she didn't care about it, but right now?

'You like to do the unpredictable.' She twisted her hands together and gripped hard, trying to hold onto reality. 'You delight in doing that.'

'Doesn't everyone like to buck convention sometimes? Not conform to the stereotype others have put them in?'

He was too astute because now she thought of those bullies—her cousins and those girls at school—who'd attacked her looks, her lack of sporting prowess, her lack of *parents*…the ones who'd been horrifically mean.

'I *really* don't want to be used as a joke.' She'd been that before and was sure the world would see their marriage that way—it was how he was seeing it, right? Nothing to be taken seriously. And she was too far from being like any woman he'd make his bride.

'Again, I'm not a jerk. I'll take you seriously and I'll ensure everyone around us does too. I'll make a complete commitment to you for the full year. I promise you my loyalty, honesty, integrity and *fidelity*. I only ask for the same in return. We could be a good team, Hester.' He glanced again at her desk. 'I know you do a good job. Fi raves about you.'

Hester's pride flickered. She did do a good job. And she knew she was too easily flattered. But this was different, this was putting herself in a vulnerable position. This was letting all those people from her past *see* her again. She'd be more visible than ever before—more vulnerable.

But hadn't she vowed not to let anyone hurt her again?

'Working for Princess Fiorella is a good job for me,' she reminded herself as much as informed him. 'I won't be able to come back to it.'

'You won't need to,' he reasoned. 'You'll be in a position to do anything you want. You'll have complete independence. You'll be able to buy your own place, fill it with cats and books about serial killers. All I'm asking for is one year.'

One year was a long time. But what she could do for Lucia and Zoe? She could change their lives *for ever*. If someone had done that for her parents? Or for her? But no one had and she'd spent years struggling. While she was in a better place now, Zoe wasn't.

Hester squared her shoulders. If she could survive what she already had, then she could survive this too. And maybe, with a little change in 'packaging', she could subvert that stereotype those others had placed on her—and yes, wouldn't that be a little 'fun'?

That long-buried seed unfurled, forming the smallest irrepressible bud. An irresistible desire for adventure, a chance impossible to refuse. She couldn't say no when he was offering her the power to change everything for someone so vulnerable. And for herself.

'I think you'll like Triscari,' he murmured easily. 'The weather is beautiful. We have many animals. We're most famous for our horses, but we have cats too...'

She gazed at him, knowing he was wheedling because he sensed success.

'All right,' she said calmly, even as she was inwardly panicking already. 'One year's employment.'

Predatory satisfaction flared in his eyes. Yes. This was a man who liked to get his way. But he was wise enough not to punch the air with an aggressive fist. He merely nodded. Because he'd expected her acquiescence all along, hadn't he?

'It'll cost you,' she added quickly, feeling the sharp edge of danger press.

'All the money?' His smile quirked.

'Yes,' she answered boldly, despite her thundering heart. 'So much money.'

'You have plans.' He sounded dispassionately curious. 'What are you going to do with it?'

'You want your privacy, I want mine,' she snapped. 'If I want to bathe in a tub full of crisp, new dollar bills, that's my prerogative.' She wasn't telling him or anyone. Not even Lucia and Zoe, because she didn't want any of this to blow back on them. This would be a secret gift.

'Wonderful. Let me know when you want them delivered.' He looked amused. 'Shall we shake on it?'

Gravely she placed her hand in his, quelling the shiver inside as he grasped her firmly. He didn't let her go, not until she looked up. The second she did, she was captured by that contrary mix of caution and curiosity and concern in his beautiful eyes. She had the horrible fear they were *full* of soul.

It didn't seem right for him to bow before her and, worse, she couldn't make herself respond in kind, not even to incline her head. She couldn't seem to move—her lungs had constricted. And her heart? That had simply stopped.

'Let's go get married, Hester,' he suggested, his lightness at odds with that ever-deepening intensity of his gaze. 'The sooner the better.'

CHAPTER TWO

ALEK COULDN'T QUITE believe what he'd just established. But that reckless part of him—that sliver of devilishness—felt nothing but euphoria. Here she was. The method by which he'd finally please the courtiers and parliamentarians who'd been pestering him for months. The means by which he'd find his freedom and fulfil his destiny at the same time.

Ms Hester Moss.

Personal assistant. Calm automaton. Perfect wife. Yes, he was going to give his country their most inoffensive, bland Queen. In her navy utility trousers, her crisp white tee shirt, her large-rimmed glasses and her hair in that long, purely functional ponytail at the nape of her neck, she looked least like any royal bride ever. Not tall, not especially slender, not styled and definitely not coated in that sophisticated confidence he was used to. In that sense she was right, she was nothing like the women he usually dated. And that was perfect. Because he didn't want to date her. And she definitely didn't want to date him. This would be a purely functional arrangement. No sex. No complications.

She had something better to offer him. She was self-contained, precise, earnest, and—he'd bet—*dutiful*. She'd be efficient, discreet, courteous and they'd co-exist for this

limited time in complete harmony And she wasn't a dragon
or a bitch; she seemed too bloodless to be either. Actually,
now he thought about it, she struck him as *too* controlled,
too careful altogether. Irritation rippled beneath his skin.
He knew she judged him—hell, who didn't? But he wanted
to scratch the surface and find *her* faults. After all, everyone had flaws and weaknesses. Everyone had something
that made their blood boil. He'd seen it briefly when she'd
referenced his 'lifestyle', when she'd called him out for
being 'spoiled', when she'd felt the need to snap *no* at him.

But he'd just got her to say yes to him and damn if it
didn't feel good. Only now he was wondering *why* she
wanted the pots of gold.

He could pull her file from security but immediately
rejected the idea. His father would never have allowed Fiorella near someone unsuitable, so there could be nothing
in her past to cause concern. He'd satisfy his curiosity the
old-fashioned way. Face to face. The prospect of breaking
through her opaque, glass façade and making her reveal
the snippets of herself that she seemed determined to keep
secret was surprisingly appealing. The only question was
how he'd go about it.

Now he had her hand in his and he was gazing into her
eyes—a breath away for the first time. Even behind the
large-framed glasses, he could appreciate their colour—
pure gold, a warm solid hue—and it seemed she wasn't
averse to a little smoke and mirrors because she had to be
wearing mascara. Her eyelashes were abnormally thick.
Heat burned across the back of his neck and slowly swept
down his spine, around his chest, skimming lower and
lower still. Startled by the unexpected sensation, he tensed,
unable to release her cool hand, unable to cease staring
into her amazing, leonine eyes.

'Alek?'

He blinked and turned his head. 'Fi.'

His sister was gaping at their linked hands.

He felt a tug and turned back to see awkwardness swarm over Hester's face. Slowly he obeyed her wordless plea and released her hand.

'What are you doing here?' Fiorella stepped forward, her astonishment obvious. 'What's going on?'

He drew a sharp breath and slammed into a snap decision. He would do this with supreme discretion. No one but he and Hester would know the truth and if they could pass the Fifi test here and now, they'd be fine with the rest of the world. 'We didn't intend to surprise you this way,' he said smoothly. 'But Hester and I are engaged.'

'Engaged? To *Hester*?' Fi's eyes bugged. *'No way.'*

'Fi—'

'You don't even *know* each other.' Fi was clearly stunned.

'That's where you're wrong. Again,' he muttered. 'We know each other far better than you think.'

'But...' Fi looked from him to Hester and that frown deepened on her face. 'No way.'

He glanced at Hester and saw she'd paled. She shoved her hands into the horrendously practical pockets of her cotton drill trousers and stood eerily still, her façade determinedly uncrackable.

'Hester?' Fiorella gazed at her assistant, a small frown formed between her brows. 'I know you've been distracted lately and not as available...'

Alek glanced at Hester and saw she'd gone paler still. His instincts were engaged—what had been distracting her? The whisper of vulnerability prickled his senses.

'She works for *me*.' Fifi pulled his attention back with her quiet possessiveness. 'And I don't want you to...mess her around.'

Hester's eyes widened and colour scurried back into her cheeks. But to his astonishment, a pretty smile broke through her tense, expressionless façade. His jaw dropped and for a moment he had the oddest wish that he'd been the one to make her smile like that. She'd suddenly looked luminous and *soft*. But then the smile faded and her self-contained neutrality was restored.

'I'm a big girl, Princess Fiorella,' Hester said in that careful, contained way she had. 'I can take care of myself.'

Alek realised Hester had feared Fi disapproved of *her*. And she was hugely relieved to discover she didn't.

'I know you had no idea,' Hester added as she gestured towards him. 'But we had our reasons for that.'

Instinctively he reached out and clasped her hand back in his. A stunningly strong ripple of possessiveness shimmered through him. Again acting on instinct, he laced his fingers through hers and locked his grip. For the proof in front of Fifi, right?

His sister now stared again at their interlinked hands, her eyes growing round before she flashed a hurt look up at Alek. 'Is this because of that stupid requirement?'

'This is because it is what both your brother and I *want*.'

Hester's faintly husky emphasis on the 'want' tightened his skin.

'I'm so sorry to have kept this from you, but it's been quite…tough.'

'And I'm sorry for the short notice,' Alek added as Hester faltered. 'But I'm taking Hester back with me immediately.'

'To Triscari? Now?' Fi clasped her hands in front of her chest. 'You're for real? Like really for real?'

That light flush swept more deeply across Hester's face as Alek confirmed it with a twinge of regret. His sister was young and unspoiled but he found himself watching Hester more closely for clues as to what was going on beneath her still exterior.

'It's like a fairy tale,' Fifi breathed. 'Oh, Alek, this is wonderful.'

Hester's hand quivered in his and he tightened his hold.

'You're really leaving right away?' Fi asked.

'It's been difficult,' Alek said honestly. 'It's best we get back to Triscari. There's a lot for Hester to take in.'

Worry dulled the delight in Fi's eyes.

'It's okay. Everything's in your diary and you can always text me with any problems,' Hester said earnestly. 'I can keep answering your correspondence—that's the bulk of what I do for you and there's no reason why I can't continue.'

Alek bit his tongue to stop himself interrupting with all the reasons why she wasn't going to be able to keep working for his sister.

'Are you sure?' Fi's relief was audible.

'Hester can help train someone up to take over from her quite quickly.' He sent Hester a shamelessly wicked smile. 'After all, you'll be busy managing your own mail shortly.'

A mildly alarmed look flickered in her eyes before she smiled politely back.

'Well.' Fi drew breath. 'I have to go, I'm late to meet my friend. I only called in to tell Hester I need her to...never mind. I can do it. I'll leave you to...go.' She glanced again between him and Hester. 'I still can't believe it.'

Fi stepped in and Alek gave her a one-armed hug.

He met Hester's gaze over the top of Fi's head and saw the glint of amusement in her eyes. She was very good at managing her emotions and at managing a volatile Fiorella. A volatility he knew he had in common with his sister on occasion.

When Fi left, he released Hester's hand—with a surprising amount of reluctance.

'Thank you,' he said. He needed to focus on the important things. Like fabricating their story. 'You're good at lying.'

'I'm good at saying what's necessary for self-preservation,' she replied. 'That's a different skill.'

His senses sharpened. Self-preservation? Why was that?

'You really want us to maintain this "relationship" in front of Princess Fiorella?' she asked too calmly.

'For now.' He nodded. 'I don't want to risk any inadvertent revelations and I don't want her to worry.'

'She's your sister, she's going to be concerned about your *happiness*.'

'I thought she seemed more worried about you than me.' He shot her an ironic glance.

'She doesn't need to worry about me.' Hester gazed down at her desk. 'I'm fine. I can handle anything.'

He had the odd feeling she could but that didn't mean that she *should*. 'It seems the pretence is under way, Hester. This is your last chance to back out.'

She was silent for a moment, but then lifted her serene face to his. 'No, let's do this. You should be crowned.'

Really? He didn't think she was in this for *his* benefit. She'd become rich; that was the real reason, wasn't it? Except he didn't think it was. What did she plan to do with the money?

He frowned. It shouldn't matter, it wasn't his business.

But what had she been so 'distracted' with lately? Not a man, or she'd not have said yes to him. He'd bet it was someone else, someone she wanted the money for.

He huffed out a breath and willed his curiosity to ebb. He didn't need to know any more. She was palace employed, therefore palace perfect. Contained, aloof, efficient. She even maintained a polite distance from Fi, who he knew was physically demonstrative. He now realised part of Fi's shock—and reason for her eventual belief—had been because he and Hester were *touching*. Fiorella hadn't hugged Hester when she'd left. He was sure the reserve came from Hester—strictly observing her role as employee, not confidante or friend. Doubtless she was all about 'professional boundaries', or something. It was evident in the way she dressed too. The utilitarian clothes and sensible black canvas shoes were almost a services uniform from the nineteen-forties. But her hourglass figure couldn't quite be hidden even by those ill-tailored trousers. Her narrow waist and curving hips held all the promise of soft, lush pillow for a man...that *stability* she'd made him think of.

But she made him think about other things too—like why did she live in that prison-like cell of a bedroom? Why was it so lacking in anything personal other than a mangy stray cat, a broken wooden box and a pile of second-hand books?

She was like a walled-off puzzle with several pieces missing. Happily, Alek quite enjoyed puzzles and he had a year to figure her out. Too easy—and there was no reason they couldn't be *friends*. He could ignore the unexpected flares of physical interest. If his desperate speed-dating of the last month had proven anything to him, it was that the last thing he wanted was anything remotely like a real relationship. Definitely not a true marriage. Not for a very long time. As for that vexed issue providing his kingdom with an heir...that he was just going to put off for as long as possible. Somehow he'd find a way to ensure any child of his didn't suffer the same constraints he had.

'We should make plans.' He moved forward to her desk. 'I need to contact the palace. You need to pack.' He glanced over to where she stood worryingly still. 'Or...?'

'How are we going to end this?' she asked pensively. 'In a year. What will we say?'

He was relieved she wasn't pulling out on him already. 'I'll take the blame.'

'No. Let me,' she said quietly. 'You're the King.'

'No.' He refused to compromise on this. 'You'll be vili-fied.'

Double standards abounded, wrong as it was, and he wasn't having her suffer in any way because of this. He'd do no harm. And she was doing him a huge favour.

'I don't want to be walked over,' she said a little un-evenly. *'I'll* do the stomping. Keep your reputation. Mine doesn't matter.'

He stared at her. She stood more still than ever—de-fensively prim, definitely prickly—and yet she wanted to be reckless in that?

'You'd sacrifice everything,' he tried to inform her gently.

'Actually, I'll sacrifice nothing,' she contradicted. 'I don't care what they say about me.'

No one didn't care. Not anyone human, anyway. And he'd seen her expression change drastically when Fi had returned, so Hester was definitely human. She'd been ter-rified of his sister's reaction—of her disapproval. Which meant she liked and cared about Fi. And she cared about doing the stomping.

Now he studied her with interest, opting not to argue. He'd had all the wins so far, so he could let this slide until later because he was totally unhappy with the idea of her taking the responsibility for their marriage 'breakdown'.

'We'll finalise it nearer the time.'

She softened fractionally.

'You know they'll want all the pomp and ceremony for this wedding.' He rolled his eyes irreverently, wanting to make her smile again. 'All the full regalia.'

'You really don't think much of your own traditions, do you?'

'Actually, I care greatly about my country and my peo-ple and *most* of our customs. But I do find the feathers on the uniform impede my style a little.'

'Feathers?' She looked diverted and suddenly, as he'd hoped, her soft smile peeked out. Followed by a too-brief giggle. 'So, you really mean smoke and mirrors?'

'It's a little ridiculous, I'm afraid.' He nodded with a grin. 'But not necessarily wrong.'

'Okay. Smoke. Mirrors. Feathers.' But she seemed to steel herself and shot him a searching look. 'You don't think everyone will know the wedding is only for the coronation?'

'Not if we convince them otherwise.'

'And how do we do that?'

'We just convinced Fi, didn't we?'

'She's a romantic.'

'So we give them romance.' Fire flickered along his limbs and he tensed to stop himself stepping closer and seeing what kind of 'romance' he could spontaneously conjure with her. What he might discover beneath her serene but strong veneer. 'Trust me, Hester. We'll make this believable. We'll make it brilliant.' He cocked his head. 'I think with some work we can look like a couple in love.'

Her eyes widened. 'But there's no need for us to *touch*.' She sounded almost breathless with horror. 'Nothing like that. We'll be very circumspect, won't we?'

Alek suppressed his laugh. His officials were going to love her, given how much they loathed his usual less than circumspect affairs. And if she presented this shy, blushing bride act to the public, she'd melt all hearts.

'You mean no public displays of affection?' he queried more calmly than he felt.

'That's right.'

Was she serious? 'None at *all*?'

He keenly watched her attempt to maintain her unruffled expression, but tell-tale colour surged over her skin and ruined her proud attempt. But she didn't reply and he realised she was utterly serious. So what about *private* displays of affection?

The fierce desire to provoke her came from nowhere and astounded him. The ways he'd make her blush all over? To make her smile and sigh and *scream*?

The immediate cascade of thoughts was so hot and heady, he tensed all over again. It was just the challenge, right? She'd initially told him no with unapologetic bluntness, while excoriating his social life. Now she reckoned she didn't want him to touch her?

Okay, no problem.

Yet surely he wasn't the only one feeling this shocking chemistry? The magnetic pull was too strong to be one-sided. Her colour deepened as the silence stretched and thickened. Of course she felt it, he realised, feeling a gauche fool. It was the whole reason for her complete blushathon.

Hester stared as he hesitated for what felt like for ever. Her whole body felt on fire—with utter and absolute mortification—but this was something she needed not just to clarify, but to make certain—iron-clad in their agreement. It suddenly seemed *essential*.

'Okay,' he agreed, but amusement flitted around his mouth. 'I wasn't about to suggest we practise or anything.'

'Good.' She finally breathed out. 'That would just be stupid.'

'Indeed. I don't need to practise. I know how to kiss.'

Hester didn't quite know how to respond. She wasn't about to admit how totally lacking in kissing experience she was. That heat beat all over her body, but she counted breaths in and out, to restore outward calm at least. Inside she was still frying.

'Because, just so you know, we will have to kiss. Twice, if you can bring yourself to agree.' He gazed at her steadily. 'During the wedding service, which will, of course, be live-streamed. We'll need to kiss after the commitment during the ceremony and once again on the steps outside the church afterwards.'

'Live-streamed?' Her lungs constricted. 'From a church?'

'In the palace chapel, yes. It's just the part we're both playing, Hester.'

The palace chapel? It really was the stuff of fairy-tale fiction. As long as she remembered that was all it was, then she could go through with it, right? As long as she remembered what she could do for Lucia and Zoe.

'Two kisses,' she conceded briefly.

She was sure they'd be chaste pecks, given they were going to be live-streamed and all. Not even the outrageous Prince Alek would put on a raunchy show for the world with his convenient bride. There was no need for him to ever know she'd never been kissed before.

'Do you think I can hold your hand at the banquet afterwards? Look at you? Smile?'

He was teasing her so she answered with even more determined seriousness. 'Depending on the circumstances, I might even smile back.'

'Depending on the circumstances?' he echoed idly. 'There's a challenge.'

But he sat down at her desk, grabbed a blank piece of paper, borrowed one of her favourite pens and began writing. She watched, fascinated as the paper filled with small squares and a task or reminder beside each. Efficiency, list-making and prioritising? Who'd have thought? After a few moments he studied the list and nodded to himself before pulling out his phone and tapping the screen.

'Good news, Marc. I'm to be married after all. I know you've had the wedding plans in place for months so now you can press "go",' he said with a bitter-edged smile. 'We'll journey home this afternoon.' He paused for a long moment. 'You think that's achievable? Is that long enough for—?' He paused again. 'You flatter me, Marc, but if you're sure.' A few moments later he rang off. 'We're getting married in ten days and the coronation will take place in the week after.'

'Ten days?' Hester echoed.

'I know, sooner than I'd have thought too. But it seems to have been planned since before I was born. It's going to be a state holiday apparently.' He scribbled more items on his ever-increasing list. 'They've got plans for everything—processions, funerals, baptisms.' He glanced across at her with a laughing grin. 'My obituary is already written. They just update it every so often.'

'You're kidding.'

'No. They're prepared for everything. I think they thought I'd get killed in a plane crash or something a few years ago.' He suddenly chuckled. 'Don't look so shocked.'

'It just seems...' She trailed off, wary of expressing her thoughts. But it seemed sad somehow, to have your life so meticulously planned, documented, constrained. Was it so surprising he'd rebelled against it?

'Don't you have every eventuality covered in your management of Fi's correspondence?' He gestured at her immaculate desk. 'I'm assuming you're a lists and contingencies person.'

'Well, yes, but—'

'They just have more lists than you.' He gazed down at his list. 'You'll need a wedding dress. It would be diplomatic if you choose a Triscarian designer. Would that be tolerable?'

'Of course,' she mumbled, but a qualm of panic struck. What had she been thinking? How could she pull off a live-streamed wedding with millions of people watching? Every last one would pick apart, not just her outfit, but every aspect of her appearance. She wasn't a leggy beautiful brunette like Princess Fiorella. She was on the shorter, wider sides of average—as her aunt had so often commented when comparing her to her gazelle-like, mean cousins.

She took a breath and squared her shoulders. She *didn't* care. She'd resolved long ago never to care again. Because the simple fact was she could never live up to the expectation or never please all of them, so why worry about *any*?

'My assistant will arrange for some samples to be brought to the palace.' He wrote yet another item in his harsh scrawl.

'There's not much time to make a dress or adjustments in ten days.' There wasn't much time to get her head around anything, let alone everything.

'They'll have a team. We'll do some preparation as well, how to pose for photos and the like.'

How to *what*? 'You mean you're going to put me through some kind of princess school?'

'Yes.' He met her appalled gaze with laughter. 'There'll be lots of cameras. It can be blinding at first.'

'Perhaps Princess Fiorella can guide me,' she suggested hopefully.

'*I* will,' he replied firmly. 'Fi needs to meet her obligations here. She'll join us only for the ceremony.'

'But it's okay for me to walk out on her right away?'

'Your obligations to me and to Triscari now take precedence.' He added something else to his endless list.

Hester glanced about the room, suddenly thinking about all the things *she* was going to need to achieve. 'I'll have to—'

'Find someone to feed the cat.' He nodded and wrote that down too.

'Yes,' she muttered, internally touched that he'd remembered.

'At my expense, of course,' he added. 'Do you have other work obligations we need to address?'

'I can sort it.' She didn't flatter herself that she was indispensable. No one was. She could disappear from the college and very few people would notice. She'd disappeared before no trouble at all. But she was going to need to sort out Lucia. 'Um…' She cleared her throat. 'I'm going to need…'

'The money?' He lifted his head to scrutinise her and waggled his pen between forefinger and thumb. 'You want your first bathtub full of dollar bills?'

The intensity in his eyes made it hard to keep her equilibrium.

'A few bundles would be good,' she mumbled.

He tore another piece of paper from the pad and put it on the opposite side of the desk in front of her. 'Write down the details and I'll have it done.'

He didn't ask more about why she wanted it. She half hoped he understood it wasn't for her.

'What family would you like to invite?' he asked. 'You can have as many as you like. Write the list and I'll have them arrange invitations, transport and accommodation.'

She froze, her pen hovering just above the paper. Family?

She eventually glanced at him. He'd stopped writing and was watching her as he waited for her reply with apparently infinite patience. She wanted to look away from his eyes, but couldn't. And she'd said this so many times before, this shouldn't be different. But it was. Her breathing quickened. She just needed to say it. Rip the plaster off. That way was best. 'My parents died when I was a child.'

He didn't bat an eyelid. 'Foster parents, then? Adoptive? Extended family?'

She swallowed to push back the rising anxiety. 'Do I have to invite them?'

His gaze remained direct and calm. 'If you don't invite anyone, there will be comment. I'm used to comment, so that doesn't bother me. But if it will bother you, then I'd suggest inviting but then keeping them at a distance. That would be the diplomatic route that the courtiers will prefer.'

'What would you prefer?' Her heart banged against her ribcage.

'I want you to do whatever will help you get through the day.'

That understated compassion shook her serenity and almost tempted her to confide in him. But she barely thought about her 'family'. She couldn't bear to. And she hadn't seen them in years. 'If they do come, will I have to spend time much with them...?'

He looked thoughtful and then the corners of his eyes crinkled. 'I can be very possessive and dictatorial.'

'You mean you'll abuse your power?' She couldn't supress another giggle.

'Absolutely.' His answering grin was shameless and charming and pleased. 'That's what you'd expect from me, right?'

Her heart skipped. 'The perks of being a prince...'

But her own smile faded as she considered the ramifications. She'd never wanted to see those people again, but this was an extremely public wedding. If she didn't invite them there'd be more than mere speculation: journalists would sniff about for stories. If they dug deep old wounds might be opened, causing more drama. Anyway, her extended family liked nothing more than status, so if she invited them to the royal wedding of the decade, they'd be less likely to say anything. They'd never admit they'd disowned her father, spurned her pregnant mother, and caused her teenage parents to run away like some modern-day Romeo and Juliet. They'd never admit that they'd only taken her in after the accident for 'the look of it'. Or that they'd never let her forget how she was the unplanned and unwanted 'trash' who'd ruined the perfect plan they'd had for her father's life.

'Do you have someone you'd like to escort you down the aisle?' he asked.

She noted with a wry smile that he didn't suggest she be given away. 'It's fine, I'll do that alone.' She looked at the paper in front of her. 'But perhaps Princess Fiorella might act as bridesmaid?' She wasn't sure if it was appropriate, but there really wasn't anyone else she could think of.

'That would work very well.'

'Perfect for your pining heart narrative,' she joked to cover the intensity of the discussion.

'The media will seize on this as soon as they hear anything,' Alek said solemnly. 'They will pry into your private life, Hester. Are you prepared for that?'

'It's fine.' She went back to writing her own list to avoid looking at him. 'They can say what they like, print what they like.'

'No skeletons in the closet?' he queried gently. 'It wouldn't bother me if there were. Heaven knows I have them.' She heard his smile in his voice before it dropped lower. 'But I wouldn't want you to suffer.'

She shook her head and refused to look up at him again. 'It's fine.'

'There are no ex-boyfriends who are going to sell their stories about you to the press?'

Her blush built but she doggedly kept looking down. Why did he have to press this? He didn't need to know.

'They're harder on women,' he said huskily. 'Wrong as that is.'

'There are no skeletons. I was lonely as a teenager. I wasn't really close to anyone.' Uncomfortable, she glanced up to assure him and instantly regretted it because she was caught in the coal-black depths of his eyes. 'My life to date has been very boring,' she said flatly. 'There's literally nothing to write about.'

Nothing in her love life anyway. She couldn't break free of his unwavering gaze and slowly that heat curled within her—embarrassment, right? But she also felt an alarming temptation to lean closer to him. Instead she froze. 'Is it a problem?'

'Not at all.'

She forced herself to focus on listing the details he'd asked for, rather than the strange sensations burgeoning within her.

This marriage was a few months of adventure. She had to treat it like that. If she'd been crazy enough to say yes to such an outlandish, impulsive proposal, she might as well go all the way with it. 'Will your assistant be able to find me a hairdresser?' She pushed past her customary independence and made herself ask for the help she needed. 'And maybe some other clothes...'

'You'd like that?'

She glanced up again and saw he was still studying her intently.

'All the smoke and mirrors?' she joked lamely again. 'I'd like all the help I can get to pull this off.'

'Then I'll have it arranged. Write down your size and I'll have some things brought to the plane.'

Heat suffused her skin again but she added it to her list before pushing the paper towards him. 'I think that's everything.'

'Good,' he said briskly. 'Start packing. I have several calls to make.'

Relieved, she escaped into her small bedroom. With an oblique reference to 'a family matter', her volunteer coordinator at the drop-in centre expressed regret but understanding. It took only a moment to open an anonymous email account from which she could make the arrangements for her support for Lucia. Packing her belongings took only a moment too. She picked up the antique wooden box Alek had touched and carefully put it into the small backpack she'd used when she'd run away all those years ago. Her clothes fitted easily into the one small suitcase she'd acquired since.

'That's everything?' He stared in frank amazement at her suitcase when she returned to the lounge.

'I don't need much.'

'You're going to need a little more than that.' He reached out to take the case from her. 'It's probably good that we leave before Fi gets back. Saves on all the questions she'll have been stockpiling over the last hour.'

But Hester didn't follow him as he headed towards the door. 'Are you absolutely certain about this, Your Highness?'

He turned back to face her. 'Of course I'm certain,' he said with absolute princely arrogance. 'And you need to call me Alek.'

'Okay.' She hoisted her backpack and walked towards the door.

But he blocked her path. 'Do it now. Practise so it slips off your tongue naturally. Call me Alek.'

'I will.'

He still didn't move to let her past. A frisson of awareness, danger, defiance, shivered within her as she defiantly met his gaze.

'Say, *Alek is wonderful*. Now,' he commanded.

She glared harder at him. 'Alek is bossy.'

'Good enough.' He stepped back, the distance between them enabling her to breathe again. But his slow smile glinted with full wickedness. 'For now.'

CHAPTER THREE

SWIFT WASN'T THE word for Alek's modus operandi. When he'd decided something, he moved. Fast.

'You're very used to getting your own way,' Hester said as she followed him downstairs out of the campus residence she'd called home for the last three years.

'You think?' He shot her a look. 'I have the feeling I might not get everything quite on my terms for a while.'

'Is that such a threat?' Without thinking, another small smile sparkled free.

'Not at all,' he denied with relish. 'I enjoy a challenge.'

Oh, she wasn't a *challenge*. She was never going to be some kind of toy for this notorious playboy. But she forgot any flattening reply she was mulling when she saw the entourage waiting outside. Large, almost armoured vehicles were staffed by a phalanx of ferociously physical suited and booted men armed with earpieces and dark eyewear and who knew what else beneath the black fabric of their jackets. Alek guided her directly to the middle car. She was absurdly glad of its size and comfort, air conditioning and sleek silence. Her pulse hammered as they drove through the streets and she tried to stop herself snatching looks at him.

Lucia and Zoe will be secure and together.

That was what she needed to focus on. *Not his dimples*.

But her nerves mounted. The fluttering in her tummy was because she'd never flown in a plane before, that was all.

That's not all.

This whole thing was insane. She needed to tell him she'd made a mistake. Back out and beg him to help that family—surely he would once he heard about Lucia's struggle?

'Okay?' Alek was watching her with astute amusement.

She thought about Lucia and Zoe again. She thought about living on a warm island for a while. She thought about full financial freedom and independence for the rest of her life.

'Okay.' She nodded.

They went through a side door of the airport terminal. A uniformed woman escorted them directly to the plane.

'Everyone is aboard?' Alek asked.

'Yes, sir. We're cleared for departure as soon as you're seated.'

Hester paused in the doorway and frowned. This wasn't a small private jet like ones she'd seen in the movies. This was a commercial airliner. Except it wasn't. There weren't rows of cramped seats and masses of people. This was a lounge with sofas and small armchairs around wooden tables. Accented with back-lit marble and mirrors, it was so beautiful, it was like a *hotel*.

She gaped. 'Is this really a plane?'

He smiled as he gestured for her to sit in one of the wide white leather armchairs and showed her where the seat belt hid. 'I'll give you the tour once we're in the air. Can I take your bag?'

'Can I keep it with me?' Her box was in there and it contained her most precious things.

'In this compartment, here.' He stowed it and took the seat opposite hers. 'I've arranged for a stylist to fly with us, so you can make a start, and I've had an assistant pull together a report on some key staffers so you can get ahead of the game on who's who at the palace.' He pulled a tablet from another hidden compartment. 'I don't find the palace intimidating, but I was born there so it's normal for me.' He shrugged his shoulders.

She nodded, unable to speak or smile. It was enough effort to stay calm. Was she really about to leave the country? About to marry a man who was destined to become a king? About to launch into the air in a giant tin can?

'Nervous?'

'Of course,' she muttered honestly. 'But once I've done some preparation I'll feel better.'

His pilots would have years of expertise behind them. She breathed carefully, managing her emotions. After a while she could glance out of the window. They'd climbed steeply and now the plane levelled out.

'Follow me,' Alek said, unfastening his seat belt.

She fumbled and he reached across and undid her belt for her.

'Are you—?'

'I'm fine,' she interrupted and quickly stood, taking a pace away from him. He was too close and she was unable to process the spaciousness. 'Are all private planes this big?'

'No,' he smirked. 'Mine's the biggest.'

'Of course it is,' she muttered. 'Your ego could handle nothing less.'

'Miaow.' He laughed. 'I see why you're friends with that grumpy cat.'

Beyond the private lounge he pointed out a bedroom suite—with more marble and mirrors—then led her through another lounge to another cabin that was more like the business-class seating she'd seen in the movies. Half the seats were full—several of those suited bodyguard

types, then others who looked like assistants. As she and
Alek neared, they all scrambled to stand.

'Please.' Alek smiled and gestured for them to remain
seated. 'Is your team ready, Billie?'

'Of course, Your Highness.' A slim jeans-clad woman
stood, as did another couple of people.

'This is Hester,' Alek said briefly when they were back
in the second lounge. 'I'll leave you to introduce your team.
Please take good care of her.' He sent her a small mocking
smile and headed back to the front of the plane.

That was it? There were no instructions? She had no
idea what she was supposed to do.

'We're here to help you, Ms Moss,' Billie said confidently.

And there was indeed a team. A hairdresser, a make-up
artist, a beautician and a tailor. They were doing a wonderful job of hiding their curiosity but it was so strong she
could almost taste it.

'Would you mind if we untie your hair?'

Hester paused. She had to trust Alek's choice, and in
their professionalism. 'Of course.' She pulled the elastic
tie to free her ponytail. 'I just need you to make me presentable as consort to the King.'

All four of them just stared at her, making her feel
awkward.

'That's not going to be a problem,' Billie replied after
endless seconds. 'Not a problem.'

She didn't pretend she could reach for anything more
than presentable. But she'd been around Princess Fiorella
long enough to understand a few tricks. Tailored clothing
and some polish could make her passable.

'We have some dresses,' Billie said. 'Would you try
them on first so I can make alterations while you're with
the beautician?'

'Of course, thank you.' Hester watched, stunned, as

Billie unzipped several garment bags while Jon the hair-dresser began laying out his tools on the table. 'You must have run to get all this together so quickly.'

'An assignment like this?' A huge smile spread across Jon's face. 'Once in a lifetime.'

Once in a lifetime was right. And it was an assignment for her as much as it was for them. She could learn to do what was necessary, she could even excel in some areas. But she definitely needed help with this. She'd never had the desire to look good before; frankly she'd never wanted people to notice her. Blending in was safer. Hiding was safer still.

But now people were going to be looking so she needed armour. That was what clothing and make-up could be, right?

Hester spent the best part of an hour turning this way and that and holding still while Billie pinned her waist and hem. The fabrics were so soft and sleek, slowly her trepidation ebbed and she actually began to enjoy herself.

'Now I have your measurements, I can get you some more when we land in Triscari,' Billie said.

Hester glanced at the pile of clothes laid out on the table. 'Do I need more?'

'Much more.' Billie swiftly hung the dresses. 'It's not all photo shoots and public engagements. You'll still have day-to-day life at the palace.'

Hester bit back a nervous giggle. It sounded fantastical and her usual navy utility trousers weren't exactly palace proper. 'Okay, some more casual items would be wonderful. And...' she fought back her blush '...perhaps some new underwear.'

'Leave it with me.' Billie smiled.

Hester smiled shyly. As the beautician waxed, plucked, buffed and massaged her, hours of flight time passed by and she was able to avoid conversation by studying the information on the tablet Alek had given her. Wrapped in a white fluffy robe, she sat in one of the chairs in the boardroom while Jon settled a towel around her shoulders.

She'd never coloured her hair or had any sort of stylish cut because she'd never been able to afford it. So now she sat still for hours as Jon and his assistant hovered over her while Billie hand-sewed alterations to the stunning dresses.

'Okay,' Jon said. 'Take as long as you like in the shower and then we'll get to drying it.'

'Shower? Seriously?' On an airplane?

'Apparently so.' Jon grinned. 'I've been in some planes...but this?'

The biggest and the best. She bit back her grimace.

As she dressed, Hester tried not to wonder what Alek would think of her make-over. He didn't need to find her *attractive*. She just needed to pass inspection.

But inside, she felt oddly different. There was something sensual about her smooth skin, rendered silky by the luxuriant lotions the beautician had rubbed in. For the first time in her life she felt pampered—almost precious.

Alek sprawled back in the recliner, absurdly satisfied with the day's events. He'd gone from frustrated and angry to being in complete control of the situation. Flying off last minute to vent to Fi after another monster row with his chief advisor, Marc, had turned out to be the best idea he'd ever had.

He'd forgotten all about his sister's prim secretary but she was perfect for this assignment. It didn't matter if she wasn't the most beautiful bride the world had ever seen because she was, after all, the one student his father had approved of. Back when Alek had been fighting to get his irascible control-freak father to allow Fiorella to study overseas, he'd come up with the idea of having an approved older student act as a mentor. His father had selected Hester from the pile of student records. So what better temporary wife could Alek produce now? The irony of it delighted him. And not having any emotional entanglement would make this 'marriage' wonderfully straightforward.

Though her determined reserve still fuelled his curiosity. He suspected she was more inexperienced than he'd first realised, but she had a smart head on her shoulders and it was insulting of him to think she couldn't handle this. She was a tough, brave little cookie.

His curiosity deepened as he wondered what personal fire she'd been through to make her so. Because there had to have been something. Why else had she been less than enthusiastic to invite what little family she had left?

He thought again about that barren little bedroom. There was minimalist simplicity and there was plain sad. He knew she had no education debt because she'd been on a scholarship and worked her way through her degree. She was clearly frugal and knew how to live on only a little. Yet she'd wanted a bundle of money in a hurry. Maybe one day she'd tell him why. Though he had the extraordinary inclination to make her tell him sooner. How would he get her to do that? She was so reticent he'd have to tease it out of her. He eased further back in the chair, enjoying the possibilities when the door opened. He glanced up as a goddess walked into his lounge.

Hester Moss.

At least he thought it was Hester. His brain had suddenly been starved of oxygen and he had to blink a couple of times and force his slack jaw actually to suck in a hit of air before he could quite believe his eyes.

'Do I pass?' She gestured to her outfit in an offhand way, her gaze not quite meeting his. 'Am I ready for the media onslaught?'

Her glasses were gone. Her hair was loose. Her baggy, boring clothing had hopefully been consigned to an incinerator because he only wanted her to wear items that fitted her as gorgeously as this dress did. He noticed all these things, but somehow he couldn't actually *think*. He could only stare.

Her expression pinched. 'That much of a difference, huh?'

'We're arriving early—they won't get much in the way of pictures,' he muttered almost incoherently before clearing his throat and reaching for his glass of water.

'Are you saying I just sat through an hour-long hair-drying session for nothing?' She finally looked him directly in the eyes.

'Not for nothing.' Oddly breathless, he detangled the tie in his tongue. 'I think it looks lovely.'

'Oh, that makes it so worth it.' She sat down in the recliner next to his. 'Lovely.'

He grinned, appreciating the lick of sarcasm in her tone. He'd deserved it with that inane comment, but he could hardly be honest. He didn't even want to face that raw and uncontrollable response himself.

Her unruffled composure had swiftly returned and he ached to scrape away that thin veneer because the leonine spark in her eyes a second ago had looked—

'Can you see without the glasses?' he muttered.

'Well enough. Just don't ask me to read my own handwriting,' she quipped.

He stared, leaning closer. 'Your eyelashes are—'

'Weird. I know.'

Her increase in visible tension was so small you'd have to be paying close attention to notice. Fortunately, Alek was paying extremely close attention.

'It's a genetic thing,' she said dismissively, but intriguingly her fingers had curled into fists. 'Don't pull an eyelash out to check they're real.'

As if he'd ever think to do that. Whoever would? 'I believe you.' He forced his stiff face into a smile.

Had someone done that to her in the past? He blinked in disbelief. They really were the thickest, most lush lashes he'd ever seen. 'And your transformation hasn't been a waste of time. We need a portrait shot to go with the media release.'

'You want to take that now?' She looked startled. 'You have a professional photographer on board too, don't you?' She nodded to herself. 'Unreal.'

He chuckled, appreciating the light relief. 'You'll get used to it.'

He buzzed for the photographer, who bounded in with more enthusiasm than usual and keenly listened as Alek explained what he wanted.

'Okay, we can use the white background over here,' the photographer said. 'What about the engagement ring?'

'We'll display that later,' Alek answered swiftly. 'Work around it for now.'

'We can do head and shoulders, but then some relaxed shots—more modern, arty, from the side—'

'Whatever you think,' Alek interrupted. 'Just get them as quickly as you can.'

Hester looked so stiff and uncomfortable, Alek had to suppress both his smile and frustration. He could think of one way of helping her relax but he didn't think she'd appreciate it. Besides, he'd ruled that out, hadn't he? He'd glibly assured her that of course he could be celibate for a year.

A *year*. The term hit him with the force of an asteroid.

'You *will* get used to it, Hester,' he repeated to reassure her.

But he was the one facing the grim reality of his impetuous decision. No sex. No touching. Just a measly two kisses—what did he think he was, twelve? And did he really think he was in 'complete control' of the situation? Because somehow, something had changed. It had only been a few hours and he was already seeing Hester in a new light. Was he so shallow it was all about the make-over? Or, worse, was it a case of wanting what was off limits—as if he were some spoilt child?

But as he stood next to her his temperature rose. He never sweated through photo sessions; he was too used to them. But she was close enough for him to catch her scent and she seemed to be glowing and it wasn't just the make-up. His fingers itched to touch and see if her skin was as silky soft as it looked.

'Can we try it with you looking at each other?' The photographer sounded frazzled. 'Um...yes, like that.'

Alek gazed at her upturned face. He couldn't think for the life of him why he'd thought her anything less than stunning. She wasn't just beautiful, she was striking. Her golden eyes with those incredible lashes? Her lush pouting lips? That infuriating serenity and stillness of her very self? He couldn't resist putting a careful hand on her waist and drawing her a little closer. He heard the slight catch in her breath but she didn't frown.

'Better,' the photographer muttered. 'Do you think you might be able to smile?'

Alek glanced up from his appallingly lustful stare at her lips to her eyes and amusement flashed between them. He chuckled the same split second she did. And there it was—that soft, enchanting smile he'd not seen enough of. A hot, raw tsunami swept through him at the sight. He wanted more of it.

'Yes!'

Now the photographer sounded far too ecstatic for Alek's liking.

'We'll get changed for the next few shots.' He wanted

to be alone with her. He wanted to make her smile again and he didn't want witnesses.

'Good idea.' Hester bit her lip and walked from the room.

Alek automatically followed her into the bedroom, unbuttoning his shirt as he went. 'What colour are—?'

'Oh!' She started and then stared bug-eyed at his chest.

Her eyes grew so round he almost preened as he shrugged his shirt all the way off.

'Is there a problem?' He couldn't help teasing her. But he was beginning to realise the real problem was all his.

No sex for a year?

'I n-need to get changed,' she stammered.

'So get changed.' With exaggerated civility he bowed and then turned his back to her and unlocked the wardrobe for a fresh shirt.

'This is your bedroom?' she choked. 'I'm so sorry, I didn't realise when we put all the clothes...'

'I don't mind, Hester.'

But it was obvious *she* minded very much. All that efficient poise of hers had vanished and he couldn't help enjoying the moment. It was because of *him*.

'Let me know when it's safe to turn around again,' he offered with a self-mocking smile. He'd prove his 'gentleman' credentials—to *himself* as much as to her.

The following silence was appallingly long. He waited, his new shirt buttoned up all the damn way, for what felt like decades for her to give him the all-clear.

'Um...' She finally coughed. 'Would you mind helping me with the zip?'

Oh, was that the problem? 'Sure.' Smothering a laugh, he turned, only to freeze at the sight of her smooth bare back. A gorgeous expanse of creamy skin was edged by the curling sweep of her voluminous golden brown hair—inviting him closer, to touch. Instead he carefully took the dress in the tips of his fingers so as not to inadvertently touch her skin. To prove his restraint to himself. Slowly he pulled the zip up, hiding her from his hungry eyes again. The desire to lean closer, to touch where he had no permission, almost overwhelmed him. By the time he finished the simple task he could barely breathe. He stepped back, coldly furious with himself. Damn if he didn't need to clear his head.

At that moment she turned and he glimpsed fire gleaming in her eyes. That barely hidden blaze of desire slammed the brakes on his breathing all over again.

'You look…' He couldn't think of an adjective—he could only think of action. Impossible action.

'Let's finish this,' she muttered, quickly turning to leave the room.

'Right.' He'd never been rendered speechless before and it took him several minutes to catch his breath. Several minutes in which he had to look into a camera and smile as if this were the happiest day of his life. And then he just gave up. 'Give us a second.'

He took Hester by the hand and walked her down to the other end of the lounge.

'You get sick of it,' she said.

'Utterly,' he admitted, so happy to see her sweet smile flash instantly.

'It must be intense, knowing absolutely everyone around is watching you all the time.'

'You learn to tune it out.'

'And pretend it's normal?' She glanced away, her smile impish as she took in the artwork adorning the plane's interior. 'As if any of this is normal?'

'Well…' he shrugged '…it is normal for me.' He nudged her chin so she looked back at him. 'It bothers you?'

To his gratification, she leaned a little closer as she shook her head, her gaze locked on his.

'That looks amazing.' A masculine voice interrupted from a distance.

Alek froze. He'd completely forgotten the photographer was still down the other end of the lounge. The startled look in Hester's face revealed she'd forgotten too and the half-laugh that escaped from her glossy pout was the sexiest thing he'd ever heard. Smiling back, he pulled her close on pure instinct. The temptation to test the softness of her lips stormed through his reason. Time stopped as he stared into her eyes, trying to read her soft heat and stillness. Could he coax her into—?

'So perfect,' the photographer muttered.

'Enough,' Alek snapped, enraged by the second intrusion. 'We'll be landing soon.' He dragged in a calming breath to recover his temper.

But it was too late. Hester had already pulled free and that fragile promise was lost.

The photographer quickly retreated to the rear of the plane.

'Everyone will assume this marriage is only because of the coronation requirement.' Her cheeks were still flushed as she sat in the seat and picked up that damn tablet again. He wished he'd never given it to her. 'Do you think it's really necessary for us to try to sell this as a love match?'

'You don't want to be treated as a joke. I have no desire for that either.' Oddly he felt more responsibility about that now. A flicker of protectiveness towards her had surged. 'I think we can pull it off. Who's to say it's not so?'

She hesitated. 'Okay, but the agreement is just between us. Not written down anywhere. I don't want lawyers getting involved and leaking information.'

'You trust that I won't renege on our deal?'

'You have more to lose than I do.' She leaned back into the corner of her chair, still staring at the tablet screen. 'Your reputation actually matters.'

She determinedly studied the information he'd put together for her to do a good job. Yet at the same time, she was determined not to care what anyone thought. Not even him. She seemed to care, yet not.

Intrigued, he studied her. Even in that gorgeous green silk dress, she reminded him of a little sparrow, carefully not taking up too much space in case she was chased away. Only taking crumbs and not demanding anything more. Why was that? Why wasn't she close to her family? Why had she not invited any friends to the wedding? It puzzled him because she was kind. Her friendliness to that feral cat showed that. And more telling, was her relationship with Fi. Fiorella, for all her faults, was a good judge of character. And it wasn't that she hadn't wanted to lose Hester as her assistant. It was that she'd been concerned for her. Was that because Fi saw vulnerability beneath that serenity as well?

The insidious warmth steadily built within him. He could go without intimacy for a year, of *course* he could. But his body rebelled at the thought. He was attracted to her and that attraction seemed to be building by the second. He gritted his teeth, determined to master it, because he was going to have to keep his fiancée close over these next few days and there could be no risk of complicating what should be a perfectly amicable agreement.

'This isn't enough.' She glanced up at him.

'Pardon?'

'I understand more about Triscari's population, economy and geography than I ever thought I'd want to. I know the potted history of your royal family and all that drama with the palace and the castle stuff. But I don't know about *you.*'

A ripple of pleasure skittered down his spine. She was curious about him?

'If I'm to convince people we're a couple then I need to know some facts,' she added primly.

Oh, she just wanted meaningless facts?

'You want my dating profile?' he teased, then chuckled at the glowering look she shot him. 'I enjoy horses, playing polo. My star sign is Scorpio. Apparently that makes me passionate—'

'What are your weaknesses?' she interrupted with a bored tone. 'What do you hate?'

So there *was* a little real curiosity there.

'I hate pickles. And I hate being told what to do.' He stared at her pointedly. 'By anyone.'

She gazed limpidly at him, not backing down. 'What else?'

'You're not taking notes,' he said softly.

'I'm not taking the risk of anyone finding them.'

'Very untrusting, aren't you?'

'Don't worry. I won't forget. *Passionately loathes pickles. And don't tell him what to do,*' she parroted and then shrugged. 'Not so difficult.'

Perversely he decided he wouldn't mind a few commands to fall from her lips. 'Tell me about you. What are your weaknesses?'

Her gaze slid to the side of him. 'I don't have any.'

He chuckled at her flat-out bravado. But it was also a way of keeping him shut out. Ordinarily he didn't mind not getting to know all that much about a woman he was dating, but Hester was going to be his *wife*. And he needed to trust her more than he'd trusted anyone in a long time. Yet she had no hesitation in lying to his face—to protect herself.

'So you expect to learn personal things about me, but won't share any of your own?' He equably pointed out her hypocrisy.

'I've already told you everything personal that's relevant. I told you my parents died when I was a child, that I'm not close to what family I have left, that my life to date has been pretty quiet. There really isn't much else.'

Rigidly determined, wasn't she? That flickering spark within her fired *his* determination. He could quiz her on the meaningless facts too. And he could push for more beyond that. 'Favourite pizza topping?' he prompted.

'Just plain—tomato and cheese.'

'Really? You don't want capers, olives, chilli oil?' He shook his head. 'You're missing out.'

'I don't need a whole bunch of extras.'

'No frills? No added luxuries—just the bare necessities? That's what you'll settle for?' He was stunned and yet when he thought of that dire bedroom of hers, it made sense. 'Tempt your palate a little, Hester. Why not treat yourself to a little something more, or don't you think you deserve it?'

Her jaw dropped. 'It's not about whether I deserve it—'

'Isn't it?' He leaned forward, pleased at her higher pitch. 'Why shouldn't you have all the extras? Other people take them all the time.'

'What if you end up with all the frills and no foundations? Then you discover you've got nothing of substance. Nothing to sustain you.' She put the tablet on the table between them. 'Keeping things simple works for me. The basics suffice.'

The basics? Was that what she considered that soulless cell of a bedroom? But that she didn't even seem to want to *try* something new was interesting. 'Are you afraid to take risks, Hester?'

'Yes,' she said baldly. 'I've fought too long and hard for what I have.'

Her admission surprised him on two counts—firstly, she didn't seem to *have* all that much. And secondly, she'd taken a massive risk with him and she was nailing this with a stunningly cool ability to adapt and handle all the challenges he was flinging at her. 'Yet you said yes to me—to this impulsive marriage.'

'Because it was an offer too good to pass up.' She gazed at him directly.

'You mean the money. Not the pleasure of my company?'

She blinked rapidly but through those glorious lashes she kept her golden focus on him. 'Yes.'

She sounded breathy and he'd like to think she was lying again because he really didn't think she was the materialistic type. He'd bet even more money that this wasn't about what she could buy but what she could *do*. Was this about freedom—so she didn't have to live on campus any more, helping first-year students get their heads around essay requirements and bibliographic details? Was this because she wanted freedom, not just from work, but from being around other people?

'Well, I'm sorry, Ms Moss, but we're going to have to spend quite a lot of time together over the next few days.' He reached forward, fastened her seat belt for landing and flashed a wicked smile at her. 'I don't know about you, but I can't wait.'

CHAPTER FOUR

TRISCARI SAT LIKE a conglomerate of emeralds and sapphires in the heart of the Mediterranean Sea. As if that giant jeweller in the sky had gathered her most prized stones in the cup of her hand and cast them into the purest blue sea in the most sun-kissed spot on the earth. And in their heart, she'd placed treasure in the form of more valuable minerals. It was incredibly attractive, wealthy and secure.

Hester already knew a lot, having researched it when she first found out she'd been selected as Princess Fiorella's safe college roommate and tutor. But now she'd read more closely about the economic success story and envy of all other small European nations. The royal family had maintained their place on the world stage and now, as ruler of a democracy, the King was mostly a figurehead and facilitator, overseeing the rights of all its people. And promoting it as a destination of course. But that was easy given the world had long been captivated by, not only the kingdom's beauty, but the luxury and the lifestyle it offered. Visiting Triscari topped absolutely everyone's bucket list.

Today the sun peeked above the horizon and turned the sea gold, making the islands look like the literal treasure they were. Hester decided she'd entered a dream world. She'd survived her first ever flight—travelling in pure luxury for hours—to arrive in the most perfect, pristine place in the world.

Ten minutes after the plane had landed, Hester followed Alek down the flight of stairs and onto the tarmac. The air was balmy even this early in the morning—the atmosphere radiated golden warmth. She got into the waiting vehicle and gazed out of the window, hungry to take in more. The stunning scenery suppressed her nerves as the car sped along the street. She knew the palace was in the centre of the town while a clifftop castle was at the water's edge. The twin royal residences had been constructed for the King and Queen of four hundred years ago. According to the legends, that arranged marriage had spectacularly failed. The couple had determinedly lived separate lives and set up their own rival courts, vying for the title of 'best'. Both had grand halls and opulent gardens and stunning artwork that had been added to over the ages.

'This would have to be the most beautiful place…' Hester said, her breath taken away by the vista. She glanced at him. 'You must love it.'

'I am very lucky.' His eyes glittered like the night sky. 'I'll do anything for this country.'

'Even get married?'

'Even that.' He nodded. 'Thanks to you.'

'Who'll be meeting us?'

'Senior palace officials.' His expression turned rueful. 'We'll ignore them for the most part, but some things will be unavoidable.'

'You live in the palace?'

'It is where the King resides.' He nodded. 'The Queen's castle is purely for display these days, but the night before the wedding you'll have to stay there. You'll process from there to the palace for the marriage ceremony. People will line the streets to watch. It's the symbolism of unity…no warring with the wife…mainly, it's just tradition.'

The men waiting for them in the vast room were all older than Alek and were all failing to mask their incredibly curious expressions. They watched her approach as if they were judge, jury and executioner in their funereal clothing and they bowed deeply as Alek introduced them.

'Very little is known about Hester and our relationship,' Alek said smoothly. 'I'm aware that where there is a vacuum, the media will fill it with fantasy over fact so we'll fill it. We'll undertake one official appearance to celebrate the engagement. Hester cannot go straight into full-time duties, certainly not right before the wedding. We have a few days but it's not long. She needs time to adjust.'

Hester watched surprise flash over the men's faces.

'Of course, Alek. It is customary for a princess to have attendants to guide her. I thought perhaps—'

'I'll guide her.' Alek cut him off.

'But—'

'We want to be together,' Alek added with a silken smile. 'If we need further support, I'll let you know. I'll meet with you shortly to discuss other issues, but I need to settle Hester into her rooms.'

As the men left Hester turned to face him. 'Do you expect me to speak at this engagement?' The thought terrified her but she was determined to hide that fact. She'd keep calm, carry on.

He glanced at her, amusement flickering in his eyes. 'Only to one person at a time, you won't address a whole room. We will need to do one pre-recorded interview, but I'll be beside you and we'll vet the questions beforehand so you have time to prepare an answer. If you smile, then we'll get through it easily.'

'All I need to do is smile?'

'You have a nice smile.'

'I can do more than smile.'

'Yeah?' His mouth quirked. 'Well, if you could look at me adoringly, that would also help.'

She rolled her eyes.

'And call me Alek.'

'You're quite stuck on that, aren't you?'

'I'm not the one who's stuck.' But his smirk slipped as he sighed. 'I inherited my father's advisors and they're used to things being done a certain way. Change is inevitable, but it's also inevitably slow.'

'Some people find change hard,' she said primly. 'It frightens them.'

'Does it frighten you?' He cocked his head.

'Of course.' She laughed. 'But I'm determined to hide it.'

'Why?' He stepped closer to her. 'You do that a lot, right? Hide your feelings. You do it well.'

'Is that a compliment or a criticism?' she asked lightly.

'Maybe it's just a comment.' His voice dropped to that delicious softness again that implied seductive intimacy— laced with steel.

'With no sentiment behind it?' She shook her head. 'There's always a judgement. That's what people do.'

'True.' He nodded. 'You judged me.'

She stared at him.

'My lifestyle.' He flicked his eyebrows suggestively.

She fought back the flush. 'I never thought you'd be so sensitive to an idle comment.'

'It wasn't idle and you're still judging me right now,' he teased. 'You don't know me, Hester.'

Her heart thudded. 'I know all I need to.'

'A bullet list of preferences that might change in an hour? That's not knowing me.'

'It's just enough detail to give this believability. I don't need to get to know you any more...'

'Intimately?' he suggested in that silken voice. *'Personally?'*

Those dimples were winking at her again. He was so unfairly handsome. And she'd never stood this close to someone in years. Never trusted that someone wouldn't hurt her—with words, or a pinch or a spiteful tug of her hair. So personal space was a thing. Wary, she stepped back, even though there was a large part of her buried deep inside that didn't want her to move in that direction at all.

'I'm going to be your husband,' he pointed out quietly.

'No. You're going to be my boss.'

'Partner.'

'Boss,' she argued. 'You're paying me.'

'You *are* afraid.' He brushed the back of his hand across her jaw ever so lightly. 'Tell me why.'

She froze at his caress, at his scrutiny. She couldn't think how to answer as tension strained between them. She was torn between the desire to flee or fall into his arms. Just as she feared her control would snap, he stepped back.

The dimples broke his solemnity. 'Come on, I have something to show you.'

She traipsed after him along endless corridors with vaulted ceilings and paintings covering every inch of the walls. Even the doors were massive. 'I'm never going to find my way back here. I need breadcrumbs or something.'

He laughed and pushed open yet another door. 'This is your space.'

'My space?'

'Your apartment.'

Her what? She stepped inside and took a second to process the stunningly ornate antechamber.

'It spans two stories within this wing of the palace, but is fully self-contained.' Alek detailed the features. 'You have a lounge, study, small kitchen, bedroom plus a spare, inward-facing balconies for privacy and of course bathroom facilities. You can redecorate it however you wish.'

She couldn't actually get past this initial reception room. 'I have all this to myself?'

'A year is a long time.' Alek circled his hand in the air as he stepped forward. 'I want you to be happy. I want you to feel like it's your home. You can have privacy and space.' He faced her. 'You can build your own library of thrillers in here if you wish.'

Hester stared at the massive room. No one had ever offered her anything like this in her life. When she'd moved to her aunt's house, she'd not been offered the same kind of welcome. And she'd tried *so* hard to fit in. But it had been awkward and they'd made her feel as if it was such a sacrifice to have her take up some of their precious space. She'd felt uncomfortable, unable to change anything for fear of offending them. She'd accumulated nothing much of her very own and that was good, given what had happened. And that minimalist habit had extended to her time at the campus. The rooms were so small, and she'd not cluttered them with anything other than books. So now, confronted with this kind of generosity, emotion choked, not just her throat, but her thinking. It was too much. Everything he'd already done was too much. He'd submerged her in an abundance that she couldn't handle. She gripped her little backpack as her limbs trembled. Frozen and tongue-tied, she couldn't trust herself to move.

'They've brought your suitcase in already,' he said.

She saw it next to one of the enormous comfortable-looking armchairs. She had such little stuff for such an opulent space it was ridiculous.

His eyebrows pulled together and he hesitated a moment before stepping towards the window. 'There's good views across to the ocean and the balcony in your bedroom is completely private. No one will be able to see you.' He paused again and she felt him gazing at her. 'Do you not like it?'

'No.' She could hardy speak for the emotion completely clogging her up. She stared hard at the floor, knowing that if she blinked some of that hot, burning liquid was going to leak from her eyes and she really didn't want that to happen. Then she realised she'd said the wrong thing. 'Not no. I meant… I just…it's fine.'

'Fine,' he echoed, but his voice sounded odd. 'So why do you look like…?' He trailed off and stepped closer than before and there was nothing for her to hide behind. 'You look like you're about to cry.'

She felt that wall of awkwardness rise and slick mortification spread at the realisation he could read her all too easily. Why could she suddenly not hide her feelings? And worse, why couldn't she hold them back?

'I don't cry.' It wasn't a lie—until now.

'Not ever—?'

'Do you?' she interrupted him, forcing herself to swallow back the tears and throw him off guard the way he was her.

He gazed at her intently and it was even worse. 'Hester—'

'I'm *fine*.' She dragged in a breath, but couldn't pull it together enough to keep it all back. 'It's just that I've never had such a big place all to myself.'

The confession slithered out, something she'd never trusted anyone enough to tell before. She didn't want him to think she didn't appreciate the effort he'd gone to. She knew he had insane wealth and property, but he'd thought this through for her. He'd taken time to consider what she might like. No one had done that for her. Not since she'd lost her parents. So she deeply appreciated this gesture, but she really needed to hold herself together because she couldn't bear to unravel completely before him.

She sensed him remain near her for a strained moment but then he strolled back towards the window.

'Personally I think the wallpaper in here is a bit much.' He casually nodded at the ferociously ornate green and black pattern.

Startled, she glanced across at him.

'You have to agree,' he added drolly. 'The word would be gaudy.'

She couldn't contain the giggle that bubbled up, a fountain of pure silliness. As her face creased, that tear teetered over the edge and she quickly wiped its trail from her cheek.

'I'm right, aren't I?' If he'd noticed her action, he didn't comment. Instead he wriggled his finger at the seam where wallpaper met window frame until he tugged enough loose to tear it.

'*Alek!*'

'Oh, the press are going to love it if you say my name with that hint of censure,' he teased in an altogether different tone.

A shock wave of heat blasted through her. Its impact was explosive, ripping through her walls to release the raw awareness. She'd been determined to ignore it. She knew he was an outrageous flirt, but it wasn't his tone or his teasing jokes that caused this reaction within her. It was *everything* about him. He made her wonder about the kind of intimacy she'd never known. The kind she'd actively avoided. And she'd never wanted to step *closer* to a person before.

'Don't be afraid to ask for what you want, Hester,' he said softly.

She stared at him blankly, her mind going in all kinds of searing directions.

'You can do what you like,' he offered. 'Take out walls, rip up the carpet, whatever.'

Oh. Right. He meant the rooms. Only she hadn't been thinking about the décor and what she feared she *wanted* was far too forbidden.

'Don't worry about the budget. I can just sell one of my horses to cover it.'

'Don't you love your horses more than anything?' She tried to break her unfortunate fixation.

'Other than my crown and my sister?' he teased. 'Or my playboy lifestyle?'

She licked her dried lips and refused to continue along that track. 'Do you have an apartment in here too?'

'Right next door.' He nodded. 'It's best if we're near each other.'

'I understand, it needs to look okay.' She made herself agree. 'Because this is a job,' she reiterated. But it was a lie already. 'It's just an act.'

With no intimacy—emotional or otherwise.

His gaze narrowed. 'I'd like to think we can be friends, Hester.'

She didn't have friends. Acquaintances and colleague, yes. But not friends. Since the rejection she'd suffered after her parents' deaths, she'd not been able to trust people, not got to know anyone well. Not even Princess Fiorella.

But she sensed that Alek expected a little more from her and perhaps that was fair enough. It wasn't right for her to judge him based on the actions of others he didn't even know. Or on the salacious reports the media wrote about him. She had to take him on his own actions around her and so far she had to admit he'd been decent. He'd done everything in his power to make this as easy as possible for her. And it wasn't his fault she was attracted to him like *that*. That element was up to her to control.

'I'm sure we can.' But inwardly she froze, petrified by her own internal reaction to him.

Her brain was fixed along one utterly inappropriate

track. She had the horrible feeling it was like the teen girl's first crush she'd never actually had. The fact was he didn't need to do or say anything but he'd half seduced her already. Could she really be so shallow as to be beguiled by his looks alone?

'It's going to be fine,' she said firmly. 'We have a whole year and most of the time I'll stay safe inside the palace, right?' She moved into the room, faking her comfort within the large, luxurious space. 'Actually I'm happy to stay here while you go to that meeting now, if you like.'

His eyes widened. 'Are you dismissing me, Hester?'

She smiled at his mild affront. 'Are you not used to that?'

'You know I'm not.'

'You'll get used to it.' She couldn't help a small giggle as she echoed his own reassurance.

'What if I don't want to?' He stepped closer.

Hester swallowed her smile and stilled. For a long moment they just stared at each other. Then, once more, he took a step back and the dimples flickered ever so briefly.

'I'm afraid I need you for another few minutes to show you something else.' He gestured towards the door.

'Do I need string?' She grimaced.

He chuckled. 'It's very near.'

She followed him through another doorway and then down a curling flight of stairs and blinked on the threshold of a huge airy space. There was a gorgeous pool—half indoor, half out, surrounded by lush plantings and private sun loungers.

'My father had this built for Fiorella's privacy, but she wanted her freedom. After my mother died, my father became overprotective and the palace became a bit of a prison for her.'

Hester swallowed at the mention of his mother. She'd

not been brave enough to ask him about her at all. 'Was it a prison for you too?'

'I was older. And—as bad as it sounds—I was a guy. He didn't have the same concerns for me as he did for her.'

'Seriously?'

'I know,' he sighed. 'Double standards suck. She was a lot younger though and she'd lost her mother. Everyone needs some freedom of choice, don't they? Fi definitely did.'

'She told me you helped her get your father's approval for her to study abroad,' Hester said. 'That it was only because you promised to stay and do all the royal duties that she could go. And that now your father's gone, you've told her she can do whatever she wants.'

He glanced out across the water. 'She enjoys her studies. She should have the freedom and opportunity to finish them. She's a smart woman.'

Hester's curiosity flared. 'What would you have done if you'd had the same freedom of choice that Fiorella now does?'

His smile was distant. 'There was never that choice for me, Hester.'

Alek's phone buzzed and he quickly checked the message. 'The wedding dress designers have arrived.'

Oh. She'd forgotten about that. But she found herself anticipating the planning—she'd very recently decided that there was something to be said for smoke and mirrors. The look on his face when she'd appeared after her airplane make-over had been both reward and insult. She'd quite like to surprise him some more.

'Is there a particular style you'd like for my dress?' she asked demurely.

He gazed at her for a moment, his eyes narrowing. 'I'm sure you'll look amazing in whatever you choose to wear.'

But his dimples suddenly appeared. 'Though I do wonder if you'll dare to go beyond the basics for once.'

'Feathers and frills?'

'Why not?' He led her back to her apartment where Hester found the women waiting. Hester drew in a deep breath and followed them in.

Four hours later Alek was hot and tired from going through the military-like wedding arrangements with his advisors and answering all their incessant questions. The media had already begun staking out the palace. The news had reverberated in a shock wave around the world. The news channels were running nothing but the photo that had been taken in the plane on the way over and digging deep for nuggets about Hester already. Fortunately her family were already on their way over and unable to comment because he'd ensured Wi-Fi wasn't available on their flight so he still had time to guide their speculation.

Though he'd learned more about her in the small pieces being published as soon as they were written than from her own too-brief mentions of her past. The bald facts were there, but the real truth of her? The depth? He doubted the investigative reporters would get anywhere near it. She was so self-contained even he was struggling and he was the one *with* her. What had happened to her parents? Why was she so alone? What did she keep in that broken little box that she kept nearby at all times?

'Alek?'

He blinked, recalling his concentration. He couldn't waste time wondering what made her tick—what secrets and hurts she held close—he had to run the palace, reply to invitations to tour another country, clarify Triscari's position on a new European environmental accord, and not least decide the next steps for the stud programme at his stables. Too much at the best of times.

Yet he still couldn't help thinking about Hester, concerned about how she was dealing with all those designers and the decisions she had to make, wondering how else he could make her comfortable. He'd liked being able to do something that had truly moved her—seeing her real response pierce her calm exterior had been oddly exhilarating. He wanted to mine more of that deeply buried truth from her and know for sure he'd pleased her.

In the end he called an assistant to check on his fiancée's movements and report back. Five minutes later he learned she'd been cloistered in her rooms this whole time. Stifling a grimace, Alek turned back to the paperwork spread on the vast table before him. The prospect of their impending marriage strangled him, fogging his usual sharp decision-making ability, making everything take longer. Another hour passed and he was almost at the point of bursting in on Hester himself, just to ensure they hadn't accidentally suffocated her in all that silk.

'Enough.' He pushed back when his advisors raised another thorny problem.

He'd been issuing instructions for hours and he was done.

If it were an ordinary day, he'd go for a ride to clear his head. But today wasn't anything like ordinary and he couldn't leave the confines of the palace, what with all the media gulls gathering. Irritated with being even more tightly constrained than usual, he impatiently stalked towards his wing. The tug deep inside drawing him there was desperation for his own space, wasn't it? It wasn't any need to see her.

He gritted his teeth as he reached her door and pushed himself past it. But once he was in his own room he heard soft splashes through the open window. He paused. Was someone in the pool?

He swiftly glanced out of the window. The view all but

killed his brain as his blood surged south. Those utility trousers and tee had done a good job of hiding her figure. So had those two dresses, even, with their floaty fabric and draping styles. Because now, in that plain, black, purely functional swimsuit, Hester Moss was even more lush in particular parts than he'd expected. She truly was a goddess. And maybe this marriage wasn't going to be as awful as he'd imagined. Already teasing her was a delight, while touching her a temptation he was barely resisting.

For the first time in his life he was pleased his father had been so overprotective towards his sister. That he'd ensured the pool was completely secure from prying eyes— beyond these private apartments, of course. In fact, the whole palace was a fortress. No one could see in and, with the air restrictions in place, no helicopters could fly over with cameras on board. He opened the door to his balcony and lightly ran down the curling stone steps to the private courtyard.

She was swimming lazy lengths and apparently hadn't noticed his arrival. It wasn't until she rolled onto her back that she saw him. Her eyes widened and she sank like a stone beneath the surface before emerging again with a splutter. He was so tempted to skim his hands over her creamy skin and sensual curves. He ached to test their silkiness and softness for himself. Except she now hid— ducking down in the blue so only her head poked above the gentle ripples she'd caused.

'What are you doing?' Her gold eyes were huge.

Uninhibited—and frankly exhilarated—he'd undone his shirt buttons before he'd even thought about it. Now he laughed at the look on her face. 'Relax. It's just skin. And it's a pool.'

'You can't swim naked,' she said, scandalised.

'I told you, the pool is completely private. No one can

see us—it's designed so only our private apartments over-
look it. Mine, yours, Fi's. And Fi isn't here.'

'You still can't swim naked,' she choked.

'Relax, Hester.' He laughed, amused by her blushing
outrage.

'You just do everything you want, don't you?'

'Not all the time. Not everything.'

She had no idea how well behaved he was being right
now. Another bolt of attraction seared through him. He
kept his black knit boxers on but swiftly dived into the
pool to hide the very direct effect she was having on him.

'How'd the fitting go?' he asked once he swam to the
surface again. The thought of her in a fancy wedding dress
intrigued him. The dresses on the plane had been stunning, but some white lacy bridal thing? He suspected she'd
slay it.

'It was fine.'

Of course she'd say that—it was her fall-back phrase
to conceal every real thought and emotion. He gazed into
her eyes, wishing he could read her mind. Only the softest
signs gave her away—her pupils had swollen so there was
only a slight ring of colour visible; her cheeks had reddened
slightly; her breath sounded a little fast and shallow. But
he wanted to provoke a *real* reaction from her—powerful,
visceral, *uncontrollable*.

'Alek?' she asked.

Despite the uncertainty in her tone, primal satisfaction
scoured his insides, tightening every muscle with anticipation. He really did like his name on her lips. That small
success would be the first of many. And he understood the
reason for her uncertainty and slight breathlessness. She
had a similar effect on him.

He swam closer, hiding his straining body beneath the
cool water. Her eyelashes were so amazing—droplets glis-
tened on the ends of a few, enhancing their lushness even

more and framing her jewel-like irises to mesmerising perfection. She was every inch a luscious lioness.

'What are you doing?' she muttered as he floated closer still.

'Tell me how the fitting went,' he said softly. 'Tell me something more than a mere platitude.'

'Why?'

'Because I want to know how you're feeling.'

That wary look entered her eyes, but at the same time the water's warmth rose a notch. The tension between them was now half exposed and she couldn't tear her gaze from him any more than he could peel his from her.

'Why?' Her lips parted in a tempting pout—ruby red berries promising delectable, juicy softness.

'Because we're going to be a team, Hester,' he muttered, struggling to focus and to keep his hands off her. 'I'd like to know how you're feeling, how you're coping with everything. We should be able to communicate openly with each other.' He cocked his head. 'I get that you're quite self-contained, but this doesn't need to be difficult.'

Except it felt complicated. Something drew him closer even when he shouldn't. This should be straightforward. Where had this vast curiosity come from? Or this gnawing desire that now rippled through every cell in his body? It hadn't been there yesterday when he'd proposed. But now? Now he wanted to *know* her—and not just in that biblical sense. He wanted to understand what she was thinking and why. Drawing her out was a challenge. It wasn't unlike detangling Fi's glass Christmas tree lights for her when he was younger—careful focus, gentle hands and infinite patience were required.

But Alek wasn't feeling brilliantly patient this second. His heart was thudding too fast. He couldn't resist reaching out to feel for himself how soft she was, placing his hands on her slender waist and pulling her closer to where he stood.

Hester braced her hands on his broad forearms, feeling the strength of his muscles beneath her palms. Her pulse quickened and, despite the cool water, her temperature soared.

'Have you decided to seduce me?' Her voice was the barest thread of a whisper.

He gazed at her intently but said nothing.

Old fears slithered in, feeding doubt and fattening the insecurity that he could never possibly *mean* it. This was just a game for him. He was so used to winning, wasn't he?

'What are you going to do once you've succeeded?' She couldn't hold back the note of bitterness. 'Discard me like disposable cutlery?'

He didn't flinch at her lame dig. His gaze was unwavering and she was drowning in the depths of darkness in his eyes. 'Are you saying I'm going to succeed?'

'A man with your experience is always going to succeed against someone like me.'

He gazed at her relentlessly and something dangerous flickered from him to her. 'You're really not experienced?'

'Of course not,' she snapped as the unfamiliar tension in her body pushed her towards rejection—it was that or something so reckless. So impossible. She'd all but told him back in Boston. 'In your impossible quest for an appropriate bride you've found a virgin fit for a king.' The bitter irony rose within her.

His hands tightened on her waist. 'You're a *virgin*?'

What else did 'not experienced' mean?

'Don't act like you didn't guess already,' she angrily snapped.

'How? And why would I?' He shook her gently. 'You said you'd had a quiet life, but this is...'

'Irrelevant,' she slammed back at him. 'We have an

agreement. You're paying me to do a job. Physical intimacy, other than those two kisses, is off the table.'

But she was finding it impossible to breathe, impossible to tear her gaze from his. And it was impossible to do this 'job' when he kept stripping off and smiling at her all the time.

'Is it, Hester?' he breathed.

Why did he have to be so beautiful? Why did her body have to choose this moment to spark to life and decide it wanted touch? The sort of touch she'd never craved before. Not like this—not with a bone-deep driving need that was almost impossible to restrain.

'Please let me go.' And the worst thing happened—because it wasn't the assertive command she wanted. It was a breathless plea, totally undermined by the thread of desire that was so obvious to her that she knew it was evident to him as well.

But he didn't release her.

'Just so you know, sweetheart, it will not be my "experience" that sees me succeed with you,' he said firmly and then swept her up to sit her on the side of the pool. 'It's not *me* at all.'

He pushed back, floating away from her, leaving her with a parting shot so powerful she was glad she wasn't still standing.

'It'll happen only when *you* decide that I'm the one you want.' He levered up out of the pool on the opposite side and she watched him stride away in all his sopping, masculine beauty. 'You're the one with the power. You're the one who will need to say yes.'

CHAPTER FIVE

HESTER GRIPPED HER new clutch purse tightly. Her dress was suitable, she could walk in her mid-heeled nude shoes, and she'd practised not blinking so she could cope with banks of cameras…it was going to be fine. It was one sequence of appearances on one day—TV interview, public outing and back to the palace. She could manage that. She'd been practising often enough. The last few days had whizzed by in a flurry of meetings and planning. Alek had been with her much of the time but he was constantly interrupted and often completely called away. But she'd hidden in the palace, preparing for the performance of a lifetime, practising the walk down the long aisle of the chapel, climbing into the carriage, then swimming in the pool each afternoon. But he'd not joined her there again.

Now he was already waiting in the corridor. As always her tummy flipped when she saw him, but it was the burn building *below* her belly—that restless, hot ache—that was the real problem. She couldn't look at him without that appalling temptation to slide closer, to soften completely and let him touch… She still couldn't believe she'd made that embarrassing confession the other day. Her virginal status had surprised him and he hadn't denied he was interested in her physically. But he could have any woman he wanted. So she needed to forget all that and remember that this was a *job*.

His appraisal of her was uncharacteristically serious— all jet-black eyes, square jaw and no dimples. She sensed his leashed power; after all, he was a man who could move mountains with the snap of his fingers.

'Your hair's down.' He finally spoke. 'I like it.'

'I'm so glad to hear that,' she muttered, letting her tension seep out with uncharacteristic acidity. 'All I ever wanted was your approval.'

'Excellent.' He smiled wolfishly, soaking up her faux sweetness and ignoring the blatant sarcasm. 'You have it. I knew you'd deliver.'

Gritting her teeth, she wished she wouldn't react to his low chuckle but warmth pooled deep inside regardless. She liked it when he teased her with this sparkle-tipped talk that turned tension into bubbling moments of fun. The kind she'd never had with anyone before.

'Ready to hold hands?' He tilted his chin at her, his eyes gleaming with challenge.

'To stop me running away?' she cooed, then snapped on some seriousness. 'Good idea.'

He took her hand in a firm grip and led her into a vast room filled with fascinating sculptures and books. She could lose herself happily in here for days but she barely had time to blink at all the gold-framed art on the walls because he swiftly guided her to a lamp-lit polished wooden desk. 'Come on, you need to choose something.'

She gaped at the velvet-lined display cases carefully placed on the table before glancing up to see a liveried man with white kid gloves discreetly leaving the room.

'Wow, you've presented so many options…' She didn't quite know what to say. There were dozens of stunning rings—diamond solitaires, sapphire clusters, ruby squares and others she had no idea of.

'I'm hoping one will fit.' Alek's brows drew together as he looked down at her. 'You have small hands.'

'Did you raid all the jewellery shops in a thousand-mile radius?'

'No, these are from the palace vault.' He smiled at her horrified expression. 'There are a number of things in there. You'll choose a tiara for the wedding later this afternoon. We don't have time for that right now and it's supposed to be a secret from me, I think.'

There was a whole vault full of priceless treasure? She stared brainlessly at the tray, stunned yet again by the extreme wealth of his lifestyle—and of his ancient heritage, steeped in tradition. As impossible to believe as it was, she knew all those gleaming stones were real. Just as their impending marriage was real.

'Which do you like?' he prompted.

She shook her head, dazed. 'Any of them. They're all amazing.'

And it was impossible to decide. Still silence followed her comment, but she was frozen with fear and awe and stinging embarrassment.

'Would you like me to help?'

She heard the smile in his voice but she couldn't smile back. 'You can just choose.'

'You should have something you actually like,' he said dryly and then lowered his voice. 'You *deserve* something you like, Hester.' He turned her to face him, making her look up to meet his gaze. 'There's no wrong answer here. You can pick whichever you want…'

It was very kind of him, but way too overwhelming. Pearls, diamonds, emeralds, sapphires, rubies…she was stunned and speechless and so deeply discomfited by his careful concern. It made it worse somehow—that he knew she wasn't used to people consulting her on what she would like, or giving her beautiful rooms to sleep in, or choices of sublime designer gowns and now priceless, beautifully crafted jewels.

'Why don't you start by trying some on to see if they even fit?' He plucked the nearest ring from the tray and grasped her cold hand.

Hester remained motionless as he slid the ring down her finger before removing it again and selecting another with rapid decisiveness. The enormous oval emerald was too enormous. The square ruby's band was too big... As he tested and discarded several options, he kept a firm grip on her hand as if he thought she really might run away if he didn't. Maybe she would've too, because her core temperature was rising and her breathing shortening. He was too near and she was too tense. She just wanted one to fit well enough so this could be done and she could get away from him.

'This makes you feel awkward, Hester?' he murmured, glancing up into her eyes.

Yes, because he was standing so close and it felt too intimate, not the businesslike process it ought to be. Her imagination was working overtime, reading too much into every look, every word—that he was subtly teasing her by lingering as if he knew how much his proximity affected her and he was playing on it.

'Of course it does.' She tried to match his careless confidence but her voice wouldn't get above a whisper. She fell back on practicalities to answer half honestly. 'I'm going to be too scared to go anywhere with something like this on my finger. What if I lose it?'

'You only need to wear it to the events today and the wedding ceremony. The rest of the time, it'll remain safe in the vault.'

Okay. Good. That made it a little better. So she nodded and held still as he tried another that had a too-large band.

'You don't have a favourite colour?' he asked as he cocked his head to study how the next option looked on her small hand.

She shook her head, too embarrassed to articulate anything. It was impossible to think when he was this near to her and holding her with firm gentleness.

'Okay, then I'm going to decide,' he said. 'And you're not getting any say.'

She would've laughed if she weren't so flummoxed by his intense effect on her. With exaggerated movements he angled his body to hide her own hand from her. She felt the sensuous slide of his fingers down hers as he tried a few more rings. But his broad shoulders and masculine body blocked her view. Then he slowed, trying one, then another—then another and taking far longer with one. All the while she stared at the fine stitching on the seam of his jacket.

He turned his head to glance at her, a smile flitting around his lips in a mysterious way. 'I'm done.'

With a flourish, he pivoted to face her, sliding his hold to the tips of her fingers so she could see the ring he'd placed on her.

'What do you think?' he gently prompted.

She just stared. But inside while her heart pounded, her brain was starved of anything useful. It was stunning. One she'd been unable to see at first glance because she'd been blinded by so many gleaming options. It was a fine gold band and a solitary diamond. But the massive stone was cut into a teardrop shape—it didn't glitter brilliantly, wasn't gaudy, but rather the multifaceted cut ensured it gleamed and gave it a depth she'd not thought possible from a mere mineral. She could get lost looking into it. It was exquisite and delicate and moved her unbearably.

'Hester?'

Unable to resist responding to that commanding thread in his voice, she glanced up. Her tongue was cleaved to the roof of her mouth. Her pulse thudded through her body with such ferocity she had to stay completely still to control it—to stop that overwhelming emotion exploding out of her in an ugly mess. It was too risky to reveal anything vulnerable—that something might *matter* to her. But the warmth in the backs of Alek's eyes was different now. There wasn't only that flicker of flirtation and teasing awareness. There was something deeper than both those things and as the seconds passed in silence it only strengthened.

'It's fine,' she croaked.

She knew her response was so woefully inadequate it was almost rude, but no way could she utter the incoherent, incomplete thoughts battling in her head amongst the swirl of confusion. She expected him to either frown or tease, but he didn't. His face lit up and he smiled. Her heart stopped. Those dimples were going to be the death of her.

'Yes, it is.' He curled his arm around her waist and walked her towards the big heavy doors at the other end of the room. 'I'm glad you like it.'

Like it? Total understatement. She couldn't help sneaking peeks at it as she walked with him into a reception room that had been prepared for the interview, but she still couldn't verbalise the hot mess of feeling inside.

The journalist was waiting with only two crew—one for camera, one for sound. Hester perched on the edge of the sofa and hoped her nerves didn't show too much. Alek kept one arm around her and drew her closer to his side while holding her hand throughout. She was so aware of his heat and strength and his smile melted everything and everyone else away until somehow it was over and he was laughing and releasing her only to shake hands with the presenter.

'You did well,' Alek said as he escorted her through the palace maze back to her apartment.

Hester couldn't actually remember a word she'd said in response to the questions, she'd been too aware of him and the slippery direction of her private thoughts. 'Oh, yes, I was amazing. I don't think I said more than three words.'

'Are you fishing for compliments? That wasn't enough for you?' He whirled to face her. 'Ask me for more.' He dared her up close. 'You have no idea how much I want you to ask me for more.' His smile deepened as she gaped at him. 'Oh, you've gone silent again.'

'Because you're a tease.'

'Yeah? Perhaps. But that doesn't mean I don't mean it.' His hand tightened around her wrist. 'Your pulse is quickening.'

'It's terror,' she muttered.

'Liar.' He grinned.

'You're so conceited.'

'Maybe because you've mastered the art of looking at me so adoringly...' He chuckled as she flicked her wrist free of his hold.

'Don't we have to go on this visit now?' She pushed herself back into work mode.

'In an hour, yes.' He leaned closer. 'That's just enough time for—'

'Me to get changed, that's right.' She all but ran back to her apartment to where her stylists were waiting.

'You're nervous?' Alek glanced at her keenly as the car drove them out of the palace gates and through the banks and banks of cameras just over an hour later.

'Is it really obvious?' She worried even more and clutched her bag strap tightly.

'Honestly, I imagine everyone would expect you to be nervous and it's not a bad thing. People like to see the humanity in others.' He reached for her hand and shot her that charming smile.

'They forgive you your sins?' She tried to answer lightly, but beneath it she was glad of the way he rubbed his thumb back and forth over her tense fingers. It was soothing, like when she counted her breathing. But better.

But bad too. Because she didn't want him to stop.

'Nerves aren't a sin.' He laughed. 'They're normal. Everyone has them.'

'Even you?'

'Even me.' He gave an exaggerated nod. 'Does it surprise you that I might feel normal things, Hester?'

That sense of danger as those undercurrents of heat and temptation swirled too close to the surface.

'So this is the paediatric ward visit,' she confirmed needlessly. Just to remember the *job*. Just to stop staring at him. Since when was she so seduced by physical beauty? She'd always tried not to judge people based on their appearance—she knew how it felt to be bullied about things.

'You don't think it's cynical to use sick children to sell us as a couple?' she asked.

'I think that most of these little guys have a really rough road ahead of them, so why shouldn't they get a little joy out of this? I'd far rather spend an hour with them than with some of the captains of industry who don't think I can live up to my father's legacy.'

'You think people don't take you seriously?'

'I'm just the Playboy Prince, aren't I?'

'Wow, I wonder why they have reason to think that?'

'I know, right?' He sent her a mocking look. 'If only they knew I now have a pure and innocent bride to mend me of my disreputable ways...'

'Very funny.'

Except she was revising her opinion on his reputation. It

hadn't taken long to see that Alek considered his country and his people in almost every decision he made.

It seemed there were thousands waiting behind police-guarded barriers and every one held a camera or phone up. As she passed them she was terribly glad of her long dress and the firmness with which her hair was pinned. Alek released her hand so they could engage with the people in the receiving line and she received a small bouquet from a sweet young girl. She heard a child bellowing and glanced quickly to see a small boy being carried away by a nurse but she maintained her smile and pretended she hadn't noticed. There was no need to draw attention to someone else's sensory overload.

Alek compelled attention like a black hole, sucking everyone, everything—all the light—into his vortex and onwards he spun, ever more powerful. But she also felt the people watching her, assessing, judging—she could only hope she passed. After a tour of the ward, they spent some time in the hospital classroom where a few children sat at tables working on drawings. At a table near the back, she could see the small boy who'd been hurried away at their arrival. With the 'freedom' to walk around, Hester gravitated towards where he was, subdued and firmly under the control of the teacher standing beside him. Belligerent sadness dimmed his eyes. Hester didn't make eye contact with the teacher, she just took the empty chair at his table. She drew a piece of paper towards her and selected a pencil to colour in with. The boy paused his own colouring to watch her work then resumed his until they reached for the same emerald pencil.

'I think it's a really nice colour,' she said softly, encouraging the boy to take it.

'It's my favourite,' he muttered.

'Mine too,' she whispered with a conspiratorial smile. 'But don't tell anyone.'

She glanced up and encountered Alek's inscrutable gaze. She'd not realised he was nearby.

'Time for us to leave, Hester,' he bent and said quietly. 'But we'll come back again.'

As they were driven back to the palace he turned in his seat to study her face. She was sure it was only for all those cameras along the route.

'You did very well. Again,' he said.

She inclined her head with exaggerated regal poise to accept the compliment.

He suddenly laughed and picked up her hand, playing with the ring on her finger in an intolerably sweet gesture. 'I mean it. Being able to make someone smile or respond— to make a connection like with that boy who'd been distressed?' Alek nodded. 'That was skilled.'

'Not *skilled*.' Hester shook her head. 'I had no clue. I just tried to give him the time to let him get himself together.'

'Natural kindness, then.' Alek ignored the photographers calling outside the car as it slowly cruised through the crowd. 'You told him your favourite colour. Or was that just a lie to make him feel good?'

She paused. 'It was the truth.'

'So you could tell him something you couldn't tell me?'

She paused, startled by the soft bite in that query. 'Have I hurt your feelings?' She tried to deflect him with a smile.

'Yes.'

She shot him a worried glance. Surely he was joking? He intently watched her—not smiling, not glowering either.

'I just wanted to be kind to him.' She drew in a breath. 'Some people get all the attention, right? The loud ones, or the ones confident enough to smile and call out, and the ones who have the tantrums like him. The ones I feel bad for are the quiet ones—who don't push forward or act out, who are so busy being good or polite or scared…

sometimes they need to know someone has seen them and I didn't today.'

'I did,' he said softly. 'I went around and saw some of those ones.'

Of course he had—because he'd been doing it all his life. Sharing his attention.

'Were you one of those kids?' he asked. 'One who was being so good she became invisible?'

'Good but not good enough?' She wouldn't have minded being that kid. 'No, that wasn't me.'

'I can't see you confidently calling out things in front of everyone.'

'No, not that one either.'

'Tantrums?' He lifted an eyebrow and sent her a sideways smile. 'No? But what else is there?'

In the safety of the car, riding on the success of her morning and the fact the worst of today was now over, she was relaxed enough actually to answer. 'I was the kid who ran away.'

He watched her. 'You really mean it.'

'I really do.' She drew in a slightly jagged breath, regretting the confession.

'Did they find you and bring you home again?'

'They had to,' she replied lowly. 'I was young and they had an image to maintain. But that didn't stop me trying again.'

'Did you ever succeed in running away for good?'

'Eventually, yes.'

She wanted to gaze out of the window. She wanted to end this conversation. But his coal-black eyes were so full of questions that she couldn't answer and so full of compassion that she didn't have the strength to pull back from him either.

'Will you run away if you don't like it here?' he asked.

'No. I'm grown up now and I'll see this through.' She

made herself smile and clear the intensity. 'I think it's more likely that you'll banish me like your ancestor did his rebel Queen.'

To her relief, he followed her lead and laughed. 'I have to banish you to her castle. I'll take you after dinner. It'll be a dark-windowed car tonight. Tomorrow is the glass carriage.'

'The fairy-tale element?'

'Absolutely.'

After another dinner devoted to preparation and planning, this time with several advisors attending and in which Alek refused to release her hand, they were driven to the castle on the edge of the city for Hester's final night as a single woman.

'Welcome to Queen Aleksandrina's home.' Alek spread his arms wide as the enormous wooden doors were closed behind them.

Hester knew the story of Aleksandrina well. Her marriage had taken place after the King's coronation and was such an unmitigated disaster that a law had been passed stipulating that any future prince could not claim the King's throne before being married. Furthermore, at the King's coronation, his bride must bow before him—before all his other subjects did; she was to be prime symbol of deference to his rule. It was appalling, but 'tradition'.

'The rebel Queen who defied her husband and decided to build her own castle at the other end of town?' Hester nodded in approval. 'She sounds *amazing.*'

Alek grinned. 'You know I'm named after her?'

'Really?' That surprised her. She'd thought the rebel Queen was frowned upon. 'And you don't want to live here?'

She hoisted her little backpack on her shoulder and

gazed up in awe at the carved constellations in the vaulted ceiling of the castle's great room. Where the palace was gilded and gleaming, the castle was hand-carved curves and lush plantings. It was softer somehow and very feminine. Carved into the coastline, it had a wild element to it; part of it actually overhung a cliff.

'There's a tunnel to the beach below. I'll show you.' He grinned at her. 'The rumour was it was how the Queen smuggled her lovers in without the King knowing.'

'Lovers—plural?'

'Apparently she was insatiable.'

'And did you say you're named after her?' Hester clarified a little too meekly.

He chuckled. 'My mother always said those rumours were just slut-shaming to steal her powerful legacy from her. The fact was she was a better queen than he was a king and he couldn't handle it.'

Hester stilled at the mention of his mother. She sensed she was an off-limits subject and Hester of all people understood the desire to protect those precious memories. 'It sounds like your mother was quite a woman too,' she said lightly.

'She was.' He turned and headed towards a doorway. 'Come to the ballroom.'

Yes, he wasn't about to elaborate and Hester didn't blame him. 'This isn't the ballroom?'

Two minutes later Hester gazed around the vast, ornate room, uttered moved by gorgeous wooden carvings and low-hanging candelabra. 'I...wow... I just...' She trailed off; her throat was too tight. It was so incredible.

Alek stepped in front of her and brushed her cheek with his hand as he gazed into her eyes. 'You really do struggle to express yourself sometimes, don't you?'

Of course, he saw that. Somehow he was right there, too close. Making her want...too much. Everything she *felt* around him was too strong and so easily he weakened the bonds with which she held herself together.

His hand on her waist was so light, so gentle, she couldn't quite be sure it was even there. But the electricity racing along her veins confirmed it. 'What are—?'

'Practising for our first dance,' he answered before she'd even finished asking.

'You're kidding—we have to dance?' She groaned. 'I can't dance, Alek. I don't know how to.'

'Just relax and follow my lead.' His dimples appeared. 'It'll be fine.'

She put her hand on his chest, keeping him at that distance as he stepped fractionally closer. But the tips of her fingers burned with the temptation to spread, to stroke. And they weren't dancing at all, they were standing still as still, close but not breathing, not blinking either. Somehow time evaporated. Somehow he was nearer still and she'd got lost in the depths of his dark eyes and the current of his energy coiling around her.

'Why try to fight it?' he whispered.

Of course he knew, of course he saw the terrible yearning within her. But self-preservation made her deny it. 'Fight what?'

'The inevitable.'

'I refuse to be inevitable,' she muttered hoarsely, her instinctive self-preservation instincts kicking in.

'There's a saying for that,' he countered with a smile. 'Cutting off your nose to spite your face.'

'You think I'm missing out on something amazing just because I won't fall for your flirting?'

'I think it's interesting that you're making it such a big deal.'

'Maybe I want something meaningful.'

'You think I don't mean it?' A frown entered his eyes.

'Because I do. There's something about you…you're growing on me, Hester.'

'Like a kind of bacteria? Fungus?'

'Not fungus.' Beneath her fingertips she felt the laughter rumble in his broad chest. 'Are you trying to put me off?'

'You know I am.'

'I do.' He shot her a look. 'And I love that you feel the need to try so hard. It makes me think I'm getting beneath that prickly shell of yours.'

'So now I'm a porcupine? And here I was thinking you were supposed to be impossibly charming and irresistible.'

'You know what I think? I think you've decided I'm some big, bad philanderer. And that makes me terrible, for some reason. Sorry for liking sex, sweetheart. Maybe if you tried it, you'd discover it's not so awful. But instead you feel you have to keep me at a distance and not explore the fact that we have quite spectacular chemistry.' He leaned closer. 'Sparks, Hester. Every time we touch. Every time we even see each other.'

She ducked her gaze. 'I just don't think it's wise for us to blur the boundaries. We have a *contract*. That's all.'

'A contract that contains two kisses.' He smiled happily.

Something swooped low in her belly. 'Only two.' And they were both going to be in public so it wasn't as if they were going to develop into anything out of control.

'But you're a lot more fun to be around than I imagined you'd be, Hester.'

'I'm so glad, given I live to please you, my lord.'

He laughed and lightly tapped her on the nose. 'Call me Alek.' He leaned closer and breathed, 'Always.'

Her smile faded. She wished he wouldn't get like this—the combination of playful and serious that was so seductive it shut down her brain and made those dormant secret parts of her roar to life.

'I…don't—' She broke off as a shiver ran down her

spine. She stepped back, seeking distance from his intensity.

He stayed where he was, studying her intently. 'Are you afraid of me?'

'Surprisingly, no.' She was too shaken to lie. She didn't fear him so much as how she *felt* when he was near.

'So you're worried about…?' A frown knitted his brows.

It was easier to talk about everything else other than the riot of emotion he invoked within her. 'The press, the Internet trolls.'

'You're such a liar, Hester. No, you're not. You never would have put yourself in their firing line if you really were. Tell me the real reason.'

'Words *can* hurt,' she argued.

'Maybe. Sometimes.' He nodded. 'Depending on who's doing the talking, right?'

He was very right. And now her voice was stolen by memories she had no wish to recall.

The teasing light in his eyes dimmed and he stepped closer. 'You can tell me,' he assured her quietly. 'I know you're prickly, you won't believe even the littlest of honest compliments. I know you don't let many people into your life.' He paused. 'I know this is an arrangement. I know I'm effectively paying for your company. And I know I tease you…but you *can* trust me. I hope that you might be able to trust me enough to be able to tell me *why* you've built such high barriers.'

She knew she shouldn't let the past constrain her future. And even though she had no real future with him, there was here and *now*. And she didn't want to lie to him any more. 'Because I've had my trust broken before.'

He waited, watching her. She knew she didn't have to explain it to him if she really didn't want to, but he was patient and quiet and somehow compelling.

'You're right,' she growled. 'I'm not really worried

about the cameras or all the crowds or the online commentators. It's my three cousins.' She breathed out. 'I shouldn't have invited them.'

'You don't see them much?'

'I haven't seen them in years.' She didn't want to tell him how weak and vulnerable she'd been. And it wasn't all their fault, right? She probably hadn't made enough effort and they couldn't understand her and it had been too easy for her to shut down.

'I know no one is perfect, but they pretty much are.' She glanced at him quickly, offering superficial detail. 'And I wasn't. I was like a troll in the elven realm. They were a party of extroverted sporting elite. I liked reading in the corner. We just couldn't relate.'

He blinked, his expression perplexed. 'But how did they break your trust?'

She'd forgotten she'd admitted that first. She swallowed. 'With words.'

It wasn't a lie—it was very true. But it wasn't all of the truth.

'They've all accepted the invitation. They're here,' he said after a while. 'I've put them up at the hotel, rather than the palace. I've already issued a personal request that they don't speak to the media but I can't muzzle anyone completely. If they get seduced by the offer of an exclusive with a news agency—'

'I know.' She licked her lips nervously. 'I know you can't control everything.'

Of course they'd accepted the invitations. Who could turn down a flight in a private jet to attend something so high profile in the incredible country of Triscari? Even she hadn't been able to turn down his offer.

'I'm sorry I can't,' he murmured. 'I'm sorry they hurt you.'

She stiffened, holding back that yearning opening

within with every step he took closer towards her. She didn't want his sympathy. She didn't want to think about any of that.

'But I'm not going to do that,' he added. 'I'm not saying anything I don't mean to you. When I talk about our inevitability, Hester, I'm not trying to flatter you. I'm just being honest.'

The trouble was his honesty was so naturally charming, so instinctively seductive. And while he was arrogant and confident, she didn't think even he really realised his potency. He was used to it, wasn't he? Flirting and having affairs. She just wasn't. She didn't think she could handle him.

'There are still only two kisses in our contract,' she breathed, clinging to that flimsy fact.

She had to keep him at that wafer-thin distance. He couldn't change the agreement before they'd even signed the marriage certificate.

'Trust me, I know.' He remained close for the merest moment more. 'And for what it's worth, I think you're going to slay them all tomorrow.'

Truthfully all she wanted was to slay *him*.

Fairy tales indeed.

CHAPTER SIX

HESTER SWAYED GENTLY as the glass carriage carried her along the castle route with its cobblestones and beautiful flower-strewn path to her waiting prince. The fine lace veil covering her face softened her focus so the vast crowds waving and watching blurred, but they were all there hoping to catch a glimpse of her—Prince Alek's mysterious bride.

She'd slept surprisingly well in the large wooden castle. Fiorella had arrived there too late in the evening for them to catch up and then Billie and her team had arrived first thing, along with an army of dressmakers. So she'd had no chance to talk to Fiorella—they were both too busy being beautified for the wedding. This was good because when she'd first spotted her soon-to-be sister-in-law, she'd veered dangerously close to hugging her. And Hester didn't hug anyone.

Before getting ready this morning she'd read only a few of the news stories about her that had been printed over the last few days. They'd not had that much time to dig up too much drama, but there was enough to make her shiver. But, worse, the real truth was there—some whispered of Alek's requirement to marry. That he'd picked someone biddable and shy and inoffensive. 'The bland bride', some bitchy bloggers had labelled her.

The romantics on the other side, however, wanted to believe the fairy tale and drowned out that truth with the fantasy. Their outing to the hospital had silenced many doubters and the body-language experts had had a field day. Apparently their light touch and laughing smiles showed 'intimacy and genuine love' between them.

And her moment with that distressed boy had some-how been leaked—still images taken by a long-range lens through a window while one of the teachers had spoken on condition of anonymity and talked of her natural affin-ity with the children...while Alek was apparently smitten and protective. Hester had put the tablet down, unwilling to read any more.

'We're almost there. Deep breath, Hester.' Fiorella smiled. 'This is going to be amazing.'

Contrarily Fiorella's soft reassurance sharpened Hes-ter's nerves. Too late she realised the princess had been abnormally quiet all morning. Was she worried—or pre-occupied? 'Are you okay Fiorella?'

'Okay?' The princess's deep brown eyes widened and curiously a rush of colour swept into her cheeks. 'You mean about the wedding?'

What else would she have meant? Fiorella's gaze dipped but before Hester could ask more, the carriage slowed and then stopped.

'You're the best person in the world for Alek,' Fiorella whispered quickly before a footman appeared at the door.

Hester was glad of the veil—it gave her soft focus too. She could literally hide behind it.

She climbed the stone steps slowly as instructed, though mainly it was because the silk train of her dress was heavy. Then she saw Alek waiting at the end of the long aisle and was unable to tear her gaze from him. Every step drew her closer to him and revealed more detail of his appearance. He wore full royal regalia—gleaming gold trim, military medals and that scarlet sash of power across his chest and, yes, even one feather. He stood straight and strong and so serious, but as she finally drew alongside him she saw the smile in his eyes and a teasing twitch of his lips.

The ceremony was full of pomp just as he'd promised. There were trumpets, choirs, a cellist...but she barely noticed them. Nor did she really see the beautiful floral arrangements and the stunningly attired guests. *He* sucked all her attention.

It seemed to take for ever, yet passed in a flash. She was vitally aware of him breathing beside her, so close yet distant, and every moment watched by millions. She grew stupidly nervous after reciting her vows. Her mouth dried and she swallowed back her anxiety. Why had she shot down the idea of a practice kiss? They'd probably bump noses, or clash teeth or something even more awkward in front of the world. It was mortifying. And it would be replayed over and over, immortalised in memes on the Internet for ever. The 'world's worst kiss'.

Terrified, she looked at Alek. That knowing glint of good humour in his eyes grew and his lips curved enough to set the dimples free. She couldn't hold back her own impish smile in response. This whole thing? It *was* ridiculous. And suddenly it was fun, this secret contract between them.

He bent nearer, so very slowly. Utterly still, she expected only a brief peck.

It was a gossamer brush of his lips over hers, so gentle that she wouldn't have been sure it had happened if she hadn't seen him. But he lingered and her eyes drifted shut as intimacy was unleashed in that lightest, purest of touches. She yearned to capture it—to stop time and bask in the warmth and connection from such slight pressure.

He pulled back and smiled again right into her eyes as she blinked and returned to the world. The roaring cheers of the crowd seeped through the stone walls and a ripple of audible pleasure ran through the guests present in the magnificent palace chapel. He drew her hand through his arm and escorted her down the long aisle. The noise of the applause boomed tenfold as the church door was opened for them to exit. They stood for a long moment on the top step, smiling at the scores and scores of people—the crowd stretched as far as she could see.

'Hester.'

She heard his soft command and faced him. The wicked laughter in his eyes was for her alone.

'Steel yourself, sweetheart,' he muttered.

She was ready and more willing than she wanted to admit. But he knew, didn't he? She saw the triumph in his eyes as he bent towards her.

This kiss lingered. This kiss lit something else—there was more than a gossamer caress, there was a hint of intent and she couldn't stop her own response—the parting gasp of delight that allowed him in.

But instead he pulled back. She saw his face only briefly but the smile was gone from his eyes—replaced by blazing intensity and an arrogant tilt to his jaw and suddenly he was back. Stealing a third. This last kiss was not chaste. He crushed her lips with his in a too-brief stamp of passion that promised so much more than it ought to—the sweep of his tongue commanding a response that she couldn't withhold. Heat and power surged through her as his hands tightened—holding her firm while promising even more. Still dignified, but so, so dangerous. It was only a moment, but one that changed her irrevocably. Because she'd been the one to moan in regret when it ended. She'd never wanted it to end.

'That was three, not two,' she breathed, trying to whip up some fury but failing. She was too floored, too unstable in containing her feelings.

'So sue me,' he breathed back before laughing delightedly. 'What are you going to do about it standing here in front of the world?'

'Stop it, all the lip-readers will interpret what you're saying and they'll know this is—'

'You stop talking. I'm not even moving my lips. Ventriloquising is a talent of mine. Learned it from a very early age. You do when you're filmed and photographed at every possible opportunity.'

She giggled as she knew he'd intended. 'Is it even a word?'

'You bet. Formal study required.' He turned his head so no cameras could get between either of them and gazed into her eyes; his own were dancing. 'Now seriously, be silent, or I'll have to employ emergency tactics and I don't know that it would be wise for me to do that here and now.'

His voice had an edge and she knew what he meant. He raised his free hand and waved to the crowds, who cheered again, then he helped her down the marble steps and into the glass carriage. He sat close, his arm tight around her while she rationalised that extra kiss. He was pleased with the afternoon's events, that was all. That kiss had been a moment of pure male satisfaction—of pleasure and power.

'Hester?'

'No.' She glinted at him. 'You've had more than your lifetime allowance.' She smiled and waved to the crowd.

'But—'

'You can't ventriloquise your way out of this, Alek,' she scolded. 'You broke the deal.'

'Why, Hester Moss, are you chastising me?'

'I'm no longer Hester Moss.' She flashed her teeth at him in a brilliant smile. 'And I'm putting on a good show, aren't I?'

The woman formerly known as Hester Moss was putting on far more than 'a good show'. She was glittering. And almost flirting. And Alek discovered he could hardly cope. All he wanted was to pull her back into his arms and kiss her again. Again. And again. And ideally everywhere. Instead he had to smile and wave and grit his teeth because there were millions watching them.

In the safe privacy of a palace antechamber, he studied the tablet for the few minutes they'd factored ahead of the formal reception, taking time to settle his own rioting emotions the way he knew Hester did—with distraction and avoidance. But he couldn't deny her radiance—or his primal response to her.

He realised now—far too late—that he hadn't noticed any other woman in days and he *always* noticed women. Now he didn't seem to give a damn. He hadn't even seen them. And it wasn't just about ensuring Hester's comfort in a difficult situation. It was as if she were some giant magnet, while his eyeballs were iron filings. With no will of their own they just kept focusing on her. It was as if she'd obliterated anyone else out of existence. He laughed a little bitterly to himself. Served him right, didn't it? That he hadn't wanted a wife at all, but now he had one and he wanted his wife more than he'd wanted any other woman? And she was so off-limits—she was effectively an employee, she was a virgin, she was clearly vulnerable because she'd been hurt somehow and was isolated now... yes, the reasons why he shouldn't lay a finger on her were probably insurmountable. But that didn't stop his body from wanting her anyway.

'Are you okay?' she asked.

'Oh, I'm dandy,' he mocked himself. And he had to survive spending the night with her in his wing because there was no way they could sleep in separate apartments on their wedding night.

Was it only because she was out of bounds? As if he truly were some spoilt child who was so used to getting everything that he wanted that he couldn't cope the first time he'd heard the word no from a woman?

No. He simply ached to seduce her. He'd been skimming closer to seducing her with every passing day, more deeply intrigued as she'd opened up so fractionally, so slowly. Those sparks of humour, of spirit, fascinated him. He wanted to break her open and bask in the warmth and wit he knew she kept locked inside. And he wanted to test the intensity of this chemistry that made mush of his synapses, made every muscle tense and turned his guts to water.

Instead he had to endure a long celebratory feast in front of hundreds.

He glanced up from the screen and saw her hips and the curve of her bottom and was hit by a rush of lust so severe he had to freeze. No. It wasn't anything as superficial as simply being told he couldn't have something and only then wanting it. He wasn't a child any more. He'd outgrown the pursuit of challenges just for the sake of toppling them. This was all about her. He wanted to see her melt in pleasure. He wanted her to turn to him, to offer him her luscious mouth again. He wanted to coax more of the passion he'd discovered just beneath her still surface.

Instead he glared back at the screen.

The world was absolutely lapping it up—they were trending on all social media sites. Images of them spiralled throughout the web—one picture, just after the kiss, was being shared hundreds of thousands of times a second, it seemed.

When she'd smiled at him, it was like a revelation— all sparkle and beauty. It helped that her dress fitted as if she'd been poured into it—cinched at her waist and flaring over her full hips. It was absolute femininity. She was no rail-thin princess but rather a slim bundle of curves that were almost too sexy for the circumstance. The heels gave her a little extra height but she still barely made it to his shoulder. Her hair had been left mostly loose—all lush, lightly curled beauty—while the fragile tiara with its droplet diamonds added to the overall picture of princess perfection. How had he ever thought she wasn't beautiful?

'What is it?' She stepped over and he tilted the tablet so she could see them too.

She assessed the pictures silently, critically, showing no obvious emotion, but he knew she was thinking and feeling. He craved to know what. His heart still beat horrifically fast. Those two kisses had been the most chaste of his life—yet somehow the most erotic and they'd forced him into stealing that third. That too-brief statement of what he really wanted—to get her alone, away from all the watching people.

As alone as they were now.

He gripped the tablet tightly, resisting the wave of desire ricocheting through him. And the fierce regret. He wanted to start again. To forget the whole damn marriage requirement and instead take the simple pleasure of seducing her slowly and completely. All he wanted was her absolute surrender—for her to be his in the most basic sense of the word. She was the most exquisite temptation—a mystery, as the press had rightly labelled her. But the contract between them imposed rules and boundaries. He wanted to break every one here and now. It was appalling—he'd never imagined that she'd fascinate him so.

'It's amazing what properly fitting clothes and expertly applied make-up can do,' she muttered, oblivious to his turmoil as she swiftly scrolled through the photographs. 'I look okay.'

The dress and make-up merely accentuated the perfection beneath. 'I thought you didn't care what they think.' He managed to push through his tension to half-smile at her.

'Well, I don't want to let you down.'

'So you care what *I* think?' he asked more harshly than he intended.

She drew a slow breath and he knew she was settling her response to him, trying to keep her façade still. 'I care about doing a good job.'

'And that's all this still is to you? Just a job?' He didn't want to believe that. He refused to.

He fought the urge to haul her close—to make her flush, to make that serenity flare in a burst of satisfaction. He ached to see her shudder, to hear her scream as ecstasy overcame her. He wanted her warm and soft and smiling, no more cool, fragile façade. That first kiss had given him the briefest hint of what pleasure they could find together and had seared his nerve endings. He wanted to crack her open and release the warmth he was now certain was at her core.

They'd effectively laughed their way back down the aisle with an intimacy built on something other than physical. It had rendered him unable to resist the need to kiss her the way he'd ached to—stealing that third kiss to feel the heat of her response.

Now she was attempting to rebuild her personal barriers, to hide the fiercely deep feelings she didn't want to express. But she wasn't going to be able to deny them for too much longer. He'd felt the ferocity of her fire.

'I'm sorry about the article,' she said quietly, sidestepping his question.

'Your cousins.' He knew the one she meant. 'They said you ghosted them,' he said. 'That you emotionally shut them out.' He watched her expression stiffen and strove to reassure her. 'Hester, I of all people know not to believe everything I read in the media.'

'But it's true.' She lifted her chin but didn't meet his eyes. 'I did.'

Defensiveness radiated from every pore and his arms ached with the urge to hold her close.

'I'm sure you had good reason to,' he said carefully.

Now liquid gleamed in her eyes and smote his heart.

'It was silly, wasn't it? To have expected them to care for me, just because of blood.'

He took in what she'd said. They hadn't cared for her—they hadn't wanted her. And she'd been so unhappy she'd run away and locked herself in that ivory tower at the university. Quietly assisting students who lived fuller lives and cared less for their studies than she did.

'I didn't think they'd speak to the press.' Her whisper rushed. 'I thought inviting them would...' She shook her head. 'I should have known better.'

'They've gone the "friend of the family" route,' he said, cynically aware of how the media worked. 'So they can say it wasn't them.'

'But it was.' She looked at him directly and he saw the hurt she'd tried to bury. 'I'm sorry if they've caused problems.' She pressed her lips together. 'Do I have to see them?'

'There's a receiving line.' He nodded. 'There'll be other eyes and ears but no cameras. We'll keep them moving quickly. I'll be on one side of you. Fi will be on the other.'

'She's been wonderful today.'

'She understands what it's like.' Alek nodded, but the strain was still etched on her face.

'She said she wants to stay in the States,' she murmured.

He let her lead the distraction, realising she needed it. 'Yes. I want her to do whatever she wants. She seemed distracted, said it's because she's thinking of doing post-graduate study.'

'She's super capable,' Hester agreed softly before turning her gaze back on him. 'What would you have chosen?' She inched closer. 'To do, I mean.'

'The crown chose me, Hester. That's why we're here.'

'But if you were free? If you didn't have to be a full-time royal?'

The wildness clawing inside him soothed a little under her gaze. He'd always wanted Fi to have the freedom he couldn't have. It was the sacrifice he'd made and he didn't regret it. What he regretted right now was the tension lingering around Hester's beautiful eyes. He never talked about all this impossibility; there was no point. But he desperately needed to stop thinking about kissing her. Distraction from difficulty was always good. And he needed to distract her too. Because that was what she was really asking him to do. So he did.

'I wanted to study medicine,' he blurted.

'You wanted to be a doctor?' Her jaw dropped and as she snapped it shut a frown furrowed her brow. 'How was that going to work?'

'I know, right? The idealism of youth.' He shook his head.

'It was a good ideal.' She curled her hand on his arm. 'You would have been—' She shook her head and broke off. 'What stopped you?'

'My father.' He smiled ruefully. 'I didn't ever think he'd disapprove of such a worthy profession, right? Literally trying to save people's lives.'

'You wanted to save lives?'

Dredging this up was infinitely preferable to facing the unrequited lust shivering through him like a damn fever. And thinking of this made him feel nothing but cold.

'I watched cancer slowly suffocate my mother, stealing her vitality and joy. It was horrendous and there was nothing I could do to help her. I hated feeling so inept. I never wanted to feel that useless again.' He glossed over the most painful memories of his life. 'And honestly, I liked science. But my father didn't think I could get the grades—before Mother got sick I'd pretty much mucked around.'

He'd not discussed his mother's death with anyone, ever. Yet it was somehow easier to talk about this than acknowledge the storm of emotion swirling within him. And Hester was in a realm of her own now in his life. Maybe he was a fool but he felt he could trust her. Besides, she'd lost both her parents and that was a pain he couldn't imagine.

'What happened to her motivated me. I wanted to make a difference and I finally got my head together. I was so proud when I got the grades that guaranteed my entry into medical school. I presented them to him. I thought he'd be proud too.'

'But he wasn't?' she whispered.

Her words somehow pushed aside the mocking self-pity to salve the true hurt beneath. He'd laughed it off to himself in recent years, but it had never really been a joke. It had broken his heart.

'He said it would take far too long to study. Eight years, minimum, before any real speciality. I had to devote more time to my country. You can't be King and have a career. Your career *is* being King. Even though I didn't expect to take the crown for a long time.' He shrugged. 'So obviously I couldn't do veterinary school either. Horses were my other passion.' His stud farm on the neighbouring island was world renowned. 'I learned to ride before I could walk.' He made himself brag with a brash smile because he regretted bringing this up.

The lingering empathy in her eyes told him she still saw through to his old hidden pain but then she smiled. 'And what other amazing accomplishments does a prince have to master? Geography, I bet. Languages?'

'Five.' He nodded.

'Ventriloquism being one of them?' Her smile quirked.

'Of course.' That tension in his shoulders eased.

'Piano? Art?'

'Actually I do play the piano but I can't draw.'

'Well, I'm glad to discover you do have an imperfection or two,' she teased. 'So what did you do after he said no to everything you wanted?'

'I went into the military. Always acceptable. I trained with both navy and land-based forces.'

'But not air? You mean even with all your amazing accomplishments you can't fly a plane?'

'I occupied my very little spare time with polo. And other off-field pursuits.'

'Women.'

'I was going to say partying.' He maintained his smile through gritted teeth. 'I was bored and bitter and I felt stuck. I resented him for saying no to every damn thing that I truly wanted to do. So I did my work, but I had frequent blow-outs—and, yes, in part it was to piss him off.' He glanced at her ruefully. 'Predictable, right?'

'I can understand why you'd resent him and want to rebel. It's horrible being denied what you want all the time.'

'It is.' He glanced at her again and smiled faintly to himself. 'I'd wanted to do something meaningful and I wasn't allowed.' He sighed. 'I was angry. I was angry that Fi was so constrained. I was angry that he was always so distant and no matter what I did it was always a disappointment. He disapproved of my straight As, for heaven's sake. What was left to do other than rebel? But then it just became a habit and what everybody expected. It sure kept Triscari in the news—I maintained our high profile. There were just other consequences as well.'

'You were lonely,' she said softly.

'Hester.' He rolled his eyes. 'I was surrounded by people.'

'People who you couldn't really talk to. Your father was distant. Fi was too young and then you helped her get away to study, your mum had gone, there was nothing but party women and yes-men. I think that would get lonely.'

He rubbed his shoulder. 'You're too generous, Hester. I revelled in being the Playboy Prince.'

She studied him. 'You still want to do something meaningful?'

'My only job now is to be a good king for my country. I was angry about the marriage thing but perhaps, now it is done, I can get on and prove that this will all be good.'

'I don't think you need to prove yourself, Alek,' she said. 'I think what you do is very meaningful.'

He had no idea how the conversation had got so side-tracked. He'd meant to distract her from her distress about her family and himself from his desire for her. Yet somehow this had turned heavy and he'd told her far more than he'd intended. And somehow she'd soothed an old wound within him that he hadn't realised was still aching.

He gazed at her—her beautiful leonine eyes were more luminous than ever and how was it he wanted her more than ever? The ache to lean close, to touch her, was unbearable.

Instead he put down the tablet and stalked towards the door, remembering far too late that they had a palace full of people to please. 'We'd better get this over with.'

CHAPTER SEVEN

HESTER WATCHED HER husband charm everyone—hustling the receiving line through while making every guest believe he'd paid them extra special individual attention. She was fascinated by his skill—and so busy contemplating what he'd told her, the depth of his secrets and sadness and sacrifice, that she didn't spot her cousins until they were right there, confronting her with their fake smiles and stabbing eyes.

All the noise of the room receded as Joshua, Kimberly and Brittany stared at her. Hester froze, struck dumb as Kimberly executed a tart curtsey that exuded total lack of respect.

'Thanks for the invitation.' Brittany's faux polite opener was so barbed.

Hester still couldn't speak. They were older yet hadn't changed a bit. And how was it that they could make her feel so inept and small, even here and now?

'Our pleasure.' Alek filled the small silence and extended his hand to Joshua. 'We're grateful you could join us in celebrating our special day.'

In the face of Alek's ruthless charm the three of them were rendered speechless. Hester watched with relief as they continued on into the reception room. It was good they'd shut up, but *she'd* not silenced them. And to her horror she discovered she still cared just a tiny bit too much. But Alek held her hand tightly, glued to her side in an outrageous display of possessiveness and protectiveness that she was enjoying far too much.

'I instructed Fi to spread the rumour that we're sneaking away early,' he muttered near her ear as they took to the dance floor. 'Which we are, by the way.'

'Okay.' It was silly to feel nervous. This wasn't a *real* wedding night, but a charade.

Less than thirty minutes later they walked through the corridors to their private apartments. 'You'll have to stay with me tonight,' he said softly. 'I'll sleep...'

'On the sofa?' she finished for him.

'Something like that.'

'We survived.'

'We did more than survive, we nailed it. Did you see their faces? They loved it.' He threw her a satisfied smile.

'Wonderful.' She'd hardly noticed anyone else. She'd hardly eaten anything at the dinner. And she'd managed only a couple of mouthfuls of champagne.

She glanced around his apartment, taking in the details to divert her thoughts. The set-up was similar to her own, only his had been refurbished in a modern style—no old-fashioned gaudy wallpaper for him.

'I might go straight to bed,' she murmured awkwardly.

'That's what you want?'

She froze. She couldn't even swallow.

His expression suddenly twisted. 'Relax, Hester. It's okay. Take the bedroom, second door on the left.'

She ought to have felt relief; instead hollow regret stole her last smile. But she'd only taken two steps into the bedroom when she realised the problem. Heat beat into her cheeks, but there was no getting around it. She walked back out to the lounge. Alek was exactly where she'd left him, staring moodily at the table.

'I'm going to need help to get out of this dress,' she said.

He lifted his chin and speared her with that intense gaze.

'I'm sewn into it.' She bit her lip, so embarrassed because it felt stupidly intimate and he seemed reluctant to move nearer. 'I'm sorry.'

'No, it's okay.' He cleared his throat and walked over to her. 'Let me see.'

She turned her back, so crazily aware that she held her breath as he ran his finger down the seam of her dress.

'I think I need scissors or something,' he said.

'You could always use your ceremonial sword.' She tried to lighten the atmosphere but it didn't work. Nothing could ease the tension she felt.

'Or my teeth,' he muttered.

She tried to quell her shiver but his hands stilled on her skin. For an endless profound moment, awareness arced between them.

'Come on,' he finally growled. 'I have scissors in the bathroom.'

He meant the bathroom that was en suite to his massive bedroom. Hester hovered on the edge of the room, trying not to stare at that huge bed, while he retrieved the scissors. Then she turned her back to him again.

'I don't want to ruin it,' he said in a low voice that purred over her.

She closed her eyes. 'I'm not going to wear it again—it won't matter if it gets a little torn.'

He worked silently for a moment longer. 'They'll put it on display at the palace museum eventually.'

'Really?' Even with her back to him his magnetism almost suffocated her. She wanted him to touch her more. She wanted another kiss…

'I really need to get out of this dress,' she begged desperately. 'I can't breathe any more.'

'Then let's get you out of it.'

She felt a tug and then he swore. 'I ripped a button off. Sorry.'

'It's fine.'

She heard his sharp intake of breath. And then she heard another unmistakable tearing sound. Her dress loosened, then slipped and she clutched the bodice to her chest. Gripping the silk tightly against her, she slowly turned to face him.

He was so near, so intent, so still. And she could so relate. She had to stay still too or else she was going to tumble into his arms like some desperate, over-sexed...*virgin*.

'Hester...'

She stared up at him.

'Just so we're clear,' he said softly. 'I didn't steal the third kiss for the cameras.'

She didn't move. She couldn't.

'It was pure selfish want on my part. I know I ought to apologise, but I think you enjoyed it as much as I did.'

He was so close she could feel his breath on her skin.

'I want to think you want another,' he said. 'Not on any stupid contract. Not limited.'

She couldn't reply.

'Your lips clung to mine.' Emotion darkened his eyes as he stared down at her, solemn and so intense, pressing his will on hers. 'I think you want me to kiss you and I sure as hell want to kiss you.'

He still didn't move. But he was right. She wanted him to touch her again. She ached to feel the electricity that had sizzled in that too-brief kiss. She wanted to know if it was real or if she'd imagined it. She *needed* to know that. 'Yes.'

'Yes?'

She knew he was warring within himself the same way she was.

'I do.' She whispered a vow more honest than the other one she'd given today.

He swooped down on her instantly. She'd never know how it happened but somehow she was backed up against the wall and he was kissing her and she was kissing him back as best she could because everything she'd been holding back for so long was released in a massive rush. All the want. All the heat. Sensual power burgeoned between them. She could no longer think, she no longer cared about anything other than keeping him kissing her. Keeping him close.

'Tell me to stop,' he groaned, lifting his head to gaze at her. 'Or do you want me to keep going? You know what I want, Hester. And while I'd like to think I know what you want, I *need* to hear it from you.' His breathing was rough but the touch of his hands at her waist was so gentle. 'I need to hear your voice.'

Even though she really wanted to, she couldn't make herself answer. She was so locked inside herself because what she wanted was so huge and she wanted it so much, she was terrified to ask for it.

'Hester?' His hands tightened on her waist.

As she gazed at the restraint in his eyes a trickle of power ran through her veins. And that trickle was enough to make her walls crack.

'I'm stronger than you,' he growled. 'I have you pinned against the wall. I could—'

'It's fine.'

His pupils flared. 'It's *what*?'

'Fantastic,' she corrected in a desperate rush. 'Please, Alek…'

She needed his touch—needed him to take her, *completely*. She wanted all of him for just this one night. Because she was so tired of being alone. She'd not realised how lonely she was until he walked into her life and made her want all kinds of impossible things. Things she could never have for good, but maybe just for now. Just for a night.

'Please what?' he growled, leaning closer. 'Tell me, Hester. I need you to tell me.'

He remained locked before her, waiting—silently *insisting*. His fierce expression forced her own fiery need to burst free.

'I'm *tired* of feeling nothing,' she cried at him breathlessly. 'I want to feel good. *This* feels good. I want to feel more good. Like *this*. With you.'

His eyes widened but he nodded. 'Okay.'

He lifted his hands from her waist to her wrists. She was holding her dress tightly to her chest but she knew what he was about to do. He applied gentle pressure to her wrists; he pulled her arms away from her body, making her beautiful dress slither to the floor. The tight bodice had meant she'd not needed underwear so now her breasts were bared. His coal eyes blazed into hers for a long moment before his gaze then lowered. His tension tripled as he stared at her. Stark, savage hunger built in his expression—an echo of her own. With a muffled groan he bent and pressed his mouth to her—kissing, caressing, caring. Unable to resist, she leaned back against the wall, shuddering with the intensity of the sensations he was arousing in her with every hot breath, each slide of his tongue and tease of his fingers. Her body arched as she was lost in the delight of it. Of *him*. He was so overpowering, so perfect.

'Oh…' She closed her eyes as his hands roved lower.

She was almost scared at how incredible it felt. 'Alek.' She couldn't stand it any more. *'Alek.'*

'Yes,' he muttered, as breathless as she. 'Yes, darling.'

She tumbled into incoherence, into nothing but heat and light, burgeoning sensations of pleasure and want. She arched against him as he slipped his hand beneath her silk panties, writhing until he had to hold her hips still with a hard hand so he could pleasure her, so he could coax her to the very crest of that most incredible feeling. He stroked her hard until she shook in his arms and screamed out the agony of ecstasy.

'You are *so* hot,' he said as he picked her up and carried her to his bed as if she weighed nothing. 'I knew you were.'

She didn't care what he knew, she just needed him closer. She needed more. 'Alek.'

She pulled him down to her. She'd never been this close to anyone and she didn't want it to end yet, not now she'd only just begun to discover him. Her hand slid up his chest, gingerly spreading her fingers to explore him.

'You can touch me.' He drew a shaking breath. 'Anywhere you want. Anyhow.'

She realised he *wanted* her to touch him. As much as she wanted him to touch her. This was give and take. Desire and hunger. She slid her hand further and watched him tense with pleasure at her touch. And then all reticence fled and she was driven to discover more. She helped him out of his suit, relishing the slow revelation of his gorgeous body. She caressed every inch of his muscled beauty, pausing when she ran her fingers over a jagged scar on his rump—not wanting to hurt him but wondering what had happened. He smiled, pulling her closer, and she forgot her question in the heat and tease of his kisses. He'd locked her in a dungeon of desire—hidden deep inside the heart of the palace, she was a prisoner to the overwhelming lust he aroused.

'Please,' she whispered. Her throat was so dry the word hardly sounded.

'Hester,' he groaned. 'I need you to tell me what you want me to do.'

'I thought you didn't like being told what to do?' She shuddered as he slid his leg between hers.

'I can make an exception for you.' He gazed into her eyes, his hips grinding delightfully against hers in a slow, tormenting motion. 'Do you want me to kiss you?'

'Yes.'

So he did—so thoroughly and lushly that she arched, unable to resist the urges of her body. He kissed, not just her mouth, but her neck and her chest. He kissed, nipped and nibbled, working his way lower and lower, kissing parts of her that had never been kissed before.

'Do you want me to touch you?' he breathed huskily against her belly.

'Yes.'

His hands swept over her—more and more intimately teasing and tormenting her until she writhed beneath him and even though he'd made her soar only minutes before, that empty ache inside was utterly unbearable.

And somehow he knew. He lifted himself up above her and looked directly, deeply into her eyes. 'Do you want me inside you?'

She wanted everything. Most of all she didn't want this good feeling to end. *'Yes.'*

But he didn't smile. 'You're sure?'

'This is like a dream, Alek. Just for tonight.'

'A dream?' He shook his head. 'This isn't a dream you can wake up from and take back, Hester.'

Her anger built. She'd not had this—not opened herself up to anyone—ever. And all she wanted was him. Now. And she didn't want him to make her wait any longer. 'Don't say anything more,' she moaned. 'Don't spoil it.'

He tensed.

'And don't stop,' she demanded fiercely. 'Yes. I want you.'

His smile spread across his face and then he kissed her again. Until she arched, until she moaned, until she couldn't form words. For a moment he paused—vaguely she realised he was protecting them both—but then he was back, big and heavy against her, and she revelled in it. He slid his hand beneath her bottom and held her still enough for him to press close. She gasped as she felt his thickness sear into her.

'Hester?' he breathed.

'Yes. Alek.' She wanted this. Him.

As he pushed closer still she trembled. He was so big and so strong and she was suddenly overwhelmed. But he moved so slowly, so carefully and then he kissed her again—in that deep, lush way, as if he'd wanted nothing more in all his life than to kiss her. As if she were the very oxygen he needed to survive. That was when everything melted within her and he slid to the hilt, so they were as deeply connected as they could possibly be. Her need coalesced again into a cascading reaction of movement. He pushed her to follow his sweet, hard, slick rhythm—into a dance she'd never known, but discovered she could do so damn well with him. His breathing roughened as she clutched him back, as she understood more the give and take, the meet and retreat of this magic. Together they moved faster, deeper...until she cried out as he brought unbearable, beautiful pleasure down upon her. As he broke through every last one of her boundaries to meet her right there—where there was light and heat and sheer physical joy.

And finally, when she couldn't actually move, when her body was so wrung out, so limp from that tornado of ecstasy, a small smile curved his gorgeous lips. He rolled but pulled her close, draping her soft body over his. And he kissed her again—a sweet intimacy she was still so unused to, and still so desperately hungry for. So hungry, in fact, that it took only one long, lush kiss to stir her hips into that primal circling dance again.

'Oh, Hester,' he muttered and swept his hands down her yearning body. 'You're magnificent.'

CHAPTER EIGHT

ALEK RESTED ON his side, watching her sleep—half impatient, half fascinated—until she finally stirred. Her gaze skittered away from his as she sat up. For the first time in his life he was unsure how to handle the morning after.

'Sorry I slept in.' She slithered from the bed and swiftly reached for the robe lying across the nearby chair. 'I had an amazing time. Thank you.'

Amazing? She had no idea what amazing was. But he supposed it was better than her telling him it had been 'fine'.

'No regrets?' He pushed for more than this awkward politeness from her.

'I don't think it would be right to regret something that felt that good.' She belted his favourite robe tightly around her waist, hiding her perfection from him again. 'I'll go back to my room now.'

'You don't have to,' he said huskily, rubbing a sore spot he felt in his chest.

Ordinarily he'd be relieved to have a lover leave him with such little fuss, but he wanted Hester to stay. But every ounce of her shy reserve had returned.

'I know…but I…um…' She drew breath. 'My clothes are in there.' She silently sped from the room—as if she daren't leave a mark or a sound.

And he just let her.

He stared into the blank space. Breaking through

her shell had been difficult and this morning it had just bounced back into place. Maybe she needed some time alone to process what had happened? Honestly, maybe he did too. Maybe letting her leave now might mean she'd be comfortable coming back soon.

Just this once.

That was what she'd whispered last night and if he were being sensible, that was how he'd leave this. But he rubbed his chest again as the reality of the situation hit hard. His sexual attraction to her hadn't been assuaged but exacerbated. Worse was his burgeoning curiosity about everything else about her. He wanted to understand it all—her bag and her box and the books she'd not kept. Why did she have so few belongings?

And the emptiness of his bedroom hurt. Suddenly he hated that she'd walked out on him. That he'd made it so easy for her to be able to. He should have stopped her. He should have seduced her. He should have stripped back her protective prickles again and found that hot, sweet pleasure with her.

He gazed out of the window, noting the blazing sun and blue sky. Personal temptation stirred harder. He'd just married for his country—didn't he deserve a few moments of private time?

He phoned his assistant, Marc. 'I know we have meetings this morning, but I plan to take Hester to the stud this afternoon. Make the arrangements.'

'Sir?'

'Two nights,' he repeated. 'Make the arrangements.'

A minute later he knocked on the door of her apartment and turned the handle. 'Hester?'

She'd not locked it and he found her in the centre of her lounge, that wooden box in her hand. He watched as she awkwardly secured the loose lid in place with two thick rubber bands.

'Sorry,' she apologised and put the box on a nearby table. 'How can I help?'

He disliked her deferential attitude and the reminder of that 'contract' between them. Hadn't they moved past that last night?

'Come breakfast with me by the pool,' he invited. 'Then I have a few meetings, but this afternoon we're taking a trip. You'll need to pack enough for a couple of days.'

'A trip?' Hester could hardly bring herself to look at him; all she could think of was what they'd done last night. All night. How good he'd made her feel. 'I thought we had to stay in the city to oversee the coronation plans and practise everything a million times.' She doggedly tried to focus on their responsibilities. 'Do I really have to kneel before you all by myself?'

'All citizens of Triscari do, but especially the King's wife.'

'It's a wonder you don't want me to lie prostrate on the floor,' she grumbled.

'Well, of course I do, but perhaps not in front of every-one else.' He sent her a wicked double-dimpled look. 'We can do that alone later. Anyway, apparently the plans are in hand so we can steal a couple of days for a honeymoon.'

A honeymoon? Her stomach somersaulted. Was he jok-ing? She stood frozen but he bent and brushed his lips over hers briefly, pulling away with a shake of his head.

'No.' He laughed. 'You can't tempt me yet.'

'I didn't tempt you,' she muttered. 'I didn't do anything.'

'Hester,' he chided softly. 'You don't have to *do* any-thing to tempt me.' He cocked his head and gave her a little push. 'Now, head to the pool. I'll meet you there shortly.'

Hester stretched out on a sun lounger, trying to read, but her brain was only interested in replaying every second of the previous night. Her body hummed, delighting in the recollections. She'd not realised the extent of what she'd been missing out on. No wonder people risked so much for sex. But she knew it would never be like that with just anyone. It hadn't just been Alek's experience or 'expertise'. It had felt as if he'd cared—not that he was in love with her, of course, but that he was concerned for her feelings, for her to receive pleasure. That he desired to see her *satisfied*. She'd not had that courtesy, that caring, from anyone in so long. It was partly her own fault—she'd not let anyone get close in years. She'd not intended to let Alek get close either, but somehow he'd swept aside all her defences. Swiftly. Completely. So easily.

She knew sleeping with her meant nothing truly meaningful to him, not really. This was merely a bonus to their arrangement. She'd consider it that way as well. She could keep her heart safe—not fancy that she was falling for him, like a needy waif who'd never been loved…

But some distance right now was so necessary—which was why this talk of a honeymoon terrified her.

It's just one year.

And last night had been just that once. They'd blurred the lines and perhaps that had been inevitable. While she didn't regret it, she couldn't get carried away on a tide of lust and mistake his actions for meaning anything more than mere physical attraction.

But Alek fascinated *her* far beyond that. She'd instinctively believed he had more depth than he let show and she'd been right. He'd been hurt by his mother's death, frustrated by his father's control over him, protective of his sister. And now of her.

There was meaningful intention in most of his actions. The playboy persona was part rebellion, only one element of his whole. He was also honourable, loyal, diligent and he did what was necessary for his country.

Okay, yes, just like that she was halfway to falling for him.

She swam, trying to clear her head and ease the stiffness in her body. Lunch was delivered on a tray to the table beside her lounger. After eating, she went back to her apartment to pack. But when she went to put her wooden box in her bag, it wasn't on the table where she'd left it. She stared at the empty space, confused. She'd opened it only this morning, but now? She whirled, quickly scanning every possible surface but the box wasn't on any. She broadened her search but it was fruitless. Finally she hit panic point—repeating the search with vicious desperation, tipping out her bag and tearing up the place.

'Hester? What's happened?'

She froze. She'd not heard him knock and now he was in the middle of her mess with his eyes wide.

'It's missing.' She hugged herself tightly, but couldn't claw back any calm. 'I can't go.'

He didn't answer as he slowly stared around her room. Hester followed the direction of his gaze and realised what a mess she'd made of the place. She'd opened and emptied every cupboard and drawer in the apartment and still not found it. Cushions and pillows were strewn across the floor alongside books and blankets.

His focus shot back to her. 'Your box?'

'Yes,' she breathed, stunned that he realised what she meant so quickly. 'Who would take it?' Her anxiety skyrocketed all over again.

'You were going to pack it? You take it everywhere with you?'

'Yes.' She couldn't bear to lose it—it held everything.

A strange expression flashed across his face. 'Wait here. Just wait. Two minutes.'

'Alek?' Confused, she leaned against the wall, her arms still wrapped around her waist as his footsteps receded.

It was more than two minutes before he returned but she was locked in position, blinking back tears. She stared as she realised what he was holding. *'Why?'* Her voice cracked. 'Why would you take it?'

'I thought I could get it back before you noticed it was gone. I'm sorry for upsetting you.'

'Why would you—?' Furious, she broke off and struggled to breathe as she took the box from him and saw it close up. The lid was open while the interior was empty. Heat fired along her veins and her distress grew. 'Where's everything gone?'

'I have it all, just in my room. I'll get them now.'

'Why?' The word barely sounded but he'd already gone.

Hester sank onto the sofa, snatching a breath to study the box properly. She closed then reopened the lid. It didn't fall off any more, while the rubber bands were gone altogether.

Her bones jellified as she realised what he'd done.

Alek returned and carefully set a small tray on the low table in front of her sofa. It held everything she'd kept. All the little things. All her precious memories.

'The lid opens and closes again.' She blinked rapidly as he sat beside her. 'It has a new hinge.'

'Yes.' He cleared his throat. 'I took it this morning after you went to the pool. I thought...' He paused and she felt him shift on the sofa. 'I knew it was precious to you. I knew it was broken. So I—'

'Had it fixed.' Her voice almost failed.

'I wanted it to be a surprise...' He trailed off and blew out a breath. 'I should've asked you,' he muttered roughly. 'I'm so sorry. You probably loved it as it was.'

'Broken?' She shook her head and her words caught on another sob as she was unable to restrain the truth. 'It broke my heart when it happened.'

He gazed at her and the empathy in his eyes was so unbearable, she had to turn away from it.

'I can't even see where the crack was.' She stared hard at the box, refusing to let her banked tears tumble.

'We have an amazing craftsman—he maintains the woodwork in the castle. He's exceptionally skilled,' Alek explained.

'And so fast…' She ran her finger over the lid of the box. How had he done this in only a few hours?

'I talked to him about it before the wedding so he knew the issues.'

'Before the wedding?' Her heart skipped. He'd noticed her box and planned this?

'I wanted to get a wedding gift that you would like.'

Her throat was so tight it wouldn't work. That he'd thought to do this for her? It was more precious than any jewels, any other expensive, exquisite item. And she wasn't used to someone wanting to do something so nice for her.

'I didn't get you anything.' She finally looked at him directly, instantly trapped in his intent gaze.

He shook his head gently. 'You've done enough by marrying me, Hester.'

That was enough? Just that contract? Somehow she didn't want that to be enough for him. She wanted him to want more from her. That dangerous yearning deepened inside—renewed desire for that intimacy they'd shared last night. But he'd let her leave this morning. He'd barely said anything. Horribly insecure, she tore her gaze from his and turned back to the table, taking in the contents of the second tray.

'Did your craftsman put these here for you?' Her heart skidded at the thought. She needed to touch each talisman and make them hers again.

'No. I didn't want him going through your things,' he said softly. 'I took them out before giving him the box.'

Something loosened inside. She was glad it was only he who'd touched them. He'd been thoughtful and kind and suddenly the walls within crumbled and her truth, all her emotion, leaked out—sadness and secrets and sacrifice.

'The box was my father's,' she said quietly. 'Actually it was his great-grandfather's, so it's really old. It was for keeping a pocket watch and cufflinks and things. I loved it as a child and Dad gave it to me for my treasures. Marbles I had, sea glass I found. We found this piece together when I was…' She trailed off as she held the piece in her hand. Memories washed over her as they always did when she opened the box—which wasn't often at all purely because of the intensity of emotion it wrought within her. But it was also why she loved it, why it was so very precious and so personal and she couldn't help whispering the secrets of more. 'The pencil was my mother's.' It was only a stub of a pencil. And the remnant of the thin leather strap from her purse. 'You must think I'm pathetic.' She quickly began putting the other items away. 'All these broken little things—'

'What? No.' He put his hand on hers and stopped her from rapidly tossing everything back into the box haphazardly. Slowly he put one item at a time into her palm so she could return them to their special place.

'Everything around me,' Alek said quietly. 'This palace—my whole life—is a memorial to my family. There are portraits everywhere…everything is a reminder of who I am, where I'm from and who I must be. You don't have that, so you keep all these. There are treasured memories in every one, right?'

She nodded, unable to speak again. Emotion kept overwhelming her and she hated it.

He picked up the white-silk-covered button from the tray and held it out for her to take. 'I'm glad this was something you wanted to remember.'

He'd recognised it? She'd scooped it from the floor on her way out of his apartment this morning. Her fingers trembled as she took the button from her wedding dress and put it into the box.

'I'm never going to forget last night,' she whispered. Just as she was never going to forget anything associated with all her broken treasures. She closed the lid, amazed again at how perfect the repair was.

He watched her close the box. 'How did it get broken?'

She traced the carved lid with the tip of her finger as he'd done that day they'd met. 'It even used to lock. I wore the key around my neck on a ribbon, hoping they couldn't see it under my shirt.'

'They?'

'My cousins.' She shrugged. 'They didn't like it when I went to live with them after my parents died.'

'They didn't welcome you?' He paused.

'My aunt and uncle were sure to publicise that they'd "done the right thing" in taking me in. But they already had three children and none of them wanted me there.'

'So they didn't give you a nice room, or let you make their home your own.'

'No.' She swallowed. 'My uncle sold most of my parents' things, but I had the box. I always kept it near me. I never left it in my room or anything because I knew not to trust them. But the ribbon was worn and one day I lost it. They teased me about never being able to open the box again because I'd lost the key—so then I knew they had it and they knew I knew. That was their fun, right? My helplessness. My desperation. There was nothing I could do and they enjoyed that power.' She shivered. She'd hated them so much. 'So I tried not to show them how much it mattered.'

'I'm guessing you told them that it was "fine" for them to have it?' He rubbed her hand. 'That's your fall-back, right? When you don't want to say what's really going on inside there.' He pressed his fist to his heart.

She nodded sadly. 'My cousin Joshua snatched the box off me, he said he'd open it for me, but he was mocking and mean. He tried to prise it open by force but couldn't, so he got a knife. He broke the hinge and the lid splintered and everything fell on the ground. The three of them laughed at all my things. They said it was all just unwanted rubbish. All broken, with no value. Like me.'

Alek muttered something beneath his breath.

'I ran away,' she confessed sadly. 'There was nothing else I could do, I just ran.'

'I don't blame you.' He gazed at her, his dark eyes full of compassion that she couldn't bear to see, yet couldn't turn away from. 'I would've done the same.'

She shook her head with a puff of denial. Because he wouldn't have. He'd have fought them or something. He was so much stronger, so much more powerful than her. He'd never have let himself get stomped on the way she had. 'I went back hours later, when it was dark and it was all still there on the ground where they'd dumped it.'

'Hester—'

'I knew then that I had to get away for real.' Pain welled in her chest and she gazed down at the box. She'd never understood why they'd been so mean—what it was she'd ever done. Why it was that she'd not been welcomed.

'Were these the cousins who attended the wedding yesterday?'

She nodded.

'If I'd known…' He muttered something harsh beneath his breath. '*Why* did you invite them?'

'It would have caused more harm if I hadn't. Imagine what they'd have said to the media then?'

'I don't give a damn *what* they'd have said.'

'It's fine, Alek. They can't hurt me any more.'

He glanced at her. 'It's not *fine*, Hester. And you know that's not true.'

'Well…' she smiled ruefully '…they can't hurt me as much as they used to. I'm not a child. I'm not as vulnerable. I do okay now.'

'You do more than okay.' He blew out his tension. 'Were these the people who tested whether your eyelashes are real by pulling them out?'

She stared at him, her heart shrivelling at the realisation that he'd seen so much. 'How did you—?'

'No one normal would ever think to do that. You only mentioned it because some cruel witch had actually done it.'

She stared into space, lost in another horrible memory. 'It was girls at school,' she mumbled. 'Pinned me down.'

'At school?'

His horror made her wince.

'I got myself a scholarship to an elite boarding school. It was supposed to be my great escape—a wonderful fresh start away from the cousins.'

'And it wasn't?' He clenched his jaw.

'It was worse.'

She felt the waves of rage radiating from him and opted to minimise what she'd confessed. 'They were just mean. I ran away from the school. I worked. I studied. I did it myself.'

'You shouldn't have had to.'

'It's okay.'

'It's not okay, Hester.'

'But *I'm* okay. Now. I truly am.' And she realised with a little jolt that it was true. If she could handle getting married in front of millions of people, she could handle anything, right?

He looked into her eyes for a long moment and finally sighed. 'My craftsman said he'd fixed the lock too,' he said, drawing a tiny ornate key from his pocket. 'So now you can lock it again and keep it safe.' He held the key out to her. 'And you could put the key on a chain this time.'

She curled her fingers around the key and pressed it to her chest. 'This was so kind of you, Alek.'

His smile was lopsided so the dimples didn't appear and he didn't kiss her as she'd thought he was about to. Instead he stood.

'We need to get going or it'll be too dark.'

'Of course,' she breathed, trying to recapture control of herself, but there was a loose thread that he seemed to have tugged and still had a hold of so she couldn't retie it. 'I need a minute to tidy up.'

'The staff will tidy up.'

'I'm not leaving this mess for them.' She sent him a scandalised look. 'They'll think we had a massive fight or something.'

He grinned as he scooped up an armful of pillows and put them away with surprising speed. 'Or something.'

CHAPTER NINE

HESTER GAZED UP at the double-storeyed mansion set in the centre of green lawns and established trees. 'I didn't think there could be anything more beautiful than the palace or the castle, but this is—'

'Very different from either of those places.' Alek said.

'Yes, it's…' She trailed off, unsure she wanted to elaborate; he seemed oddly distant.

Only then he wasn't.

'What?' He stepped in front of her, his gaze compelling. 'Tell me what you think.'

It was impossible to deny him anything when he stood that close.

'It doesn't seem like a royal residence. It's more like a home.' Admittedly a beautiful, luxurious home—but there was something warm and welcoming and *cosy* about it.

'It was home.' Something softened in his eyes. 'My mother designed it and my father had it built for her before I was born.' His lips twisted in a half-smile.

'You grew up here?'

He nodded. 'She wanted us here as much as possible. School had to be in the city, of course, but before then and every holiday during. It was our safe place to be free.'

Hester was fascinated and honoured that he'd brought her somewhere clearly so special to him. 'Was?'

'My father never returned here after she died.' He gazed across the fields before turning to walk towards the homestead. 'Because she died here.'

Hester stilled. But he strode ahead and clearly had no desire to continue the conversation.

She couldn't catch her breath as she followed him through the living area. The interior of the homestead was much more personal than the palace. Large, deep sofas created a completely different space—it was luxurious and comfortable and she felt as if she was encroaching on something intimate and deeply personal.

'You really love horses,' she muttered inanely when it had been silent too long and because out of every window she saw the beautiful animals grazing in the fields.

He chuckled at her expression. 'You've never ridden?'

'I'm nowhere near co-ordinated enough. I've seen video of Fiorella, though. She's amazing.'

'She likes show jumping. I prefer polo.'

'Whacking things with your big stick?' She smirked.

He eyed her, that humour and wickedness warming his gaze. 'At least I'm not *afraid* of them.'

'They're huge and powerful and they could trample me to death. Of course I'm afraid of them.'

'They'll sense your fear. Some will behave badly.'

'A bit like people, really,' she muttered.

'True.' He laughed as he led her up the stairs. 'Come up and appreciate the view. All the staff have gone away for these couple of nights so we're completely alone.'

His phone pinged and he frowned but paused to check the message.

'It never ends for you, does it?' she asked.

'I imagine it's the same for you,' he replied as he tapped out a quick reply. 'Students pulling all-nighters wanting help with their due essays. Fi's correspondence is mountainous.'

'I like being busy,' she said. 'I always took extra sessions at the drop-in centre.'

'What drop-in centre?' He glanced up and pocketed his phone. 'For the students?'

'No, an advice bureau in the city. I helped people fill in forms and stuff.'

'Is that where you sent that first tranche of money?'

'Yes.' She blushed. 'Something charitable, as you said. I couldn't ignore that.'

But his gaze narrowed. 'I had the feeling it was more than charitable. That it might've been personal.'

'Okay.' Her heart thudded; of course he'd seen that. 'You're right. I've asked the centre to give it to a young mother and her daughter,' she confessed. 'Lucia's on her own. She's trying to make a better life for her daughter. I used to hold the strap of my mum's bag the way Zoe holds Lucia's.'

Alek soaked up the information. The trust blooming in Hester's eyes was so fragile but he couldn't resist seeking more. 'Tell me about her—your mother.' He wanted to understand everything.

She looked at him, her golden eyes glowing with soft curiosity of her own. 'Tell me about yours,' she countered.

His jaw tightened, but at the same time his lips twisted into a reluctant smile. Her question was fair enough. 'Her name was Aurora and she was from a noble family on the continent. Apparently my father saw her riding in an equestrian event and fell for her instantly. She loved her horses so he built these stables for her to establish a breeding programme. It was his wedding gift to her.'

'Wow.'

'Yeah.' He nodded. 'They struggled to have me and it was a long time before they got Fiorella after me. So I'll admit I was very spoiled.'

'Everyone should be spoiled sometimes.' Hester suddenly smiled. 'Especially by parents, right?'

Warmth blossomed in his chest and he took her by the hand and led her to the second-storey veranda.

'My mother passed her love for horses on to me—they were our thing,' he said as he tugged her to sit down on the large sofa with the best view in the world—over horse-studded fields, to his favourite forest and the blue sea beyond. 'She had such a gift with them. Meanwhile, my father was very busy and dignified.' He rolled his eyes but was actually warming to the topic because he'd not spoken of her in so very long. 'She was vivacious—he was the shadow, the foil to her light.'

'They sound like they were good together.'

He stretched his feet out on the sofa and tucked her closer to his side, kind of glad he couldn't see her face, and he watched as the sky began to darken.

'Yeah, they were. She softened him, kept him human. But then she got sick. It was so quick. My father wouldn't reduce his engagements. Wouldn't admit what was happening. Wouldn't speak to me about it. But I was fourteen and I wasn't stupid. I stayed with her here. I'd bring the horses by her window downstairs and we'd talk through the programme...' He'd missed months of school that year.

'And Fiorella?'

'Came and went. She was young and my mother wanted to protect her. So did I. She'd go for long rides every day—she had a governess. And I sat with Mother and read to her. But she deteriorated faster than any of us expected. I wanted to call her specialists, for my father, but she wouldn't let me. It was just the two of us.'

The horror of that morning—that rage against his powerlessness resurged—breaking out of the tiny box he'd locked it in all these years. 'I couldn't help her. I couldn't stop it.'

What did titles or brains or money or anything much matter when you were reduced to being so completely *useless* in a moment of life and death? 'I couldn't do anything.'

He was still furious about it.

'You did do something, Alek,' Hester eventually said softly. 'You were *there* for her. She wasn't alone. Isn't that the best thing anyone could have done? You were *with* her.'

He couldn't answer.

'Nothing and no one can stop death,' she added quietly. 'And being alone in that moment must be terrifying. But she wasn't alone, because she had you. That's not nothing, Alek. That's about the furthest from nothing that you can get.'

He turned. In the rising moonlight her eyes were luminous. This was someone who knew isolation. Who understood it—within herself, and within him. And she was right. A slip of peace floated over his soul, slowly fluttering into place, like the lightest balm on an old sore, a gossamer-thin layer of solace.

He'd never allowed himself to think of that moment. Even the threat of recollection hurt too much. But now that memory screened slowly, silently in his head and for once he just let it.

'And then what happened?' Hester finally asked.

He looked at her blankly.

'Afterwards. Your father, Fiorella, you. How did you all cope?'

They hadn't. None of them had.

'Your father didn't come for you?' Hester asked.

'He never returned here.' Alek coughed the frog from his throat. 'He stayed at the palace and they brought her body to him. He made them bring me too.' He'd never wanted to leave. He'd wanted to hide here for ever. 'I fought to come back from then on because I didn't want the stables to close. People had jobs and there were the thoroughbreds...'

'And it was your mother's project,' she said.

'Right.' He released a heavy sigh. 'She loved it.' How could he let it fall to ruin? 'I didn't want to lose her legacy.'

But it had been hard to come back and see that small room downstairs where she'd spent her last days. Awful to be here alone when she'd gone for ever and his family had almost disintegrated.

'And Fiorella?'

'The governesses kept her away and kept her busy. She was okay. But as my father retreated into his work he became even more strict and controlling over our lives. Over every aspect. I guess it was his way of handling it.'

'And what was your way of handling it?' she murmured.

He flexed his shoulders. 'I didn't have one really.'

'No?'

'You're thinking my social life?' he asked—feeling weary and oddly hurt at the suggestion. 'Maybe. It didn't mean anything.'

'Maybe that was the point,' she said lightly. 'If it didn't mean anything, then it couldn't hurt, right?'

'Not gonna lie—it felt *good*, Hester.'

'Well, wouldn't it suck if it didn't?' She smiled. 'And when things really hurt you'll do almost anything to feel better even for a little while, right?'

He felt raw. Maybe she was right. Maybe it had been more than escape. He'd been burying frustration and grief. But he'd *liked* being the Playboy Prince. He'd liked encouraging zero expectations of him settling down. Only then his father had died. And then that stupid requirement had come into play and he'd been forced to create a relationship he'd never wanted. That he still didn't want—right?

'You don't need to apologise for it,' she said. 'It just was what was, right? I locked myself away. That was my choice. Neither of us were right or wrong necessarily, it was just how we each coped with a really crappy time.'

'Yeah.' He'd not stopped to think about what a really crappy time it had been in so long.

'So now you run the stud.' She looked across the grounds. 'And that was the other way of handling it—building on her legacy. Keeping something that she loved very much alive.'

He swallowed, unable to reply.

'And you freed Fiorella from that royal burden.'

'Of course I did.' He could breathe again. 'That was easy. She didn't need to be stuck in Triscari the same as...'

'The same as you.'

'It's just fate.' He shrugged. 'An accident of birth. I just have to do the best I can.'

'Do you worry about your ability to do the job?' She stared at him. 'Seriously?'

'What, you have dibs on feeling insecure?' He half chuckled. 'Of course I worry I won't be good enough. Being the firstborn Prince means you're going to end up King. It's a full-time job that starts from the moment you're born and it takes up every minute. I'm not saying that to summon your sympathy. I know how privileged I am and I want to do what's right for my country.'

'And you do. They love you. They ask for your thoughts all the time and they trust your answers. Everyone loves you. Everyone knows you do what's best for the country because you care. And as long as you keep caring, then you'll do what's right for Triscari. You're not selfish, Alek.' She paused. 'You've given your life for duty.'

He shot her a look. 'I thought I was a rapscallion play-boy.'

'Maybe you were when you could snatch a second to yourself, but mostly you've done the job forced upon you. And the job you wanted to do for your mother.' Hester realised he couldn't separate his role as Prince from his *self*. It was a career like no other—too enmeshed with his very existence and it brought with it a kind of pressure she'd not stopped to consider. 'You're building on your father's legacy too, by being a good king. But you're more important than just your crown, you know—'

'I know,' he interrupted and reached out to stroke her hair back from her face. 'Don't worry too much, my ego is perfectly healthy.'

She actually wasn't so sure about that. 'But it's isolating, isn't it?' she said passionately. 'Living with grief.'

His eyes widened. 'I'm not—'

'Yes, you are. For your mother. For the life you're never going to be able to have.'

And somehow in the course of this conversation her own loneliness had been unlocked. 'I grieve for the life I might've had if the accident hadn't happened,' she confided in an unstoppable swirl of honesty. 'I was at the library, happily reading and waiting for them to pick me up. They never did and I never got to go home again. I was taken to the police station and after a few hours my uncle arrived and took me. Five hours of flight time later I landed in a place I didn't know, to meet people who didn't want me.'

Alek just stared at her, and this time his eyes were so full of care and compassion and she wanted to share with him—because it wasn't all awful. She'd been so lucky in so many ways.

'My parents were a runaway love match.' She smiled impishly, delighting in the romance they'd had. 'He was the second youngest, destined to uphold their place in society, right? His family were snobs. My mother was new to town, moved into the wrong suburb...she totally wasn't from the right background. They met at school and it was true, young love. But when she got pregnant his family came down so hard and they ran away—living transiently, working seasonal jobs, barely keeping themselves housed and fed, fighting hard to stay afloat and keep me with them. But they did it. They loved each other and they loved me. They decided they couldn't afford more so there was just me and...not going to lie, Alek...' she smiled cheekily at him '... I was spoiled too.'

'Oh, sweetheart,' he said huskily. 'I'm so glad to hear that.'

'Yeah, we had nothing but we had everything, you know? And we certainly never visited his home town. So after the accident when I turned up, all that old bitterness was still real. I didn't fit in—I looked more like my mother than my father. I had her vixen eyes. I was part of who and what stole him away and that made me bad. But they were determined to "do the right thing". Except they had nothing good to say about my mum and they went on about my father's selfishness and weakness. I couldn't tell them how wonderful they really were—they didn't want to listen and they never would've believed me. In the end the only way to get through it was to lock my grief away, shut it down.' She shook her head. 'I put everything into my studies, hoping that would lead to a way out, and eventually it did, but only once I got to university and by then... I was good at keeping others at a distance. I put the treasures into my box and I'd go for long walks.'

'Walks? *That* was your way to feel good?' He half laughed.

'Sure. Mostly...' She smiled more ruefully this time. 'But a couple of times I ran.'

'You shouldn't think running away is something to be ashamed of. Or that it's cowardly.'

'Isn't it though? Shouldn't I have stood up for myself or fought harder to be heard?'

'How were you supposed to do that when there were a

tonne of them and only one of you?' He shook his head.
'I think what you did was actually more brave. Escaping
that abuse, and going out on your own. Lots of people
wouldn't have the courage or the skills to be able to do
that without support.'

Alek hadn't known it was possible to feel supremely
content and disconcerted at the same time. He was both
assuaged and unsatisfied. Most of all he was confused.
This was not the way he'd envisaged this evening going.
He'd thought they'd have been in bed hours ago—that he'd
have stripped her and satisfied them both several times already. Instead they'd shared something far more intimate
than if they'd spent hours having simultaneous orgasms.

And somehow he couldn't stop speaking. 'Tell me
more,' he asked. 'What were their names?'

To his immense relief she answered—and asked questions of her own. He shared old anecdotes he hadn't realised he'd even remembered. Making her laugh over silly,
small things that were too personal to keep back. As the
stars emerged he leaned back lower on the sofa, curling
her closer into his side—soft and gentle and warm and appallingly tired and still talking.

Yet the discomfort was still there. All kinds of aches
weighed down his limbs as he discovered that an old hurt
he'd forgotten had only been buried. It had taken so little
to lift it to the surface. He wanted to resist—to pull free
again. Drowsily he gazed across the fields. He'd go riding
as soon as it was light. He needed to feel that liberation—
the complete freedom as the wind whipped and knocked
the breath from his lungs, racing faster than he could ever
run, jumping high enough to feel as if he were flying for
the briefest of seconds. Yes. He needed that escape. He
needed to ride—hard and fast and free.

CHAPTER TEN

'HESTER.'

Hester blinked drowsily. 'Mmm…?'

'Are you awake?'

Her vision focused. Alek was in the doorway, fully dressed and looking vitally handsome in slim-fit black jeans and a black shirt and gleaming black boots.

'What time is it?' She coughed the question because her insides had turned to jelly.

'Mid-morning.' He leaned against the doorframe and shot her a lazy smile.

Hester gaped—she'd slept like the dead. She didn't even *remember* coming to bed or if he'd even been in this bed *with* her. Disappointment struck. So much for thinking he might want her again or that he'd intended this to be a real honeymoon. She glanced at the table to avoid his eyes. Her box sat in the centre of it and she knew he'd put it there for her to see first thing so she wouldn't fret about it.

'I wondered if you'd like to ride with me,' he said.

'On a horse?' The question slipped out before she thought better of it and her heart hollowed out the second she realised the implication of what she'd said.

'Uh…' He looked diverted but then his smile flashed back. 'Yes. A horse.'

'Um…' She paused, prevaricating while she tried to think of…anything. Ideally a reason or excuse to say no.

But her brain was failing her. She'd not wanted anything from anyone in so long and it was safest that way but now she felt heat and confusion and awkwardness and that *fear*.

'Are you afraid to try something in case you're not good at it?' He tilted sideways to take up residence against the doorframe in that gorgeous way of his.

She gave up on any pretence and just let the truth slip out. 'No. I'm afraid of everything.'

And what she was most afraid of was that what had happened between them wasn't going to happen again. When they'd talked last night she'd felt as if they'd crossed into another level—her heart had ached for what he'd been through. In opening up with him she'd thought they'd forged even more of a connection than the fireworks of their physical compatibility the night before. She'd developed faith in him and every one of her barriers had fallen. She'd relaxed so much in his company that she'd actually fallen *asleep* on him in the middle of a conversation. She'd never been that relaxed with anyone, *ever*.

'I don't believe that,' Alek challenged. 'Not for a second.'

'It's true.'

'Then you're even braver than I already believed.' He cocked his head. 'Because you do it anyway. Even terrified, you get on with what's necessary.'

She willed her brain to work so she could push back her own weakness. 'Yes, but fortunately I don't consider sitting on a massive animal as *necessary*, Alek.'

'But it's so much *fun*,' he goaded with that irresistible grin. 'Come on, Hester, it's just another little adventure and we adventure quite well together, don't you think?'

She gazed at him, sunk already. She couldn't say no to him. She'd never been able to. Not the day he'd made his convenient proposal to her. And not now. 'I'll come watch you.'

'Oh?' Triumph lit his eyes. 'See you down there in five.'

She pulled on jeans and a tee. Downstairs she picked up a pastry from the platter that was on the table and headed out to the beautiful yard. To her relief there was no one there other than Alek. She took one look at the two enormous horses saddled and tethered behind him and almost choked on her chunk of croissant.

'Uh… I'm really not sure.' She shook her head.

'Bess is very old, very gentle,' he assured her, gently patting the chestnut horse.

'And the other one?' She glanced at the jet-black gigantic creature on the other side of him.

'Is mine.'

She didn't need to look at him to know he was smiling and somehow her pride flared.

'Okay.' She drew in a breath and squared her shoulders. 'I'm fine. This'll be fine.'

'Hester,' he said softly.

She looked at him, confused by his gently warning tone.

'Don't hide again. Not with me. Not now.'

'Hide?'

'You've just assumed your calm demeanour. It's the way you keep yourself at a distance. You don't need to do that with me any more. I know the truth.'

'The truth?' Her lungs shivered. He knew how much she wanted him?

'You've already told me you're scared.'

To avoid meeting his gaze and revealing that *other* truth, Hester moved quickly. She could do this. Lots of people got on horses all the time—how hard could it be? She looked at the horse and stepped on the small stool waiting beside it. She held onto the saddle, eyed the stirrup and braced. But suddenly the horse shifted, she missed the stirrup, lost balance and in a flash had fallen. It turned out the ground was hard.

She shut her eyes, utterly mortified as she heard Alek crouch beside her. 'Are you hurt?'

'No.' But she realised she was unconsciously rubbing her rump. 'And don't even think about kissing it better.'

Embarrassment swamped her the following second. What was it with her mouth running off before her brain kicked in? He probably hadn't thought of doing *that* at all. *She* was the one fixated on the thought of kissing—and touching, and everything else.

'Only this would happen to me,' she groaned.

'I can't tell you how many times I've fallen off.' He laughed.

'I didn't even manage to get *on*, Alek.'

'Just sit there for a moment.' He turned his head. 'It's okay.' He raised his voice. 'We're okay.'

Oh, heavens, he wasn't talking to her. 'Are there people watching? They saw that? Great.'

His eyes crinkled at the corners and their coal-black centres gleamed. 'I thought you didn't care what people thought.'

'Of course I do. I mean, I try very hard not to and most of the time that works, but sometimes it doesn't and I... don't know what I'm saying when you're just sitting here grinning at me.' She rubbed her head, feeling so hot and embarrassed while wishing he were closer still and she was still rabbiting on in a way that she never normally did. That 'calm demeanour' he reckoned she had? Shattered. Toasted in the fiery brilliance that was Alek himself.

'Didn't you see my scar the other night? You know, the one on my butt?' He chuckled as the heat spread further over her face. 'I took the most stupid tumble off my pony onto a very pointy stick when I was about seven. Everyone laughed so hard.'

'Everyone?'

'My parents, the staff...' He shrugged. 'It's a good scar. I'm sure you saw it...or do you want me to show you now?'

'No,' she lied, then laughed, then sighed. 'You're going to make me try and get on that horse again, aren't you?'

'I'm not sure anyone can make you do anything,' he teased.

'Don't try to make me feel competent at this when we both know I'm not. It's all right for you,' she muttered quietly. 'You're used to it. You know what to do.'

'It's just practice, Hester.' He reached out to brush her face and whispered, 'What if you ride with me?'

She stared into his bottomless eyes. 'On Bess?'

'No, on Jupiter.' That wickedness gleamed again. 'He's named for his size.'

'Of course he is.' She rolled her eyes. 'If I can't get on Bess, how do you think I'm going to get on Gigantor?'

'Jupiter,' he corrected with another laugh. 'I'll help you.' He took her hand and tugged her to her feet.

She stood nervously as Alek shifted the small stool. His hands were firm on her waist as he hoisted her with ease, ensuring she was safely astride the animal before releasing her. She clung to the reins nervously as Alek vaulted up behind her with superhuman agility.

'You can let go now. I've got him. And you.' Alek's breath was warm in her ear and she heard his amusement as he put his arms around her. He pressed his palm against her belly and pulled her back to lean against his chest.

She drew a shaky breath in because this felt extremely intimate and precarious. They were up *high*.

'Don't worry,' he murmured. 'We'll start slow.'

She closed her eyes for an instant, transported back to that magical night when he'd turned her in his arms and made her feel impossibly good things. But then she blinked as Alek made a clicking noise with his mouth and the horse moved.

She heard his laughter as she tensed. He pulled her back against him firmly again and kept his hand pressed on her stomach. She gave up resisting and just leaned against him. He talked endlessly, telling her the names of the horses grazing in the fields as they passed them but she didn't remember a single one. His voice simply mesmerised her as he pointed out other features of the ranch as Jupiter carried them along a pathway that narrowed as they headed towards a forested area.

'These islands are volcanic,' Alek explained. 'While there's apparently no threat of an eruption any time soon, we do get some interesting geographical features.'

'Really?' She mocked his tour-guide tone. 'Such as?'

'Such as wait and see.'

She felt his laughter rumble again and her stomach somersaulted. Being held in his arms like this just made all her unrequited-lust feelings burn brighter still. It would take nothing to turn her head and press her lips to his neck. It took everything to stop herself from doing it.

Alek pressed his knees, urging Jupiter forward, faster. He wanted to get to the forest sooner. Having Hester in front of him like this was pure torture. He'd been pacing downstairs for hours waiting for her to wake up, yet not wanting to disturb her too soon because she'd obviously been exhausted. And now she was in his arms but not the way he really wanted. The battle within was long lost. He wanted her again and damn any complicated consequences. Yet he still ached. With what he'd told her? What she'd told him?

'I'm sorry we brought your cousins to Triscari,' he blurted.

'I wanted to be a princess for a day,' she said ruefully. 'I wanted to look like I had the fairy tale. Just for that moment. Just for once. Because I do still care, just a little. That's pretty stupid, right?'

'No, I think it's pretty normal.' He totally understood that she'd want to prove herself to them. 'I always wanted *not* to be a prince for a day, so I get it.'

'Does it ever happen? Do you ever get to have a day off?'

'I have one now.'

She was quiet for a while, but he felt her stiffness slowly return.

'When this ends, I want everyone to think I walked away from you. I don't want to be the victim all over again. I'd rather be seen as the evil cow who broke your heart. That it was me who chose. That I had the power.' Slight laughter shook her slim body. 'Can your ego handle that battering?'

'Absolutely.' But he felt choked. He didn't want to think about this ending yet. He didn't want to consider the moment when she'd walk out and not look back. But at the same time he wanted her to feel the power that she sought. He wanted her to know she actually had it already. She was strong and beautiful.

'They'll never believe it, of course,' she groaned. 'But I can pretend.'

'They'll believe it,' he said. 'It wouldn't surprise them to hear I've been a jerk.'

She shook her head. 'You weren't that bad. You just needed to find some fun, right? A blow-out now and then. Especially given you never get a day off.'

He didn't regret his past actions, but he didn't feel any desire to replicate them. The thought of being with anyone else now was abhorrent. Irritation needled his flesh. He didn't understand how everything had changed in such a short amount of time. He urged Jupiter to move faster, taking the excuse to hold her more tightly. Her breathing quickened, but her body moved with his. In the forest it was quiet and felt even more intimate. Through the trees he spied the blue sea and felt that familiar exhilaration and peace. 'The view is amazing, isn't it?' he said.

'Yes.'

'And then there's this.' His very favourite place in the world.

'Is that steam?' Hester asked. 'Is it a thermal pool?'

'Yeah.' He smiled; smart cookie. He guided Jupiter carefully around the large rocks and to the left of the small steaming pond.

'Can we swim in it?'

'Yes. No one else comes here. It's completely private.' It was his.

'And those rocks—they're amazing.'

'Yeah—there's volcanic glass—obsidian—in them. Sometimes I find pieces broken off.'

'It's the colour of your eyes,' she murmured. 'This is your wait-and-see moment.' She was very still against him and her voice was the thinnest whisper. 'It's like some ancient fairyland. It's just incredible, Alek. It's like…a fantasy. There's nothing more, is there? Because what with the palace and the castle and the homestead and now this?'

'This is the best place in the world, Hester.' His chest warmed as she softly babbled on, for once not holding back on expressing anything. And he was happy to confess his own secret love for it. 'I think so, anyway.'

'But am I going to have to get off this horse now?' Her voice had gone even smaller.

He chuckled, tightening his arm across her waist. 'It wasn't so unbearable, was it?'

It had been *completely* unbearable. The raw sexuality Hester felt emanating behind her was making her steamier than the gorgeous-looking thermal pool. She hadn't been able to resist pressing back, indulging in his heat and strength, the security in his hold and the danger in the press of his thighs as he'd guided the horse to a faster pace. The wind had whipped her hair and stolen her breath before it could reach her lungs, exhilarating and liberating. She'd become appallingly aroused and he'd brought her here— to paradise. She never wanted to return to reality.

'Stay there a sec.' He swung and leapt off the horse, landing so easily all the way down there on the ground.

He turned back to face her and held his arms out to help her down. She literally slithered off the saddle and into his embrace—somehow ended up pressed against his chest. His hands ran down her back, pushing her closer against him, and she shut her eyes tightly, savouring the moment before he pulled fractionally away.

'Hester.'

She didn't answer, didn't move, didn't open her eyes.

'Look at me,' he said softly.

Neither her fight nor flight instincts were working. She'd frozen with the worst emotion of all—*longing*.

'Hester.'

She opened her eyes, lifting her chin to gaze at him, pinioned by a riot of yearning. She'd thought—so naively— that once that curiosity had been quenched, it would end. That it had mostly been only curiosity driving her to let him in. Instead, she'd discovered the utter delight of him and she wanted more. There were myriad things she secretly desired to do with him now. To do *to* him. She'd not thought she'd ever want to share any part of herself, ever. But with him?

'You know you can practise your riding skills on me any time,' he said huskily.

Oh, he was just pure temptation.

'What, as if you're some stallion who needs breaking in?' she muttered, but couldn't hide her breathlessness.

His eyebrows lifted and his eyes widened. 'Maybe. While you're the skittish filly who needs a gentle touch to bring her round.'

'Maybe I don't need that gentle of a touch.'

His smile vanished, leaving only raw intensity. 'And maybe I don't need to be controlled.'

The electricity between them crackled. The tension tore her self-control to shreds.

Why should this be difficult? Why shouldn't she reach out and take what *she* wanted? She'd been isolated and alone and denied touch for so long. And while she knew this wasn't going to last, why shouldn't she enjoy everything this arrangement with him could offer?

She couldn't deny herself. She reached for him, tilting her chin to kiss him. His arms swept back around her, pulling her right off her feet. She clung to him as every ounce of need unravelled—forcing her to ensnare him. To keep him close. She kissed him as if there were no tomorrow. But he tore his mouth free.

'I need to…uh… I need to sort Jupiter… It'll just take a moment.' He shook his head and firmly set her at a distance but she saw the tremble in his hands as he released her.

The strongest sense of liberation swept over her as she faced the thermal springs. She stripped off her tee and her trousers, sliding her underwear off too. She wanted to be *free*. She carefully stepped into the narrow pool and then sank lower, letting the silken, warm water soothe her oversensitive body.

'Hester?'

She turned at his choked sound and saw him standing at the edge of the small pond. He was still and intent.

Her awareness heightened and a deeply buried instinct kicked in. She stood, suddenly certain of her own sensuality as she stepped out of the water. She had no designer dress, no make-up. She was just plain, unadorned Hester. Completely bared. But the way he was looking at her? The response that he couldn't conceal?

He believed she was beautiful. He *wanted* her. He ached the same way she did.

Pride and power exploded within her.

For the first time in her life she was *unafraid* to take what she wanted. He could take it—more than that, she knew he willed it for her. For her to find that freedom to explore, to claim, even to conquer. It was almost anger that built within her—a reckless force so fierce and hot she couldn't contain it. That searing need drove her to take what she wanted. And that was simply to get closer to him. To seek that sensual obliteration and satisfaction from him, with him.

She unbuttoned his shirt with a dexterity she'd never imagined possessing. He said nothing but the rise and fall of his glorious chest quickened and suddenly he moved to kick off his boots. But then he was hers again. She unfastened his trousers, freeing him to her gaze, her touch, her total exploration. And she kissed him everywhere.

She pushed and he tumbled. She rose above him, savouring the sensation of having his strength between her legs. She didn't just open up and allow him in, but actively claimed what he was offering. She took, her hands sweeping over him, and she drew on the hot, slick power of him. She couldn't contain her desire any more—it was utterly unleashed and she was hungry. *So* hungry she was angry with it. With the depth of the need she felt for him. The ache that only he filled yet that grew larger every moment she spent with him. She wanted to end it—this *craving*. The sheer ferocity of it stole her breath so for a second she stilled.

He reached up and cupped the side of her face. 'Don't stop. Do what you want.'

'I want you.'

'You already have me. Hester.'

The way he sighed her name was her undoing. She

slid on him—taking him right into her soul. She heard his muttered oath, the broken growls of encouragement as he urged her on, fiercer. Faster. His sighs of pleasure scorched her, catapulting her beyond her own limits. Until she shrieked as he exploded her world.

Dazed, she collapsed on him. She'd felt nothing like this kind of physical exhaustion or satisfaction.

'Hester,' he whispered. 'Hester, Hester, Hester.' He shuddered and his arms tightened again. 'What you do to me.'

Alek sprawled on the ground, holding her close, shattered by the most elemental experience of his life. He wasn't sure his heart rate would ever recover. She was a chaotic bundle of limbs in his arms. He didn't want this fragile connection to be severed—for her to retreat behind her emotional walls again. So he slid his hand beneath her jaw, tilting her face so he could kiss her and keep her soft and pliable and warm. But she shivered. He moved, gathering her properly into his arms and rising to his knees, then feet. He carried her to the pond and carefully stepped in, holding her to him so they were both warmed and soothed by the thermal water. She floated in his arms and he teased with pushing her away only to pull her close and kiss her over and over and over until, impossible as it was, his body hardened with need again and he slid deep into her, locking her close on him, rocking them together until the pleasure poured between them and through them, brilliant and free.

A long while later he lifted her from the water. As he climbed out after her, something dug into his heel. He reached down and picked up the small chunk of obsidian. He weighed it in his palm for a moment. He could give it to her so she could put it in that box of hers and remember this even when she'd walked away from Triscari. When she left him.

He glanced at her—she looked shattered by the passion

that had exploded between them. She didn't speak. Nor did he. For once he had no idea what to say—no smooth little joke or something to lighten the intensity. He'd lost all charm, all calm. It felt as if he were still standing on something sharp and the only way to ease it was by touching her.

So he dressed alongside her in silence, pocketing the stone and swiftly readying Jupiter because he needed to feel Hester resting against him again soon.

They still didn't speak as they rode back to the homestead. He knew they were going to have to address their 'contract' at some point. But that time wasn't now. Now was the time to keep holding her in his arms and pleasuring her.

But that was a fantasy too far. Instead the world was waiting for him. As soon as he saw his assistant together with his housekeeper, he knew duty had come knocking, otherwise they'd still be off-site. He cursed inwardly as Hester stiffened. Of course she understood what the welcome committee meant.

'Your Highness.' His assistant bowed stiffly while looking apologetic at the same time. 'An issue has arisen. We need to return to the palace immediately.'

CHAPTER ELEVEN

ALEK GLANCED AT his watch and grimaced. His eyes felt gritty and he could hardly concentrate on what it was his advisor was asking.

The 'issue' dragging them back after only one measly night away was nothing that couldn't have waited another day or three. It had just been palace officials stressed about his absence and using the smallest drama to summon him back. And that annoyed him. Why couldn't he spend a full day making love to his wife? But now he'd stopped to think about it, that he'd *wanted* to do that was even more of a concern.

It had been Hester who'd solved the foreign dignitaries issue—with a few quiet suggestions to him that he'd amplified to his advisors. She was intelligent and diligent and a damn good problem-solver. He'd selfishly kept her with him as he was consumed by meetings and obligations until he'd seen her losing colour and remembered how tired she'd been. So he'd sent her in the direction of her apartment and continued without her late into the evening. She'd been fast asleep when he'd returned to the apartment and he hadn't had the heart to wake her.

And now he was back there was no escape from the duties, the questions, the decisions that everyone wanted from him. He'd ended up back in conference with courtiers first thing. Which was good. Space from her would shake off that lingering concern, wouldn't it? He'd concentrate on the multitude of tasks at hand and push back that creeping sense of discomfort.

But it felt as if a craggy boulder were slowly and inexorably rolling into his gut, weighing him down further and further as every second ticked by. Those conversations he'd had with Hester at Triscari Stud had been too raw, raising elements of his past that were better off buried. Things he'd not thought of in for ever. Things that, now he'd recalled them, didn't seem inclined to return to that safe stasis easily or quickly.

He'd forgotten so much. And now he'd remembered? That stuff hurt. That stuff wouldn't be shaken. So it was good to lurch from meeting to meeting, to force every brain cell to focus on debates and decisions and stupid, tiny details that really didn't matter.

Except his brain kept returning to Hester. To those moments at the thermal springs. Her unfettered incredible response had been a searing delight. He'd wrapped around her, holding her close—not wanting her to retreat. Wanting no barrier to build between them again.

He stilled, suddenly realising there'd literally been nothing between them physically at all. He'd not used contraception. In that wild, free moment, he'd not stopped to consider *anything* other than getting closer to her. In all his years, in all his exploits, he'd never once failed to use protection. He'd never once risked it. But at the time it hadn't even occurred to him. He couldn't have cared less in his haste to have her.

Which meant he might've got her pregnant. Hester might be carrying his child.

His vision tunnelled. He'd not wanted children. Ever. Even though he knew he was going to have to at some point, he'd figured he could delay it for as long as possible. But now?

Now he had Hester. And she might be pregnant.

He felt as if parts of a puzzle had slid into place without him paying attention. But now he did. If she'd got pregnant would it really matter? Wouldn't they just stay married?

Surprising as it was, that thought didn't horrify him at all. In fact, completely weirdly, that rock weighing on his gut actually eased off. They worked well together—she was skilled and capable. There was no reason why this couldn't become a successful marriage long term. It would answer all their issues, wouldn't it?

She would have the security and safety she'd never had. The viciousness of her cousins and her school bullies appalled him and, while she seemed well free of them now, he didn't want her to suffer like that ever again. He could keep her safe with him. The media might have their moments, but they could shake that off. His life was constricted and that would impact on her—but surely it was better than what she'd had. Surely what he could offer her outweighed those negatives?

He glanced up as the door opened, half hoping Hester might've come to check on him—drawn to him in the same way he was to her. But it was his private assistant who entered.

'I apologise for the interruption, Your Highness, but you requested we update you on your wife if—'

'What's happened?' Alek's instincts sharpened.

'She's walking in the gardens, sir.' His assistant flashed a deferential but reassuring smile. 'But I don't think she realised that it's public viewing time.'

Alek frowned. 'Has she been seen by someone?'

'Her bodyguard believes they might be family members, sir.'

'Damn.' Alek strode straight to the door.

* * *

'I didn't realise you were still here.' Hester remained still, refusing to obey the urge to run away. She didn't have Alek and Fi either side of her, but she could handle the unholy cousinly trinity of Joshua, Brittany and Kimberly now, right?

'The invitation included staying for the coronation,' Joshua said with the faintest edge of belligerence. 'We're looking around the gardens.'

Hester nodded, momentarily unable to think of a reply. They reminded her of crocodiles with their toothy smiles and tough skin and she was instantly cast into freeze mode.

'You look pale,' Kimberly commented with a concern that was a touch *too* solicitous. 'Are you feeling well?'

'Very well.' Hester breathed slowly to regulate her skipping pulse. 'Thank you.'

'I imagine it's been frantic,' Kimberly added. 'Such an unexpected whirlwind wedding, Hester. How *fortunate* he found you.'

'Yes.' Brittany had been watching closely with her sharp eyes. 'You've done so well for yourself, I could hardly believe it was *you* when you walked into that chapel. What an *amazing* dress and make-up job.'

Their peals of laughter reverberated with a cruel edge and Hester all but choked. Because they knew and she knew—it was all a façade, as *fake* as their flattery and smiles were now. Smoke and mirrors.

'And now Alek can be crowned King.' Brittany sent another stabbing look towards Hester. 'But I'd have thought you'd look more like a blushingly happy bride.'

Her cousins had said nothing overtly cruel. Not even they would dare spit bare barbs and bitchiness at her in the palace grounds. No, this was a subtle poison, wrapped in layers of saccharine politeness. But they'd always known where to strike for maximum hurt—mean girls from the moment she'd met them.

Don't reply. Don't give them ammunition.

But that was the old Hester whispering. The one who'd been too afraid to speak or stand up, who'd hidden every reaction, who'd run away...

As Alek had pointed out, there was nothing wrong with choosing not to stick around to be abused. It had taken strength for her to walk out and because she had, she was even stronger now. So she wasn't going to let them chip away her new-found confidence. She'd taken on a huge job here and nailed it. What was more, while Alek mightn't love her, he liked her and he respected what she could offer.

'Oh, I'm very happy,' Hester dredged up enough serenity to assure them. 'Just a little tired from our secret honeymoon. We weren't supposed to go away, what with the coronation so soon, but—' she shrugged and her oh-so-polite tone matched theirs '—Alek's very used to doing and having what he wants.' She paused for a moment to bestow them with a smile as brilliantly fake as theirs had been. 'And he wants me.'

It was true, after all. Even if only for now.

The satisfaction she felt wasn't from seeing her cousins slack-jawed, but from the sudden lightening of her soul. What these people thought of her *truly* didn't matter and she didn't need to bother any more.

'If you'll excuse me...' She stepped past her cousins only to see her security officer standing at a slight distance behind them. Worse, *Alek* was standing beside him.

She froze. She'd been so focused on her cousins she'd not noticed him arrive. Now she saw the question in his eye and knew he'd heard some of that conversation. Her composure began to crumble.

'Is everything all right, Hester?' he asked, his gaze fixed on her.

'Perfectly fine, Alek,' she said clearly, despite her pulse pounding again in her ears. 'But Kimberly, Brittany and Joshua were just explaining that unfortunately they're unable to stay for the coronation. They need to return home tonight.'

'Oh, I see.' Alek swiftly turned to their security officer. 'Could you please escort our guests back to their hotel now and ensure they get on the next available flight this afternoon?'

'Of course, Your Highness.' The security stepped forward with an authoritative air.

Hester watched as her cousins—with furious wordlessness—walked out of her life.

'Are you okay?' Alek asked softly once they were beyond earshot.

She nodded. 'I'm fine.' She flashed a wobbly grin at him. 'I actually mean that. I handled them *fine*.'

'Not fine, Hester.' A chuckle broke his tense expression. 'You eviscerated them.'

Alek watched a raft of expressions cross Hester's face. She was much easier to read now—anger melded with satisfaction, but quickly faded to wispy sadness, to settle on bittersweet relief. It was a mash-up of conflicting emotions that made her so very human. He'd watched, frankly awed, as she'd stood her ground and despatched her former bullies. She'd breathed ice-cool fire.

Those flames within her were so well hidden, but when she let them show? She was incredible. He guided her through the gardens to the terrace and into his private study. He closed the door, determined to be alone with her again.

'I was thinking,' he muttered. 'I don't think this should end.'

'Pardon?' She shot him a confused look.

'Our marriage.' He cleared his throat and discovered

how truly horrible awkwardness felt. 'You realise we had unprotected sex yesterday.'

Her skin mottled and she ducked her head, brushing the swing of her hair back with a shaking hand. 'Oh, I should have told you at the time but I... I wasn't thinking,' she mumbled. 'I won't get pregnant. I'm on contraception for other reasons. I'm sorry if you've been worried.'

'Worried? No.' He needed a moment to absorb the hit of disappointment. It was startling and he had to clear his throat again. 'Well, I think that we should tear up the contract.'

Her eyes widened. 'Tear it up?' she echoed. 'You want this to end already?'

'No. I mean stay married,' he clarified.

'Stay married.'

She seemed to be stuck on repeat.

'That's right.' He nodded. 'For good.'

She just stared at him.

'I will have to have children some day,' he said.

She didn't even blink. 'I thought you had years to figure that out.'

'I think perhaps I've figured it out already.' He watched her closely. 'I'm not going to lie. I didn't think I wanted them. Partly because I don't want to burden them with... everything. But perhaps the sooner I have children, the longer I'll be around to be King, so they can have as long as possible to shape their own lives, have their own careers, their own dreams.'

She was still staring at him, still unmoving.

'We work well together, Hester. We could make a good team.'

Why wasn't she smiling? Why was she staring at him aghast, as if he'd said something insane? Why did he feel as if he'd just tried to run through a boggy field wearing woollen socks?

'You're willing to settle for...' She trailed off. 'Just for that?'

'What do you mean "settle"?' This made sense. 'I don't think I'd be settling, Hester.'

'What about *your* dreams, Alek?'

'My what?'

'Your dreams.'

He shook his head blankly, because that wasn't the point. That wasn't ever the point.

'You don't have any?' she asked softly.

His gaze narrowed as she stepped closer. She'd done a magnificent job of masking her emotions with her hideous cousins, but her façade had truly cracked wide now. Now there was pure golden fire. 'What about *mine*?' she asked.

'Uh...um...'

'You want me to stay married to you?' she clarified. 'To have children with you? So are you saying you're in love with me?'

Hester held her breath, but for once in his life her charming, usually so smooth husband was lost for words.

'Didn't think so,' she muttered. 'You rebelled so much against the control the Crown—that tradition, your father—all exerted over you. Would you really just accept that little now? Really agree to live such an empty life?'

His gaze narrowed. 'Who's to say it would be empty?'

Had he been concerned he'd got her pregnant and decided he'd better offer to make this a permanent deal? Her heart ached because for a second there, just for a second, she'd wanted to believe he meant it for *real*.

'For so long, I've felt like I didn't fit in,' she said.

'You fit in just fine here. You know we could make this work.'

'I want more than to just make something *work*.'

And when he bored of her? What then?

'We're a lot alike, Hester,' he argued. 'You don't really want all that either. You were happy to accept a convenient marriage.'

'Temporarily, yes. But, actually, I *do* want "all that".'

She wanted the whole package—marriage and children, a family built on a foundation of love. The love she'd not had since her parents died. And the irony of it was that it was thanks to the confidence and appreciation Alek had given her that she finally recognised that she could and should.

'I deserve "all that".'

'You could have *everything* here.'

'And what's that? What's "everything"?'

'Security. Safety.'

'That's what you think I need?' She gazed at him. 'Because that's *not* everything. That's not the most important thing to me.'

'Hester, it's what you need.'

'Is that really what you think?' She gazed at him, horrified. Did he think he was 'helping' her somehow? Rescuing her? Trying to fix her life for her because he'd been unable to do that in his past? Because he'd seen her horrible cousins? 'Am I just a win for your wannabe doctor ego?' she asked, hurt. 'I don't want to be that. I don't want your pity.'

'You don't have it.' Arrogance glittered.

She didn't believe him. 'When we first met, you were furious at the fact you had to get married. You thought a marriage of convenience was the worst thing ever and you wanted to fling your own choice in their faces. But now you've decided it's everything you've ever wanted? What, something superficial, some purely contractual, cool paperwork?'

'We're hardly cool paperwork between the sheets, Hester.'

'That's just… That's not anything more than sex for you. You don't want anything actually emotional.'

His jaw hardened and a wary look entered his eyes. 'And you do?'

She looked at him sadly. 'I've not let anyone close to me in a long, long time. Do you truly think I don't feel anything more than just lust for you?'

He stilled and his expression shuttered. 'Hester—'

But she was struggling to maintain her composure. 'I don't want to settle for safety and security. I want it *all*, Alek.'

He pressed his lips together. 'What is it "all", Hester? Moonbeams and fairy tales?'

'Love isn't an impossible fairy tale to me.' She gazed at him. 'My parents loved each other. I think yours did too.'

He'd turned into a statue. But she couldn't stop her emotions from seeping through her once formidable control as in this most terrible of moments her feelings crystallised. Her ability to stay calm—to maintain her mask—vanished.

'And yes, that's the "everything", the "all" I want. Love. And, honestly, I want it with you.'

He looked winded—as if *she'd* sucker-punched *him* instead of the other way round.

'I can't…say the same to you.'

Of course he couldn't. It was the cruellest moment of her life—when she was so close, but so far from the one thing she really wanted.

'It's not you—'

'Don't.' She held up her hand.

'I can't offer that to anyone, Hester.' He overrode her furiously. 'I never have, never will. It's not in my make-up.'

'That's such a cop-out. Why? You're that afraid?'

'It's not about being afraid,' he snapped. 'I just wanted—'

'What? To make me feel better? To make me feel safe?'

He glared at her. 'And what is so wrong with that?'

'I don't need you to keep me safe. I don't need you to feel secure in my life. I just stood up to the worst people ever...and I didn't need you there to do that.'

He swallowed.

'I can do more than survive now, Alek. I can fight for what I want. The irony is that's because of you.' She shook her head. 'You've made me feel like I can.'

He didn't love her. He wanted her, yes, but that wasn't enough.

'And what I want—what I really want—is everything, "all that" and more with *you*. But because you don't feel that deeply for me, you can't understand that you're hurting me without even realising it. That? That you couldn't see that? You might be happy to live such a superficial, safe existence, Alek, but I'm not.'

'You think I'm shallow?'

'I'd hoped you weren't. You're good to your sister. I get that you're trying to be good to me. You don't understand how heartless it really is.'

'Heartless?' He scowled and his control began to slip. 'Would you rather I lied to you?'

'Of course not.'

He was angry. 'Are you going to run away because I can't give you what you want?'

'No. I only run away from abuse, and I know you won't hurt me more now. I made a commitment to you and I won't renege on our contract. But we go back to business.'

'What does that mean?'

'I won't sleep with you any more.'

'No more kissing? No more touching? You really think that's possible?'

He looked so disbelieving it was insulting.

'It's the only way I will stay for the duration until our divorce.'

'You'll need to lock the door, Hester. But not from me.'

'I know I will. But I'll lock the door and I'll throw away the key.'

'If it's going to be that much of a challenge, then why fight it? Why not just accept that we're good together, Hester? There's no real reason why *that* can't last.'

But it wasn't enough for her. She'd told him how she really felt and he still didn't understand.

'You're really not used to not getting your own way, are you?' She gaped at him. 'Listen to me, Alek. I want more. And I'm worth more. And I will never settle for the little you're offering.'

She fled from the room, slamming the door behind her before she stared at him too long and surrendered everything regardless.

Almost all her life she'd not had it all. She'd not felt secure and cared for. She'd not felt safe enough to care for others too. He'd opened her up. She'd allowed herself to fall for someone. To love.

But she wanted to be loved in return. Loved the way other people were. She knew she'd shut down and hidden away, but she'd not realised how entrenched her defensiveness had become. She'd forgotten that she actually had things to offer people. Alek had reminded her. And made her believe she was beautiful. She could open up and share in joy and pleasure. She could engage with people beyond a quick moment in which to help someone in some superficial way. He'd made her feel warmth again—from companionship and closeness and, above all, humour. He'd changed her.

But while she'd changed him—it wasn't in the same way. The adjustment to his offer wasn't enough. And it hurt more than anything.

CHAPTER TWELVE

HESTER STARED AT her reflection, barely recognising the sleek, stylish woman in the mirror as herself. This coronation was more important than their wedding. It was the reason *for* the wedding—so Alek could fulfil the duty conferred on him from birth.

This was what he'd wanted and truthfully it was *all* he'd wanted. Their affair had been a mere cherry on his already massive cake. No doubt he'd have plenty more cherries in the future.

He might've thought they'd make a good team but it would never last. Because what he'd offered wouldn't be enough for her. She'd be hurt more and more and more knowing that she loved him in a way he would never return. When she'd had so little for so long, she couldn't do that to herself.

The teardrop diamond necklace that had been sent to her room earlier hung like an icy noose around her neck, reminding her of the heartbreak she faced. A year was an interminable amount of time. She wished he'd see that there was no need for them to wait that long. But she'd promised him she'd stay. In public, she'd hold her head high and play her part. Thankfully the palace was large enough for her to avoid him at all other times. She would run away to her apartment and survive. Eventually she'd return to the States—or maybe somewhere else entirely. Then she'd start again. She just had to get through this coronation today.

All the years of hiding her emotions were going to stand her in good stead. It was the only way she was going to get through this and do her job. Because that was her one thing—she was damn good at her job.

It was worse than if she'd run away. She was still present, still doing everything he'd initially asked, but she'd become like a will-o'-the-wisp around the palace. He heard her footsteps but never spoke to her. Caught her scent but never saw her. She was incredibly skilled at making herself invisible. Because she knew what she had to do to survive—and for her that meant not seeing him.

That hurt.

And how badly *he* wanted to see her hurt too. When he was with her, he felt good. She'd slipped under his skin and exposed old wounds to sunlight. It had hurt, tearing off those crusted wrappers. But the salve was Hester herself.

He'd not given anyone real meaning in his life in a long time because it hadn't been a risk he'd been prepared to take. He hadn't even realised how hurt he'd been. He'd not seen the truth. He'd accused her of being prickly and defensive when he was the one holding back. He'd thought he was whole and happy. But he'd been a heartless coward.

But she'd asked him what his dreams were. No one had asked him that, ever, he didn't think. And he hadn't thought he had any. Until now. *She'd* ignited new dreams, enabling him to imagine beyond merely passing personal pleasure. She'd made him realise the emptiness in his life that he'd have denied he felt only a few short weeks ago.

She'd wakened within him the possibility of a future that held more than duty. The prospect of private happiness—of laughter and fulfilment for himself. He wanted—

ached—to inspire that in her. He wanted to be the one *she* dreamed about in the way he dreamed about her. He actually wanted this marriage—with her. And children—with her. He wanted to be the father he'd not had—one who was there. One who *listened*.

She made him want everything he'd deluded himself into believing he dreaded—one woman. Children. Love.

He'd been so wrong about her. He'd thought her shy— she wasn't shy; biddable—where she was intractable, and dutiful—when she could be so defiant it made his blood sing. He'd been unable to admit how much she'd come to mean to him—not to himself. Not to her. Which mean she was right and he was a coward. It took strength to leave a situation, to speak up for what you wanted. He'd been weak in offering less than what either of them wanted or deserved. And in not opening up properly—in not allowing himself to be vulnerable the way she had—he'd hurt her. And he couldn't stand to know that.

The solution had dawned on him early this morning— after another long, sleepless, heart-searching night.

Now, as she slowly made her approach towards him in front of millions again, he realised she'd retreated further behind her walls than ever before.

Her ball gown was of epic proportions—it was the colour of the ocean surrounding the islands while the scarlet regal sash crossed her breast. This time her hair was swept up high. Long silk gloves hid, not just her fingers, but her wrists, right to her elbows. It was impenetrable armour.

But while her face was beautifully made up, he saw through to the emotion-ravaged pallor beneath. He saw the tearful torment in her eyes for that snippet of a second before she looked to the floor again. She was so formal. So correct. So dutiful. And he hated it.

He'd hurt her too badly and the knowledge gutted him. He curled his hands into fists, barely containing the self-directed anger building within him. Barely restraining his urge to run to her and haul her into his arms and beg her forgiveness.

He had to do this properly.

He didn't want her to kneel in front of him. He wanted her to stand beside him. He *needed* her beside him. She strengthened him and he hoped he could strengthen her.

For so long she'd been able to hide behind those walls. Self-contained and in control, masking her emotions, trying to bury everything so deeply so nothing and no one could hurt her. But he knew her walls were built with the thinnest of glass now and with one false move of his, they'd shatter. He didn't want to do that to her. Not here, not now. He'd hurt her too much already. He'd never seen anyone as brittle and as fragile. Or as determined.

So while he was filled with pain for hurting her, he was also consumed with pride and awe. Because she walked towards him smoothly, hidden courage lifting every step. She was loyal and considerate and frankly loving, even when he didn't deserve it.

He was determined to deserve it. And he was determined to show her how much she mattered.

Hester couldn't hold Alek's gaze. He looked so stern it scalded her heart. The last thing she wanted was to walk towards him in front of the world. This packed room was enough, but this was being broadcast again to millions over the Internet. But she had to lead the way for the rest of the citizens in his kingdom. Tradition dictated she display deference before him. Before all of them.

Her blood burned as she kept her eyes on the floor. Slowly she walked to the edge of the dais on which he stood in his cloak and crown. She couldn't look at him even then. The media would probably interpret her body language as submission and that was fine by her. Because she didn't want anyone to guess that it was pure pain and hopeless love.

Slowly she knelt before him. There was a moment of complete silence, then she heard movement as all those people behind her lowered to their knees as well.

She couldn't bear to look at him. It was all just a pretence anyway—just the part she'd promised to play. She'd grit her teeth through the final act and in a year's time she'd leave and, fingers crossed, never see him again.

'Hester.'

His soft call was a command she had to obey. Looking up, she saw he'd moved closer, right to the edge of the dais. But his solemn stare still left welts on her heart.

'I will not let you kneel before me.' His harsh whisper rasped against her flayed skin, stinging like salt rubbed across raw cuts.

She stared at him blankly.

He bent and took her hand and tugged, but she frowned and didn't move. With an impatient grunt he put his hands on her waist and physically lifted her to her feet, pressing her against him for the merest moment.

'What—?'

'Not long and we'll be alone, Hester. Trust me until then, okay?'

It was the quickest whisper in her ear so that no camera could capture the movement of his lips and no distant microphone could amplify the secret speech.

Why was he insisting she stand? Why he was going so far off-script of this massive pantomime they'd been preparing for?

Murmurs rippled across the crowd behind her. The courtiers and guests had remained kneeling, but they were looking up. Alek had stepped to the side briefly but now turned. She saw he held a crown in his hands—a smaller one than his but no less ornate.

He met her gaze for only a moment before looking beyond her to his wide-eyed citizens.

'Allow me a moment to explain,' Alek said. 'I am proud of Triscari's traditions and I will honour them but I also look forward to building new ones.' His face was ashen and his smile so faint. 'I do not wish for my most important partner to bow before me.'

Another murmur rippled across the crowd, but Alek kept talking and they silenced.

'It is a bittersweet time, this coronation, because it only happens because we have lost my father and he was a great king. He was devoted to our country and you, his people. But he was also a lonely man after my mother died. As my sister is, my mother was intelligent, progressive and loving. Losing her was very difficult for us as a family. We do not speak of her enough. I will confess, I thought the requirement for the monarch to be married was archaic—that it was a constraint and a form of control. It is only recently that I've realised it was never for the country's benefit, but for my own. To find a partner, a woman with whom I could share everything—riches and rewards, hope and dreams, and also the weight of this crown. So it is my honour, my privilege, to bow before *you*. To offer my life in service to my people, my country. And finally to offer my love to my Queen—Hester.'

Vaguely she heard cheering through the stone walls—the crowds outside were shouting his name over and over again. Not just his name. Her name too.

'Alek and Hester!'
'Alek and Hester!'
'Alek and Hester!'

Now he was staring straight at her, willing her to move. She couldn't ignore him, yet it hurt, this public display of unity that was so false. But his intense, unwavering gaze and the emotion emanating from him were all-encompassing. Surely it was something she had to reject?

But she couldn't. Not because of the crowds watching, but because of *him*. He compelled her to move with just that promise in his eyes. And even though she couldn't trust it, she couldn't deny him. So she stepped forward and took her place on the dais beside him. He turned and placed the crown on her head—the fine-wrought gold the delicate mate of his.

To her amazement, he then bowed before her. Without prompting, without even thinking about it, she dropped into a curtsey before him. They rose together and he reached out to take her hand. This was good because the air was rushing around her and she felt faint. To the beat of those chanting voices, they walked the length of the grand hall and out to the balcony. Time sped crazily as they stood in front of the gathered crowds and the clicking cameras and listened to the hum of reporters broadcasting their commentaries.

Eventually he turned and guided her back into the palace and into the nearest escape room.

'We need a few minutes.' He shut the door in the face of the palace official seeking to follow them.

Keeping her back to him, Hester stepped further into the room to gather herself.

'You…' She trailed off, realising she couldn't speak about anything too personal without losing it. 'That was an amazing spectacle,' she said harshly, indescribably angry all of a sudden. 'You really nailed it.'

His muttered oath sounded suspiciously close.

'Hester, look at me.' His hands were on her shoulders and he spun her to face him.

His eyes blazed with an emotion she couldn't hope to analyse and couldn't bear to face.

'It's wasn't a *spectacle*,' he said furiously. 'It wasn't

some show for public consumption. I meant it. Every word. Not for them. For you.'

She stared up at him, stunned into rigidity.

'I don't want to do any of this without you. I was a jerk. I'm sorry. I was never more serious in my life than when I said you are my Queen. *You're* who I want by my side, always.'

She got that he thought they were a good fit. That she could complement him. But it wasn't enough. She shook her head. 'I can't—'

'I know what I offered wasn't enough for you, Hester. I thought I understood, but I didn't. It wasn't until we were apart these last few days that I realised just how hollow my words were. How stupid.'

Her mouth dried.

'I had my walls too, Hester, I just didn't realise. All those women? It was avoidance. I didn't want to get close to anyone and never stopped to think why. You helped me— you opened me up and I realise I never dealt with any of it: the ache of losing Mother of watching Dad retreat into isolation and control. And that I'd done the exact same thing in my own way. I thought I was so clever when, actually, I'm a coward.' He huffed out a powerful sigh. 'I thought you were the one who was shut off—and you were. But you're braver than I've ever been. You realised what more you really need and you decided to fight for it.'

'That was only because you got through to me. *You* made me realise how much I was worth. And how much I really want.'

'How much you *deserve*.' His chest rose and fell. 'I know it's all been too fast but give me a chance, Hester. Give *us* time. We're amazing together.'

Amazing together? She blinked.

'Hester, I've fallen in love with you.'

She stared at him fixedly. 'That's not possible.'

'Why?' That old smile twitched. 'Haven't you fallen for me?'

She swallowed. 'Yes, but—'

'The only problem was I couldn't admit it to *myself*. I couldn't admit how much *you* mattered. I was able to keep anyone from mattering much for a very long time. But you slid into my life and suddenly everything was upside down and inside out. Me, *I'm* inside out—I'm unable to exist the way I used to. Because it isn't enough for me any more either. I want you right with me. I can't stand the thought of losing you. I hate this distance we've had.' He was shaking. 'I know it's a lot to ask. I know my life comes with a whole lot of pressure and complication. But you belong here—this could be your home. Stay with me, Hester. Please.'

'You didn't really want me to before. Not like this.'

'Because I was an idiot. Because I didn't know how to handle my own feelings. Because I was afraid. Losing someone you love hurts, Hester. I didn't realise how much I was avoiding letting myself love someone. But the fact is, I can't stop myself and I don't want to any more. I love you. And I want you to let me love you.'

She shrivelled inside. Not believing him while at the same time wanting to.

'Is it so hard to believe that I could love you?' he asked.

'It's been a long time…'

'I know.' He brushed her cheek with the backs of his fingers in the way that made her feel *precious*. 'But I think a lot of other people are going to love you, if you let them. A whole country full.'

That scared her, a lot. 'I don't want all that…' she mumbled. It felt like such pressure and all that mattered to her was him. 'I just want you.'

'And you have me.' He drew in a deep breath. 'You're

so beautiful.' He leaned closer. 'You're loyal and brave and funny and kind and so very organised.'

She almost smiled.

'But if you don't want to stay here, we can work something out.' He glanced at her. 'I don't quite know—' He broke off.

'Of course I want to stay, Alek.' Of course she would stand beside him, do anything she could to help him. Just as she was beginning to realise that he would for her. 'I want to be with you. To work with you.'

His hands swept to her waist to hold her still, but it was the look in his eyes that transfixed her. She didn't notice their finery; the gold and jewels faded into insignificance because all that mattered was the emotion shining so clearly in his eyes.

'I have something for you.' He unfastened the top two buttons of his jacket and reached into the inside breast pocket. He pulled his fist out and unfurled his fingers in front of her. A small shard of obsidian sat in his palm. 'It's from that afternoon at the springs.'

'You took a piece?'

'At the time I thought...'

'Thought what?'

'That you might put it with that button in your box.' He gazed into her eyes, his own a little shy. 'But *I* wanted the reminder, that's why I didn't give it to you then. And now I know we should collect more memories *together*.'

Little treasures from little moments that meant so much more than any precious jewels ever could.

He put the obsidian in her palm and locked his hand around hers. What he'd given her was beyond precious—it was access to his heart, his soul. And she would always keep it safe. Just as he was offering to keep her heart safe in his hand too.

He was here for her. He wanted her. He loved her.

Her eyes filled as he swept her into his arms. But he kissed the tears away. He pressed her close against him as if he were afraid she'd disappear if he didn't; his grip was almost painful. But she revelled in it—rising to meet his mouth with hers. To pour every ounce of soaring emotion back into him. She loved him. And he loved her.

'I should've known when I realised I wasn't terrified by the thought of you being pregnant,' he confessed with a breathy laugh. 'I never thought I wanted kids, now I can't wait. I want to see you cradling our babies. I want to see a whole bunch of miniature Hesters curled up in a big chair and reading their favourite books.'

She laughed through her tears. 'While mini Aleks will wow everyone with their ventriloquism?'

'Something like that.' He pulled her close again. 'You believe me?'

She rested her head against his chest and wrapped her arms around his waist, needing to feel him against her and know he was solid and real. 'I will.'

'I know, we need some time together alone.' He sighed. 'But right now we have to go in there for a while. Can you handle it?' He sounded apologetic.

She lifted her face to smile up at him. They'd have their time alone together soon enough and she couldn't wait for that magic. But she understood that right now Alek had the obligations of that heavy crown upon him. It was a burden she'd gladly help him shoulder.

His answering smile reflected the joy rippling through her veins. She rose up on tiptoe to kiss him and whisper her absolute truth.

'I can handle anything when I have you beside me.'

EPILOGUE

Two years later

'COME RIDE WITH ME.'

Hester glanced up and registered the heat of intent in her husband's eyes. 'I thought you had meetings all afternoon?' she asked, faking cool serenity. But she put down the book she'd been reading and quickly stood.

'Finished early.' Alek smiled knowingly.

She knew that smile so well and every time he sent it her way, it hit her right in the solar plexus. He didn't just love her, he *adored* her—making her feel beautiful inside and out. And with him at her side, she didn't just handle everything—all the good and the bad—that life had to offer, she *revelled* in it.

So now she drank in the sight of him in the black trousers and shirt he preferred to ride in. Sensual attraction fluttered as she felt ruthless desire emanating from him. Their need for touch hadn't dissipated in the two years since their mad, quick and convenient marriage—in fact it had increased.

After the coronation they'd had to escape—stealing a full month of a real honeymoon at the stud, replying to any arising issues via phone and emails. And even then, upon their return, it had been a challenge to concentrate for longer periods of work again.

Together they'd formed their alliance. She'd accompanied him more on engagements and she'd found a purpose of her own in reinvigorating the city's literacy programmes. Then, just this year, she'd opened the children's library of her dreams—using a room in Queen Aleksandrina's castle, to bring life and love and laughter back to the place, so that more people could take time out there and appreciate the beauty built by an untameable woman who'd refused to fit in.

And every weekend they could, they came back here to Triscari Stud to oversee the breeding programme and take some time for themselves. So now Hester walked with him to the yard. Jupiter was saddled and waiting not quite patiently. They always rode together when staying at the stud even though Hester had learned to ride on her own and actually found she wasn't just getting better, she enjoyed it.

Today Jupiter carried them both. Alek steered him in the direction of the clifftop forest that they'd gone to on her first visit here. Hester's heart sang as, sure enough, they went to the hot springs where they'd come together again in that desperately passionate way. She treasured that piece of obsidian that rested safely in her box. But today it wasn't only the striking rock formations and steaming water that caught her attention. A circular white tent was set up near the pool and a small sofa actually sat outside in the warm sun, smothered in plump cushions and rugs.

'What's this?'

'Our anniversary escape.' He tightened his hold on her. 'Or did you think I'd forgotten?'

'I didn't think you'd forgotten,' she murmured. 'I

thought you were probably planning something for later. I figured your meeting was a cover.'

'Were you planning something?'

She smiled coyly and leaned back against him. 'Of course.'

She loved dreaming up nice things to show she cared. Small things, to treat him, and he did the same for her— slowly building their own language of care and love and collecting the trinkets to put in their shared memory box. But this time she had the most perfect secret to surprise him with.

She slipped down from Jupiter and walked towards the tent. Fairy lights were wound around the wooden poles while the interior was filled with fresh flowers and a pile of soft-looking wool throws artfully strewn on a bed. There was a small table with a wicker basket beside it that she knew would be filled with their favourite picnic food.

'Going for comfort this time?' she teased him.

'Going to stay the whole night.' He nodded. 'Maybe even two nights.'

She curled her toes with delight. There was nothing better than stealing time for just the two of them. She'd never known such fulfilment and happiness.

'So...' He leaned back to look into her eyes. 'Has my bringing you here caused any problem for what you had planned?'

She shook her head. 'My plan was vague but portable.' Her heart pounded and to her amazement tears formed, bathing her eyeballs in hot acid that spilled before she could speak any more.

Alek's eyes widened. 'Hester?'

She nodded quickly. 'I'm fine.' All the emotion clogged her throat so she could only whisper. 'I'm better than fine. You know...'

He still frowned but a small smile curved his mouth

and his hold on her tightened. The contact strengthened her. She trusted him completely—knew she could expose herself, reveal her greatest vulnerability—because he always caught her. He always listened. He cared.

'I'm pregnant,' she blurted.

He stared, frozen for eternity before his expression exploded with intensity. 'Say it again.'

'We're having a baby.'

Because this was *them*, together, and their little unit of two was going to become three.

A huge rush of air hissed from his lungs and she felt the impact as relief and joy and incredulity radiated from him.

'It's been hideous keeping it from you these last couple of days.' She lifted her hands to frame his beloved face. 'But I wanted to save it just long enough to tell you today.' She rose on tiptoe and pressed her tear-stained mouth to his.

They'd decided to delay trying for a little while after their wedding so they could discover and delight in each other and solidify the intense connection they'd forged so quickly. But a few months ago they'd discarded any contraception. And now? Now her joy was so fierce, it burgeoned, encompassing him too.

'Not going to lie—I'm terrified. But I can't wait, Hester.'

He pressed her to him and she felt his strong muscles shaking.

'We can still make love? Is it safe—?'

'There'll only be danger if we don't!' She laughed and growled at the same time. 'I need to have my way with you, my King.'

'Well, you are my Queen and I will always bow before you.' He didn't just bow, he dropped to his knees, his hands firm on her hips as he gazed up the length of her still-slim body. 'I can't wait to meet our child, Hester.'

'Neither can I.' She dropped to her knees too—desperate to feel again the pleasure that was only theirs.

With him she was free and utterly unafraid to reveal everything—her body, her soul, her secrets—all the things that scared her, all the things that delighted her. He didn't just accept them, he embraced them, and he shared his own so together they were stronger still.

'Alek...' she breathed, enraptured by the fantasy world into which he'd cast her.

'I'm here, Hester.'

And he was.

Because beneath it all—the crowns, the diamonds, the palaces and castles...everything—their love was real.

* * * * *

CONVENIENTLY
HIS PRINCESS

OLIVIA GATES

To my family and friends, who give me all I need…
love, understanding, encouragement and space, to
keep on writing…and enjoying it. Love you all.

One

"You want me to marry Kanza the Monster?"

Aram Nazaryan winced at the loudness of his own voice.

Not that anyone could blame him for going off like that. Shaheen Aal Shalaan had made some unacceptable requests in his time, but *this* one warranted a description not yet coined by any language he knew. And he knew four.

But the transformation of his best and only friend into a meddling mother hen had been steadily progressing from ignorable to untenable for the past three years. It seemed that the happier Shaheen became with Aram's kid sister Johara after they had miraculously reunited and gotten married, the more sorry for Aram he became and the more he intensified his efforts to get his brother-in-law to change what he called his "unlife."

And to think he'd still been gullible enough to believe that Shaheen had dropped by his office for a simple visit. Ten minutes into the chitchat, he'd carpet bombed him with emotional blackmail.

He'd started by abandoning all subtlety about enticing him to go back to Zohayd, asking him point-blank to come *home*.

Annoyed into equal bluntness, he'd finally retorted that Zohayd was Shaheen's home, not his, and he wouldn't go back there to be the family's seventh wheel, when Shaheen and Johara's second baby arrived.

Shaheen had only upped the ante of his persistence. To prove that he'd have a vital role and a full life in Zohayd, he'd offered him his job. He'd actually asked him to become Zohayd's freaking minister of economy!

Thinking that Shaheen was pulling his leg, he'd at first laughed. What else could it be but a joke when only a royal Zohaydan could assume that role, and the last time Aram checked, he was a French-Armenian American?

Shaheen, regretfully, hadn't sprouted a sense of humor. What he had was a harebrained plan of how Aram could *become* a royal Zohaydan. By marrying a Zohaydan princess.

Before he could bite Shaheen's head off for that suggestion, his brother-in-law had hit him with the identity of the candidate he thought *perfect* for him. And *that* had been the last straw.

Aram shot his friend an incredulous look when Shaheen rose to face him. "Has conjugal bliss finally fried your brain, Shaheen? There's no way I'm marrying that monster."

In response, Shaheen reeled back his flabbergasted expression, adjusting it to a neutral one. "I don't know where you got that name. The Kanza I know is certainly no monster."

"Then there are two different Kanzas. The one I know, Kanza Aal Ajmaan, the princess from a maternal branch of your royal family, has earned that name and then some."

Shaheen's gaze became cautious, as if he were dealing with a madman. "There's only one Kanza…and she is delightful."

"Delightful?" A spectacular snort accompanied that exclamation. "But let's say I go along with your delusion and agree that she is Miss Congeniality herself. Are you out of your mind even suggesting her to me? She's a kid!"

It was Shaheen's turn to snort. "She's almost thirty."

"Wha…? No way. The last time I saw her she was somewhere around eighteen."

"Yes. And that was over ten years ago."

Had it really been that long? A quick calculation said it had been, since he'd last seen her at that fateful ball, days before he'd left Zohayd.

He waved the realization away. "Whatever. The eleven or twelve years between us sure hasn't shrunk by time."

"I'm eight years older than Johara. Three or four years' more age difference might have been a big deal back then, but it's no longer a concern at your respective ages now."

"That may be your opinion, but I…" He stopped, huffed a laugh, shaking his finger at Shaheen. "Oh, no, you don't. You're not dragging me into discussing her as if she's actually a possibility. She's a monster, I'm telling you."

"And I'm telling you she's no such thing."

"Okay, let's go into details, shall we? The Kanza I knew was a dour, sullen creature who sent people scurrying in the opposite direction just by glaring at them. In fact, every time she looked my way, I thought I'd find two holes drilled into me wherever her gaze landed, fuming black, billowing smoke."

Shaheen whistled. "Quite the image. I see she made quite an impression on you, if after over ten years you still recall her with such vividness and her very memory still incites such intense reactions."

"Intense *unfavorable* reactions." He grunted in disgust. "It's appalling enough that you're suggesting this marriage of convenience at all but to recommend the one…creature who ever creeped the hell out of me?"

"Creeped?" Shaheen tutted. "Don't you think you're going overboard here?"

He scowled, his pesky sense of fairness rearing its head. "Okay, so perhaps *creeped* is not the right word. She just… disturbed me. *She* is disturbed. Do you know that horror once went around with purple hair, green full-body paint and pink contact lenses? Another time she went total albino rabbit with white hair and red eyes. The last time I saw her she had blue hair and zombie makeup. *That* was downright creepy."

Shaheen's smile became that of an adult coddling an unreasonable child. "What, apart from weird hair and eye color and makeup experimentation, do you have against her?"

"The way she used to mutter my name, as if she was casting a curse. I always had the impression she had some... goblin living inside her wisp of a body."

Shaheen shoved his hands inside his pockets, the image of complacency. "Sounds like she's exactly what you need. You could certainly use someone that potent to thaw you out of the deep freeze you've been stuck in for around two decades now."

"Why don't I just go stick myself in an incinerator? It would handle that deep freeze much more effectively and far less painfully."

Shaheen only gave him the forbearing, compassionate look of a man who knew such deep contentment and fulfillment and was willing to take anything from his poor, unfortunate friend with the barren life.

"Quit it with the pitying look, Shaheen. My temperature is fine. It's how I am now.... It's called growing up."

"If only. Johara feels your coldness. I feel it. Your parents are frantic, believing they'd done that to you when you were forced to remain with your father in Zohayd at the expense of your own life."

"Nobody forced me to do anything. I chose to stay with Father because he wouldn't have survived alone after his breakup with Mother."

"And when they eventually found their way back to each other, you'd already sacrificed your own desires and ambitions and swerved from your own planned path to support your family, and you've never been able to correct your course. Now you're still trapped on the outside, watching the rest of us live our lives from that solitude of yours."

Aram glowered at Shaheen. He was happy, incredibly so, for his mother and father. For his sister and best friend. But when they kept shoving his so-called solitude in his face, he felt nothing endearing toward any of them. Their solicitude only chafed when he knew he couldn't do anything about it.

"I made my own choices, so there's nothing for anyone to feel guilty about. The solitude you lament suits me just fine. So put your minds the hell at ease and leave me be."

"I'll be happy to, right after you give my proposition serious consideration and not dismiss it out of hand."

"Said proposition deserves nothing else."

"Give me one good reason it does. Citing things about Kanza that are ten years outdated doesn't count."

"How about an updated one? If she's twenty-eight—"

"She'll be twenty-nine in a few months."

"And she hasn't married yet—I assume no poor man has taken her off the shelf only to drop her back there like a burning coal and run into the horizon screaming?"

Shaheen's pursed lips were the essence of disapproval. "No, she hasn't been married or even engaged."

He smirked in self-satisfaction at the accuracy of his projections. "At her age, by Zohaydan standards, she's already long fossilized."

"How gallant of you, Aram. I thought you were a progressive man who's against all backward ideas, including ageism. I never dreamed you'd hold a woman's age against her in anything, let alone in her suitability for marriage."

"You know I don't subscribe to any of that crap. What I'm saying is if she is a Zohaydan woman, and a princess, who didn't get approached by a man for that long, it is proof that she is generally viewed as incompatible with human life."

"The exact same thing could be said about you."

Throwing his hands up in exasperation, he landed them on his friend's shoulders. "Listen carefully, Shaheen, because I'll say this once, and we will not speak of this again. I will not get married. Not to become Zohaydan and become your minister of economy, not for any other reason. If you really need my help, I'll gladly offer you and Zohayd my services."

Shaheen, who had clearly anticipated this as one of Aram's answers, was ready with his rebuttal. "The level of involvement needed has to be full-time, with you taking the top job and living in Zohayd."

"I have my own business…"

"Which you've set up so ingeniously and have trained your deputies so thoroughly you only need to supervise operations from afar for it to continue on its current trajectory of phenomenal success. This level of efficiency, this uncanny ability to employ the right people and to get the best out of them is exactly what I need you to do for Zohayd."

"*You* haven't been working the job full-time," he pointed out.

"Only because my father has been helping me since he abdicated. But now he's retreating from public life completely. Even with his help, I've been torn between my family, my business and the ministry. Now we have another baby on the way and family time will only increase. And Johara is becoming more involved in humanitarian projects that require my attention, as well. I simply can't find a way to juggle it all if I remain minister."

He narrowed his eyes at Shaheen. "So I should sacrifice my own life to smooth out yours?"

"You'd be sacrificing nothing. Your business will continue as always, you'd be the best minister of economy humanly possible, a position you'd revel in, and you'll get a family…something I know you have always longed for."

Yeah. He was the only male he knew who'd planned at

sixteen that he'd get married by eighteen, have half a dozen kids, pick one place and one job and grow deep, deep roots.

And here he was, forty, alone and rootless.

How had that happened?

Which was the rhetorical question to end all rhetorical questions. He knew just how.

"What I longed for and what I am equipped for are poles apart, Shaheen. I've long come to terms with the fact that I'm never getting married, never having a family. This might be unimaginable to you in your state of familial nirvana, but not everyone is made for wedded bliss. Given the number of broken homes worldwide, I'd say those who are equipped for it are a minority. I happen to be one of the majority, but I happen to be at peace with it."

It was Shaheen who took him by the shoulders now. "I believed the exact same thing about myself before Johara found me again. Now look at me…ecstatically united with the one right person."

Aram bit back a comment that would take this argument into an unending loop. That it was Shaheen and Johara's marriage that had shattered any delusions he'd entertained that he could ever get married himself.

What they had together—this total commitment, trust, friendship and passion—was what he'd always dreamed of. Their example had made him certain that if he couldn't have that—and he didn't entertain the least hope he'd ever have it—then he couldn't settle for anything less.

Evidently worried that Aram had stopped arguing, Shaheen rushed to add, "I'm not asking you to get married tomorrow, Aram. I'm just asking you to consider the possibility."

"I don't need to. I have been and will always remain perfectly fine on my own."

Eager to put an abrupt end to this latest bout of emotional wrestling—the worst he'd had so far with Shaheen—he started to turn around, but his friend held him back.

He leveled fed-up eyes on Shaheen. *"Now what?"*

"You look like hell."

He felt like it, too. As for how he looked, during necessary self-maintenance he'd indeed been seeing a frayed edition of the self he remembered.

Seemed hitting forty did hit a man hard.

A huff of deprecation escaped him. "Why, thanks, Shaheen. You were always such a sweet talker."

"I'm telling it as it is, Aram. You're working yourself into the ground…and if you think I'm blunt, it's nothing compared to what Amjad said when he last saw you."

Amjad, the king of Zohayd, Shaheen's oldest brother. The Mad Prince turned the Crazy King. And one of the biggest jerks in human history.

Aram exhaled in disgust. "I was right there when he relished the fact that I looked 'like something the cat dragged in, chewed up and barfed.' But thanks for bringing up that royal pain. I didn't even factor him in my refusal. But even if I considered the job offer/marriage package the opportunity of a lifetime, I'd still turn it down flat because it would bring me in contact with *him*. I can't believe you're actually asking me to become a minister in that inhuman affliction's cabinet."

Shaheen grinned at his diatribe. "You'll work with me, not him."

"No, I won't. Give it up, already."

Shaheen looked unsatisfied and tried again. "About Kanza…"

A memory burst in his head. He couldn't believe it hadn't come to him before. "Yes, about her and about abominations for older siblings. You didn't only pick Kanza the Monster for my best match but the half sister of the Fury herself, Maysoon."

"I hoped you'd forgotten about her. But I guess that was asking too much." Wryness twisted Shaheen's lips. "Maysoon was a tad…temperamental."

"A tad?" he scoffed. "She was a raging basket case. I barely escaped her in one piece."

And she'd been the reason that he'd had to leave Zohayd and his father behind. The reason he'd had to abandon his dream of ever making a home there.

"Kanza is her extreme opposite, anyway."

"You got that right. While Maysoon was a stunning if unstable harpy, Kanza was an off-putting miscreant."

"I diametrically differ with your evaluation of Kanza. While I know she may not be…sophisticated like her womenfolk, Kanza's very unpretentiousness makes me like her far more. Even if you don't consider those virtues exciting, they would actually make her a more suitable wife for you."

Aram lifted a sarcastic brow. "You figure?"

"I do. It would make her safe and steady, not like the fickle, demanding women you're used to."

"You're only making your argument even more inadmissible, Shaheen. Even if I wanted this, and I consider almost anything admissible in achieving my objectives, I would draw the line at exploiting the mousy, unworldly spinster you're painting her to be."

"Who says there'd be any exploitation? You might be a pain in the neck that rivals even Amjad sometimes but you're one of the most coveted eligible bachelors in the world. Kanza would probably jump at the opportunity to be your wife."

Maybe. Probably. Still…

"No, Shaheen. And that's final."

The forcefulness he'd injected into his voice seemed to finally get to Shaheen, who looked at him with that drop-it-now-to-attack-another-day expression that he knew all too well.

Aram clamped his friend's arm, dragging him to the door. "Now go home, Shaheen. Kiss Johara and Gharam for me."

Shaheen still resisted being shoved out. "Just assess the

situation like you do any other business proposition before you make a decision either way."

Aram groaned. Shaheen was one dogged son of a king. "I've already made a decision, Shaheen, so give it a rest."

Before he finally walked away, Shaheen gave him that unfazed smile of his that eloquently said he wouldn't.

Resigned that he hadn't heard the last of this, Aram closed the door after him with a decisive click.

The moment he did, his shoulders slumped as his feet dragged to the couch. Throwing himself down on it, he decided to spend yet another night there. No need for him to go "home." Since he didn't have one anyway.

But as he stretched out and closed his eyes, his meeting with Shaheen revolved in his mind in a nonstop loop.

He might have sent Shaheen on his way with an adamant refusal, but it wasn't that easy to suppress his own temptation.

Shaheen's previous persuasions hadn't even given him pause. After all, there had been nothing for him to do in Zohayd except be with his family, who had their priorities—of which he wasn't one. But now that Shaheen was dangling that job offer in front of him, he could actually visualize a real future there.

He'd given Zohayd's economy constant thought when he'd lived there, had studied it and planned to make it his life's work. Now, as if Shaheen had been privy to all that, he was offering him the very position where he could utilize all his talents and expertise and put his plans into action.

Then came that one snag in what could have been a once-in-a-lifetime opportunity.

The get-married-to-become-Zohaydan one.

But…should it be a snag? Maybe convenience was the one way he *could* get married. And since he didn't want to get married for real, perhaps Shaheen's candidate *was* exactly what he needed.

Her family was royal but not too high up on the tree of

royalty as to be too lofty, and their fortune was nowhere near his billionaire status. Maybe as Shaheen had suggested, she'd give him the status he needed, luxuriate in the boost in wealth he'd provide and stay out of his hair.

He found himself standing before the wall-to-wall mirror in the bathroom. He didn't know how he'd gotten there. Meeting his own eyes jogged him out of the preposterous trajectory of his thoughts.

He winced at himself. Shaheen had played him but good. He'd actually made him consider the impossible.

And it was impossible. Being in Zohayd, the only place that had been home to him, being with his family, being Zohayd's minister of economy were nice fantasies.

And they would remain just that.

Miraculously, Shaheen hadn't pursued the subject further.

Wonders would never cease, it seemed.

The only thing he'd brought up in the past two weeks had been an invitation to a party he and Johara were holding in their New York penthouse tonight. An invitation he'd declined.

He was driving to the hotel where he "lived," musing over Shaheen dropping the subject, wrestling with this ridiculously perverse sense of disappointment, when his phone rang. Johara.

He pressed the Bluetooth button and her voice poured its warmth over the crystal-clear connection.

"Aram, please tell me you're not working or sleeping."

He barely caught back a groan. This must be about the party, and he'd hate refusing her to her ears. It was an actual physical pain being unable to give Johara whatever she wanted. Since the moment she'd been born, he'd been a *khaatem f'esba'ha,* or "a ring on her finger," as they said in Zohayd. He was lucky that she was part angel or she would have used him as her rattle toy through life.

He prayed she wouldn't exercise her power over him, make it impossible for him to turn down the invitation again. He was at an all-time low, wasn't in any condition to be exposed to her and Shaheen's happiness.

He imbued his voice with the smile that only Johara could generate inside him no matter what. "I'm driving back to the hotel, sweetheart. Are you almost ready for your party?"

"Oh, I am, but…are you already there? If you are, don't bother. I'll think of something else."

He frowned. "What is this all about, Johara?"

Sounding apologetic, she sighed. "There's a very important file that one of my guests gave me to read, and we'd planned to discuss it at the party. Unfortunately, I forgot it back in my office at Shaheen's building, and I can't leave now. So I was wondering if you could go get the file and bring it here to me?" She hesitated. "I'm sorry to take you out of your way and I promise not to try to persuade you to stay at the party, but I can't trust anyone else with the pass codes to my filing cabinets."

"You know you can ask me anything at all, anytime."

"Anything but come to the party, huh?" He started to recite the rehearsed excuse he'd given Shaheen, and she interjected, "But Shaheen told me you did look like you needed an early night, so I totally understand. And it's not as if I could have enjoyed your company anyway, since we've invited a few dozen people and I'll be flitting all over playing hostess."

He let out a sigh of relief for her letting him off the hook, looking forward to seeing them yet having the excuse to keep the visit to the brevity he could withstand tonight.

"Tell me what to look for."

Twenty minutes later, Aram was striding across the top floor of Shaheen's skyscraper.

As he entered Johara's company headquarters, he

frowned. The door to her assistants' office, which led to hers, was open. Weird.

Deciding that it must have been a rare oversight in their haste to attend Johara and Shaheen's soiree, he walked in and found the door to his sister's private office also ajar. Before he could process this new information, a slam reverberated through him.

He froze, his senses on high alert. Not that it took any effort to pinpoint the source of the noise. The racket that followed was unmistakable in direction and nature. Someone was inside Johara's office and was turning it upside down.

Thief was the first thing that jumped into his mind.

But no. There was no way anyone could have bypassed security. Except someone the guards knew. Maybe one of Johara's assistants was in there looking for the file she'd asked him for? But she had been clear she hadn't trusted anyone else with her personal pass codes. So could one of her employees be trying to break into her files?

No, again. He trusted his gut feelings, and he knew Johara had chosen her people well.

Then perhaps someone who worked for Shaheen was trying to steal classified info only she as his wife would be privy to?

Maybe. Calling the guards was the logical next step, anyway. But if he'd jumped to conclusions it could cause unnecessary fright and embarrassment to whomever was inside. He should take a look before he made up his mind how to proceed.

He neared the door in soundless steps, not that the person inside would have heard a marching band. A bulldozer wouldn't have caused more commotion than that intruder. That alone was just cause to give whomever it was a bit of a scare.

Peeping inside, he primed himself for a confrontation if need be. The next moment, everything in his mind emptied.

It was a woman. Young, slight, wiry. With the thickest

mane of hair he'd ever seen flying after her like dark flames
as she crashed about Johara's office. And she didn't look in
the least worried she'd be caught in the act.

Without making a conscious decision, he found himself
striding right in.

Then he heard himself saying, "Why don't you fill me
in on what you're looking for?"

The woman jumped in the air. She was so light, her
movement so vertical, so high, it triggered an exaggerated
image in his mind of a cartoon character jumping out of her
skin in fright. It almost forced a laugh from his lips at its
absurdity yet its appropriateness for this brownie.

The laugh dissolved into a smile that hadn't touched his
lips in far too long as she turned to him.

He watched her, feeling as if time was decelerating, like
one of those slow-motion movie sequences that signified a
momentous event.

He heard himself again, amusement soaking his drawl.
"I hear that while searching for something that evidently
elusive, two sets of hands and eyes, not to mention two
brains, are better than one."

With his last word, she was facing him. And though
her face was a canvas of shock, and he could tell from her
shapeless black shirt and pants that the tiny sprite was un-
armed, it felt as if he'd gotten a kick in his gut.

And that was before her startled expression faded, before those fierce, dark eyes flayed a layer off his skin and
her husky voice burned down his nerve endings.

"I should have known the unfortunate event of tripping
into your presence was a territorial hazard around this place.
So what brings you to your poor sister's office while she's
not around? Is no one safe from the raids of The Pirate?"

Two

Aram stared at the slight creature who faced him across the elegant office, radiating the impact of a miniature force of nature, and one thing reverberating through his mind.

She'd recognized him on the spot.

No. More than that. She *knew* him. At least knew *of* him.

She'd called him "The Pirate." The persona, or rather the caricature of him that distasteful tabloids, scorned women and disgruntled business rivals had popularized.

She seemed to be waiting for him to make a comeback to her opening salvo.

A charge of electricity forked up his spine, then all the way up to his lips, spreading them wider. "So I'm The Pirate. And what do you answer to? The Tornado? The Hurricane? You did tear through Johara's office with the comparative havoc of one. Or do you simply go with The Burglar? A very messy, noisy, reckless one at that?"

She tilted her head, sending her masses of glossy curls tumbling over one slim shoulder. He could swear he heard them tutting in sarcastic vexation that echoed the expression on her elfin face.

It also poured into her voice, its timbre causing something inside his rib cage to rev. "So are you going to stand there like the behemoth that you are blocking my escape route and sucking all oxygen from the room into that ridiculously massive chest of yours, or are you going to give a fellow thief a hand?"

His lips twitched, every word out of hers another zap lashing through his nerves. "Now, how is it fair that I assist you in your heist without even having the privilege of knowing who I'm going to be indicted with when we're caught? Or are formal introductions not even necessary? Perhaps your spritely self plans on disappearing into the night, leaving me behind to take the fall?"

Her stare froze on him for several long seconds before she suddenly tossed her hair back with a careless hand. "Oh, right…I remember now. Sorry for that. I guess having you materialize behind me like some genie surprised me so much it took me a while to reboot and access my memory banks."

He blinked, then frowned. Was she the one who'd stopped making sense, or had his mind finally stopped functioning? It *had* been increasingly glitch riddled of late. He had been teetering on the brink of some breakdown for a long time now, and he'd thought it was only a matter of time before the chasm running through his being became complete.

So had his psyche picked now of all times to hit rock bottom? But why *now,* when he'd finally found someone to jog him out of his apathy, even if temporarily; someone he actually couldn't predict?

Maybe he'd blacked out or something, missed something she'd said that would make her last words make sense.

He cleared his throat. "Uh…come again?"

Her fed-up expression deepened. "I momentarily forgot how you got your nickname, and that you continue to live down to it, and then some."

Though the jump in continuity still baffled him, he went along. "Oh? I'm very much interested in hearing your dissection of my character. Knowing how another criminal mastermind perceives me would no doubt help me perfect my M.O."

One of those dense, slanting eyebrows rose. "Invoking the code of dishonor among thieves? Sure, why not? I'm charitable like that with fellow crooks." That obsidian gaze poured mockery over him. "Let's see. You earned your moniker after building a reputation of treating other sentient beings like commodities to be pillaged then tossed aside once their benefit is depleted. But you reserve an added insult and injury to those who suffer the terrible misfortune of being exposed to you on a personal level, as you reward those hapless people by deleting them from you mind. So, if you're seeking my counsel about enhancing your performance, my opinion is that you can't improve on your M.O. of perfectly efficient cruelty."

Her scathing portrayal *was* the image that had been painted of him in the business world and by the women he'd kept away by whatever measures necessary.

When his actions had been exaggerated or misinterpreted and that ruthless reputation had begun to be established, he'd never tried to adjust it. On the contrary, he'd let it become entrenched, since that perceived cold-bloodedness did endow him with a power nothing else could. Not to mention that it supplied him with peace of mind he couldn't have bought if he'd projected a more approachable persona. This one did keep the world at bay.

But the only actual accuracy in her summation was the personal interactions bit. He didn't crowd his recollections with the mundane details of anyone who hadn't proved worth his while. Only major incidents remained in his memory—if stripped from any emotional impact they might have had.

But…wait a minute. Inquiring about her identity had triggered this caustic commentary in the first place. Was she obliquely saying that he didn't remember *her,* when he should?

That was just not possible. How would he have ever forgotten those eyes that could reduce a man to ashes at thirty paces, or that tongue that could shred him to ribbons, or that wit that could weave those ribbons into the hand basket to send him to hell in?

No way. If he'd ever as much as exchanged a few words with her, not only would he have remembered, he would probably have borne the marks of every one. After mere minutes of being exposed to her, he felt her eyes and tongue had left no part of him unscathed.

And he was loving it.

God, to be reveling in this, he must be sicker than he'd thought of all the fawning he got from everyone else—especially women. Though he knew *that* had never been for *him.* During his stint in Zohayd, it had been his exotic looks but mainly his closeness to the royal family that had incited the relentless pursuit of women there. After he'd become a millionaire, then a billionaire… Well, status and wealth were irresistible magnets to almost everyone.

That made being slammed with such downright derision unprecedented. He doubted if he would have accepted it from anyone else, though. But from this enigma, he was outright relishing it.

Wanting to incite even more of her verbal insults, he gave her a bow of mock gratitude. "Your testimony of dishonor honors me, and your maligning warms my stone-cold heart."

Both her eyebrows shot up this time. "You have one? I thought your species didn't come equipped with those superfluous organs."

His grin widened. "I do have a rudimentary thing somewhere."

"Like an appendix?" A short, derogatory sound purred in the back of her throat. "Something that could be excised and you'd probably function better without? Wonder why you didn't have it electively removed. It must be festering in there."

As if compelled, he moved away from the door, needing a closer look at this being he'd never seen the likes of before. He kept drawing nearer as she stood her ground, her glare one that could have stopped an attacking horde.

It only made getting even closer imperative. He stopped only when he was three feet away, peering down at this diminutive woman who was a good foot or more shorter than he was yet feeling as if he was standing nose to nose with an equal.

"Don't worry," he finally said, answering her last dig. "There is no reason for surgical intervention. It has long since shriveled and calcified. But thank you from the bottom of my vestigial heart for the concern. And for the counsel. It's indeed reassuring to have such a merciless authority confirm that I'm doing the wrong thing so right."

He waited for her ricocheting blitz, anticipation rising. Instead, she seared him with an incinerating glance before seeming to delete *him* from her mind as she resumed her search.

By now he knew for certain that she wasn't here to do anything behind Johara's back. Even when she'd readily engaged him in the "thieves in the night" scenario he'd initiated, and rifling through the very cabinets he himself was here to search…

It suddenly hit him, right in the solar plexus, who this tempest in human form was.

It was *her*.

Kanza. Kanza Aal Ajmaan.

Unable to blink, to breathe, he stood staring at her as she kept transferring files from the cabinets, plopping them down on Johara's desk before attacking them with a speed and focus that once again flooded his mind's eye with images of hilarious cartoon characters. He had no clue how he'd even recognized her. Just as she'd accused him, his memories of the Kanza he'd known over ten years ago had been stripped of any specifics.

All he could recall of the fierce and fearsome teenager she'd been, apart from the caricature he'd painted for Shaheen of her atrocious fashion style and the weird, bordering-on-repulsive things she'd done with her hair and eyes, was that it had felt as if something ancient had been inhabiting that younger-than-her-age body.

A decade later, she still seemed more youthful than her chronological age, yet packed the wallop of this same primal force. But that was where the resemblance ended.

The Mad Hatter and Wicked Witch clothes and makeup and extraterrestrial hair, contact lenses and body paint were gone now. From the nondescript black clothes and the white sneakers that clashed with them, to the face scrubbed clean of any enhancements, to the thick, untamed mahogany tresses that didn't seem to have met a stylist since he'd last seen her, she had gone all the way in the other direction.

Though in an opposite way to her former self, she was still the antithesis of all the svelte, stylish women who'd ever entered his orbit, starting with her half sisters. Where they'd been overtly feminine and flaunting their assets, she made no effort whatsoever to maximize any attributes she might have. Not that she had much to work with. She was small, almost boyish. The only big thing about her was her hair. And eyes. Those were enormous. Everything else was tiny.

But that was when he analyzed her looks clinically. But when he experienced them with the influence of the being they housed, the spirit that animated them…that was when his entire perception changed. The pattern of her features, the shape of her lips, the sweep of her lashes, the energy of her movements… Everything about her evolved into something totally different, making her something far more interesting than pretty.

Singular. Compelling.

And the most singular and compelling thing about her was those night eyes that had burned to ashes any preformed ideas of what made a woman worthy of a second glance, let alone constant staring.

Though he was still staring after she'd deprived him of their contact, he *was* glad to be relieved of their all-seeing scrutiny. He needed respite to process finding her here.

How could Shaheen bring her up a couple of weeks ago only for him to stumble on her here of all places when he hadn't crossed paths with her in ten years? This was too much of a coincidence. Which meant…

It wasn't one. Johara had set him up.

Another realization hit simultaneously.

Kanza seemed to be here running his same errand. Evidently Johara had set her up, too.

God. He was growing duller by the day. How could he have even thought Shaheen wouldn't share this with Johara, the woman where half his soul resided? How hadn't he picked up on Johara's knowledge or intentions?

Not that those two coconspirators were important now. The only relevant thing here was Kanza.

Had she realized the setup once he'd walked through that door? Was that why she'd reacted so cuttingly to his appearance? Did she take exception to Johara's matchmaking, and that was her way of telling her, and him, "Hell, no!"?

If this was the truth, then that made her even more interesting than he'd originally thought. It wasn't conceit, but as Shaheen had said, in the marriage market, he was about as big a catch as an eligible bachelor got. He couldn't imagine any woman would be averse to the idea of being his wife—if only for his status and wealth. Even his reputation was an irresistible lure in that arena. If women thought they had access, it only made him more of a challenge, a dangerous bad boy each dreamed she'd be the one to tame.

But if Kanza was so immune to his assets, so opposed

to exploring his possibility as a groom, that alone made her worthy of in-depth investigation.

Not that *he* was even considering Shaheen and Johara's neat little plan. But he *was* more intrigued by the moment by this…entity they'd gotten it into their minds was perfect for him.

Suddenly, said entity looked up from the files, transfixed him in the crosshairs of her fiercest glare yet. "Don't just stand there and pose. Come do something more useful than look pretty." When she saw his eyebrows shoot up, her lips twisted. "What? You take exception to being called pretty?"

He opened his mouth to answer, and her impatient gesture closed it for him, had him hurrying next to her where she foisted a pile of files on him and instructed him to look for the very file Johara had sent him here to retrieve.

Without looking at him, she resumed her search. "I guess pretty is too mild. You have a right to expect more powerful descriptions."

He gave her engrossed profile a sideways glance. "If I expect anything, it certainly isn't that."

She slammed another file shut. "Why not? You have the market of *halawah* cornered after all."

Halawah, literally sweetness, was used in Zohayd to describe beauty. That had him turning fully toward her. "Where *do* you come up with these things that you say?"

She flicked him a fleeting glance, closed another file on a sigh of frustration. "That's what women in Zohayd used to say about you. Wonder what they'd say now that your *halawah* is so exacerbated by age it could induce diabetes."

That had a laugh barking from his depths. "Why, thanks. Being called a diabetes risk is certainly a new spin on my supposed good looks."

She tsked. "You know damn well how beautiful you are."

He shook his bemused head at what kept spilling from those dainty lips, compliments with the razor-sharp edges of insults. "No one has accused me of being beautiful before."

"Probably because everyone is programmed to call men handsome or hunks or at most gorgeous. Well, sorry, buddy. You leave all those adjectives in the dust. You're all-out beautiful. It's really quite disgusting."

"Disgusting!"

"Sickeningly so. The resources you must devote to maximizing your assets and maintaining them at this…level…" She tossed him a gesture that eloquently encompassed him from head to toe. "When your looks aren't your livelihood, this is an excess that should be punishable by law."

An incredulous huff escaped him. "It's surreal to hear you say that when my closest people keep telling me the very opposite—that I'm totally neglecting myself."

She slanted him a caustic look. "You have people who can bear being close to you? My deepest condolences to them."

He smiled as if she'd just lavished the most extravagant praise on him. "I'll make sure to relay your sympathies."

Another withering glance came his way before she resumed her work. "I'll give mine directly to Johara. No wonder she's seemed burdened of late. It must be quite a hardship having you for an only brother in general, not to mention having to see you frequently when she's here."

His gaze lengthened on her averted face. Then suddenly everything jolted into place.

Who Kanza *really* was.

She was the new partner that Johara had been waxing poetic about. Now he replayed the times his sister had raved about the woman who'd taken Johara's design house from moderate success to household-name status, this financial marketing guru who had never actually been mentioned by name. But he had no doubt now it was Kanza.

Had Johara never brought up her name because she didn't want to alert him to her intentions, making him resistant to meeting Kanza and predisposed to finding fault with her if he did? If so, then Johara understood him better than Shaheen did, who'd hit him over the head with his intentions and Kanza's name. That *had* backfired. Evidently Johara had reeled Shaheen in, telling her husband not to bring up the subject again and that she'd handle everything from that point on, discreetly. And she had.

Another certainty slotted into place. Johara had kept her business partner in the dark about all this for the same reason.

Which meant that Kanza had no clue this meeting wasn't a coincidence.

The urge to divulge everything about their situation surged from zero to one hundred. He couldn't wait to see the look on her face as the truth of Johara and Shaheen's machinations sank in and to just stand back and enjoy the fireworks.

He turned to her, the words almost on his lips, when another thought hit him.

What if, once he told her, she became stilted, self-conscious? Or worse, *nice?* He couldn't bear the idea that after their invigorating duel of wits, her revitalizing lambasting, she'd suddenly start to sugarcoat her true nature in an attempt to endear herself to him as a potential bride. But worst of all, what if she shut him out completely?

From what he'd found out about her character so far, he'd go with scenario number three as the far more plausible one.

Whichever way this played out, he couldn't risk spoiling her spontaneity or ending this stimulating interlude.

Deciding to keep this juicy tidbit to himself, he said, "Apart from burdening Johara with my existence, I was actually serious for a change. Everyone I meet tells me I've never looked worse. The mirror confirms their opinion."

"I've smacked people upside the head for less, buddy." She narrowed her eyes at him, as if charting the trajectory of the smack he'd earn if he weren't careful. "Nothing annoys me more than false modesty, so if you don't want me to muss that perfectly styled mane of yours, watch it."

Suddenly it was important for him to settle this with her. "There is no trace of anything false in what I'm saying—modesty or otherwise. I really have been in bad shape and have been getting progressively worse for over a year now."

This gave her pause for a moment, something like contrition or sympathy coming into her eyes.

Before he could be sure, it was gone, her fathomless eyes glittering with annoyance again. "You mean you've looked better than this? Any better and you should be...arrested or something."

Something warm seeped through his bones, brought that unfamiliar smile to his lips again. "Though I barely give the way I look any thought, you managed what I thought impossible. You flattered me in a way I never was before."

She grimaced as if at some terrible taste. "Hello? Wasn't I speaking English just now? Flattering you isn't among the things I would ever do, even at gunpoint."

"Sorry if this causes you an allergic reaction, but that is exactly what you did, when I've been looking at myself lately and finding only a depleted wretch looking back at me."

She opened her mouth to deliver another disparaging blow, before she closed it, her eyes narrowing contemplatively over his face.

"Now I'm looking for it. I guess, yeah, I see it. But it sort of...roughens your slickness and gives you a simulation of humanity that makes you look better than your former overly polished perfection. Figures, huh? Instead of looking like crap, you manage to make wretched and depleted work for you."

He abandoned any pretense of looking through the files and turned to her, arms folded over his chest. "Okay. I get it. You despise the hell out of me. Are you going to tell me what I ever did to deserve your wrath, Kanza?"

When she heard her name on his lips, something blipped in her eyes. It was gone again before he could latch on to it, and she reverted back to full-blast disdain mode. "Give the poor, depleted Pirate an energy bar. He's exerted himself digging through his hard drive's trash and recognized me. And even after he did, he still asks. What? You think your transgressions should have been dropped from the record by time?"

"Which transgressions are we talking about here?"

"Yeah, with multitudes to pick from, you can't even figure out which ones I'm referring to."

"Though I'm finding your bashing delightful, even therapeutic, my curiosity levels are edging into the danger zone. How about you put me out of my misery and enlighten me as to what exactly I'm paying the price for now?"

Her lips twisted disbelievingly. "You've really forgotten, haven't you?" At his unrepentant yet impatient nod, she rolled her eyes and turned back to the files, muttering under her breath. "You can go rack your brains with a rake for the answer for all I care. I'm not helping you scratch that itch."

"Since there's no way I've forgotten anything I did to you that could cause such an everlasting grudge…" He paused, frowned then exclaimed, "Don't tell me this is about Maysoon!"

"*And* he remembers. In a way that adds more insult to injury. You're a species of one, aren't you, Aram Nazaryan?"

Before he could say anything, she strode away, clearly not intending to let him pursue the subject. He could push his luck but doubted she'd oblige him.

But at least he now knew where this animosity was coming from. While he hadn't factored in that this would be her stance regarding the fiasco between him and Maysoon, it seemed she had accumulated an unhealthy dose of prejudice against him from the time he'd been briefly engaged to her half sister. And she'd added an impressive amount of further bias ever since.

She slammed another filing cabinet shut. "This damn

file isn't here." She suddenly turned on him. "But you are. What the hell are you doing here, anyway?"

So it had finally sunk in, the improbability of his stumbling in on her here in his sister's office.

Having already decided to throw her off, he said, "I was hoping Johara would be working late."

She frowned. "So you don't know that she and Shaheen are throwing a party tonight?"

"They are?" This had to be his best acting moment ever.

She bought it, as evidenced by her return to mockery. "You forgot that, too? Is anything of any importance to you?"

He approached her again with the same caution he would approach a hostile feline. "Why do you assume it's me who forgot and not them who neglected to invite me?"

"Because I'd never believe either Johara or Shaheen would neglect anyone, even you."

When he was a few feet away, he looked down at her, amusement again rising unbidden. "But it's fully believable that I got their invitation and tossed it in the bin unread?"

She shrugged. "Sure. Why not? I'd believe you got a dozen phone calls, too, or even face-to-face invitations and just disregarded them."

"Then I come here to visit my sister because I'm disregarding her?"

"Maybe you need something from her and came to ask for it, even though you won't consider going to her party."

He let out a short, delighted laugh. "You'll go the extra light-year to think the worst of me, won't you?"

"Don't give me any credit. It's you who makes it exceptionally easy to malign you."

Hardly believing how much he was enjoying her onslaught, he shook his head. "One would think Maysoon is your favorite sister and bosom buddy from the way you're hacking at me."

The intensity of her contempt grew hotter. "I would have

hacked at you if you'd done the same to a stranger or even an enemy."

"So your moral code is unaffected by personal considerations. Commendable. But what *have* I done exactly, in your opinion?"

Her snort was so cute, so incongruous, that it had his unfettered laugh ringing out again.

"Oh, you're good. With three words you've turned this from a matter of fact to a matter of opinion. Play another one."

"I'm trying hard to."

"Then *el'ab be'eed.*"

This meant *play far away.* From her, of course.

Something he had no intention of doing. "Won't you at least recite my charges and read me my rights?"

She produced her cell phone. "Nope. I bypassed all that and long pronounced your sentence."

"Shouldn't I be getting parole after ten years?"

"Not when I gave you life in the first place, no."

His whole face was aching. He hadn't smiled this much in…ever. "You're a mean little thing, aren't you?"

"And you're a sleazy huge thing, aren't you?"

He guffawed this time.

Wondering how the hell this pixie was doing this, triggering his humor with every acerbic remark, he headed back to Johara's desk. "So are we done with your search mission? Or going by the aftermath of your efforts, search-and-destroy operation?"

"Just for that," she said as she placed a call, "you put everything back where it belongs."

"I don't think even Johara herself can accomplish that impossibility after the chaos you've wrought."

She flicked him one last annihilating look, then dismissed him as she started speaking into the phone without preamble. "Okay, Jo, I can't find anything that might be the file you described, and I've gone through every shred of paper you got here."

"You mean *we* did." Aram raised his voice to make sure Johara heard him.

An obsidian bolt hit him right between the eyes, had his heart skipping a beat.

He grinned even more widely at her. He had no doubt Johara *had* heard him, but it was clear she'd pretended she hadn't, since Kanza's wrath would have only increased if Johara had made any comment or asked who was with her.

And he'd thought he'd known everything there was to know about his kid sister. Turned out she wasn't only capable of the subterfuge of setting him and her partner up, but of acting seamlessly on the fly, too.

Kanza was frowning now. "What do you mean it's okay? It's not okay. You need the file, and if it's here, I'll find it. Just give me a better description. I might have looked at it a dozen times and didn't recognize it for what it was."

Kanza fell silent for a few moments as Johara answered. He had a feeling she was telling Kanza a load of ultra-convincing bull. By now, he was 100 percent certain that file didn't even exist.

Kanza ended the conversation and confirmed his deductions. "I can't believe it! Johara is now not even sure the file is here at all. Blames it on pregnancy hormones."

Hoping his placating act was half as good as Johara's misleading one, he said, "We only lost an hour of turning her office upside down. Apart from the mess, no harm done."

"First, there's no *we* in the matter. Second, I was here an hour before you breezed in. Third, you *did* breeze in. Can't think of more harm than that. But the good news is I now get to breeze out of here and put an end to this unwelcome and torturous exchange with you."

"Aren't you even going to try to ameliorate the destruction you've left in your wake?"

"Johara insisted I leave everything and just rush over to the party."

So she was invited. Of course. Though from the way she was dressed, no one would think she had anything more glamorous planned than going to the grocery store.

But it was evident she intended to go. That must have been Johara and Shaheen's plan A. They'd invited him to set him and Kanza up at the soirée. And when he'd refused, Johara had improvised find-the-nonexistent-file plan B.

Kanza grabbed a red jacket from one of the couches, which he hadn't noticed before, and shrugged it on before hooking what looked like a small laptop bag across her body.

Then, without even a backward glance at him, she was striding toward the door.

He didn't know how he'd managed to move that fast, but he found himself blocking her path.

This surprised her so much that she bumped into him. He caught an unguarded expression in those bottomless black eyes as she stumbled back. A look of pure vulnerability. As though the steely persona she'd been projecting wasn't the real her, or not the only side to her. As though his nearness unsettled her so much it left her floundering.

A moment later he wondered if he'd imagined what he'd seen, since the look was now gone and annoyance was the only thing left in its place.

He tried what he hoped was the smooth charm he'd seen others practice but had never attempted himself. "How about we breeze out of here together and I drive you to the party?"

"You assume I came here...how? On foot?"

"A pixie like you might have just blinked in here."

"Then I can blink out the same way."

"I'm still offering to conserve your mystic energies."

"Acting the gentleman doesn't become you, and any attempt at simulating one is wasted on me since I'm hardly a damsel in distress. And if you're offering in order to score points with Johara, forget it."

"There you go again—assigning such convoluted motives to my actions when I'm far simpler than you think. I've decided to go to the party, and since you're going, too, you can save your pixie magic, as I have a perfectly mundane car parked in the garage."

"What a coincidence. So do I. Though mine is mundane for real. While yours verges on the supernatural. I hear it talks, thinks, takes your orders, parks itself and knows when to brake and where to go. All it has left to do is make you a sandwich and a cappuccino to become truly sentient."

"I'll see about developing those sandwich- and cappuccino-making capabilities. Thanks for the suggestion. But wouldn't you like to take a spin in my near-sentient car?"

"No. Just like I wouldn't want to be in your near-sentient presence. Now *ann eznak*...or better still, *men ghair eznak*." Then she turned and strode away.

He waited until she exited the room before moving. In moments, his far-longer strides overtook her at the elevators.

Kanza didn't give any indication that she noticed him, going through messages on her phone. She still made no reaction when he boarded the elevator with her and then when he followed her to the garage.

It was only when he tailed her to her car that she finally turned on him. *"What?"*

He gave her his best pseudoinnocent smile and lobbed back her parting shot. "By your leave, or better still without it, I'm escorting you to your car."

She looked him up and down in silence, then turned and took the last strides to a Ford Escape that was the exact color of her jacket. Seemed she was fond of red.

In moments, she drove away with a screech right out of a car chase, which had him jumping out of the way.

He stood watching her taillights flashing as she hit the

brakes at the garage's exit. Grinning to himself, he felt a rush of pure adrenaline flood his system.

She'd really done it. Something no other woman—no other person—had ever done.

She'd turned him down.

No…it was more that that. She'd *rebuffed* him.

Well. There was only one thing he could do now.

Give chase.

Three

Kanza resisted the urge to floor the gas pedal.

That…rat was following her.

That colossal, cruelly magnificent rat.

Though the way he made her feel was that *she* was the rat, running for her life, growing more frantic by the breath, chased by a majestic, terminally bored cat who'd gotten it in his mind to chase her…just for the hell of it.

She snatched another look in the rearview mirror.

Yep. There he still was. Driving safely, damn him, keeping the length of three cars between them, almost to the inch. He'd probably told his pet car how far away it should stick to her car's butt. The constant distance was more nerve-racking than if he'd kept approaching and receding, if he'd made any indication that he was expending any effort in keeping up with her.

She knew he didn't really want to catch her. He was just exercising the prerogative of his havoc-inducing powers. He was doing this to rattle her. To show her that no one refused him, that he'd do whatever he pleased, even if it infringed on others. Preferably if it did.

It made her want to slam the brakes in the middle of the

road, force him to stop right behind her. Then she'd get down, walk over there and haul him out of his car and... and... What?

Bite mouthfuls out of his gorgeous bod? Swipe his keys and cell phone and leave him stranded on the side of the road?

Evidently, from the maddening time she'd just spent in his company, he'd probably enjoy the hell out of whatever she did. She *had* tried her level worst back in Johara's office, and that insensitive lout had seemed to be having a ball, thinking every insult out of her mouth was a hoot. Seemed his jaded blood levels had long been toxic and now any form of abuse was a stimulant.

Gritting her teeth all the way to Johara and Shaheen's place, she kept taking compulsive glances back at this incorrigible predator who tailed her in such unhurried pursuit.

Twenty minutes later, she parked the car in the garage, filled her lungs with air. Then, holding it as if she was bracing for a blow, she got out.

Out of the corner of her eye she could estimate he'd parked, too. Three empty car places away. He was really going the distance to maintain the joke, wasn't he?

Fine. Let him have his fun. Which would only be exacerbated if she made any response. She wouldn't.

When she was at the elevator, she stopped, a groan escaping her. Aram had frazzled her so much that she'd left Johara and Shaheen's housewarming present, along with the Arabian horse miniature set she'd promised Gharam, in the trunk.

Cursing him to grow a billion blue blistering barnacles, she turned on her heel and stalked back to the car. She passed him on her way back, as he'd been following in her wake, maintaining the equivalent of three paces behind her.

Feeling his gaze on her like the heaviest embarrassment she'd ever suffered, she retrieved the boxes. Just as the tailgate clicked closed, she almost knocked her head against it in chagrin. She'd forgotten to change her sneakers.

Great. This guy was frying her synapses even at fifty paces, where he was standing serenely by the elevator, awaiting her return. Maybe she should just forget about changing the sneakers. Or better still, hurl them at him.

But it was one thing to skip around in those sneakers, another to attend Johara and Shaheen's chic party in them. It was bad enough she'd be the most underdressed one around, as usual.

Forcing herself to breathe calmly, she reopened the tailgate and hopped on the edge of the trunk. He'd just have to bear the excitement of watching her change into slightly less nondescript two-inch heels. At least those were black and didn't clash like a chalk aberration on a black background.

In two minutes she was back at the elevators, hoisting the boxes—each under an arm. Contrary to her expectations, he didn't offer to help her carry them. Then he didn't even board the elevator with her. Instead, he just stood there in that disconcerting calm while the doors closed. Though she was again pretending to be busy with her phone, she knew he didn't pry his gaze from her face. And that he had that infuriating smile on his all the time.

Sensing she'd gotten only a short-lived respite since he was certain to follow her up at his own pace, she knew her smile was on the verge of shattering as Johara received her at the door. It must have been her own tension that made her imagine that Johara looked disappointed. For why would she be, when she'd already known she hadn't found her file and had been the one to insist Kanza stop searching for it?

Speculation evaporated as Johara exclaimed over Kanza's gifts and ushered her toward Shaheen and Gharam. But barely three minutes later, Johara excused herself and hurried to the door again.

Though Kanza was certain it was *him,* her breath still

caught in her throat, and her heart sputtered like a mal-
functioning throttle.

Ya Ullah... Why was she letting this virtuoso manipula-
tor pull her strings like this?

The surge of fury manifested in exaggerated gaiety with
Shaheen and Gharam. But a minute later Shaheen excused
himself, too, and rushed away with Gharam to join his wife
in welcoming his so-called best friend. She almost blurted
out that Aram was here only to annoy her, not to see him or
his sister, and that Shaheen should do himself a favor and
find himself a new best friend, since *that* one cared about
no one but himself.

Biting her tongue and striding deeper into the penthouse, she forced herself to mingle, which usually rated
right with anesthesia-free tooth extractions on her list of
favorite pastimes. However, right now, it felt like the most
desirable thing ever, compared to being exposed to Aram
Nazaryan again.

But to her surprise, she wasn't.

After an hour passed, throughout which she'd felt his
eyes constantly on her, he'd made no attempt to approach
her, and her tension started to dissipate.

It seemed her novelty to him had worn off. He must be
wondering why the hell he'd taken his challenge this far—
at the price of suffering the company of actual human beings. Ones who clearly loved him, though why, she'd never
understand.

She still welcomed the distraction when Johara asked
her to put the horse set in their family living room away
from Gharam's determined-to-take-them-apart hands. The
two-and-a-half-year-old tyke was one unstoppable girl who
everyone said took after her maternal uncle. Clearly, in nature as well as looks.

She'd finished her chore and was debating what was
more moronic—that she was this affected by Aram's presence or that her relief at the end of this perplexing interlude

was mixed with what infuriatingly resembled letdown—when it felt as if a thousand volts of electricity zapped her. His dark, velvety baritone that drenched her every receptor in paralysis.

It was long, heart-thudding moments before what he'd said made sense.

"I'm petitioning for a reopening of my case."

She didn't turn to him. She couldn't.

For the second time tonight, he'd snuck up on her, startling the reins of volition out of her reach.

But this time, courtesy of the building tension that had been defused in false security, the surprise incapacitated her.

When she didn't turn, it was Aram who circled her in a wide arc, coming to face her at that distance he'd been maintaining, as if he was a hunter who knew he had his quarry cornered yet still wasn't taking any chances he'd get a set of claws across the face.

And as usual with him around, she felt the spacious, ingeniously decorated room shrink and fade away, her senses converging like a spotlight on him.

It was always a shock to the system beholding him. He was without any doubt the most beautiful creature she'd ever seen. Damn him.

She'd bet it was beyond anyone alive not to be awed by his sheer grandeur and presence, to not gape as they drank in the details of what made him what he was. She remembered with acute vividness the first time she'd seen him. She *had* gaped then and every time she'd seen him afterward, trying to wrap her mind around how anyone could be endowed with so much magnificence.

He lived up to his pseudonym—a pirate from a fairy tale, imposing, imperious, mysterious with a dark, ruthless edge to his beauty, making him…utterly compelling.

It still seemed unbelievable that he was Johara's brother. Apart from both of them possessing a level of beauty that was spellbinding, verging on painful to behold, they looked nothing alike. While Johara had the most amazing golden hair, molten chocolate eyes and thick cream complexion, Aram was her total opposite. But after she'd seen both their parents, she'd realized he'd manifested the absolute best in both, too.

His eyes were a more dazzling shade of azure than that of his French mother's—the most vivid, hypnotic color she'd ever seen. From his mother, too, and her family, he'd also inherited his prodigious height and amplified it. He'd added a generous brush of burnished copper to his Armenian-American father's swarthy complexion, a deepened gloss and luxury to his raven mane and an enhanced bulk and breadth to his physique.

Then came the details. And the devil was very much in those. A dancing, laughing, knowing one, aware of the exact measure of their unstoppable influence. Of every slash and hollow and plane of a face stamped with splendor and uniqueness, every bulge and sweep and slope of a body emanating maleness and strength, every move and glance and intonation demonstrating grace and manliness, power and perfection. All in all, he was glory personified.

Now, exuding enough charisma and confidence to power a small city, he towered across from her, calmly sweeping his silk black jacket out of the way, shoving his hands into his pockets. The movement had the cream shirt stretching over the expanse of virility it clung to. Her lips tingled as his chiseled mouth quirked up into that lethal smile.

"I submit a motion that I have been unjustly tried."

Aram's obvious enjoyment, not to mention his biding his time before springing his presence on her again, made retaliation a necessity.

Her voice, when she managed to operate her vocal cords, thankfully sounded cool and dismissive. "And I submit you've not only gotten away with your crimes but you've been phenomenally rewarded for them."

"If you're referring to my current business success, how are you managing to correlate it to my alleged crimes?"

She fought not to lick the dryness from her lips, to bite into the numbness that was spreading through them. "I'm managing because you've built said success using the same principles with which you perpetrated those crimes."

His eyes literally glittered with mischief, becoming bluer before her dazzled ones. "Then I am submitting that those principles you ascribe to me and your proof of them were built around pure circumstantial evidence."

Her eyebrows shot up. "So you're not after a retrial. What you really want is your whole criminal record expunged."

He raised those large, perfectly formed hands like someone blocking blows. "I wouldn't dream of universally dismissing my convictions." His painstakingly sculpted lips curled into a delicious grin. "That would be pushing my luck. But I do demand an actual primary hearing of my testimony, since I distinctly remember one was never taken."

Although she felt her heart sputtering out of control, she tried to match his composure outwardly. "Who says you get a hearing at all? You certainly didn't grant others such mercy or consideration."

The scorching amusement in those gemlike eyes remained unperturbed. "By others you mean Maysoon, I assume?"

"Hers was the case I observed firsthand. As I am a stickler for justice, I will not pass judgment on those I know of only through secondhand testimonies and hearsay."

His eyes widened on what looked like genuine surprise.

Yeah, right. As if he could feel anything for real.

"That's very…progressive of you. Elevated, even." At her baleful glance, something that simulated seriousness took over his expression. "No, I mean it. In my experience, when people don't like someone, they demonize them wholesale, stop granting them even the possibility of fairness."

She pursed her lips, refusing to consider the possibility of his sincerity. "Lauding my merits won't work, you know."

"In granting me a hearing?"

"In granting you leniency you haven't earned and certainly don't deserve." He opened his mouth, and she raised her hand. "Don't you think you've taken your joke far enough?"

For a moment he looked actually confused before a careful expression replaced uncertainty. "What joke, exactly?"

She rolled her eyes. "Spare me."

"Or you'll spear me?" At her exasperated rumble, he raised his hands again, the coaxing in his eyes rising another notch. "That *was* lame. But I really don't know what you're talking about. I am barely keeping up with you."

"Yeah, right. Since you materialized behind me like some capricious spirit, you've been ready with something right off the smart-ass chart before I've even finished speaking."

He shook his head, causing his collar-length mane to undulate. "If you think that was easy, think again. You're making me struggle for every inch before you snatch it away with your next lob. For the first time in my life I have no idea what will spill out of someone's lips next, so give me a break."

"I would ask where you want it, but I have to be realistic. Considering our respective physiques, I probably can't give you one without the help of heavy, blunt objects."

The next moment, all her nerves fired up as he proceeded to subject her to the sight and sound of his all-out amusement, a demonstration so…virile, so debilitating, each peal was a new bolt forking through her nervous system.

When he at last brought his mirth under control, his lips remained stretched the widest she'd seen them, showing off that set of extraordinary white teeth in the most devastating smile she'd had the misfortune of witnessing. He even wiped away a couple of tears of hilarity. "You can give me compound fractures with your tongue alone. As for your glares, we're talking incineration."

Hating that even when he was out of breath and wheezing, he sounded more hard-hitting for it, she gritted out, "If I could do that, it would be the least I owe you."

"What have I done *now?*" Even his pseudolament was scrumptious. This guy needed some kind of quarantine. He shouldn't be left free to roam the realm of flimsy mortals. "Is this about the joke you've accused me of perpetrating?"

"There's no accusation here—just statement of fact. You've been enjoying one big fat joke at my expense since you stumbled on me in Johara's office."

His eyes sobered at once, filling with something even more distressing than mischief and humor. Indulgence? "I've been relishing the experience immensely, but not as a joke and certainly not at your expense."

Her heart gave her ribs another vicious kick. She had to stop this before her heart literally bruised.

She raised her hands. "Okay, this is going nowhere. Let's say I believe you. Give me another reason you're doing this. And don't tell me that you care one way or the other what I think in general or what I think of you specifically. You don't care about what anyone thinks."

The earnestness in his eyes deepened. "You're right. I care nothing for what others think of me."

"And you're absolutely right not to."

That seemed to stun him yet again. "I am?" At her nod, he prodded, "That includes *everyone?*"

She nodded again. "Of course. What other people think of you, no matter who they are, is irrelevant. Unsolicited opinions are usually a hindrance and a source of discontentment, if not outright unhappiness. So carry on not caring, go take your leave from Johara and Shaheen and return to your universe where no one's opinion matters…as it shouldn't."

"At least grant me the right to care or not care." Those unbelievable eyes seemed to penetrate right through her as his gaze narrowed in on her. "And whether it comes under caring or not, I do happen to be extremely interested in your opinion of me. Now, let me escort you back to the party. Let me get us a drink over which we'll reopen my case and explore the possibility of adjusting your opinion of me—at least to a degree."

She arched a brow. "You mean you'd settle for adjusting my opinion of you from horrific to just plain horrid?"

"Who knows, maybe while retrying my case, your unwavering sense of justice will lead you to adjusting it to plain misjudged."

"Or maybe just downright wretched."

He hit her with another of his pouts. Then he raised the level of chaos and laughed again, his merriment as potent as everything else about him. "I'd take that."

Trying to convince her heart to slot back into its usual place after its latest somersault, she again tried her best glower. It had no effect on him, as usual. Worse. It had the opposite effect to what she'd perfected it for. He looked at her as if her glare was the cutest thing he'd seen.

She voiced her frustration. "You talk about my incinerating glares, but I could be throwing cotton balls or rose petals at you for all the effect they have on you."

"It's not your glares that are ineffective. It's me who's discovering a penchant for incineration."

Instead of appeasing her, it annoyed her more. "I'll have you know I've reduced other men to dust with those scowls. No one has withstood a minute in my presence once I engaged annihilate mode." She lifted her chin. "But you seem to need specifically designed weapons. If I go along with you in this game you got it in your mind to play, it'll be so I can find out if you have an Achilles' heel."

"I have no idea if I have that." His gaze grew thoughtful. "Would you use it to...annihilate me if you discovered it?"

She gave him one of her patented sizing-up glances and regretted it midway. She must quit trying her usual strategies with him. Not only because they always backfired, but it wasn't advisable to expose herself to another distressing dose of his wonders.

She returned to his eyes, those turquoise depths that exuded the ferocity of his intellect and the power of his wit, and found gazing into them just as taxing to her circulatory system.

She sighed, more vexed with her own inability to moderate her reactions than with him. "Nah. I'll just be satisfied knowing your Achilles' heel exists and you're not invulnerable. And maybe, if you get too obnoxious, I'll use my knowledge as leverage to make you back off."

That current of mischief and challenge in his eyes spiked. "It goes against my nature to back off."

"Not even under threat of...annihilation?"

"Especially then. I'd probably beg you to use whatever fatal weakness you discover just to find out how it feels."

"Wow. You're jaded to the point of numbness, aren't you?"

"You've got me figured out, don't you? Or do you? Shall we find out?"

It was clear this monolith would stand there and spar with her until she agreed to this "retrial" of his. If she was in her own domain or on neutral ground, or at least somewhere without a hundred witnesses blocking her only escape route, she would have slammed him with something cutting and walked out as she'd done in Johara's office.

But she couldn't inflict on her friends the scene this gorgeous jerk would instigate if he didn't have his way. She bet he knew she suffered from those scruples, was using the knowledge to corner her into participating in his game.

"You're counting on my inability to risk spoiling Johara and Shaheen's party, aren't you?"

His blink was all innocence, and downright evil for it. "I thought you didn't care what other people thought."

"I don't, not when it comes to how I choose to live my

life. But I do care about what others think of my actions that directly impact them. And if I walk out now, you'll tail me in the most obvious, disruptive way you can, generating curiosity and speculation, which would end up putting a damper on Johara and Shaheen's party." Her eyes narrowed as another thought hit her. "Now I am wondering if maybe they *didn't* extend an invitation to you after all because they've been burned by your sabotage before."

He pounced on that, took it where she couldn't have anticipated. "So you're considering changing your mind about whether I was invited? See? Maybe you'll change your mind about everything else if you give me a chance."

She blew out a breath in exasperation. "I only change my mind for the worse...or worst."

"You're one tiny bundle of nastiness, aren't you?" His smile said he thought that the best thing to aspire to be.

She tossed her head, infusing her disadvantaged stature with all the belittling she could muster. "Again with the size references."

"It was you who started using mine in derogatory terms. Then you moved on to my looks, then my character, then my history, and if there were more components to me, I bet you'd have pummeled through them, too."

Refusing to rise to the bait, she turned around and stomped away.

He followed her. Keeping those famous three steps behind. With his footfalls being soundless, she could pinpoint his location only by the chuckles rumbling in the depths of his massive chest. When those ended, his overpowering presence took over, cocooning her all the way to the expansive reception area.

Absorbed in warding off his influence, she could barely register the ultraelegant surroundings or the dozens of chic people milling around. No one noticed her, as usual, but everyone's gaze was drawn to the nonchalant predator behind her. Abhorring the thought of having everyone's eyes on her by association once they realized he was following her, she continued walking where she hoped the least amount of spectators were around.

She stepped out onto the wraparound terrace that over-looked the now-shrouded-in-darkness Central Park, with Manhattan glittering like fiery jewels beyond its extensive domain. Stopping at the three-foot-high brushed stainless steel and Plexiglas railings, gazing out into the moonlit night, she shivered as September's high-altitude wind hit her overheating body. But she preferred hypothermia to the burning speculation that being in Aram Nazaryan's company would have provoked. Not that she'd managed to escape that totally. The few people who'd had the same idea of seeking privacy out here did their part in singeing her with their curiosity.

She hugged herself to ward off the discomfort of their interest more than the sting of the wind. He made it worse, drenching her in the dark spell of his voice.

"Can I offer you my jacket, or would I have my head bitten off again?"

Barely controlling a shudder, she pretended she was flipping her hair away. "Your head is still on your shoulders. Don't push your luck if you want to keep it there."

His lips pursed in contemplation as he watched her suppress another shudder. "You're one of those independent pains who'd freeze to death before letting people pay them courtesies, aren't you?"

"You're one of those imposing pains who force people into the cold, then inflict their jackets on them and call their imposition courtesy, aren't you?"

"I would have settled for remaining inside where it's toasty. You're the one who led me out here to freeze."

"If you're freezing, don't go playing Superman and volunteering your jacket."

That ever-hovering smile caught fire again. "How about we both mosey on round the corner? Since you're the one who decided to hold my retrial thirty floors up and in the open, I at least motion to do it away from the draft."

"You're also one of those gigantic pains who love to marvel at the sound of their own cleverness, aren't you?" She tossed the words back as she walked ahead to do as he'd suggested.

His answer felt like a wave of heat carrying on the whistling wind. "Just observing a meteorological fact."

As he'd projected, the moment they turned the corner, the wind died down, leaving only comfortable coolness to contend with.

She turned to him at the railings. "Stop right there." He halted at once, perplexity entering his gaze. "You're in the perfect position to shield me from any draft. A good use at last for this superfluous breadth and bulk of yours."

Amusement flooded back into his eyes, radiated hypnotic azure in the moonlight. "So you're only averse to voluntary courtesy on my part, but using me as an unintentional barrier is okay with you."

"Perfectly so. I don't intend to suffer from hypothermia because of the situation you imposed on me."

"I made you come out here?"

"Yes, you did."

"And how did I do that?"

"You made escaping the curiosity, not to mention the jealousy, of all present a necessity."

"Jealousy!" His eyebrows disappeared into the layers of satin hair the wind had flopped over his forehead.

"Every person in there, man or woman, would give anything to be in my place, having your private audience." She gave an exaggerated sigh. "If only they knew I'd donate the *privilege* if I could with a sizable check on top as bonus."

His chuckle revved inside his chest again and in her bones. "That *privilege* is nontransferable. You're stuck with it. So before we convene, what shall I get you?"

"Why shouldn't I be the one to get you something?"

His nod was all concession. "Why shouldn't you, indeed?"

She nodded, too, slowly, totally unable to predict him and feeling more out of her depth by the second for it. "Be specific about what you prefer. I hate guessing."

"I'm flabbergasted you're actually considering my preferences. But I'll go with anything nonalcoholic. I'm driving." Considering he'd placed his order, she started to turn around and he stopped her. "And, Kanza…can you possibly also make it something nonpoisoned and curse free?"

Muttering "smart-ass" and zapping him with her harshest parting glance, which only dissipated against his force field and was received by another chuckle, she strode away.

On reentering the reception, she groaned out loud as she immediately felt the weight of Johara's gaze zooming in on her. She'd no doubt noticed Aram marching behind her across the penthouse and must be bursting with curiosity about how they'd met and why that older brother of hers had gotten it into his mind to follow her around.

Johara just had to bear not knowing. She couldn't worry about her now. One Nazaryan at a time.

She grabbed a glass of cranberry-apple juice from a passing waiter and strode back to the terrace, this time exiting from where she'd left Aram. As soon as she did, she nearly tripped, as her heartbeat did.

Aram was at the railing, two dozen paces away with his back to her. He was silhouetted against the rising moon, hands gripping the bar, looking like a modern statue of a Titan. The only animate things about him were the satin stirring around his majestic head in the tranquil breeze and the silk rustling around his steel-fleshed frame.

But apart from his physical glory, there was something about his pose as he stared out into the night—in the slight slump of his Herculean shoulders, dimming that indomitable vibe—that disturbed her. Whatever it was, it forced her to reconsider her disbelief of his assertion that he'd never felt worse. Made her feel guilty about how she'd been bashing him, believing him invincible.

Then he turned around, as if he'd felt her presence, and his eyes lit up again with that potent merriment and mischief, and all empathy evaporated in a wave of instinctive challenge and chagrined response.

How was it even possible? That after all these years he remained the one man who managed to wring an explosive mixture of fascination and detestation from her?

From the first time she'd laid eyes on him when she'd been seventeen, she'd thought him the most magnificent male in existence, one who compounded his overwhelming physical assets with an array of even more impressive superiorities. He'd been the only one who could breach her composure and tongue-tie her just by walking into a room. That had only earned him a harder crash from the pedestal she'd placed him on, when he'd proved to be just another predictable male, one who considered only a woman's looks and status no matter her character. Why else would he have gotten involved with her spoiled and vapid half sister? Her opinion of him would have been salvaged when he'd walked away from Maysoon, if—and it was an insurmountable if— he hadn't been needlessly, shockingly cruel in doing so.

Remembered outrage rose as she stopped before him and foisted the drink into his hand. It rose higher when she couldn't help watching how his fingers closed around the glass, the grace, power and economy of the movement. It made her want to whack herself and him upside the head.

She had to get this ridiculous interlude over with.

"Without further ado, let's get on with your preposterous retrial."

That gargantuan swine gave a superb pretense of wiping levity from his face, replacing it with earnestness.

"It's going to be the fastest one in history. Your indictment was unequivocal and the evidence against you overwhelming. Whatever her faults, Maysoon loved you, and you kicked her out of your life. Then when she was down, you kicked her again—almost literally and very publicly. You left her in a heap on the ground and walked away unscathed, and then went on to prosper beyond any expectations. While she went on to waste her life, almost self-destruct in one failed relationship after another. If I'd judged your case then, I would have passed the harshest sentence. In any retrial, I'd still pronounce you guilty and judge that you be subjected to character execution."

Four

Aram stared at the diminutive firebrand who was the first woman who'd ever fetched him a drink, then followed up by sentencing his character to death.

Both action and indictment should have elated the hell out of him, as everything from her tonight had. But the expected exhilaration didn't come; something unsettling spread inside him instead. For what if her opinion of him was too entrenched and he couldn't adjust it?

He transferred his gaze to the burgundy depths in the glass she'd just handed him, collecting his thoughts.

Although he'd been keeping it light and teasing, he knew this had suddenly become serious. He had to be careful what to say from now on. If he messed this up, she'd never let him close enough again to have another round. That would be it.

And he couldn't let that be it. He wasn't even going to entertain that possibility. He might have lost many things in his life, but he wasn't going to lose this.

He raised his eyes to meet hers. It was as if they held pieces of the velvet night in their darkest depths. She was waiting, playing by the rules he'd improvised, giving him a chance to defend himself. He had no doubt it would be his one and only chance. He had to make it work.

He inhaled. "I submit that your so-called overwhelming evidence was all circumstantial and unreliable. I did none of the things you've just accused me of. Cite every shred of evidence you think you have, and I'll debunk each one for you."

Her face tilted up at him, sending that amazing wealth of hair cascading with an audible sigh to one side. "You didn't kick Maysoon out of your life?"

"Not in the way you're painting."

"How would you paint it? In black-and-white? In full color? Or because the memory must have faded—in sepia?"

"Who's being a smart-ass now?" At her nonchalant shrug, he pressed on. "What do you know about what happened between Maysoon and me? Apart from her demonizing accounts and your own no less prejudiced observations?"

"Since my observations were so off base, why don't you tell me your own version?"

Having gotten so used to her contention, he was worried by her acquiescence.

He exhaled to release the rising tension. "I assume you knew what your half sister was like? Maybe the impossible has happened and she's evolved by age, but back then, she was…intolerable."

"But of course you found that out after you became engaged to her."

"No. Before."

As he waited for her censure to surpass its previous levels, her gaze only grew thoughtful.

There was no predicting her, was there?

"And you still went through with it. Why?"

"Because I was stupid." Her eyes widened at his harsh admission. She must have thought he'd come up with some excuse to make his actions seem less pathetic and more defensible. He would have done that with anyone else. But with her, he just wanted to have the whole truth out. "I wanted to get married and have a family, but I had no idea how to go about doing that. I thought I'd never leave Zohayd at the time and I'd have to choose a woman from those available. But there was no one I looked at twice, let alone considered for anything lasting. So when Maysoon started pursuing me…"

"Watch it." Her interjection was almost soft. It stopped him in his tracks harder than if she'd bitten it off. "You'll veer off into the land of fabrication if you use this rationale for choosing Maysoon. Using the pursuit criterion, you should have ended up with a harem, since women of all ages in Zohayd chased after you."

"Now who's taking a stroll in the land of exaggeration? Not all women were after me. Aliyah and Laylah, for instance, considered me only one of the family. And you didn't consider me human at all, I believe, let alone male."

Her eyes glittered with the moon's reflected silver as she ignored his statement concerning her. "And that's what? Two females out of two million?"

"Whatever the number of women who pursued me, they were after me as an adventure, and each soon gave up when I made it clear I wasn't into the kind of…entertainment they were after. I wanted a committed relationship at the time."

"And you're saying that none wanted that? Or that none seemed a better choice than Maysoon for said relationship?"

"Compared to Maysoon's pursuit, they were all slouches. And your sister did look like the best deal. Suitable age, easy on the eyes and very, very determined. Sure, she was volatile and superficial, but when her pursuit didn't wane for a whole year, I thought it meant she *really* liked what she saw."

"Her along with everyone with eyes or a brain wave."

Again she managed to make the compliment the most

abrasive form of condemnation, arousing that stinging pleasure he was getting too used to.

"I'm not talking about my alleged 'beauty' here. I thought
she liked *me*, and that meant a lot then. I knew how I was
viewed in the royal circles in Zohayd, what my attraction
was to the women you cite as my hordes of pursuers. I was
this exotic foreigner of mixed descent from a much lower
social class that they could have a safe and forbidden fling
with. Many thought they could keep me as their boy toy."

Something came into her eyes. Sympathy? Empathy?

It was probably ridicule, and he was imagining things.

"You were hardly a boy," she murmured.

"Their gigolo, then. In any event, I thought Maysoon
viewed me differently. Her pursuit in spite of our class differences and the fact that I was hardly an ideal groom for a
princess made me think she was one of those rare women
who appreciated a man for himself. I thought this alone
made up for all her personal shortcomings. And who was
I to consider those when I was riddled with my own?" He
emptied his lungs on a harsh exhalation. "Turned out she
was just attracted to me as a spoiled brat would be to a toy
she fancied and couldn't have. Most likely because some of
the women in her inner circle must have made me a topic
of giggling lust, maybe even challenge, and being patho-
logically competitive herself, she wanted to be the one to
triumph over them."

Kanza's eyes filled with skepticism, but she let it go un-
voiced and allowed him to continue.

"And the moment she did she started trying to strip me
bare to dress me up into the kind of toy she had in mind all
along. She started telling me how I must behave, in private
and public, how I must distance myself from my father,
whom she made clear she considered the hired help." He
drew in a sharp inhalation laden with his still-reverberating
chagrin on his father's account. "And it didn't end there.
She dictated who I should get close to, how I must kiss up

to Shaheen's brothers now that he was gone, play on my former relationship with him to gain a 'respectable' position within the kingdom and wheedle financial help in setting up a business like theirs so I would become as rich as possible."

The cynicism in Kanza's eyes had frozen. There was nothing in them now. A very careful nothing. As if she didn't know how to react to the influx of new information.

He went on. "And she was in a rabid hurry for me to do all that. She couldn't wait to have me pick up the tab of her extravagant existence—which she'd thought so disadvantaged—and informed me that as her husband it would be my duty to raise her up to a whole new level of excess." He scrubbed a hand across his jaw. "In the four months' duration of the engagement, I was so stunned by the depths of her shallowness, so taken aback by the audacity of her demands and the intensity of her tantrums, that I didn't react. Then came the night of that ball."

She'd been there that night. In one of those horrific get-ups and alien makeup. He now remembered vividly that she'd been the last thing he'd seen as he'd walked out, standing there over Maysoon, glaring at him with loathing in her eyes.

There was nothing but absorption in her eyes now. She was evidently waiting to see if his version of that ill-fated night's events would change the opinion she'd long held of him, built on her interpretation of its events.

He felt that his next words would decide if she'd ever let him near again. He had to make them count. The only way he could do that was to be as brutally honest as possible.

"Maysoon dragged me to talk to King Atef and Amjad. But when I didn't take her heavy-handed hints to broach the subject of the high-ranking job she'd heard was open, or the loan she'd been pushing me to ask for, she decided to take control. She extolled my economic theories for Zohayd and made a mess of outlining them. Then she proceeded to massacre my personal business plans, which I'd once made the mistake of trying to explain to her. She became terminally obvious as she bragged how anyone getting on with me on the ground level with a sizable investment would reap *millions*." He huffed a bitter laugh. "For a mercenary soul, she knew nothing about the real value of money, since she'd never made a cent and had never even glanced at her own bills."

There was only corroboration in Kanza's eyes now. Knowing her half sister, she must have known the accuracy of this assessment.

He continued. "Needless to say, King Atef and Amjad were not impressed, and they must have believed I'd put her up to it. I was tempted to tell them the truth right then and there, that I'd finally faced it that I was just a means to an end to subsidize her wasteful life. Instead, I attempted to curtail the damage she'd done as best I could before excusing myself and making my escape. Not that she'd let me walk away."

Wariness invaded her gaze. She must have realized he'd come to the point where he'd finally explain the fireworks that had ended his life in Zohayd and formed her lasting-till-now opinion of him.

He shoved his hands into his pockets. "She stormed after me, shrieking that I was a moron, a failure, that I didn't know a thing about grabbing opportunities and maximizing my connections. She said my potential for 'infiltrating' the higher echelons of the royal family was why she'd considered me in the first place and that if I wanted to be her husband I'd do anything to ingratiate myself to them and provide her with the lifestyle she deserved."

Her wince was unmistakable. As if, even if she knew full well Maysoon was capable of saying those things and harboring those motivations, she was still embarrassed for her, ashamed on her account.

Suddenly he wanted to go no further, didn't want to

cause her any discomfort. But she was waiting for him to go on. Her eyes were now prodding him to go on.

He did. "It was almost comical, but I wasn't laughing. I wasn't even angry or disappointed or anything else. I was just…done. So I told her that I would have done anything for the woman I married if she had married me for me and not as a potential meal ticket. Then I walked away. Maysoon wasn't the first major error in judgment I made in Zohayd, but she was the one I rectified."

He paused for a moment, then made his concluding statement, the one refuting her major accusation. "If your half sister has been wasting her life and self-destructing, it's because that's what she does with her capriciousness and excesses and superfluous approach to life—not because of anything *I* did to her. And she's certainly not spinning out of control on my account, because I never counted to her."

Kanza stared up at Aram for what felt like a solid hour after he'd finished his *testimony*.

She could still feel his every word all over her like the stings of a thousand wasps.

She'd never even imagined or could have guessed about his situation back in Zohayd, how he'd been targeted and propositioned, how he'd felt unvalued and objectified.

And she'd been just as guilty of wronging him. In her own mind, in her own way, she had discriminated against him, too, if in the totally opposite direction to those women he'd described. While they'd reduced him to a sexual plaything in their minds, or a stepping-stone to a material goal, she'd exalted him to the point where she'd been unable to see beyond his limitless potential. She hadn't suspected that his untouchable self-possession could have been a facade, a defense; had believed him confident to the point of arrogance; equated his powerful influence with ruthlessness; and had assumed that he could have no insecurities, needs or vulnerabilities.

But…wait. *Wait.* This story was incomplete. He'd left out a huge part. A vital one.

She heard her voice, low, strained, wavering on a gust of wind that circumvented the shield of his body. "But you ended up doing what she advised you to do. She just didn't reap the benefit of her efforts, since you kicked her out of your life on her ear and soared so high on your own."

"Now what the hell are you talking about?"

She pulled herself to her full five-foot-two-plus-heels height, attempting to shove herself up into his face. "Did you or didn't you seek the Aal Shalaan Brotherhood in providing you with their far-reaching connections and fat financial support on your launch into billionairedom?"

"Is this what she said I did?" His scoff sounded furious for the first time. So this was his inapproachable line, what would rouse the indolent predator—any insinuations maligning the integrity and autonomy of his success. "And why not? I did know that there was no limit to her vindictiveness, that she'd do and say anything to punish me for escaping her talons. What else did she accuse me of? Maybe that I abused her, too?"

Her own outrage receded at the advance of his, which was so palpable she had no doubt it was real. Her answer stuck in her throat.

She no longer wanted to continue this. She hadn't wanted to start it in the first place. But his eyes were blazing into hers, demanding that she let him know the full details of Maysoon's accusations. And she had to tell him.

"She said you…exploited her, then threw her aside when you had enough of her."

His eyes narrowed to azure lasers. "By exploited, she meant…sexually?" She nodded, and he gave a spectacular snort, a drench of cold sarcasm underscoring his affront. "Would you believe that I never slept with her?"

"Last I heard, 'sleeping' with someone wasn't a prerequisite of being intimate."

"All right, I did try to be a gentleman and spare you the R-rated language. But since being euphemistic doesn't work in criminal cases, let me be explicit. I never had sex with her. In *any* form. *She* did instigate a few instances of heavy petting—which I didn't reciprocate and put an end to when she tried to offer me…sexual favors. Bottom line…beyond a few unenthusiastic-on-my-part kisses, I never breached her 'purity.' And I wasn't even holding back. I just never felt the least temptation. And when I started seeing her true colors and realized what she really wanted from me, I even became repulsed."

Every word had spiked her temperature higher. To her ears, her every instinct, each had possessed the unmistakable texture of truth. But sanctioning them as the new basis for her belief, her view of the past and his character was still difficult. Mainly because it went against everything she'd believed for so long, about him, about men in general.

Feeling her head would burst on fire, she mumbled, "You're telling me you could be so totally immune to a woman as beautiful as Maysoon when she was so very willing, too? I never heard that mental aversion ever interfered with a man's…drive. Maybe you are not human after all."

"Then get this news flash. There are men who don't find a beautiful, willing woman irresistible."

"Yes. Those men are called gay. Are you? Did you maybe discover that you were when you failed to respond to Maysoon?"

She knew she was being childish and that there was no way he was gay. But she was floundering.

"I 'failed to respond' to Maysoon because I'm one of those men who recognizes black widows and instinctively recoils from said intimacies out of self-preservation. Feeling you're being set up for long-term use and abuse is far more effective than an ice-cold shower. Of course, in hindsight, the fact that I was not attracted to her from the start should have been the danger bell that sent me running. But as I said, I was stupid, thinking that marriage didn't have to include sexual compatibility as a necessary ingredient, that beggars shouldn't be choosers."

He shook his head on a huff of deep disgust. "Lord, now I know why everyone treated me as if I was a sexual predator. Even knowing what she's capable of, I never dreamed she'd go as far as slandering herself in a conservative kingdom where a woman's 'honor' is her sexual purity, in order to paint me a darker shade of black."

That was the main reason Kanza had been forced to believe her half sister. She hadn't been able to imagine even Maysoon would harm herself this way if it hadn't been true. And once she'd believed her in this regard, everything else had been swallowed and digested without any thought of scrutiny. But now she couldn't even consider *not* believing him. This was the truth.

This meant that everything she'd assumed about him was a lie. Which left her…where?

Nowhere. Nowhere but in the wrong and not too happy about being forced to readjust her view of him.

Which didn't actually amount to anything. Her opinion had never mattered to anyone—especially not to Aram. All this new information would do now was torment her with guilt over the way she'd treated him. She'd always prided herself on her sense of justice, yet she'd somehow allowed prejudice to override her common sense where he'd been concerned.

The other damage would be to have her rekindled fascination with him unopposed by that buffering detestation. Although it wouldn't make any difference to him how she changed her opinion of him, she couldn't even chart the ramifications to herself. There was no way this wouldn't be a bad thing to her. Very bad.

Snapping out of her reverie, she realized he wasn't even done "testifying" yet. "Now I come to my deposition about your other accusation—of enlisting the Aal Shalaan Brotherhood's help in 'soaring so high.'"

She waved him off, not up to hearing more. "Don't bother."

"Oh, I bother. Am bothered. Very much so."

"Well, that's your problem. I've heard enough."

"But I haven't said enough." He frowned as a shudder shook her. "For a hurricane, it seems you're not impervious to fellow weather conditions. Let's get inside, and I'll field all the curiosity and jealousy you dragged us out here to avoid."

She shuddered again—and not with cold. She was on the verge of combusting with mortification. "It's not the cold that's bothering me."

He gave her one of those patient looks that said he'd withstand any amount of resistance and debate...until he got his way. Then he suddenly advanced on her.

Trapped with the terrace railings at her back, she couldn't have moved if she'd wanted to. She was unable to do anything but stand there helplessly watching him as he neared her in that tranquil prowl, shrugging off his jacket. Then, without touching her, he draped her in it. In what it held of his heat, his scent, his...essence.

For paralyzed moments, feeling as if she was completely enveloped in him, she gazed way up into those preternatural eyes, that slight, spellbinding smile, a quake that originated from a fault line at her very core threatening to break out and engulf her whole.

Before it did, he stepped away, resumed the position she'd told him to maintain as her windshield.

"Now that you're warm, I don't have to feel guilty about rambling on. To explain what happened, I have to outline what happened after that showdown at the ball. I basically found myself a pariah in Zohayd, and I very soon was forced to take the decision to leave. I was preparing to when the Aal Shalaan Brotherhood came to me—all but Amjad, of course. They attempted to dissuade me from leaving, assured me they knew me too well to believe Maysoon's accusations, that they'd resolve everything with their family and Zohaydan society at large if I stayed. They did offer to help me set up my business, to be my partners or to finance me until it took off. But I declined their offer."

She again tried to interject with her insistence that she didn't need him to explain. She believed that had been another of Maysoon's lies. "Aram, I—"

He held up a hand. "Don't take my word for it. Go ask them. I wanted no handouts, but even more, I wanted nothing to maintain any ties to Zohayd after I decided to sever them all forever. I'd remained in Zohayd in the first place for my father, but I felt I hadn't done him any good staying, and after Maysoon's stunt, I knew my presence would cause him nothing but grief." He paused before letting out his breath on a deep sigh. "I had also given up on Shaheen coming back. It was clear that the reconciliation I'd thought being in Zohayd would facilitate wouldn't come to pass."

She heard her voice croaking a question that had long burned in the back of her mind. "Are you going to tell me that Shaheen was to blame for this breakup and alienation, too?"

She hadn't been able to believe the honorable Shaheen could have been responsible for such a rift. Learning of that estrangement after Maysoon's public humiliation *had* entrenched her prejudice against Aram, solidifying her view of him as a callous monster who cast the people who cared for him aside.

Though said view had undergone a marked recalibration, she hoped he'd blame Shaheen as he'd blamed Maysoon. This would put him back in the comfortable dark gray zone.

His next words doused that hope.

"No, that was all my doing. But don't expect me to tell you what I did that was so bad that he fled his own kingdom to get away from me."

"Why not?" she muttered. "Aren't you having a disclosure spree this fine night?"

"You expect me to spill all my secrets all at once?" His feigned horror would have been funny if she was capable of humor now. "Then have nothing more to reveal in future encounters?"

"Did I ask you to tell me *any* secrets? You're the one who's imposing them on me."

His grin was unrepentant. "Let me impose some more on you, then. Just a summation, so grit your teeth and bear it. So...rather than following Maysoon's advice and latching onto Shaheen's brothers for financing, connections and clout, I turned down their generous offers. I had the solid plan, the theoretical knowledge and some practical experience, and I was ready to take the world by storm."

Her sense of fairness reared its head again. "And you certainly did. I am well aware of the global scope of your business management and consultation firm. Many of the major conglomerates I worked with, even whole countries, rely on you to set up, manage and monitor their financial and executive departments. And if you did it all on your own, then you're not as good as they say—you're way better."

Again her testimony seemed to take him by surprise.

His eyes had taken that thoughtful cast again as he said, "Though I'm even more intrigued than ever that you know all that, and I would have liked to take all the credit for the success I've achieved, it didn't happen quite that way. The beginning of my career suffered from some...catastrophic setbacks, to say the least."

"How so?"

Those brilliant eyes darkened with something...vast and too painful. But when he went on, he gave no specifics. "Well, what I thought I knew—my academic degrees, the experience I had in Zohayd—hadn't prepared me for jumping off the deep end with the sharks. But I managed to climb out of the abyss with only a few parts chomped off and launched into my plans with all I had. But I wouldn't have attained my level of success if I hadn't had the phenomenal luck of finding the exact right people to employ. It was together that we 'soared so high.'"

Not taking all the credit for his achievements cast him in an even better light. But there was still one major crime nothing he'd said could exonerate.

"So Maysoon might have been wrong—*was* wrong—about how you made your fortune. But can you blame her for thinking the worst of you? My opening statement in this retrial stands. You didn't have to be so unbelievably cruel in your public humiliation of her."

His stare fixed her for interminable moments, something intense roiling in its depths, something like reluctance, even aversion, as if he hated the response he had to make.

Seeming to reach a difficult decision, he beckoned her nearer.

He thought she'd come closer than that to him? Of her own volition? And why did he even want her to?

When she remained frozen to the spot, he sighed, inched nearer himself. She felt his approach like that of an oncoming train, her every nerve jangling at his increasing proximity.

He stopped a foot away, tilted his head back, exposing his neck to her. She stared at its thick, corded power, her mind stalling. It was as if he was asking her to...to...

"See this?" His purr jolted her out of the waywardness of her thoughts. She blinked at what he was pointing at. Three parallel scars, running from below his right ear halfway down his neck. They'd been hidden beneath his thick, luxurious hair. A current rattled through her at the sight of them. They were clearly very old, and although they weren't hideous, she could tell the injury *had* been. It was because his skin was that perfect, resilient type that healed with minimum scarring that they'd faded to that extent.

He exhaled heavily. "I ended my deposition at the moment I walked away, thought it enough, that any more was overkill. But seems nothing less than full disclosure will do here." He exhaled again, his eyes leveled on hers, totally serious for the first time. "Maysoon gave me this souvenir. She wouldn't let me go just like that. I barely dodged before she slashed across my face and took one eye out."

Kanza shuddered as the scene played in her mind. She did know how hysterical Maysoon could become. She could see her doing that. And she was left-handed...

"I pushed her off me, rushed to the men's room to stem the bleeding and had to lock the door so she wouldn't barge in and continue her frenzy. I got things under control and cleaned myself up, but she pounced on me as soon as I left the sanctuary of the men's room. I couldn't get the hell out of the palace without crossing the ballroom, and I kept pushing her off me all the way there, but once we got back inside, she started screeching.

"As people gathered, she was crying rivers and saying I cheated on her. I just wanted out—at any cost. So I said, 'Yes, I'm the bad guy, and isn't she lucky she's found out before it was too late?' When I tried to extricate myself, she flung herself on the ground, sobbing hysterically that I'd hit her. I couldn't stand around for the rest of her show, so I turned away and left."

He stopped, drew in a huge breath, let it out on a sigh. "But my deposition wouldn't be complete without saying that I've long realized that I owe her a debt of gratitude for everything she did."

Now, *that* stunned her. "You do?"

He nodded. "If her campaign against me hadn't forced me to leave Zohayd, I would have never pursued my own destiny. My experience with her was the perfect example of *assa an takraho sha'an wa howa khairon lakkom*."

You may hate something and it is for your best.

He'd said that in perfect Arabic. Hearing his majestic voice rumbling the ancient verse was a shock. Maysoon had spoken only English to him, making her think he hadn't learned the language. But it was clear he had—and perfectly. There wasn't the least trace of accent in his pronunciation. He'd said it like a connoisseur of old poetry would.

He cocked that awesome head at her. "So now that you've heard my full testimony, any adjustment in your opinion of me?"

Floundering, wanting for the floor to split and snatch her below, she choked out, "It—it *is* your word against hers."

"Then I am at a disadvantage, since she is your half sister. Though that should be to her disadvantage, since you're probably intimate with all her faults and are used to taking her testimony about anything with a pound of salt. But if for some reason you're still inclined to believe her, then there is only one way for me to have a fair retrial. I demand that you get to know me as thoroughly as you know her."

"What do you mean, get to know you?" She heard the panic that leaped into her voice.

He was patient indulgence itself. "How do people get to know each other?"

"I don't know. How?"

The same forbearance met her retort. "How did you get to know anyone in your orbit?"

"I was thrown with them by accidents of birth or geography or necessity."

That had his heart-stopping smile dawning again. "I'm tempted to think you've been a confirmed misanthrope since you exited the womb."

"According to my mother, they barely extracted me surgically before I clawed my way out of her. She informed me I spoiled the having-babies gig for her forever."

His eyes told her what he thought of her mother. Yeah, him and everyone in the civilized world.

Then his eyes smiled again. "It's a calamity we don't have video documentation of your entry into the world. That would have been footage for the ages. So—" he rubbed his hands together "—when will our next reconnaissance session be?"

Her heart lodged in her throat again. "There will be no next anything."

"Why? Have you passed your judgment again, and it's still execution?"

"No, I've given you a not-guilty verdict, so you can go gallop in the fields free. Now, *ann eznak...*"

"Or better still, *men ghair ezni,* right?"

"See? You can predict me now. I was only diverting when you couldn't guess what I'd say next, but now that you've progressed to completing my sentences, my entertainment value is clearly depleted. Better to quit while we're ahead."

"I beg to differ. Not that I am or was after 'entertainment.' Will you suggest a time and venue, or will you leave it up to me?"

She could swear flames erupted inside her skull.

"You've had your retrial, and I want to salvage what I can of this party," she growled. "Now get out of my way."

As if she hadn't said anything, his eyes laughed at her as he all but crooned, "So you want me to surprise you?"

"Argh!"

Foisting his jacket at him, she pushed past him, barely resisting the urge to break out into a sprint to escape his nerve-fraying chuckles.

She felt those following her even after she'd rejoined the party, when there was no way she could still hear him.

And he thought she'd expose herself to him again?

Hah.

One cataclysmic brush with Aram Nazaryan might have been survivable. But enduring another exposure?

No way.

After all, she didn't have a death wish.

Five

"I see you've found Kanza."

Aram stopped midstride across the penthouse, groaning out loud.

Shaheen. Not the person he wanted to see right now.

But then, he wanted to see no one but that keg of unpredictability who'd skittered away from him again. Though he was betting she wouldn't let him find her again tonight.

While Shaheen wasn't going anywhere before he rubbed his nose in some choice I-told-you-sos.

Deciding on the best defense, he engaged offensive maneuvers. "*Found* her? Don't you mean you and your coconspirator wife threw us together?"

"*I* did nothing but put my foot in it. It's *your* kid sister who pushed things along. But she only 'threw' you two together. You could have extracted yourself in five minutes if she'd miscalculated. But obviously she didn't. From our estimations, you've spent over five hours in Kanza's company. To say you found her...compatible is putting it mildly."

"*Hold* it right there, buddy." He shook his finger at Shaheen. "You're not even going down that road, you hear? I just *talked* to the...to the... God, I can't even find a name

for her. I can't call her girl or woman or anything that...
run-of-the-mill. I don't know what the hell she is."

"As long as it's not monster or goblin anymore, that's a
huge development."

"No, she's certainly neither of those things." And Kanza
the Monster hadn't even been his name for her. It had been
Maysoon's and her friends'. That alone should have made
him disregard it. He'd adopted it only because he couldn't
find an alternative. And Kanza *had* unsettled the hell out
of him back then. She still did—if in a totally different
way. One he still couldn't figure out. "All night I've been
thinking sprite, brownie, pixie...but none of that really de-
scribes her either."

"The word you're looking for is...treasure."

Aram stared at his friend. *"Treasure?"*

Then he blinked. *Kanz* meant treasure. Kanza was the
feminine form. How had he never focused on her name's
meaning?

Though... "Treasure isn't how I'd describe her, either."

"No?" Shaheen quirked an eyebrow. "Maybe not...yet.
She can't be categorized, anyway."

"You got *that* right. But that's as right as you get. I'm not
about to ask for her hand in marriage, so put a lid on it."

"Your...caution is understandable. You met her—the
grown-up her, anyway—only hours ago. You wouldn't be
thinking of anything beyond the moment yet."

"Not yet, not ever. Can't a man enjoy the company of an
unidentifiable being without any further agenda?"

Knowing amusement rose in Shaheen's eyes. "You tell
me. Can he?"

"*Yes,* he can. And he fully intends to. And he wants you
and your much better half to butt out and stay out of this.
Let *him* have *fun* for a change, and don't try to make this
into anything more than it is. Got it?"

Shaheen nodded. "Got it."

He threw his hands in the air. "Why didn't you argue? Now I know I'm in for some nasty surprise down the road."

Abandoning his pretense of seriousness, Shaheen grinned teasingly. "From where I'm standing, you consider the surprise you got a rather delightful one."

"Too many surprises and one is bound to wipe out all good ones before it. It's basic Surprise Law." Folding his arms across his chest, he shot his friend a warning look. "Keep your royal noses out of this, Shaheen. I'm your senior, and even if you don't think so, I do know what's best for me, so permit me the luxury of running my own personal life."

Shaheen's grin only widened. "I already said I...*we* will. Now chill."

"Chill?" Aram grimaced. "You just managed to give me an anxiety attack. God, but you two are hazards."

Shaheen took him around the shoulder. "We've done our parts as catalysts. Now we'll let the experiment progress without further intervention."

He narrowed his eyes at him. "Even if you think I'm messing it up? You won't be tempted to intervene then?"

Shaheen wiggled one eyebrow. "That worry would motivate you not to mess it up, wouldn't it?"

He tore himself away. "Shaheen!"

Shaheen laughed. "I'm just messing with you. You're on your own. Just don't come crying one day that you are."

"I won't." He tsked. "And quit making this what it isn't. I only want to put my finger on what makes her so... unquantifiable."

Sighing dramatically, Shaheen played along. "I guess it's because she's nothing anyone expects a princess, let alone a professional woman, to be. Before she became Johara's partner, I only heard her being described as mousy, awkward, even gauche."

"*What?* Who the hell were those people talking about?"

"*You* had that Kanza the Monster conviction going, too."

"At least 'monster' recognized the sheer force of her character."

Shaheen shrugged. "I think she's simply nice."

An impressive snort escaped him. "Who're you calling nice? That's the last adjective in the English language to describe her. She's no such vague, lukewarm, *benign* thing."

Shaheen's lips twitched. "After an evening in her company, you seem to have become *the* authority on her. So how would *you* describe her?"

"Didn't you hear me when I said that I don't *know* what she is? All I know is that she's an inapproachable bundle of thorns. An unstoppable force of nature, like a...a... hurricane."

"That's more of a natural disaster."

He almost muttered "smart-ass" in the exact way Kanza had to him. He *was* exasperated with having his enthusiasm interpreted into what Shaheen and Johara wanted it to be. When it was like nothing he'd ever felt. It was as unpredictable as that hurricane in question.

One thing he knew for certain, though. He wasn't trying to define it or to direct it. Or expect anything from it. And he sure as hell wasn't attempting to temper it. Not to curb Shaheen's expectations, not for anything.

"Whatever. It's the one description that suits her."

"That would make her Hurricane Kanza."

With that, Shaheen took him back to Johara, where he endured her teasing, too. And he again made her and her incorrigibly romantic spouse promise that they wouldn't interfere.

Then as he left the party, he thought of the name Shaheen had suggested.

Hurricane Kanza. It described her to a tee.

After he'd compared her effect on Johara's office to one a lifetime ago, she had proceeded to tear through him with the uprooting force of one. All he wanted to do now was hurtle into her path again and let her toss him wherever she would.

But she wouldn't do it of her own accord. She must still be processing the revelations that, given her sense of justice, *must* have changed her opinion of him. But it no doubt remained an awkward situation for her, since her prejudice had been long held, and Maysoon was still her half sister.

Not that he would allow any of that to stand in his way. He fully intended to get exposed to her delightful destruction again and again, no matter what it took.

Now he just had to plan his next exposure to her devastation.

Aram eyed Johara's office door, impatience rising.

Kanza was in a morning meeting with his sister. Once that was over, he planned to…intercept her.

He'd done so every day for the past two weeks. But the sprite had given him the slip each time. He never got in more than a few words with her before she blinked out on him like her fellow pixies did. But what words those had been. Like tastings from gourmet masterpieces that only left him starving for a full meal again.

He'd let her wriggle away as part of his investigation into her components and patterns of behavior. It had pleased the hell out of him that he still found the first inscrutable and the second unforeseeable. But today he wasn't letting that steel butterfly flutter away. She was having a whole day in his company. She just didn't know it yet.

Johara's assistants eyed him curiously, no doubt wondering why he was here, *again*. And why he didn't just walk right into his sister's office. That had been his first inclination, to corner that elusive elf in there.

He'd reconsidered. Raiding Kanza's leisure time was one thing. Marauding her at work was another. He'd let her get business out of the way before swooping in and sweeping her away on that day off Johara said she hadn't taken in over a year. He'd arranged a day off himself. The first whole one he'd had in…ever.

The office door was suddenly flung open, and Johara's head popped out, golden hair spilling forward. "Aram—come in, please."

He was on his feet at once, buoyed by the unexpected thrill of seeing Kanza now, not an hour or more later. "I thought you were having a meeting."

"When did that ever stop you?" Johara's grin widened as he ruffled her hair. "But as luck would have it, the day you chose to go against your M.O., I found myself in need of that incomparable business mind of yours, big brother."

He hugged her to his side, kissing the top of her head lovingly. "At your service always, sweetheart."

His gaze zeroed in on Kanza like a heat-seeking missile the moment he entered the office. Déjà vu spread its warmth inside his chest when he found her standing by the filing cabinets, like that first night. The only difference was the office was in pristine order. It had looked much better to him after she'd exercised her hurricane-like powers.

He noticed the other two people in the room only when they rose to salute him. All his faculties converged on that power source at the end of the office, even when he wasn't looking at her.

Then he did, and almost laughed out loud at the impact of her disapproving gaze and terse acknowledgment.

"Aram."

While it no longer sounded like a curse, it was…eloquent. No, more than that. Potent. Her unique, patented method of cutting him down to size.

Johara dragged back his attention, explaining their problem. Forcing himself to shift from Kanza to business mode, Aram turned to his sister's concerns.

After he'd gotten a handle on the situation, he offered solutions, only for Kanza to point out the lacking in some and the error in others. But she did so without the least contention or malice, as most would have when they considered someone to be infringing on their domain. In fact, there was nothing in her analysis except an earnest endeavor to reach the best possible solution.

Aram ascribed his lapse to close exposure to her, but he was lucid enough to know he was in the presence of a mind that rivaled his in his field. Having met only a handful of those in his lifetime, who'd been much older and wielding far more experience, he was beyond impressed.

As the session progressed, what impressed him even more was that she didn't compete with him, challenge him or harp on his early misjudgment. She deferred to his superior knowledge where he possessed it and put all her faculties at his disposal during what became five intensive hours of discussion, troubleshooting and restructuring.

Once they reached the most comprehensive plan of action, Johara leaped to her feet in excitement. "Fantastic! I couldn't have dreamed of such a genius solution! I should have teamed you and Kanza up a long time ago, Aram."

He couldn't believe it.

How had he not seen this as another of Johara's blatant efforts to show him how *compatible* they were? Would he *never* learn?

He twisted his lips at Johara for breaching their *noninterference* pact again as he rose to his feet. "And now that you did, how about we celebrate this breakthrough? It's on me."

Johara's eyes were innocence incarnate. "Oh, I wish. I have tons of boring, artistic stuff to take care of with Dana and Steve. You and Kanza go celebrate for us."

If anyone had told him before that business with Kanza that his kid sister was an ingenious actress, he wouldn't have believed it. But though he didn't approve of her underhanded methods, he was thankful for the opportunity she provided to get Kanza alone.

He turned to the little spitfire in question, gearing up for another battle, but Kanza simply said, "Let's go, then. I'm starving. And, Aram, it's on me. I owe you for those shortcuts you taught me today."

His head went light as the tension he'd gathered for the anticipated struggle drained out of him. Then it began to spin, at her admission that she'd learned from him, at her willingness to reward the favor.

Exchanging a last glance that no doubt betrayed his bewilderment with Johara, who was doing less than her usual seamless job of hiding her smug glee, he followed Kanza the Inscrutable out of the office.

Kanza walked out of Johara's office with the most disruptive force she'd ever encountered following her and a sense of déjà vu overwhelming her.

In the past two weeks he'd been taking this "get to know him" to the limit, had turned up everywhere to trail her as he was doing now. Instead of getting used to being inundated in his vibe and pervaded by his presence, each time the experience got more intense, had her reeling even harder.

And she still couldn't find one plausible reason why he was doing this.

The possibility that he was attracted to her had been the first one she'd dismissed. The idea of Aram Nazaryan, the epitome of male perfection, being romantically interested in her was so ludicrous it hadn't lasted more than two seconds of perplexed speculation before it had evaporated. Other reasons hadn't held water any better or longer.

So, by exclusion, one theory remained.

That he was nuts.

The hypothesis was loosely based on Johara's testimony.

With his repeated appearances of late, which Johara hadn't tied to Kanza, Johara had started talking about him. Among the tales from the past, mostly of their time in Zohayd, she'd let slip she believed he'd been sliding into depression. Kanza had barely held back from correcting Johara's tentative diagnosis to *manic*-depression, according to that inexplicable eagerness and elation that exuded from him and gleamed in his eyes.

Johara believed it was because he'd long been abusing his health and neglecting his personal life by working so much. Again, Kanza had barely caught back a scoff. In the past two weeks he hadn't seemed to work at all. How else could he turn up everywhere she went, no matter the time of day? Her only explanation was that he'd set up his business with such efficiency that its success was self-perpetuating and he could take time off whenever the fancy struck him.

But according to Johara, he had been working himself to death for years, resulting in being cut off from humanity and lately even becoming physically sick. It had been why she and Shaheen came so often to New York of late, staying for extended periods of time, to try to alleviate his isolation and stop his deterioration.

Not that Johara thought they were succeeding. She felt that their intimacy as husband and wife left Aram unable to connect with either of them as he used to, left him feeling like an outsider, even a trespasser. But she truly believed he needed the level of attachment he'd once shared with them to maintain his psychological health. Bottom line, she was worried that his inability to find anyone who fulfilled that need, along with his atrocious lifestyle, was dragging him to the verge of some breakdown.

But this man, stalking her like a panther who'd just discovered play and couldn't contain his eagerness to start a game of all-out tackle and chase, seemed nothing like the morose, self-destructive loner Johara had described. Which made *her* theory the only credible explanation. That his inexplicable pursuit of her was the first overt symptom of said breakdown.

Not that she was happy with this diagnosis.

While it had provided an explanation for his behavior, it had also influenced hers.

She'd dodged him so far, because she'd thought he'd

latched on to her in order to combat his ennui, and she hadn't fancied being used as an antidote to his boredom. But the idea that his behavior wasn't premeditated—or even worse, was a cry for help—had made it progressively harder to be unresponsive.

"So where do you want to take me?"

Doing her best not to swoon at the caress of his fathomless baritone, she turned to him as they entered the garage. "I'm open. What do you want to eat?"

"You pick." He grinned as he strode ahead, leading the way to his car. Seemed it was time for that spin in his nearsentient behemoth, a black-and-silver Rolls-Royce Phantom that reportedly came with a ghastly half-million-dollar price tag.

She stopped. "Okay, this goes no further."

That dazzling smile suddenly dimmed. "You're taking back your invitation?"

"I *mean* we're not going in circles, each insisting the other chooses. I already said I'm open to whatever you want, and it wasn't a ploy for you to throw the ball back in my court, proving you're more of a gentleman. I always say exactly what I mean."

His smile flashed back to its debilitating wattage. "You have no idea what a relief that is. But I'm definitely more of a gentleman. It's an incontestable anatomical fact."

She made no response as he seated her in his car's passenger seat. She wasn't going to take this exchange that lumped him and anatomy together any further. It would only lead to trouble.

Focusing instead on being in his car, she sank into the supple seashell leather while her feet luxuriated in the rich, thick lamb's wool, feeling cosseted in the literal lap of luxury.

After veering that impressive monster into downtown traffic, he turned to her. "So why did you suddenly stop evading me?"

Yeah. Good question. Why did she?

She told him the reason she'd admitted to herself so far. "I took pity on you."

"Yes." He pumped his fist. At her raised eyebrow, he chuckled. "Just celebrating the success of my pitiful puppy-dog-eyed efforts."

"If that's what you were shooting for, you missed the mark by a mile. You came across as a hyper, blazing-eyed panther."

Those eyes flared with enjoyment. "Back to the drawing board, then. Or rather the mirror, to practice. But if that didn't work…what did?"

And she found herself admitting more, to herself as well as to him. "It got grueling calculating the lengths you must have gone to, popping up wherever I went. It had me wondering if you're one of those anal-retentive people who must finish whatever they start, and I was needlessly prolonging both of our discomfort. I also had to see what would happen if I let go of the tug-of-war."

"You'll enjoy my company." At her sardonic sideways glance, he laughed. "Admit it. You find me entertaining."

She found him…just about everything.

"Not the adjective I'd use for you," Kanza said with a sigh.

"Don't leave me hanging. Lay it on me."

Her gaze lengthened over his dominant profile. She'd been candid in her description of his outward assets. Was it advisable to be her painfully outspoken self in expounding on what she thought of his more essential endowments?

Oh, what the hell. He must be used to fawning. Her truthfulness, though only her objective opinion, wouldn't be more than what he'd heard a thousand times before.

She opened her mouth to say she'd use adjectives like *enervating,* like a bolt of lightning, and *engulfing,* like a rising flood—and as if to say the words for her, thunder rolled and celestial floodgates burst.

He didn't press her to elucidate, because even with the efficiency of the automatic wipers, he could barely see through the solid sheets of rain. Thankfully, they seemed to have arrived at the destination he'd chosen. The Plaza Hotel, where Johara had mentioned Aram stayed.

As he stopped the car, she thought they should stay inside until the rain let up. They'd get soaked in the few dozen feet to the hotel entrance. Then he opened her door, and lo and behold...an umbrella was ingeniously embedded there. In moments, he was shielding her from the downpour and leading her through the splendor of the iconic hotel. But it wasn't until they stepped into the timeless Palm Court restaurant that she felt as if she'd walked into a scene out of *The Great Gatsby.*

She took in the details as she walked a step ahead among tables filled with immaculate people. Overhanging gilded chandeliers, paneled walls, a soaring twenty-foot green-painted and floral-patterned ceiling and 24-karat gold-leafed Louis XVI furniture, all beneath a stunning stained-glass skylight. Everything exuded the glamour that had made the hotel world famous while retaining the feel of a French country house.

After they were seated and she opted for ordering the legendary Plaza tea, she leveled her gaze back on him and sighed. "Is that your usual spending pattern? This hotel, that car?"

"I am moderate, aren't I?" At her grimace, he upped his teasing. "I was eyeing a Bugatti Veyron, but since there are no roads around to put it through its two-hundred-and-fifty-miles-per-hour paces, I thought paying three times as much as my current car would be unjustified." He chuckled at her growl of distaste. "Down, girl. I can afford it."

"And that makes it okay? Don't you have something better to do with your money?"

"I do a *lot* of better things with my money. And then, it's my only material indulgence. It's in lieu of a home."

"Meaning?"

"Meaning I've never bought a place, so I consider my cars my only home."

This was news. Somewhat…disturbing news. She'd thought he'd been staying in this hotel for convenience, not that he'd never had a place to call home.

"But…if you're saying you don't splurge on your accommodations, it would be *far* more economical—and an investment—to buy a place. A day here is an obscene amount of money down the drain, and you've been here almost a *year*."

His nod was serene. "My suite goes for about twenty grand a night." At her gasp, his lips spread wide. "Of which I'm not paying a cent. I am a major shareholder in this hotel, so I get to stay free."

Okay. She should have known a financial mastermind like him wouldn't throw money around, that he'd invest every cent to make a hundred. It was a good thing their orders had arrived so she'd have it instead of crow after she'd gone all self-righteous on him.

She felt him watching her and pretended to have eyes only on the proceedings as waiters heaped varieties of tea, finely cut sandwiches, scones, jam, clotted cream and a range of pastries on the table.

They had devoured two irresistible scones each, and mellow live piano music had risen above the buzz of conversation, when he broke the silence.

"This place reminds me of the royal palace in Zohayd. Not the architecture, but something in the level of splendor. The distant resemblance is…comforting."

The longing, the melancholy in his reminiscing about the place where he'd lived a good portion of his youth, tugged at her heart…a little too hard.

Suddenly his smile dawned again. "So ask me anything."

Struggling with the painful tautness in her throat, she eyed him skeptically. "Anything at all?"

His nod was instantaneous. "You bet."

It seemed Johara had been correct. He did need someone to share things with that he felt he could no longer share with his sister or brother-in-law. And as improbable as it was, he seemed to have elected her as the one he could unburden himself to. His selection had probably been based on her ability to say no to him, to be blunt with him. That must be a total novelty for him.

But she also suspected there was another major reason she was a perfect candidate for what he had in mind. Because he didn't seem to consider her a woman. Just a sexless buddy he could have fun with and confide in without worrying about the usual hassles a woman would cause him.

She had no illusions about what she was, how a man like him would view her. But that still had mortification warring with compassion in her already tight chest. Compassion won.

Feeling the ridiculous urge to reach across the table for his hand, to reassure him she was there for him, even if he thought her a sprite, she cleared her throat. "Tell me about the rift between you and Shaheen."

He nodded. "Did Johara tell you how we came to Zohayd?"

"Oh, no! You're planning to tell me your whole life story to get to one incident in its middle?"

"Yep. So you'll understand the factors leading up to the incident and the nature of the players in it."

"Can I retract my request?" She pretended glibness.

"Nope. *Dokhool el hammam mesh zay toloo'oh.*"

Entering a bathroom isn't like exiting it. What was said in Zohayd to signify that what was done couldn't be undone.

And she was beginning to realize what that really meant.

Living life knowing a man like him existed had been fine with her as long as he'd been just a general concept—not a reality that could cross hers, let alone invade it.

But now that she was experiencing him up close, she feared it would irrevocably change things inside her.

And the peace she'd once known would be no more.

Six

Pretending to eat what seemed to have turned to ashes, Kanza watched Aram as he poured her tea and began sharing his life story with her.

"Before I came to Zohayd at sixteen, my father used to whisk me, Johara and Mother away every year or so to yet another exotic locale as he built his reputation as an internationally rising jeweler. When I told my peers that I'd trade what they thought an enchanted existence in the glittering milieus of the rich and famous for a steady, boring life in a small town, dweeb and weirdo were only two of the names they called me. I learned to keep my mouth shut, but I couldn't learn to stop hating that feeling of homelessness. My defense was to go to any new place as if I was leaving the next day, and I remained in self-imposed isolation until we left."

She gulped scalding tea to swallow the lump in her throat. So his isolation had deeper roots than Johara even realized. And she'd bet she was the first one he'd told this to.

He went on. "I had a plan, though. That the moment I hit eighteen, I'd stay put in one place, work in one job forever, marry the first girl who wanted me and have a brood of kids. That blueprint for my future was what kept me going as the flitting around the world continued."

She gulped another mouthful, the heaviness in her chest increasing. His plans for stability had never come to pass. He was forty and as far as she knew, apart from the fiasco with Maysoon, he'd never had any kind of relationship.

So how had the one guy who'd planned a family life so early on, who'd craved roots when all others his age dreamed of freedom, ended up so adrift and alone?

He served them sandwiches and continued. "Then my father's mentor, the royal jeweler of Zohayd, retired and his job became open. He recommended Father to King Atef…."

Feeling as if a commercial had burst in during a critical moment, she raised a hand. "Hey, I'm from Zohayd and I know all the stories. How your father became the one entrusted with the Pride of Zohayd treasure is a folktale by now. Fast forward. Tell me something I don't know. I hate recaps."

His eyes crinkled at her impatience—he was clearly delighted she was so riveted by his story. "So there I was, jetting off to what Father said was one of the most magnificent desert kingdoms on earth, feeling resigned we'd stay for the prerequisite year before Father uprooted us again. Then we landed there. I can still remember, in brutal vividness, how I felt as soon as my feet touched the ground in Zohayd. That feeling of…belonging."

God. The emotions that suddenly blazed from him… Any moment now she was going to reach for that box of tissues.

"That feeling became one of elation, of certainty, that I'd found a home—that I *was* home—when I met Shaheen." His massive chest heaved as he released an unsteady breath. "Did Johara tell you how he saved her from certain death that day?"

She shook her head, her eyes beginning to burn.

"She was a hyperactive six-year-old who made me age

running after her. Then I take my eyes off her for a minute and she's dangling from the palace's balcony. I was too far away, and Father failed to reach her, and she was slipping. But then at the last second, Shaheen swooped in to snatch her out of the air like the hawk he's named after.

"I was there the next second, beside myself with fright and gratitude, and that kindred feeling struck me. And from that day forward, he became my first and only friend. As he became Johara's first and only love."

She let out a ragged breath. "Wow."

"Yeah." He leaned back in his chair. "It was indescribable, having the friendship of someone of Shaheen's caliber—a caliber that had nothing to do with his status. But though he felt just as closely bonded to me, considered me an equal, I knew the huge gap between us would always be unbridgeable. I grew more uncomfortable by the day when Johara started to blossom, and I became certain that her emotions for Shaheen weren't those of a friend but those of a budding woman in love.

"By the time she was fourteen, worry poisoned every minute I spent with Shaheen, which by then almost always included Johara. Though the three of us were magnificent together, I thought Shaheen's all-out indulgence of Johara would lead to catastrophe, for Johara, for my whole family. Then my anxiety reached critical mass..."

"Go on," she rasped when he paused, unable to wait to hear the rest.

He raked a hand through his dark, satin hair. "We were having a squash match, and I started to trounce a bewildered Shaheen. The more Johara cheered him to fight back, the more vicious I became. Afterward in the changing room, I tore into Shaheen with all my pent-up resentment. I called him a spoiled prince who made a game of manipulating people's emotions. I accused him of encouraging her crush on him—which he knew was beyond hopeless—just for fun. I demanded he stop leading her on or I'd tell his father King Atef...so he'd *order* him never to come near Johara again.

"Shaheen was flabbergasted. He said Johara was the little sister he'd never had. I only sneered that his affections went far beyond an older brother's, as I should know as her *real* one. He countered that while he didn't know what having a sister was like, Johara was his 'girl'—the one who 'got' him like no one else, even me, and he did love her... in every way but *that* way.

"But I was way beyond reason, said that his proclamations meant nothing to me—I cared only about Johara—and that he was emotionally exploiting her, and I wouldn't stand idly by waiting for him to damage her irrevocably."

She couldn't imagine how he'd felt at the time. Sensing the powerful bond between his best friend and sister, having every reason to believe it would end in devastation and being forced to risk his one friendship to protect his one sister. It must have been terrible, knowing that either way he'd lose something irreplaceable.

Grimacing with remembered pain, Aram placed his forearms on the table, his gaze fixed on the past. "Outrage finally overpowered Shaheen's mortification that I could think such dishonorable things of him. His bitterness escalated as my conviction faltered, then vanished in the face of his intense affront and hurt. But there was no taking back what I'd said or threatened. Then it was too late, anyway.

"Shaheen told me he'd save me the trouble of running to his father with my demands for him to cease and desist. He'd never come near Johara again. Or me. He carried out his pledge, cutting Johara and me off, effective immediately."

It was clear the injury of those lost years had never fully healed. And though Shaheen and Johara were now happily married and Aram's friendship with Shaheen had been restored, it seemed the gaping wound where his friend had been torn out had been only partially patched. Because there was no going back to the same closeness now that Shaheen's life was so full of Johara and their daughter while Aram had found nothing to fill the void in his own life. Except work. And according to Johara, it was nowhere near enough.

"Just when I thought Shaheen's alienation was the worst thing that could happen to me, Mother suddenly took Johara and left Zohayd. I watched our family being torn apart and was unable to stop it. Then I found myself left alone with a devastated father who kept withdrawing into himself in spite of all my efforts. I tried to grope for my best friend's support, hoping he'd let me close again, but he only left Zohayd, too, dashing any hope for a reconciliation."

So she had been totally wrong about him in this instance, too. It hadn't been not caring that had caused that breach; it had been caring too much. And it had cost him way more than she'd ever imagined.

He went on. "With all my dreams of making a home for myself in Zohayd over, I wanted to leave and tried to persuade Father to leave with me, too, but I backed off when I realized his service to the king and kingdom was what kept him going. Knowing I couldn't leave him, I resigned myself that I'd stay in Zohayd as long as he lived."

It must have been agonizingly ironic to get what he wanted, that permanent stay in Zohayd, but for it to be more of an exile than a home.

As if he'd heard her thoughts, he released a slow, deep breath. "It was the ultimate irony. I was getting what I'd hoped for all my life—stability in one place, just without the roots or the family, to live there in an isolation that promised to become permanent." *Isolation.* There was that word again. "Then, six years after everyone left Zohayd, I took a shot at forging that family I'd once dreamed of…and you now know what happened next."

She nodded, her throat tight. "And you ended up being forced to leave."

He sighed deeply again. "Yeah. So much happened after

that. Too much. And I've never stayed in one place longer than a few months since. I hadn't wanted to. Couldn't bear to, even. Then three years ago, Shaheen and Johara ended up getting married. I was right about the nature of their involvement." He smiled whimsically. "I just jumped the gun by twelve years." Another deep sigh. "Then suddenly I had my friend back, Mother reconciled with Father and my whole family was put back together—just in Zohayd, where I could no longer be."

Swallowing what felt like a rock, she wondered if he'd elaborate on the intervening years, the "too much" he'd said with such aversion. He didn't.

He'd done what he'd set out to do, told her the story that explained his rift with Shaheen. Anything else would be for another day. If there would be one.

From the way her heart kept twisting, it wasn't advisable to have one. Exposure to him when she'd despised him, thought him a monster, had been bad enough. Now that she saw him as not only human but even empathetic, further exposure could have catastrophic consequences. For her.

His eyes seemed to see her again, seeming to intensify in vividness as he smiled like never before. A heartfelt smile.

"Thank you."

Her heart fired so hard it had her sitting forward in her chair. "Wh-what for?"

The gentleness turning his beauty from breathtaking to heartbreaking deepened. "You listened. And made no judgments. I think you even…sympathized."

She struggled to stop the pins at the back of her eyes from dissolving in an admission of how moved she was. "I did. It was such a tragic and needless waste, all those years apart. For all of you."

His inhalation was sharp. The exhalation that followed was slow, measured. "Yes. But they're back together now."

They. Not we.

He didn't seem to consider he had his family and friend

back. Worse, it seemed he didn't consider himself part of the family anymore. And though his expression was now carefully neutral, she sensed he was...desolate over the belief. What he seemed to consider an unchangeable fact of his life now.

After that, as if by unspoken agreement, they spent the rest of their time in the Palm Court talking about a dozen things that weren't about lost years or ruined life plans.

After the rain stopped, he took her out walking, and they must have covered all of Central Park before it was dark.

She didn't even feel the distance, the exertion or the passage of time. She saw nothing, heard and smelled and felt nothing but him. His company was that engrossing, that gratifying. The one awful thing about spending time with him was that it would come to an end.

But it didn't. When she'd thought their impromptu outing was over, he insisted she wasn't going home until she was a full, exhausted mass unable to do anything but fall into bed. She hadn't even thought of resisting his unilateral plans for the rest of the evening. This time out of time would end soon enough, and she wasn't going to terminate it prematurely. She'd have plenty of time later to regret her decision not to.

Over dinner, their conversation took a turn for the funny, then the hilarious. On several occasions, his peals of goose-bump-raising laughter incited many openmouthed and swooning stares from besotted female patrons, while *she* was leveled with what's-*she*-doing-with-that-god glares, not to mention the times the whole restaurant seemed to be turning around to see if there was a hyena dining with them.

When he drove her back to her apartment building, he parked two blocks away—just an excuse to have another walk.

As they walked in companionable silence, she felt the impulsive urge to hook her arm in his, lean on him through the wind. It wasn't discretion that stopped her but the fact that he hadn't attempted even a courteous touch so far.

At her building's entrance, he turned to her with expectation blazing in those azure eyes. "So same time tomorrow?"

Her heart pirouetted in her chest at the prospect of another day with him.

But… "We went out at *one* today!"

He shrugged. "And?"

"And I have work."

He waved dismissively. "Take the day off."

"I can't. Johara…"

"Will shove you out of the office if she can to make you take some time off. She says you're a workaholic."

"Gee. She says the same about you."

"See? We both need a mental-health day."

"We already had one today."

"We worked our asses off for five hours in the morning. Tomorrow is a *real* day off. With all the trimmings. Sleeping in, then going crazy being lazy and doing nothing but eating and chatting and doing whatever pops into our minds till way past midnight."

And he'd just described her newfound vision of heaven.

Then she remembered something, and heaven seemed to blink out of sight. She groaned, "I really can't tomorrow."

Disappointment flooded his gaze, but only for a second. Then eagerness was back full steam ahead. "The day after tomorrow, then. And at noon. No…make it eleven. *Ten.*"

Her heart tap-danced. She did her best not to grin like a loon, to sound nonchalant as she said, "Oh, all right."

He stuck his hands at his hips. "Got something more enthusiastic than that?"

"Nope." She mock scowled. "That's the only brand available. Take it or…take it."

"I'll take it, and take it!" He took a step back as if to dodge a blow, whistled. "Jeez. How did something so tiny become so terrifying?"

She gave a sage nod. "It's an evolutionary compensatory mechanism to counteract the disadvantaged size."

"Vive la évolution." And he said it in perfect French, reminding her he spoke that fluently, too.

She burst out laughing.

Minutes later, she was still chuckling to herself as she entered her apartment. God, but that man was the most unprecedented, unpredictable, unparalleled fun she'd ever had.

She met her eyes in her foyer's mirror, wincing at what she'd never seen reflected back...until now. Unmistakable fever in her cheeks and soppy dreaminess in her eyes. Aram had put it all there without even meaning to.

Yeah. He was boatloads of fun. Too bad he was also a mine of danger.

And she'd just agreed to another daylong dose of deadly exposure.

Seven

"So how's my Tiny Terror doing this fine day?"

Kanza leaned against the wall to support legs that always went elastic on hearing Aram's voice. Not to mention the heart that forgot its rhythm.

You'd think after over a month of daily and intensive exposure, she'd have developed some immunity. But she only seemed to be getting progressively more susceptible.

She forced out a steady, "Why, thank you, I'm doing splendidly. And you, Hulking Horror?"

Right on cue, his expected laugh came, boisterous and unfettered. He kept telling her that she had the specific code that operated his humor, and almost everything she said tickled him mercilessly. She'd been liberally exercising that power over him, to both their delight.

In return, the gift of his laughter, and knowing that she could incite it, caused her various physical and emotional malfunctions.

She was dealing with the latest bout when he said, laughter still permeating his magnificent voice, "I'm doing spectacularly now that my Mighty Miniature has taken me well in hand. You ready? I'm downstairs." Yeah, he never even asked to come up. "And hurry! I have something to show you."

"Uh-uh. Don't play that game with me." She took a look in the mirror and groaned. Not a good idea to inspect herself right before she beheld him. The comparison was just too disheartening. She slammed out of her apartment in frustration and ran into the elevator that a neighbor had just exited. "Tell me what it is. I have severe allergies to surprises."

"Just so we won't end up in the E.R., I'll give you a hint." His voice had that vibrant edge of excitement she'd been hearing more of late as they planned trips they'd take and projects they'd do together. "It's things people live in."

Her heart sputtered in answering excitement. "You bought an apartment! Oh, congrats."

"Hey, you think me capable of making a decision without consulting my Mini Me?"

The elevator opened to reveal him. And it hit her all over again with even more force than last time. How…shattering his beauty was.

But with the evidence of his current glory, she knew he'd been right. When she'd met him again six weeks ago, he *had* been at his lowest ebb. Ever since then, he'd been steadily shedding any sign of haggardness. He was now at a level that should be prohibited by law, like any other health hazard.

And there she was, the self-destructive fool who willingly exposed herself to his emanations on a daily basis. And without any protection.

Not that there was any, or that she'd want it if there was. She'd decided to open herself up to the full exposure and to hell with the certain and devastating side effects.

As usual, without even taking her arm or touching her in any way whatsoever, he rushed ahead, gesturing eagerly for her to follow. She did. As she knew by now, she always would.

Once in his car and on their way, he turned to her. "I'm

taking you to see the candidates. I'm signing the contract of the one you'll determine I'll feel most comfortable in."

Her jaw dropped. "And I'm supposed to know that... how?"

His sideways glance was serenity itself. "Because you know everything."

"Hey." She turned in her seat. "Thanks for electing me your personal oracle or goddess or whatever, but no thanks. You can't saddle me with this kind of responsibility."

"It's your right and prerogative, O Diminutive Deity."

She rolled her eyes. "What ever happened to free will?"

"Who needs that when I have you?"

"If it was anyone else, I'd be laughing. But I know you're crazy enough to sign a contract if I as much as say a word in preference of one place." His nod reinforced her projection. "What if you end up hating my choice?"

"I won't." His smile was confidence incarnate. "And that's not crazy, but the logical conclusion to the evidence of experience. Everything you choose for me or advise me to do turns out to be the perfect solution for me. Case in point, look at me."

And she'd been trying her best not to. Not to stare, anyway. He gestured at his clothes. "You pointed this out in a shop yesterday, said I'd look good in it."

Yeah, because you'd look good in anything. You'd make a tattered sac look like haute couture.

"Even though I thought I'd look like a cyanotic parrot in this color..." A deep, intense purple that struck incredible hues off his hair and eyes. "I bought it on the way here based solely on your opinion. Now I think I've never worn anything more complimenting."

Her lips twisted in mockery, and with a twinge at how right he was. He looked the most vital and incandescent he'd ever been. "Pink frills would compliment you, Aram."

"Then I'll try those next."

A chuckle overpowered her as imaginings flooded her mind. "God, this I have to see."

His grin flashed, dazzling her. "Then you will." Suddenly his face settled into a seriousness that was even more hard-hitting. "All joking aside, I'm not being impulsive here. I'm a businessman, and I make my decisions built on what works best. And *you* work best."

"Uh, thanks. But in exactly what way do I do that?"

"Your perception is free from the distortions of inclinations. You cut to the essence of things, see people and situations for what they are, not what you'd prefer them to be, and don't let the background noise of others' opinions distract you." He slid her that proud, appreciative glance that he bestowed on her so frequently these days. "You proved that to me when you accepted my word and adjusted your opinion of me, guided only by your reading of me against overwhelming circumstantial evidence and long-standing misconceptions. It's because you're so welcoming of adjustments and so goal oriented that you achieve the best results in everything. I mean, look at me..."

Oh, God, not again. Didn't he have any idea what it did to her just being near him, let alone looking more closely at him than absolutely necessary?

No, he didn't.

He had no idea whatsoever how he made her feel.

She sighed. "I'm looking. And purple does become you. Anything else I should be looking at?"

"Yes, the miracle you worked. You took a fed-up man who was feeling a hundred years old and turned him into that eager kid who skips around doing all the things he'd long given up on. And you did it by just being your no-nonsense self, by just reading me right and telling me everything you thought and exactly what I have to hear."

She almost winced. She wasn't telling *everything* she thought. Not by a long shot. But her thoughts and feelings where he was concerned were her responsibility. She had no right to burden him with what didn't concern him.

But he was making it harder by the minute to contain those feelings within her being's meager boundaries.

He wasn't finished with his latest bout of unwitting torment. "You yanked me out of the downward spiral I was resigned to plunge into until I hit rock bottom. So, yes, I'm sure your choice of abodes will be the best one for me. Because you've been the best thing that has ever happened to me."

The heart that had been squeezing harder with every incredible word almost burst.

To have him so eloquently reinforcing her suspicion that he'd come to consider her the replacement best friend/sister he needed was both ecstasy and agony.

Feeling the now-familiar heat simmering behind her eyes, she attempted to take this back to lightness. "What's with the seriousness? And here I was secure in the fact that you're incapable of being that way around me."

His smile was so indulgent that she felt something coming undone right in her very essence. "I'm always serious around you. Just in a way that's the most fun I've ever had. But if you feel I'm burdening you with making this choice…"

And she had to laugh. "Oh, shut up, you gigantic weasel. After all the sucking up you did, and all the puppy-dog-eyed persuasion that you *have* perfected in front of that mirror, you have the audacity to pretend that I have a choice here?"

His guffaw belted out, almost made her collapse onto herself. "Ah, Kanza, *you* are the most fun I've ever had."

Yeah. What every girl wanted to hear from the most divine man on earth. That she made him laugh.

But she'd already settled for that. For anything with him. For as long as she could have it. Come what may.

He brought the car to a stop in front of a building that felt vaguely familiar. As he opened his door, she jumped out so he wouldn't come around to open hers, since opening doors and pulling back seats for her seemed to be the only acts that indicated that he considered her female.

When he fell into step beside her, she did a double take.

They were on Fifth Avenue. Specifically in front of one of the top Italian-renaissance palazzo-style apartment buildings in Manhattan.

Forgetting everything but the excitement of apartment hunting, she turned to him with a whoop. "I used to live a block from here." And she'd found the area only "vaguely familiar." He short-circuited her brain even more than she'd thought. "God, I loved that apartment. It was the only place that ever felt like home."

His eyebrows shot up. "Zohayd didn't feel like that?"

"Not really. You know what it was like."

He frowned and, if possible, became more edible than ever. "Actually, I have no idea how it was like for you there. Because you never told me." As soon as they entered the elevator, he turned to her with a probing glance. "How did we never get to talk about your life in Zohayd?"

She shrugged. "Guess we had more important things to discuss. Like how to pick the best avocado."

His lips pursed in displeasure. "That alone makes me realize how remiss I've been and that there is a big story here. One I won't rest until I hear."

She waved him off. "It's boring, really."

His pout was adamant. "I live to be bored by you."

The last thing she wanted to do was tell him about her disappointment-riddled life in Zohayd. But knowing him, he'd persist until she told him. The best she could hope for was to distract him for now.

She took the key from his hand as they got off the elevator. "Which apartment?"

He pointed out the one at the far end of the floor.

As they sauntered in that direction, he looked down at her. "So about this old place of yours—if it felt like home, and I'm assuming your new place doesn't, why did you move?"

"A friend from Zohayd begged me to room with her, as she couldn't live alone, and the new place was right by her work. Then she up and got married on me and went back to Zohayd, and I never got around to going back to my place. But now that you might be buying a place this close, it would save us a lot of commuting if I got it back. Hope it's still on the market."

"Choose this apartment, and I'll *make* it on the market."

"Oh. Watch out, world, for the big, bad tycoon. He snaps his fingers and the market yelps and rolls over."

He gave her a deep bow. "At your service."

They laughed and exchanged wit missiles as they entered the opulent duplex through a marble-framed doorway. Then she fell silent as she beheld what looked straight out of the pages of *Architectural Digest*. Sweeping, superbly organized layouts with long galleries, an elegant staircase, lush finishes, oversize windows, high ceilings and a spacious terrace that wrapped around two sides of the apartment. It was even furnished to the highest standards she'd ever seen and very, very much to her taste.

In only minutes of looking around, she turned to Aram. "Okay, no need to see anything more. Or any other place. I hereby proclaim that you will find utmost comfort here."

He again bowed deeply, azure flames of merriment leaping in his eyes. "My Minuscule Mistress, thy will be done."

And in the next hour, it was. He immediately called the Realtor, who zoomed over with the contracts. Aram passed them to her to read before he signed, and she made some amendments before giving him the green light. From then on, it took only minutes for the check to be handed over and the Realtor to leave the apartment almost bouncing in delight.

Aram came back from walking the lady to the front door, his smile flooding his magnificent new place in its radiance.

"Now to inaugurate the apartment with our first meal." He threw himself down beside her on the elegant couch. "So what are we eating?"

She cocked an eyebrow at him and tsked. "This inability to make decisions without my say-so is becoming worrisome."

He slid down farther on the couch, reclining his big, powerful body more comfortably. "I've been making business decisions for countless employees, clients and shareholders for the past eight years. I'm due for a perpetual vacation from making minor- to moderate-sized decisions for the rest of my personal life."

She gave him her best stern scowl, which she resignedly knew he thought was the most adorable thing ever. "And I'm the one who's supposed to pick up the slack and suddenly be responsible for your decisions as well as mine?"

He nodded in utmost complacency. "You do it so well, so naturally. And it's your fault. You're the one who got me used to this." His gaze became that cross between cajoling and imploring that he'd perfected. "You're not leaving me in the lurch now, are you?"

"Stop with the eyes!" she admonished. "Or I swear I'll blindfold you."

"What a brilliant idea. Then besides making decisions for me, you'll have to lead me around by the hand. Even more unaccountability for me to revel in."

She threw her hands up. "Sushi, okay. Here's your decision before I find myself taking over your business, too, while you go indulge in the teenage irresponsibility you evidently never had."

Chuckling, he got out his phone. Then he proceeded to ask her exactly what kind of sushi they were eating, piece by piece, until she had to slam him with a cushion.

After they'd wiped off the delicious feast, he was pouring her jasmine tea when she noticed him looking at her in an even more unsettling, contemplative way.

"What?" she croaked.

"I was wondering if you were always this interesting."

"And I'm wondering if you were always this condescending. Oh, wait, you were even worse. You used to look at me like I was a strange life-form."

"You *were* a strange life-form. I mean, green body makeup? And pink contacts? Pink? Did you have those custom-made?" He rejoined her on the couch with his own cup. "What statement were you making?"

She was loath to remember those times when she'd felt alone even while deluged by people. When she used to look at him and know that *nogoom el sama a'arablaha*—that the stars in the sky were closer than he was. Now, though he was a breath away, he remained as distant, as impossible to reach.

She sighed, shaking free from the wave of melancholy. "One of my stepmothers, Maysoon's mother, popularized Kanza the Monster's name until everyone was using it. So I decided to go the whole hog and look the part."

His eyes went grim, as if imagining having his hands on those who'd been so inconsiderate with her. Knowing him, she didn't put it past him that he would act on his outrage on behalf of her former self.

"What made you give it up?" His voice was dark with barely suppressed anger. "Then go all the way in the other direction, doing without any sort of enhancement?"

She shrugged. "I developed an allergy to makeup."

His lips twitched as his anger dissolved into wry humor. "Another allergy?"

"Not a real one. I just realized that regardless of whether makeup makes me look worse or better, I was focusing too much on what others thought of me. So I decided to focus on myself. Be myself."

That pride he showered on her flooded his gaze. "Good for you. You're perfect just the way you are."

Kanza stared at him. In any romantic movie, as the hero

professed those words, he would have suddenly seen his dorky best friend in a new light, would have realized she was beautiful in his eyes and that he wanted her for more than just a friend.

Before her heart imploded with futility, she slid down on the couch, pretending she thought it a good moment for one of those silent rituals they exercised together.

Inside her, there was only cacophony.

Aram considered her perfect.

Just not for him.

Eight

Aram sank further into tranquility and relaxation beside Kanza, savoring the companionable silence they excelled at together, just as they did at exhilarating repartee.

Just by being here, she'd turned this place, which he'd felt ambivalent toward until she'd entered it and decided she liked it, into a home. He'd decided to have one at last only because she'd said she would always stay in New York and make it hers.

He sighed, cherishing the knowledge that expanded inside him with each passing hour.

She was really her name. A treasure.

And to think that no one, even Shaheen and Johara, realized how much of one she really was.

He guessed she was too different, too unexpected, too unbelievable for others to be able to fathom, let alone to handle.

She was perfect to him.

It was hard to believe that only six weeks ago he hadn't had her in his life. It felt as if his existence had *become* a life only once she'd entered it.

And it seemed like a lifetime ago when Shaheen had

suggested her as a convenient bride, convinced she'd consider his assets and agree to the arrangement. If Shaheen only knew her, he would have known that she'd sign a contract of enslavement before she would a marriage of convenience. If he'd known how unique, how exceptional she was, he wouldn't have even thought of such an unworthy fate for her.

She'd achieved her success in pursuit of self-realization and accomplishment, not status and wealth—things she cared nothing about and would certainly never wish to attain through a man. She'd even made it clear she didn't consider marriage a viable option for herself. But among the many misconceptions about her had been his own worry that his initial fascination would fade, and she'd turn out to be just another opportunistic woman who'd use any means necessary to reel in a husband.

But the opposite had happened. His fascination, his admiration, his pleasure at being with her intensified by the minute. For the first time, he found himself attracted to the *whole* woman, his attraction not rooted in sexuality or sustained by it. He had to use Shaheen's word to describe what they were. Compatible. They were matched on every level—personally, professionally, mentally and emotionally. Her every quality and skill meshed with and complemented his own. She was his equal, and his superior in many areas.

She was *just* perfect.

Just yesterday, Shaheen had asked him for an update on whether he'd changed his mind about Kanza now that he'd gotten to know her.

He'd said only that he had, leaving it at that.

What he'd really meant was that he had changed his mind about *everything*.

The more he was with Kanza, the more everything he'd believed of himself—of his limits, inclinations, priorities and everything he'd felt before her—changed beyond all recognition.

She made him work hard for her respect and esteem, for the pleasure and privilege of his presence in her life, for her gracing his with hers. She gave him what no one had ever given him before, not even Shaheen or Johara. She *reveled* in being with him as much as he did with her. She *got* him on every level. She accepted him, challenged him, and when she felt there were things about him that needed fixing— and there were *many*—she just reached inside him with the magic wand of her candor and caring and put it right.

She'd turned his barren existence into a life of fulfill- ment, every day bringing with it deeper meanings, invigo- rating discoveries and uplifting experiences.

The only reason he'd fleetingly considered Shaheen's offer had been for the possibility of filling his emptiness with a new purpose in life and the proximity of his family. Now he found little reason to change his status quo. For what could possibly be better than this?

It was just perfection between them.

So when Shaheen had asked for an update, really asking about projected developments, he couldn't bear thinking of any. How could he when any might tamper with this blissful state? He was *terrified* anything would happen to change it.

They were both unconcerned about the world and its conventions, and things were flourishing between them. He only hoped they would continue to deepen in the exact same way. So even if he wanted to, he certainly wasn't introduc- ing any new variable that might fracture the flawlessness.

For now, the only change he wanted to introduce was removing the last barrier inside him. He wanted to let her into his being, fully and totally.

So he did. "There's something I haven't told you yet. Something nobody knows."

She turned to him, her glorious mass of hair rustling as if it was alive, those unique obsidian eyes delving deep inside his recesses, letting him know she was there for him always.

Just gazing into them he felt invincible. And secure that he could share everything with her, even his shame.

"It happened a few months after I left Zohayd…." He paused, the long-repressed confession searing out of his depths. He braced himself against the pain, spit it out. "I got involved in something…that turned out to be illegal, with very dangerous people. I ended up in prison."

That had her sitting up. And what he saw on her face rocked through him. Instantaneous reassurance that, whatever had happened, whatever he told her, it wouldn't change her opinion of him. She was on his side. Unequivocally.

And as he'd needed to more frequently of late, he took a moment to suppress the desire to haul her to him and crush her in the depths of his embrace with all his strength.

The need to physically express his feelings for her had been intensifying every day. But she'd made no indication that she'd accept that. Worse. She didn't seem to want it.

It kept him from initiating anything, even as much as a touch. For what if even a caress on her cheek or hair changed the dynamic between them? What if it made her uneasy and put her on her guard around him? What if he then couldn't take it back and convince her that he'd settle for their previous hands-off status quo, forever if need be?

He brought the urge under control with even more difficulty than he had the last time it had assailed him, his voice sounding as harsh as broken glass as he went on, "I was sentenced to three years. I was paroled after only one."

Her solemn eyes were now meshed with his. He felt he was sinking into the depths of their unconditional support, felt understood, cosseted, protected. It was as if she was reaching to him through time, to offer him her strength to tide him through the incarceration, to soothe the wounds and erase his scars.

"For good behavior?" Her voice was the gentlest he'd ever heard it.

He barked a mirthless laugh. "Actually, they probably

wanted me out to get rid of me. I was too much trouble, gave them too many inmates to patch up. I almost killed a couple. I spent over nine months of that year in solitary. The moment they let me out, I put more inmates in the infirmary and I was shoved back there."

"You ended up being…solitary too many times throughout your life."

She'd mused that as if to herself. But he felt her soft, pondering words reaching down inside him to tear out the talons he'd long felt sunk into his heart. Making him realize that it hadn't been the solitude itself that had eaten at him but the notion that he'd never stop being alone.

But now she was here, and he'd never be alone again.

Her smile suddenly dawned, and it lit up his entire world. "But you still managed to make the best of a disastrous situation in your own inimitable way."

"It wasn't only my danger to criminal life-forms that got me out. I was a first-time offender, and I was lucky to find people who believed that I had made a mistake, not committed a crime. Those allies helped me get out, and afterward, they supported my efforts to…expunge my record."

The radiance of her smile intensified, scorching away any remnants of the ordeal's despondency and indignity. "So you're an old hand at expunging your record. And I wasn't the first one who believed in you."

He didn't know how he stopped himself from grabbing her hands, burying his lips and face in them, grabbing *her* and burying his whole being in her magnanimity and faith.

He expended the urge on a ragged breath. "You're the first and only one who did with only the evidence of my word."

She waved that away. "As you so astutely pointed out the first night, I do know Maysoon. That was a load of evidence in your favor, once I'd heard both sides of the story."

He wasn't about to accept her qualification. "No. You

employed this unerring truth-and-justice detector of yours without any backing evidence. You read *me*. You believed *me*."

Her eyes gleamed with that indulgence that melted him to his core. "Okay, okay, I did. Boy, you're pushy."

"And you believed me again now," he insisted, needing to hear her say it. "When I said I didn't knowingly commit a crime, even when I gave you no details, let alone evidence."

Teasing ebbed, as if she felt he needed the assurance of her seriousness. "Yes, I did, because I know you'd always tell me the truth, the bad before the good. If you'd been guilty, you would have told me. Because you know I can't accept anything but the truth and because you know that whatever it was, it wouldn't make a difference to me."

Hot thorns sprouted behind his eyes, inside his heart. Everything inside him surged, needing to mingle with her.

He had to end these sublime moments before he...expressed how moved he was by them, shattering them instead.

He first had to try to tell her what her belief meant to him. "Your trust in me is a privilege and a responsibility that I will always nurture with pride and pleasure."

Her gaze suddenly escaped his, flowed down his body.

By the time they rose back, he was hard all over. Thankfully, her eyes were intent on his, full of contemplation.

"Though you're so big, with no doubt proportionate strength, it never occurred to me you'd be that capable of physical violence."

The vice that had released his heart suddenly clamped around it again. "Does this...disturb you?"

Her laugh rang out. "Hello? Have you met me? It *thrills* me. I would have loved to see you decimate a few thugs and neuter some bullies."

His hands, his whole being itched, ached. He just wanted to squeeze the hell out of her. He wanted to contain her, assimilate her and never let her go again.

He again held back with all he had, then drawled, "And to think something so minuscule could be so bloodthirsty."

She grinned impishly. "You've got a lot to learn about just what this deceptive exterior hides, big man."

Though her words tickled him and her smile was unfettered, he was still unsettled. "Is it really no problem for you to change your perception of me from someone who's too civilized to use his brute strength to someone who relishes physical violence?"

She shook her head, her long, thick hair falling over her slight shoulders down to her waist. "I don't believe you 'relish' it, but you'll always do 'what works best.' At the time, violence was the one thing that would keep the sharks away. So you used it, and to maximum efficiency, as is your way with everything. I'm only lamenting that there's no video documentation of those events for *me* to cheer over."

The delight she always struck in his heart overflowed in an unbridled guffaw. "I can just see you, grabbing the popcorn and hollering at the screen for more gore. But I might be able to do something about your desire to see me on a rampage. I can pull some strings at the prison and get some surveillance-camera footage."

She jumped up to her knees on the couch, nimble and keen as a cat. "Yes, yes, please!"

"Uh…I'm already regretting making the offer. You might think you can withstand what you'd see, but it was no staged fight like those you see on TV. There was no showmanship involved, just brutality with only the intent to survive at whatever cost."

She tucked her legs as if she was starting a meditation session, her gaze ultraserious. "That only makes it even more imperative to see it, Aram. It was the ugliest, harshest, most humiliating test you've ever endured and your deepest scar. I need to experience it in more than imagination, even if in the cold distance of past images, so I'd be able to share it with you in the most profound way I need to."

Stirred through to his soul, he swallowed a jagged lump of gratitude. "You just have to want it and it's done."

"Oh, I so want it. Thank you." Before he pounced with a thank-*you,* she probed, "You've really been needing to confide this all this time. Why didn't you?"

She was killing him with her ability to see right into his depths. She was reviving him with it, reanimating him.

"I was…ashamed. Of my weakness and stupidity. I wanted to prove to Shaheen and his brothers that I didn't need their help after all, that I'd make it on my own. And I got myself involved in something that looked too good to be true because I was in such a hurry to do it. And I paid the price."

She tilted her head to the side, as if to look at him from another perspective. "I can't even imagine what it was like. When you were arrested, when you were sentenced, when you realized you might have destroyed your future, maybe even tainted that of your family. That year in prison…"

He wanted to tell her that she was imagining it just fine, that her compassion was dissipating the lingering darkness of that period, erasing the scars it had left behind. But his throat was closed, his voice gone.

The empathy in her gaze rose until it razed him. "But I can understand the ordeal was a link in the chain that led to your eventual decline. Not the experience itself as much as the reinforcement of your segregation. You couldn't share such a life-changing experience with your loved ones, mainly because you wanted to protect them from the agony they would have felt on your behalf. But that very inability to bare your soul to them made you pull further away emotionally, and actually exacerbated your solitude."

When he finally found his voice, it was a hoarse, ragged whisper. "See? You do know everything."

Her eyes gentled even more. "Not everything. I'm still unable to fill some spaces. You were going strong for years after your imprisonment. Was that only *halawet el roh?*"

Literally sweetness of the soul. What was said in Zohayd to describe a state of deceptive vigor, a clinging to life when warding off inevitable deterioration or death.

"Now that you mention it, that's the best explanation. I came out of prison with a rabid drive to wipe out what happened, to right my path, to make up for lost time. I guess I was trying to run hard and fast enough to escape the memories, to accumulate enough success and security to fix the chasm the experience had ripped inside me and that threatened to tear me open at any moment."

Her eyes now soothed him, had him almost begging her to let her hand join in their caress. "Johara told me you were at the peak of fitness, at least physically, three years ago when you attended their wedding in Zohayd. From her observations, you started deteriorating about two years ago. Was there a triggering event? Like when it sank in that they were a family now? Did their togetherness—especially with your parents' reconciliation—leave you feeling more alone than ever?"

He squeezed his eyes on a spasm of poignancy. "You get me so completely. You get me better than I get myself."

Wryness touched her lips. "It was Johara who gave me the code to decipher your hieroglyphics when she said she felt as if her and Shaheen's intimacy left you unable to connect with either of them on the same level as you used to."

"She's probably right. But it's not only my own hang-ups. Neither of them has enough left to devote to anyone else. A love like that fills up your being. And then there's the massive emotional investment in Gharam and their coming baby."

Something inscrutable came into her eyes, intensifying their already absolute darkness.

Seeming to shake herself out of it, whatever it was, she continued searching his recesses. "So *was* there a triggering physical event? That made your health start to deteriorate?"

"Nothing specific. I just started being unable to sleep

well, to eat as I should. Everything became harder, took longer and I did it worse. Then each time I got even a headache or caught a cold, it took me ages to bounce back. My focus, my stamina, my immunity were just shot. I guess my whole being was disintegrating."

"But you're back in tip-top shape now."

It was a question, not a statement, worry tingeing it.

He let his gaze cup her elfin face in lieu of his hands. "I've never been better. And it's thanks to you."

Her smile faltered as she again waved his assertion away. "There you go again, crediting me with miracles."

"You *are* a miracle. My Minute Miracle. Not that size has anything to do with your effect. *That's* supreme."

He jumped to his feet, feeling younger and more alive than he'd ever felt, needing to dive headfirst into the world, doing everything under the sun with her. He rushed to fetch their jackets, then dashed back to her. "Let's go run in the rain. Then let's hop on my jet and go have breakfast anywhere you want. Europe. South America. Australia. Anywhere."

She donned her jacket and ran after him out of the apartment with just as much zeal. "How about the moon?"

Delighted at her willingness to oblige him in whatever he got it in his mind to say or do, he said, "If it's what you want, then I'll make it happen."

She pulled one of those funny faces that he adored. "And I wouldn't put it past you, too. Nah...I'll settle for something on terra firma. And close by. I have to work in the morning, even if you're so big and important now you no longer have to."

He consulted his watch. "If we leave for Barbados in an hour, I'll have you at work by ten."

Her disbelief lasted only moments before mischief and excitement replaced it. "You're on."

Nine

"It's…good to hear your voice, Father."

Kanza hated that hesitation in her voice. Whatever her father's faults, she did love him. Did miss him.

Yeah. She did. But, and it was a huge but, after ten minutes of basking in the nostalgia of early and oblivious childhood when her father had been her hero, she always thudded back to reality and was ready not to see him again for months.

"It's great to hear yours, *ya bnayti*."

His calling her *my daughter,* instead of bestowing a personalized greeting with her name included, annoyed her. He called his other eight daughters that, with the same indiscrimination. She thought he used it most times because he forgot the name of the one he was talking to.

Curbing her irritation, and knowing her father never called unless he had something to ask of her, she said, "Anything I can do for you, Father?"

"*Ya Ullah,* yes. Only you can help me now, *ya bnayti*. I need you to come back to Zohayd at once."

Ten minutes later, she sat staring numbly into space.

She'd tried to wriggle out of saying yes. She'd failed.

She was really going back to Zohayd. Tonight.

Her father had begged her to board the first flight to Zohayd. Beyond confirming that no one was dead or severely injured, he'd said no more about why he needed her back so urgently.

She reserved a ticket online, then packed a few essentials. She wouldn't stay a minute longer than necessary.

Not that there was a reason to hurry back.

Not from the evidence of the past two weeks anyway.

It had been then, six weeks after that magical time in Aram's new apartment and the breakfast in Barbados, that Aram had suddenly become insanely busy. He'd neglected his work so much that the accumulation had become critical.

She understood. Of *course,* she did. She knew exactly how many people depended on him, what kind of money rode on his presence and expertise. She'd been neglecting her work, too, but Johara had picked up the slack, and she was not so indispensable that her absence would cause the same widespread ripples his had. She appreciated this fully. Mentally. But otherwise...

The fact was, he'd spoiled her. She'd gotten reliant on seeing him each and every day, on being able to pick up the phone, day or night, and he'd be eager and willing to grant her every wish, to be there with her at no notice. When that had suddenly come to an abrupt end, she'd gone into withdrawal.

God. She'd turned into one of those clingy, needy females. At least in her own mind and psyche. Outwardly, she was her devil-may-care self. At least, she hoped she was.

But she was something else, too. Moronic. The man had a life outside her, even if for three months straight it had seemed as if he didn't. She'd known real life would reassert itself at one point. So she should stop whining *now.*

And now that she thought of it without self-pity, going to Zohayd was a good thing. She'd been twiddling her thumbs until she and Johara started the next project. And by the time she was back, he would have sorted himself enough to be able to see her again—at least more than he had the past two weeks.

She speed-dialed his number. The voice she now lived to hear poured into her brain after the second ring.

"Kanza—a moment please..." His voice was muffled as he talked to someone.

Feeling guilty for interrupting him when he'd told her he wouldn't have a free moment before seven, she rushed on. "I just wanted to tell you I'm going home in a couple of hours."

More muffled words, then he came back to her. "That's fantastic. About time."

That she hadn't expected. "It—it is?"

"Sure, it is. Listen, Kanza, I'm sorry, but I *have* to finish this before the Saudi Stock Exchange opens. 'Bye now."

Then he hung up.

She stared at the phone.

Last night, he'd said he'd see her later tonight. But she'd just told him she wouldn't be able to see him because she was traveling and he'd sounded...glad?

Had she unwittingly let her disappointment show when he'd been unable to see her for the past two weeks, and he now thought it was a good idea if she did something other than wait for him until his preoccupation lightened and he could see her again?

But he hadn't even asked why she was going or how long she'd stay. Sure, he'd been in a hurry, but he could have said something other than *fantastic* or *about time*. He could have said he'd call later to get details.

So was it possible he was just glad to get her off his back? Could it be that what she'd thought were unfounded feelings of impending loss had just been premonition? Was the magical interlude with him really over?

She'd known from the start he'd just needed someone to help him through the worst slump in his life. Now that he was over it, was he over his need for her?

That made sense. Terrible sense. And it was only expected. She'd dreaded that day, but she'd known it would come. She'd just kept hoping it would not come so soon. She wasn't ready to give him up yet.

But when would she ever be? How could she ever be… when she loved him?

Suddenly a sob tore out of her. Then another, and another until she was bent over, tears raining on the ground, unable to contain the torrent of anguish anymore.

She loved him.

She would forever love him.

And she would have remained his friend forever, asking nothing more but to have the pleasure and privilege of his nearness, of his appreciation, of his completion. Of his need.

But it seemed he no longer needed her.

Now he'd recede, but never really end it as he would have with a lover. She would see him again and again whenever life threw them together. And each time, he'd expect her to be his buddy, would chat and tease and reminisce and not realize that she missed him like an amputee would a limb.

Maybe going to Zohayd now *was* a blessing in disguise.

Maybe she should stay until he totally forgot about her.

The moment Aram finished his last memo for the night, he pounced on his phone to call Kanza. Before he did, Shaheen walked into his office.

A groan escaped him that he had to postpone the call—and seeing her—for the length of Shaheen's visit.

His brother-in-law whistled. "*Ya Ullah,* you missed me *that* much?"

Aram winced. His impatience must be emblazoned across his whole body. And he'd been totally neglecting his friend as of late. But he'd been reserving every hour, every moment, every spare breath for Kanza.

"Actually I do miss you, but—" he groaned again, ran his fingers through his hair "—you know how it is."

Shaheen laughed. *"Menn la'ah ahbaboh nessi ashaboh."*
He who finds his loved ones forgets his friends.

He refused to comment on Shaheen's backhanded reference to Kanza as his loved one. "As much as I'd love to indulge your curiosity, Shaheen, I have to go to Kanza now. Let's get together some other time. Maybe I'll bring Kanza over to your home, hmm?"

Shaheen blinked in surprise. "You're going to Zohayd?"

Aram scowled. "Now, where did that come from? Why should I go to Zohayd?"

"Because you said that you're going to Kanza, who's on her way to Zohayd right now."

Aram glanced at his watch, then out of the jet's window, then back at his watch.

Had it always taken that long to get to Zohayd?

It felt as if it had been a day since he'd boarded his jet—barely an hour after Shaheen had said Kanza was heading there.

He was still reverberating with disbelief. With…panic.

His condition had been worsening since it had sunk in that the "home" Kanza had meant was Zohayd. According to Johara, Kanza was returning there at her father's urgent demand. Kanza herself didn't know why. Shaheen hadn't been able to understand why he'd be so agitated that she was visiting her family and would probably be back in a few days.

But he'd been unable to listen, to Shaheen or the voice of reason. Nothing had mattered but one thing.

The need to go after her.

A tornado was tearing through him. His gut told him something was wrong. Terribly wrong.

For how could she go like that without saying goodbye?

Even if she had to rush, even if he'd been swamped, the Kanza he knew would have let him see her before separation was imposed on them.

So why hadn't she? Why hadn't she made it clear where she was going? If he'd known, he would have rushed to her, would have paid the millions that would have been lost for a chance to see her even for a few minutes before she left. She had to know he would have. So why hadn't she given him the chance to? Hadn't it been as necessary for her to see him this last time as it was for him?

Was he not as necessary to her as she was to him?

He'd long been forced to believe his necessity to her differed from hers to him. He'd thought that as long as the intimacy remained the same, he'd just have to live with the fact that its…texture wasn't what he now yearned for.

But what if he was losing even that? What if not saying goodbye now meant that she *could* eventually say goodbye for real? What if that day was even closer than his worst nightmares?

What if that day was here?

He couldn't even face that possibility. He'd lost his solitariness from the first time he'd seen her. She'd proceeded to strip him of his self-containment, his autonomy. He'd known isolation. But he hadn't realized what loneliness was until he'd heard from Shaheen that she'd left.

She'd become more than vital to him. She'd become… home.

What if he could never be anything like that to her?

What if he caught up with her in Zohayd and she only thought he was out of his mind hurtling after her like that?

Maybe he was out of his mind. Maybe everything he'd just churned himself over had no basis in fact. Maybe…

His cell phone rang. He fumbled with it, his fingers going numb with brutal anticipation. *Kanza.* She'd tell him why she hadn't said goodbye. And he'd tell her he'd be with her in a couple of hours and she could say it to his face.

The next moment disappointment crashed through him. Johara.

He couldn't hold back his growl. "What is it, Johara?"

A silent beat. "Uh...don't kill the messenger, okay?"

"What the hell does that mean? Jo, I'm really not in any condition to have a nice, civil conversation right now. For both our sakes, just leave me alone."

"I'm sorry, Aram, but I really think you need to know, so you'd be prepared."

"Know what? Be prepared for what?" A thousand dreads swooped down on him, each one shrieking Kanza, Kanza, *Kanza*... "Just spit it out!"

"I just got off the phone with Kanza's father. He said he needed me to know as Kanza's best friend that Prince Kareem Aal Kahlawi has asked for her hand in marriage."

Kanza thought it was inevitable.

She would end up killing someone.

For now, storming through her father's house, slamming her old bedroom door behind her was all the venting she could do.

She leaned against it, letting out a furious shriek.

Of all the self-involved, self-serving, unfeeling... Argh!

To think that was why her father had dragged her back here!

Couldn't she kill him? And her sisters? Just a little bit...?

Her whole body lurched forward, every nerve firing at once.

She stopped. Moving. Breathing. Even her heart slowed down. Each boom so hard her ears rang.

That must be it. Why she thought she'd heard...

"Kanza."

Aram.

God. She was starting to hear things. Hear him. When he was seven thousand miles away. This was beyond pathetic....

"Kanza. I know you're there."

Okay. She wasn't *that* pathetic.

"I saw you tearing out of the living room, saw you going

up. I know this is your room. I know you're in there now. Come to the window. *Now,* Kanza."

That last "now" catapulted her to the French doors. She barely stopped before she shot over the balcony's balustrade.

And standing down there, among the shrubs below, in all his mind-blowing glory, was Aram.

Azure bolts arced from his eyes and a wounded lion's growl came from his lips. "What are you *doing* here?"

Her head spun at the brunt of his beauty under Zohayd's declining sun and the absurdity of his question.

She blinked, as if it would reboot her brain. "What are *you* doing here? In Zohayd? And standing beneath my window?"

He stuck his fists at his hips. He looked…angry? And agitated. Why? "What does it look like? I'm here to see you."

She shook her head, confusion deepening. He must have left New York just a few hours after she had. Had he come all the way here to find out why she had? After he'd basically told her to scram? Why not just call? What did it all mean?

Okay. With the upheaval of this past day, her brain was on the fritz. She could no longer attempt to make any sense of it.

She pinched the bridge of her nose. "Well, you saw me. Now go away before all my family comes out and finds you here. With the way you've been shouting, they must be on their way."

He widened his stance, face adamant planes and ruthless slashes. "If you don't want them to see me, come down."

"I can't. If I go down and try to walk through the front door, I'll have twenty females on my case…and I don't want the ulcer I've acquired in the last hours to rupture."

"Then *climb* down."

That last whisper could have sandpapered the manor's facade. "Okay, Aram, I know you're crazy, but even in your insanity you can see that the last foothold is twenty feet above splat level."

He shrugged. "Fifteen max. I'll catch you."

Closing her mouth before it caught one of the birds zooming back to their nests at the approach of sunset, she echoed his pose, fists on hips. "If you want to reenact Shaheen's stunt with Johara, I have to remind you that she was six at the time."

That shrug again. "You're not that much bigger now."

She coughed a chagrined laugh. "Why, thanks. Just what every grown woman wants to hear."

He sighed. "I meant the ratio of your size to mine, compared to that of fourteen-year-old Shaheen to six-year-old Johara." He suddenly snarled again, his eyes blazing. "Stop arguing. I can catch you, easy. You know I've been exercising."

Yeah, she knew. She'd attended many a mind-scrambling session, seen what he looked like with minimal clothing, flexing, bulging, sweating, flooding a mile's radius with premium, lethal testosterone.

"But even in my worst days, I would have been able to catch you. I always knew I was that big for a reason, but I just never knew what it was. Now I know. It's so I could catch you."

Her mouth dropped open again.

What that man kept *saying*.

What would he say when he was actually in love…?

That thought made her feel like jumping off the balcony—and not so he could catch her.

She inhaled a steadying, sanity-laced breath. "Oh, all right. Just because I know you'll stand there until I do. Or worse, barge into the house to come up here and have a houseful of your old fans pick your bones. I hope you know I'm doing this to save your gorgeous hide."

His smile was terse. "Yes, of course. I'm, as always, eternally indebted to you. Now hurry."

Mumbling under her breath about him being a hulk-sized brat who expected to get his way in everything, she took one last bracing breath and climbed over the balustrade.

As she inched down over the steplike ledges, he kept a running encouragement. "You're doing fine. Don't look down. I'm right here."

Slipping, she clung to the building, wailed, "Shut *up,* Aram. God, I can't believe what you can talk me into."

He just kept going. "Keep your body firm, not tense, okay? Now let go." When she hesitated, his voice suddenly dropped into the darkest reaches of hypnosis. "Don't worry, I'll catch you, *ya kanzi.*"

My treasure.

All her nerves unraveled. She plummeted.

Her plunge came to a jarring, if firm and secure, end.

He'd caught her. Easy, as he'd said. As if he'd snatched her from a three-foot drop. And she was staring up into those vivid, luminescent eyes that now filled her existence.

Without one more word, he swept her along through the manicured grounds and out of her father's estate.

She reeled. Not from the drop, but from her first contact with him. His flesh pressed to hers, his warmth enveloping her, his strength cocooning her. Being in his arms, even if in this context, was like…like…going home.

Even if the feeling was imaginary, she'd savor it. He was here, for whatever reason, and their…closeness wasn't over.

Not yet.

She let go, let him take her wherever he would.

Aram brooded at Kanza as she walked one step ahead.

He could barely let her be this far away. He'd clutched her all the way out of her father's estate, almost unable to let her go to put her into the car. As if by agreement, they hadn't said anything during the drive. But it hadn't been the companionable silence they'd perfected. By the time they'd arrived, he'd expended his decimated willpower so he wouldn't roar, demanding she tell him what was wrong.

She turned every few steps, as if to check if he was maintaining the same distance. Her glances felt like the sustenance that would save him from starvation. But they didn't soothe him as they'd always done. There was something in them that sent his senses haywire. Something...wary.

He couldn't bear to interpret this. Any interpretation was just too mutilating. And could be dead wrong anyway. So he wouldn't even try.

She stopped at the railings of the upper-floor terrace, turning to him. "Don't tell me you bought this villa in your half hour in Zohayd before popping up beneath my window."

He barely caught back a groan of relief. Her voice. Her teasing. God, he *needed* them.

"Why? Do you think I'm not crazy enough to do it?"

Her smile resembled her usual ones. But not quite. "Excellent point. Since you're crazier, you might have also bought the sea and desert in a ten-mile radius."

A laugh caught in his throat, broke against the spastic barrier of tension. "It's Shaheen's. Now tell me what the hell you're doing here. And why you left without telling me."

Her eyes got even more enormous. "I did tell you."

He threw his arms wide in frustration. "How was I supposed to know you meant Zohayd when you said home?"

"Uh...is this a new crisis? What else could I have meant?"

"Your old New York apartment, of course. The one you said felt like home, the one I got you back the lease for. I thought you were finally ready to move there again."

"That's why you thought it fantastic when I said I was going home," she said, as if to herself. "You thought it was about time I was down the street from you."

He gaped at her. "Are you *nuts?* You thought I would *actually* think it fantastic for you to come out here and leave me alone in New York? Contrary to popular belief, I'm not that evolved. I might support your doing something that doesn't involve me if it makes you happy, even accept that it could take you away from me—for a little while—but be okay, let alone ecstatic about it? No way."

Her eyes kept widening with his every word. At his last bark, her smile flashed back to its unbridled vivacity.

"Thanks for letting me know the extent of your evolution. Now quit snarling at me. I have a big enough headache being saddled with making decisions for more than you now, in not only one but *two* weddings."

It felt as if a missile had hit him.

No. She couldn't be talking about a wedding already. He couldn't allow it. He wouldn't. He'd…

Two weddings?

His rumble was that of a beast bewildered with too many blows. "What the hell are you talking about?"

"My last two unmarried sisters' weddings. With each from a different mother and with how things are in Zohayd where weddings are battlefields, they've reached a standoff with each other and with their bridegrooms' families. It seems there's more hope of ending a war than reaching an agreement on the details of the weddings. Enter me—what Father thinks is his only hope of defusing the situation."

He frowned. "Why you?"

Her lips twisted whimsically. "Because I'm what Father calls the 'neutral zone.' With me as the one daughter of the woman who gave birth to me then ran off with a big chunk of my father's wealth, I am the one who has always given him no trouble, having no mother to harass him on my behalf. And being stuck as the middle sister between eight half sisters, four each from a stepmother, it made me the one in his brood of nine female offspring that no one is jealous of, therefore not unreasonably contentious with." She sighed dramatically. "I was always dragged to referee, because both sides don't consider me a player in the family power games at all. Now Father has recruited me to get all these hysterical females off his back and hopefully get those weddings under way and over with."

What about the groom who proposed to you? That... prince? *Why aren't you telling me about him?*

The questions backlashed in his chest. He couldn't give this preposterous subject credence by even mentioning it.

There was only one thing to ask now.

"Is it me?"

She stared up at him, standing against the winter sunset's backdrop, its fire reflecting gold on her skin and striking flames from the depths of her onyx eyes and the thick mahogany satin tresses that undulated around her in the breeze. She was the embodiment of his every taste and desire and aspiration. And the picture of incomprehension.

But he could no longer afford the luxury of caution. Not when he had the grenade of that...*prince's*...proposal lying there between them. Not when letting the status quo continue could give it a chance to explode and cost him everything.

He halved the step he'd been keeping between them. "You're the only one who's ever told me the whole truth, Kanza. I need you to give it to me now."

Her gaze flickered, but she only nodded. She would give him that truth. Always.

And that truth might end his world.

But he had to have it. "I believe in pure friendship between a man and a woman. But when they share... everything, I can't see how there'd be no physical attraction at all. So, again, is it me? Or are you generally not interested?"

No total truth came from her. Just total astonishment.

He groaned. "It's clear this has never even crossed your mind. And I've been content with what we share, delighted our friendship is rooted in intellectual and spiritual harmony—and I was willing to wait forever for anything else. But I feel I don't have forever anymore. And I can't live with the idea that maybe you just aren't aware of the possibilities, that if I can persuade you to give it a try, you might…not hate it."

Still nothing. Nothing but gaping.

And he put his worst fear into words. "Were you stating your personal preferences that first night? When you said I was disgustingly pretty? Do your tastes run toward something, I don't know, rougher or softer or just not…this?" He made a tense gesture at his face, his body. "Do you have an ideal of masculinity and I'm just not it?"

Her cheeks and lips were now hectic rose. Her voice wavered. "Uh… I'm really not sure…"

Neither was he. If it would be even adequate between them. If he could even please her.

But he felt everything for her, wanted everything with her, so he had to try.

He reached for her, cupped her precious head and gazed down into her shocked eyes. "There's one way to make sure."

Then he swooped down and took her lips.

At the first contact with her flesh, the first flay of her breath, a thousand volts crackled between them, unleashing everything inside him in a tidal wave.

Lashed by the ferocity of his response and immediacy of her surrender, he captured her dainty lower lip in a growling bite, stilling its tremors, attempting to moderate his greed. She only cried out, arched against him and opened her lips wider. And her taste inundated him.

God…her *taste*. He'd imagined but couldn't have possibly anticipated her unimaginable sweetness. Or the perfume of her breath or the sensory overload of her feel. Or what it would all do to him. Everything about her mixed in an aphrodisiac, a hallucinogen that eddied in his arteries and pounded through his system, snapping the tethers of his sanity.

He could have held back from acting on his insanity, could have moderated his onslaught if not for the way she melted against him, blasting away all doubts about her capacity for passion in the inferno of her response. Her moans and whimpers urged him on to take his possession from tasting to clinging to wrenching.

His hands shook with urgency as he gathered her thighs, opened her around his bulk, pinned her against the railings with the force of his hunger. Plundering her with his tongue, he drove inside her mouth, thrust against her heat, losing rhythm in the wildness, losing his mind.

But even without a mind or will, his love for this irreplaceable being was far more potent than even his will to live. She did mean more than life to him.

Tearing out of their merging, rumbling at the sting of separation, he looked down at the overpowering sight of the woman trembling in his arms. "Do you want this, Kanza? Do you want *me?*"

Her dark eyes scorched him with what he'd never dreamed of seeing in them: drugged sensuality and surrender. Then they squeezed in languorous acquiescence.

He needed more. A full disclosure, a knowing consent.

"I will take everything you have, devour everything you are, give you all of me. Do you understand? Is this what you want? What you need? *Everything* with me, now?"

His heart faltered, afraid to beat, waiting for her verdict. Then its valves almost burst as her parted, passion-swollen lips quivered on a ragged, drawn-out sigh.

A simple, devastating, "Yes."

Ten

Kanza heard herself moaning "yes" to Aram as if from the depths of a dream. What *had* to be a dream.

For how could this be reality? How could she be in Aram's arms? How could it be that he'd been devouring her and was now asking for more, for everything?

The only reason she believed it was real was that no dream could be this intense, this incredible. And because no dream of hers about him had been anything like this.

In her wildest fantasies, Aram, her indulgent friend, had been gentle in his approach, tender in his passion.

But the Aram she'd known was gone. In his place was a marauder: wild, almost rough and barely holding back to make certain she wanted his invasion and sanctioned his ferocity.

And she did. Oh, how she did. She'd said yes. Couldn't have said more. She could barely hold on to consciousness as she found herself swept up in the throes of his unexpected, shocking passion. The thrill of his dominance, the starkness of his lust tampered with everything that powered her, body and being. Her brain waves blipped, her heartbeat plunged into arrhythmia, her every cell swelled, throbbed, screamed for his possession and assuagement.

She'd thought she'd been aroused around him. Now she knew what arousal was. This mindlessness, this avalanche of sensations, this need to be conquered, dominated, ravished. By him, only him.

Almost swooning with the force of need, she delighted in openly devouring him, indulging her greed for his splendor. He loomed above her, the fiery palette of the horizon framing his bulk, accentuating his size, setting his beauty ablaze. The tempest in his eyes was precariously checked. He was giving her one last chance to recant her surrender. Before he devastated her.

She would die if he didn't.

The only confirmation she was capable of was to melt back into his embrace, arching against him in fuller surrender.

Growling something under his breath, he bent toward her. Thinking he'd scoop her up into his arms, carry her inside and take full possession of her, she felt shock reverberate when he started undoing her shirt. He planned to make love to her out here!

There was no one around in what looked like a hundred-mile radius, but she still squirmed. One arm firmed around her only enough to still her as his other hand drifted up her body and behind her to unclasp her bra. The relief of pressure on her swollen flesh buckled her legs.

He held her up, his eyes roving her body in fierce greed as he rid her of her jacket, shirt and bra. The moment her breasts spilled out, he bared his teeth, his lips emitting a soft snarl of hunger. Before she could beg for those lips and teeth on her, his hand undid her pants. She gaped as he dropped to his knees, spanning her hips in his hands' girdle of fire; his fingers hooked into both pants and panties and swept both off her, along with her shoes.

Suddenly his hands reversed their path, inflaming her flesh, rendering her breathless, and he stilled an inch from her core.

She shook—and not with cold. If it wasn't for the cooling air, she might have spontaneously combusted.

Then he lit her fuse, raising eyes like incendiary precious stones. *"Ma koll hada'l jamaal? Kaif konti tekhfeeh?"*

Hearing him raggedly speaking Arabic, asking how she had hidden all this beauty, made her writhe. "Aram... please..."

"Aih...I'll please you, *ya kanzi."* His face pressed to her thighs, her abdomen, his lips opening over her quivering flesh, sucking, nibbling everywhere like a starving man who didn't know where to start his feast. Her fingers convulsed in his silky hair, pressed his face to her flesh in an ecstasy of torment, unable to bear the stimulation, unable to get enough. He took her breasts in hands that trembled, pressed them, cradled them, kneaded and nuzzled them as if they were the most amazing things he'd ever felt. Tears broke through her fugue of arousal. "Please, Aram..."

He closed his eyes as if in pain and buried his face in her breasts, inhaling her, opening his mouth over her taut flesh, testing and tasting, lavishing her with his teeth and tongue. *"Sehr, jonoon, ehsasek, reehtek, taamek..."*

Magic, madness, your feel, your scent, your taste...

Her mind unraveled with every squeeze, each rub and nip and probe, each with the exact force, the exact roughness to extract maximum pleasure from her every nerve ending. He layered sensation with each press and bite until she felt devoured, set aflame. Something inside her was charring.

Her undulations against him became feverish, her clamoring flesh seeking any part of him in mindless pursuit of relief. Her begging became a litany until he dragged an electric hand between her thighs, tormenting his way to her core. The heel of his thumb delved between her outer lips at the same moment the damp furnace of his mouth finally clamped over one of the nipples that screamed for his possession. Sensations slashed her nerves.

Supporting her collapsing weight with an arm around

her hips, he slid two fingers between her molten inner lips, stilling at her entrance. "I didn't think that I'd ever see you like this, open for me, on fire, hunger shaking you apart, that I would be able to pleasure you like this...."

He spread her legs, placed one after the other over his shoulders, opening her core for his pleasure and possession. Her moans now merged into an incessant sound of suffering.

He inhaled her again, rumbling like a lion maddened at the scent of his female in heat, as she was. Then he blew a gust of acute sensation over the knot where her nerves converged. She bucked, her plea choking. It became a shriek when he pumped a finger inside her in a slow, slow glide. Sunset turned to darkest night as she convulsed, pleasure slamming through her in desperate surges.

Her sight burst back to an image from a fantasy. Aram, fully clothed, kneeling between her legs...her, naked, splayed open over his shoulders, amidst an empty planet all their own.

And he'd made her climax with one touch.

Among the mass of aftershocks, she felt his finger, still inside her, pumping...beckoning. Her gasp tore through her lungs as his tongue joined in, licked from where his finger was buried inside her upward, circling her bud. Each glide and graze and pull and thrust sent hotter lances skewering through her as if she hadn't just had the most intense orgasm of her life. It was only when she sobbed, bucked, pressed her burning flesh to his mouth, opening herself fully to his double assault, that his lips locked on her core and really gave it to her, had her quaking and screaming with an even more violent release.

She tumbled from the explosive peak, drained, sated. Stupefied. What had just happened?

Her drugged eyes sought his, as if for answers.

Even in the receding sunset they glowed azure, heavy with hunger and satisfaction. "You better have really en-

joyed this, because I'm now addicted to your taste and pleasure."

Something tightened inside her until it became almost
painful. She was flabbergasted to recognize it as an even
fiercer arousal. Her satisfaction had lasted only a minute,
and now she was even hungrier. No. Something else she'd
never felt before. Empty. As if there was a gnawing void inside her that demanded to be filled. By him. Only ever him.

She confessed it all to him. "The pleasure you gave me
is nothing like I ever imagined. But I hope you're not thinking of indulging your addiction again. I want pleasure *with*
you."

All lightness drained from his eyes as he reached for
her again. He cupped her, then squeezed her mound pos-
sessively, desensitizing her, the ferocious conqueror flaring
back to life. "And you will have it. I'll ride you to ecstasy
until you can't beg for more."

Her senses swam with the force of anticipation, with the
searing delight of his sensual threat. Her heart went haywire
as he swept her up in his arms and headed inside.

In minutes, he entered a huge, tastefully furnished suite
with marble floors, Persian carpets and soaring ceilings.
At the thought that it must be Johara and Shaheen's master
suite, a flush engulfed her body.

A gigantic circular bed draped in chocolate satin spread
beneath a domed skylight that glowed with the last tendrils
of sunset. Oil lamps blazed everywhere, swathing everything in a golden cast of mystery and intimacy.

Sinking deeper into sensory overload, she tried to drag
him down on top of her as he set her on the bed. He sowed
kisses over her face and clinging arms as he withdrew, then
stood back looking down at her.

His breath shuddered out. "Do you realize how incredible you are?" Elation, embarrassment, but mainly disbelief
gurgled in her throat. "Do you want to *see* how incredible
I find you?"

That got her voice working. "Yes, *please*."

She struggled up to her elbows as he started to strip, exposing each sculpted inch, showing her how incredible *he* was. Her eyes and mouth watered, her hands stung with the intensity of need to explore him, revel in him. He did have the body of a higher being. It was a miracle he wore clothes at all, didn't go through life flaunting his perfection and driving poor inferior mortals crazy with lust and envy.

Then he stepped out of his boxers, released the...proof of how incredible he found her, and a spike of craving and intimidation had her collapsing onto her back.

She'd felt he was big when he'd pressed against her what felt like a lifetime ago back on the terrace. But this... What if she couldn't accommodate him, couldn't please him?

But she had to give him everything, had to take all he had. Her heart would stop beating if he didn't make her his now. *Now.*

His muscles bunched with barely suppressed desire as he came down onto the bed, his hunger crashing over her in drowning waves. "No more waiting, *ya kanzi*. Now I take you. And you take me."

"Yes." She held out shaking arms as he surged over her, impacted her. She cried out, reveling in how her softness cushioned his hardness. Perfect. No, sublime.

He dragged her legs apart even as she opened them for him. He guided them around his waist, his eyes seeking hers, solicitous and tempestuous, his erection seeking her entrance. Finding it both hot and molten, he bathed himself in her flowing readiness in one teasing stroke from her bud to her opening.

On the next stroke, he growled his surrender, sank inside her, fierce and full.

The world detonated in a crimson flash and then disappeared.

In the darkness, she heard keening as if from the end of

a tunnel, and everything was shuddering. Then she went nerveless, collapsed beneath him in profound sensual shock.

She didn't know how long existence was condensed into the exquisite agony. Then the world surged back on her with a flood of sensations, none she'd ever felt before.

She found him turned to stone on top of her, face and body, eyes wild with worry. "It's your first time."

As she quivered inside and out, a laugh burst out, startling them both. "As if this is a surprise. Have you met me?"

The consternation gripping his face vanished and was replaced by sensuality and tenderness. "Oh, yes, I have. And oh, yes, it is—*you* are a surprise a second."

He started withdrawing from her depths.

The emptiness he left behind made her feel as if she'd implode. "No, don't go...don't stop...."

Throwing his head back, he squeezed his eyes. "I'm going nowhere. In consideration of your mint condition, I'm just trying to adjust from the fast and furious first time I had in mind to something that's slower and more leisurely...." He opened his eyes and gazed down at her. "I would only stop if you wanted me to."

Feeling the emptiness inside her threatening to engulf her, she thrust her hips upward, uncaring about the burning, even needing it. "I'd die if you stop."

His groan was as pained, as if she'd hurt him, too. "Stopping would probably finish me, as well. For real."

She thrust up again, crying out at the razing sensations as he stretched her beyond her limits. "You'd still stop... if I asked?"

A hand stabbed through her hair, dragged her down by its tether to the mattress, pinning her there for his ferocious proclamation. "I'd die if you asked."

Her heart gave a thunderclap inside her chest, shaking her like an earthquake. Tears she'd long repressed rose and poured from her very depths.

She surged up, clung to him, crushed herself against his

steel-fleshed body. "*Ya Ullah, ya* Aram, I'd die for you, too. Take me, leave no part of me, finish me. Don't hold back, hurt me until you make it better...."

"*Aih, ya kanzi,* I'll make it better. I'll make it so much better...." He cupped her hips in both hands, tilted them into a fully surrendering cradle for his then ever so slowly thrust himself to the hilt inside her.

It was beyond overwhelming, being occupied by him, being full of him. The reality of it, the sheer meaning and carnality of it, rocked her to the core. She collapsed, buried under the sensations.

He withdrew again, and she cried out at the unbearable loss, urged him to sink back into her. He resisted her writhing pleas, his shaft resting at her entrance before he plunged inside her again. She cried out a hot gust of passion, opening wider for him.

He kept her gaze prisoner as he watched her, gauging her reactions, adjusting his movements to her every gasp and moan and grimace, waiting for pleasure to submerge the pain. He kept her at a fever pitch, caressing her all over, suckling her breasts, draining her lips, raining wonder over her.

Then her body poured new readiness and pleasure over him, and he bent to drive his tongue inside her to his plunging rhythm, quickening both, until she felt a storm gathering inside her, felt she'd shatter if it broke.

His groan reverberated inside her mouth. "Perfection, *ya kanzi,* inside and out. Everything about you, with you."

Everything inside her tightened unbearably, her depths rippling around him, reaching for that elusive something that she felt she'd perish if she didn't have it, now, now.

She cried out, "Please, Aram, please, give it to me now, everything, *everything*...."

And he obliged her. Tilting her toward him, angling his thrusts, he drove into her with the exact force and speed she needed until he did it, shattered the coil of tension.

She heaved up beneath him so hard she raised them both in the air before crashing back to the bed. Convulsion after convulsion tore through her, clamped her around him. Her insides splintered on pleasure too sharp to register at first, then to bear, then to bear having it end.

Then she felt it, the moment his body caught the current of her desperation, a moment she'd replay in her memory forever. The sight and feel of him as he surrendered inside her to the ecstasy the searing sweetness of their union had brought him.

She peaked again as he threw his head back to roar his pleasure, feeding her convulsions with his own, pouring his release on her conflagration, jetting it inside her in hot surges until she felt completely and utterly filled.

Nothingness consumed her. For a moment, or an hour. Then she was surging back into her body, shaking, weeping, aftershocks demolishing what was left of her.

He *had* finished her, as she'd begged him to.

Then he was moving, and panic surged. She clung to him, unable to be apart from him now. He pressed soothing kisses to her swollen eyes, murmuring reassurance in that voice that strummed everything in her as he swept her around, took her over him, careful not to jar her, ensuring he remained inside her.

Then she was lying on top of him, the biggest part of her soul, satiated in ways she couldn't have imagined, at once reverberating with the enormity of the experience, and in perfect peace for the first time in her life.

She lay there merged with him, fused to him, awe overtaking her at everything that had happened.

Then her heart stopped thundering enough to let her breathe properly, to raise her head, to access her voice.

She heard herself asking, "What—what was...that?"

He stared up at her, his eyes just as dazed, his lips twitching into a smile. "I...have absolutely no idea. So *that* was sex, huh?"

"Hey...that's my line."

"Then you'll have to share it with me."

He withdrew from her depths carefully, making her realize that his erection hadn't subsided. His groan echoed her moan at the burn of separation. He soothed her, suckling her nipples until she wrapped herself around him again.

Unclasping her thighs from around him, he gave a distressed laugh. "You might think you're ready for another round of devastation, but trust me, you're not." He propped himself on his elbow, gathered her along his length, looking down at her with such sensual indulgence, her core flowed again. "It's merciful I had no idea it would be like this between us or I would have pounced on you long ago."

Feeling free and incredibly wanton, she rubbed her hands down his chest and twined her legs through his. "You should have."

He pressed into her, daunting arousal undiminished, body buzzing with vitality and dominance and lust. "I should make you pay for all these times you looked at me as if I was the brother you never had."

She arched, opening for his erection, needing him back inside her. "You should."

He chuckled, a dozen devils dancing in his incredible eyes. "Behave. You're too sore now. Give it an hour or two, then I'll...make you pay."

"Make me pay now. I loved the way you made me sore so much I almost died of pleasure. Make me sore again, Aram."

"And all this time I was afraid you were this sexless tomboy. Then after one kiss, that disguise you wear comes off and there's the most perfectly formed and uninhibited sex goddess beneath it all. You almost did kill me with pleasure, too."

"How about we flirt with mortal danger some more?"

"Sahrah."

Calling her *enchantress,* he crushed her in his arms and

thrust against her, sliding his erection up and down between the lips of her core, nudging her nub over and over.

The pleasure was unimaginable, built so quickly, a sweet, sharp burn in her blood, a tightening in her depths that now knew exactly how to unfurl and undo her. She opened herself wide for him, let him pleasure her this way.

Feeling the advance tremors of a magnificent orgasm strengthening, she undulated faster against him. Her pleas became shrieks as pleasure tore through her.

He pinned her beneath him as she thrashed, bucked, gliding over his hardness to the exact pressure and rhythm to drain her of the last spark of pleasure her body needed to discharge.

Then, kneeling between her splayed legs, he pumped his erection a few last times and roared as he climaxed over her.

She'd never seen anything as incredible, as fulfilling as watching him take his pleasure, rain it over the body he'd just owned and pleasured. The sight of his face in the grip of orgasm...

Then he was coming down half over her, mingling the beats of their booming hearts.

"Now I might have a heart attack thinking of all the times I was hard as steel around you and didn't realize this—" he made an explicit gesture at all of her spread beneath him, no doubt the very sight of abandon "—was in store for me if I just grabbed you and plunged inside you."

"Sorry for wasting your time being so oblivious."

His eyes were suddenly anxious, fervent. "You wasted nothing. I was just joking. I can never describe how grateful I am that we became friends first. I wouldn't change a second we had together, *ya kanzi*. Say you believe that."

She brought him down to her. "I believe *you*. Always. And I feel exactly the same. I wouldn't change a thing."

She didn't know anything more but that she was surrounded by passion and protection and sinking into a realm of absolute safety and contentment....

* * *

She woke up to the best sight on the planet.

A naked Aram standing at the window, gazing outside through a crack in the shutters. From the spear of light, she judged it must be almost sunset again. He'd woken her up twice through the night and day, showed her again and again that there was no limit to the pleasure they could share.

As if feeling her eyes on him, he turned at once, his smile the best dawn she'd ever witnessed.

She struggled to sit up in bed as he brought her a tray. Then he sat beside her, feeding her, cossetting her. The blatant intimacy in his eyes suddenly made her blush as everything they'd done together washed over her. She buried her flaming face in his chest.

He laughed out loud. "You're just unbearably cute being shy now after you blew my mind and every cell in my body with how responsive and uninhibited you are."

"It's a side effect of being transfigured, being a first timer," she mumbled against the velvet overlying steel of his skin and flesh.

"I was a first timer, too." She frowned up at him. "I *was* as untried as you in what passion—towering, consuming, earth-shattering passion—was like. So the experience was just as transformative for me as it was for you."

Joy overwhelmed her, had her burrowing deeper in his chest. "I'll take your word for it."

He chuckled, raised her face. "Now I want to take *your* word. That you won't do what your sisters did."

"What do you mean?"

"That you won't ask for a million contradictory details. That you won't do a thing to postpone our wedding."

Eleven

"What do you mean *wedding?*"

Aram's smile widened as Kanza sprang up, sitting like the cat she reminded him of, switching from bone-deep relaxation to full-on alertness in a heartbeat. Everything inside him knotted and hardened again as his gaze roved down that body that had taught him the meaning of "almost died of pleasure."

He reached an aching hand to cup that breast that filled it as if it was made to its measurement. "I mean our wedding."

"Our…" Her face scrunched as if with pain. "Stop it right this second, okay? Just…don't. *Don't,* Aram."

His heart contracted so hard it hurt. "Don't what?"

"Don't start with 'doing the right thing.'"

He frowned. "What the hell do you mean by that?"

She rose to her knees to scowl down at him. "I mean you think you've seduced a 'virgin,' had unprotected sex with her a handful of times and probably put a kid inside her by now. Having long been infected with Zohaydan conservatism, you think it's unquestionable that you have to marry me."

He rose to his knees, too, towering over her, needing to

overwhelm her and her faulty assumptions before this got any further. "If there is a kid in there, I'd want with every fiber of my being to be its father…."

"And that's no reason to get married."

He pressed on. "And to be the best friend, lover and husband of its mother for as long as I live…and if there's really a beyond, I'd do anything to have dibs on that, too."

The chagrined look in her eyes faltered. "Well, that only applies if there was actually a…kid. I assure you there is no possibility of one. It's the wrong time completely. So don't worry about that."

He reached for her, pressing her slim but luscious form to his length. "Does this look like a worried man to you?"

She leaned back over his arm, her eyes wary. "This looks like a…high man to me."

"I am. High on you, on the explosively passionate chain reaction we shared." He ground his erection harder into her belly, sensed her ready surrender. "And it's really bad news there isn't a possibility of a kid in there right now. I really, really want to put one in there. Or two. Or more."

Her eyes grew hooded. "What's the rush all of a sudden, about all that life-changing stuff?"

"I don't know." He bent to suckle her earlobe, nip it, before traveling down her neck and lower. "Maybe it's my biological clock. Turning forty does things to a man, y'know?"

She squirmed out of his arms, put a few inches' distance between them. "Since you'll live to a gorgeous, vital hundred, you're not even at the midpoint yet, so chill."

He slammed her back against him. "I don't *want* to chill. I've been chilling in a deep freeze all my life. Now that I've found out what burning in searing passion is like, I'll never want anything else but the scorching of your being. I love you, *ya kanzi,* I more than love you. I adore and worship you. *Ana aashagek.*"

She lurched so hard, she almost broke his hold.

"You—you do?"

He stared into her eyes, a skewer twisting in his gut at what filled them. God, that vulnerability!

Unable to bear that she'd feel that way, he caught her back, holding her in the persuasion of his hands and eyes. "How can you even doubt that I do?"

That precious blush that he'd seen only since last night blazed all over her body. "It's not you I doubt, I guess."

He squeezed her tighter, getting mad at her. "How can you doubt yourself? Are you nuts? Don't you know—"

"How incredible I am? No, not really. Not when it comes to you, anyway. I couldn't even dream that you could have emotions for me. That's why I kept it so strictly chummy. I didn't see how you'd look at me as a woman, thought that I must appear a 'sexless tomboy' to you."

"I was afraid *you* thought you were that. This wasn't how *I* saw you." He filled his hand with her round, firm buttock, pushed the evidence of how he saw her against her hot flesh.

As she undulated against him, her voice thickened. "I was never sexless where you were concerned."

"Don't go overboard now. You were totally so at the beginning. Probably till last night."

Her undulations became languorous, as if he was already inside her, thrusting her to a leisurely rhythm. "If you only knew the thoughts I had where you were concerned."

"And what kind of thoughts were those?"

She rubbed her breasts against him, her nipples grazing against his hair-roughened chest. "Feverishly licentious ones. At least I thought they were. You proved me very uncreative."

He crushed her against him to stop her movements. He had to or he'd be inside her again, and they wouldn't get this out of the way. "If you'd had thoughts of even wanting to hold my hand, you hid them well. Too well, damn it."

Her hands cupped his face, her eyes filling with such tenderness, such remembered pain. "I couldn't risk putting you on edge or having you pull back if you realized

I was just another woman who couldn't resist you. I was afraid it would mar our friendship, that I wouldn't be able to give you the companionship you needed if you started being careful around me. I couldn't bear it if you lost your spontaneity with me."

The fact that she'd held back for him, as he'd done for her, was just more proof of how right they were for one another. "When did you start feeling this way about me?"

"When I was around seventeen."

That flabbergasted him. "But you hated the sight of me!"

"I hated that in spite of all your magnificent qualities you seemed to be just another predictable male who'd go for the prettiest female, no matter that she had nothing more to recommend her. Then I hated that you also seemed so callous—you could be cruel to someone who was so out of your league. But mostly, I hated how you of all men made me feel, when I knew I couldn't even dream of you."

"I beg you, dream of me now," he groaned, burrowing his face into her neck. "Dream of a lifetime with me. Let yourself love me, *ya kanzi.*"

"I far more than love you, Aram. *Ana aashagak kaman.*"

To hear her say she felt the same, *eshg,* stronger than adoration, more selfless than love, hotter than passion, was everything. What he had been born for. For her.

Lowering her onto the bed, he gazed deep into her eyes as she wound herself around him. "I've been waiting for you since I was eighteen. And you had to go get born so much later, make me wait that much longer."

Tears streamed among unbridled smiles. "You can take all the waiting out on me."

Taking her lips, her breath, he pledged, "Oh, I will. How I will."

Floating back to her father's house, Kanza felt like a totally different woman from the one who'd left it over twenty-four hours ago.

She was so high on bliss that she let her family subject her to their drama with a smile. She might have spent three years living autonomously in New York, but once on Zohaydan soil, she must act the unmarried "girl," who could do whatever she wanted during "respectable hours" provided she spent the nights under her father's roof.

To shut them up, she told them of Aram's proposal.

Her news boggled everyone's mind. It seemed beyond their comprehension that she, the one undesirable family member they'd thought would die a spinster, hadn't gotten only one, but two incredible proposals in the space of two days. One from a prince, which she'd dared turn down on the spot, and the other from Aram, someone far bigger and better than any prince. It seemed totally unacceptable to her sisters and stepmothers that she'd marry the incomparable Aram of all men, when *they* had all settled for *far* lesser men.

At least Maysoon was absent, as usual, pursuing her latest escapades outside Zohayd and unconcerned with the rest of her family or their events. Kanza would at least be spared what would have been personal venom, with her history with Aram.

Feeling decidedly Cinderella-like, she thought it was poetic when her prince strolled in. Reading the situation accurately, Aram proceeded to give her family strokes. Showing them he couldn't keep his eyes or hands or even lips off her, he declared he wouldn't wait more than three days for their wedding. A wedding he'd finance from A to Z—unlike her sisters' grooms who divided costs—and that the nuptials would be held at the royal palace of Zohayd.

As her family reeled that Kanza would get a wedding that topped that of a member of the ruling family and in the royal palace, too—where most of them had rarely set foot—Aram took her father aside to discuss her *mahr*. As the dowry or "bride's price" was paid to the father, Aram let everyone hear that her father could name *any* number.

As his *shabkah* to Kanza, the bride's gift, he was writing his main business in her name.

Kanza let him deluge her in extravagant gestures and tumbled deeper in love with him. He was defending her against her family's insensitivity and honoring her in front of them and all of Zohayd by showing them there were no lengths he wouldn't go to for the privilege of her hand.

She'd later tell him that her *mahr* was his heart and her *shabkah* was his body.

But then, he already knew that.

Now that she was as rock-stable certain of his love as he was of hers, she was ready to marry him right there on the spot. Three days felt like such an eternity. Couldn't they just elope?

Kanza really wished they *had* eloped.

Preparing for the wedding, even though Aram had taken care of most of the arrangements, was nerve-racking.

At least now it would be over in a few hours.

If only it would start *already*. The hour until it did felt like forever. Not that anyone else seemed to think so. Everyone kept lamenting that they didn't have more time.

"It's a curse."

Maram, the queen of Zohayd, and Johara's sister-in-law, threw her hands in the air as she turned from sending two of her ladies-in-waiting for last-minute adjustments in Kanza's bridal procession's bouquets. The florist had sent white and yellow roses instead of the cream and pale gold Aram had ordered, which would go with all the gowns.

"No matter what—" Johara explained Maram's exclamation "—we end up preparing royal weddings in less and less time."

Kanza grinned at all the ladies present, still shell-shocked that all the women of the royal houses of Zohayd, Azmahar and even Judar were here to help prepare her wedding. "Take heart, everyone. This is only a *quasi*-royal wedding."

"It is a bona fide royal one around here, Kanza." That was Talia Aal Shalaan, Johara's other sister-in-law. "It's par for the course when you're a friend or relative to any of the royal family members. And you and Aram are both to so many of us. But this is an all-time crunch, and there is no earthshaking cause for the haste as there was in the other royal weddings we've rushed through preparing here."

"Aram can't wait." Johara giggled, winking to her mother, then to Kanza. "That *is* earthshaking."

Talia chuckled. "Another imperious man, huh? He'll fit right in with our men's Brotherhood of Bigheadedness."

Maram pretended severity. "Since this haste is only at his whim, this Aram of yours deserves to be punished."

"Oh, I'll punish him." Kanza chuckled, then blushed as Jacqueline Nazaryan, her future mother-in-law, blinked.

Man, she liked her a lot, but it would be a while until the poised swan of a French lady got used to Kanza's brashness.

Maram rolled her eyes. "And if he's anything like my Amjad, he'll love it. I applaud you for taming that one. I never saw Amjad bristle around another man as he does around Aram. A sign he's in a class of his own in being intractable."

"Oh, Aram is nothing of the sort...." Kanza caught herself and laughed. "*Now.* He told me how he locked horns with Amjad when he lived here, and I think it's because they *are* too alike."

Maram laughed. "Really? Someone who's actually similar to my Amjad? *That* I'd like to see. We might need to put him in a museum."

As the ladies joined in laughter, Carmen Aal Masood came in. Carmen was the event planner extraordinaire whose services Aram had enlisted in return for contributing an unnamed fortune to a few of her favorite charities, and the wife of the eldest Aal Masood brother, Farooq, who gave up the throne of Judar to marry her. The Aal Masoods were also Kanza's relatives from their Aal Ajmaan mother's side.

Yeah, it was all tangled up around here.

"So you ready to hop into your dress, Kanza?" Carmen said, carrying said dress in its wrapping.

Kanza sprang to her feet. "Am I! I can't wait to get this show on the road."

Lujayn, yet another of Johara's sisters-in-law, the wife of Shaheen's half brother Jalal, sighed. "At least you're eager for your wedding to start. Almost every lady here had a rocky start, and our weddings felt like the end of the world."

Farah, the wife of the second-eldest Judarian prince, Shehab Aal Masood, raised her hand. "I had my end of the world *before* the wedding. So I was among the minority who were deliriously happy during it."

"Kanza doesn't seem deliriously happy." Aliyah, King Kamal Aal Masood of Judar's wife—the queen who wore black at her own wedding then rocked the whole region when she challenged her groom to a sword duel on global live feed—gave Kanza a contemplative look. "You're treating it all with the nonchalance of one of the guests. Worse, with the impatience of one of the caterers who just wants it over with so she can get the hell home."

Kanza belted a laugh as she ran behind the screen. "I just want to marry the man. Don't care one bit how I do it."

Feeling the groans of her half sisters flaying her, she undressed and jumped into her gown. They were almost *haybeedo*—going to lay eggs—to have anything like her wedding. And for her to not only have it but to not care about having it must be the ultimate insult to injury to them.

Sighing, she came out from behind the screen.

Her sisters and stepmothers all gaped at her. Yeah, she'd gaped, too, when she'd seen herself in that dress yesterday at the one and only fitting. If you could call it a dress. It was on par with a miracle. Another Aram had made come true.

Before she could get another look at herself in the mirror, the ladies flocked around her, adjusting her hair and veil and embellishing her with pieces of the Pride of Zohayd treasure that King Amjad and Maram were lending her.

Then they pulled back, and it was her turn to gasp.

Who was that woman looking back at her?

The dress's sumptuous gradations of cream and gold made everything about her coloring more vivid, and the incredible amalgam of chiffon, lace and tulle wrapped around her as if it was sculpted on her. The sleeveless, corsetlike, deep décolleté top made her breasts look full and nipped her waist to tiny proportions. Below that, the flare of her hips looked lush in a skirt that hugged them in crisscrossing pleats before falling to the floor in relaxed sweeps. And all over it was embroidered with about every ornament known to humankind, from pearls to sequins to cutwork to gemstones. Instead of looking busy, the amazing subtleness of colors and the denseness and ingeniousness of designs made it a unique work of art. Even more than that. A masterpiece.

Aram had promised he'd tell her how he'd had it made in only two days, if she was very, very, *very* good to him.

She intended to be superlative.

Looking at herself now—with subtle makeup and her thick hair swept up in a chignon that emphasized its shine and volume, with the veil held in place by a crown from the legendary royal treasure, along with the rest of the priceless, one-of-a-kind jewels adorning her throat, ears, arms and fingers—she had to admit she looked stunning.

She wanted to look like that more from now on.

For Aram.

The new bouquets had just arrived when the music that had accompanied bridal processions in the region since time immemorial rocked the palace.

Kanza ran out of the suite with her royalty-studded procession rushing after her, until Johara had to call out for her to slow down or they'd all break their ankles running in their high heels.

Kanza looked back, giggling, and was again dumbfounded by the magnitude of beauty those women packed. They themselves looked like a bouquet of the most perfect flowers in their luscious pale gold dresses. Those royal men of theirs sure knew how to pick women. They had been blessed by brides who were gorgeous inside and out.

As soon as they were out in the gallery leading to the central hall, Kanza was again awed by the sheer opulence of this wonderland of artistry they called the royal palace of Zohayd. A majestic blend of Persian, Ottoman and Mughal influences, it had taken thousands of artisans and craftsmen over three decades to finish it in the mid-seventeenth century. It felt as if the accumulation of history resonated in its halls, and the ancient bloodlines that had resided and ruled in it coursed through its walls.

Then they arrived at the hall's soaring double doors, heavily worked in embossed bronze, gold and silver Zohaydan motifs. Four footmen in beige-and-gold outfits pulled the massive doors open by their ringlike knobs. Even over the music blaring at the back, she heard the buzz of conversation pouring out, that of the thousand guests who'd come to pay Aram respects as one of the world's premier movers and shakers.

Inside was the octagonal hall that served as the palace's hub, ensconced below a hundred-foot high and wide marble dome. She'd never seen anything like it. Its walls were covered with breathtaking geometric designs and calligraphy, its eight soaring arches defining the space at ground level, each crowned by a second arch midway up, with the upper arches forming balconies.

At least, that had been what it was when she'd seen it yesterday. Now it had turned into a scene right out of *Arabian Nights*.

Among the swirling sweetness of *oud,* musk and amber

fumes, from every arch hung rows of incense burners and flaming torches, against every wall breathtaking arrangements of cream and gold roses. Each pillar was wrapped in gold satin worked heavily in silver patterns, while gold dust covered the glossy earth-tone marble floor.

Then came the dozens of tables that were lavishly decorated and set up in echoes of the hall's embellishment and surrounded by hundreds of guests who looked like ornaments themselves, polished and glittering. Everyone came from the exclusive realm of the world's most rich and famous. They sparkled under the ambient light like fairy-tale dwellers in Midas's vault.

Then the place was plunged into darkness. And silence.

Her heart boomed more loudly than the boisterous percussive music that had suddenly ended. After moments of stunned silence, a wildfire of curious murmuring spread.

Yeah. Them and her both. This wasn't part of the planned proceedings. Come to think of it, not much had been. Aram had been supposed to wait at the door to escort her in. She hadn't given it another thought when she hadn't found him there because she'd thought he'd just gotten restless as her procession took forever to get there, and that he'd simply gone to wait for her at the *kooshah,* where the bride and groom presided over the celebrations, keeping the *ma'zoon*—the cleric who'd perform the marriage ritual— company.

So what was going on? What was he up to?

Knowing Aram and his crazy stunts, she expected anything.

Her breathing followed her heartbeat in disarray as she waited, unmoving, certain that there was no one behind her anymore. Her procession had rustled away. This meant they were in on this. So this surprise was for her.

God, she hated surprises.

Okay, not Aram's. She downright adored those, and had,

in fact, gotten addicted to them, living in constant antici-pation of the next delightful surprise that invariably came.

But really, now wasn't the time to spring something on her. She just wanted to get this over with. And get her hands back on him. Three days without him after that intensive… initiation had her in a constant state of arousal and frus-tration. By the end of this torture session, she'd probably attack and devour him the moment she had him alone….

"Elli shoftoh, gabl ma tshoofak ainayah.
Omr daye'e. Yehsebooh ezzai alaiah?"

Her heart stopped. Stumbled. Then stopped again.

Aram. His voice. Coming from…everywhere. And he'd just said…said…

All that I've seen, before my eyes saw you.
A lifetime wasted. How can it even be counted life?

Her heart began ricocheting inside her chest. Aram. Say-ing exactly what she felt. Every moment before she was with him, she no longer counted as life.

But those verses… They sounded familiar….

Suddenly a spotlight burst in the darkness. It took mo-ments until her vision adjusted and she saw…saw…

Aram, rising as if from the ground at the far end of the gigantic ballroom, among swirling mist. In cream and gold all over, looking like a shining knight from a fantasy.

As he really was.

Music suddenly rose, played by an orchestra that rose on a huge platform behind him, wearing complementary colors.

She recognized the overture. *Enta Omri,* or *You Are My Lifetime.* One of the most passionate and profound love songs in the region. That was why the verses had struck a chord.

Not that their meaning had held any before. Before Aram, they'd just been another exercise in romantic hy-perbole. Now that he was in her heart, every word took on a new meaning, each striking right to her foundations.

He now repeated the verses but not by speaking them. Aram was *singing*. Singing to *her*.

Everything inside her expanded to absorb every nuance of this exquisite moment as it unfolded, to assimilate it into her being.

She already knew he sang well, though it was his voice itself that was unparalleled, not his singing ability. They'd sung together while cooking, driving, playing. He always sang snippets of songs that suited a situation. But nothing local.

While his choice and intention overwhelmed her with gratitude and happiness, the fact that he knew enough about local music to pick this song for those momentous moments stunned her all over again with yet another proof that Aram knew more about her homeland than she did. Not to mention loved it way more.

He was descending the steps from the platform where the orchestra remained. Then he was walking toward her across the huge dance floor on an endless gold carpet flanked by banks of cream rose petals. All the time he sang, his magnificent, soul-scorching voice filling the air, overflowing inside her.

"Ad aih men omri ablak rah, w'adda ya habibi.
Wala da'a el galb ablak farhah wahda.
Wala da'a fel donia ghair ta'am el gerah."
How much of my lifetime before you passed and was lost.
With a heart tasting not a single joy but only wounds.
She shook, tears welling inside her.
Yes, yes. Yes. Exactly. *Oh, Aram...*

He kept coming nearer, his approach a hurricane that uprooted any lingering despondencies and disappointments, blowing them away, never to be seen again.

And he told her, only her, everything in his heart.
"Ebtadait delwa'ti bas, ahheb omri.
Ebtadait delwa'ti akhaf, lal omr yegri."
Only now I started to love my lifetime.

Only now I started to fear its hasty passage.

Every word, everything about him, overwhelmed her. It was impossible, but he was even more beautiful now, from the raven hair that now brushed his shoulders, to the face that had never looked more noble, more potent, every slash carved deeper, every emotion blazing brighter, to the body that she knew from extensive hands-on…investigation was awe incarnate. To make things worse and infinitely better, his outfit showcased his splendor to a level that would have left her speechless, breathless, even without the overkill of his choice of song and his spellbinding performance.

The costume echoed her dress in colors, from the cream-and-gold embroidered cape that accentuated his shoulders and made him look as if he'd fly up, up and away at any moment to the billowing-sleeved gold shirt that was gathered by a cream satin sash into formfitting coordinating pants, which gathered into light beige matte-leather boots.

She was looking at those when he stopped before her, unable to meet his eyes anymore. Her heart had been racing itself to a standstill, needed respite before she gazed up at him and into the full force of his love up close.

His hands reached for her, burned on her bare arms. Quivers became shudders. She raised her eyes, focused on the mike in front of lips that were still invoking the spell.

His hands caressed her face, cupped it in their warmth and tenderness, imbuing her with the purity of his emotions, the power of their union. And he asked her:

"Ya hayat galbi, ya aghla men hayati.
Laih ma abelneesh hawaak ya habibi badri?"
Life of my heart, more precious than my life.
Why didn't your love find me earlier, my love?

Shudders became quakes that dismantled her and dislodged tears from her depths. She waited, heart flailing uncontrollably, for the last verse to complete the perfection.

"Enti omri, elli ebtada b'noorek sabaho."
You are my lifetime, which only dawned with your light.

Music continued in the closing chords, but she no longer heard anything as she hurled herself into his arms.

She rained feverish kisses all over his face, shaking and quaking and sobbing. "Aram…Aram…too much… too much…everything you are, everything with you, from you…" She burrowed into his containment and wept until she felt she'd disintegrate.

He hugged her as if he'd assimilate her, bending to kiss her all over her face, her lips, raggedly reciting the verses, again and again.

She thought a storm raged in the background. It wasn't until she expended her tears and sobs that she realized what it was. The thunder of applause and whistles and hoots among the lightning of camera flashes *and the video floodlights*.

Drained, recharged, she looked up at her indescribable soul mate, her smile blazing through the upheaval. "This should get record hits on YouTube."

It was amazing, watching his face switch from poignancy to elation to devilry.

Only she could do this to him. As he was the one who could make her truly live.

"Maybe this won't." He winked. "But *this* surely will."

Before she could ask what "this" was, he turned and gestured, and for the second time tonight he managed to stun her out of her wits.

Openmouthed, she watched as hundreds of dancers in ethnic Zohaydan costumes, men in flowing black-and-white robes and women with waist-length hair and in vibrant, intricately embroidered floor-length dresses, poured onto the huge dance floor from all sides, *including* descending by invisible harnesses from the balconies. Drummers with all Zohaydan percussive instruments joined in as they formed facing queues and launched into infectiously energetic local dances.

He caught her around the waist, took her from gravity's

dominion into his. "Remember the dance we learned at that bar in Barbados?" She nodded hard enough to give herself a concussion. He swung her once in the air before tugging her behind him to the dance floor. "Then let's dance, *ya kanzi.*"

Though the dance was designed to a totally different rhythm, somehow dancing to this melody worked and, spectacularly, turned out to be even more exhilarating.

Soon all the royal couples were dancing behind them as they led the way, and before long, the whole guest roster had left the tables and were circled around the dance floor clapping or joining the collective dances.

As she danced with him and hugged him and kissed him and laughed until she cried, she wondered how only he could do this—change the way she felt about anything to its opposite. This night she'd wished would be over soon, she suddenly wished would never end.

But even when it did, life with Aram would only begin.

Twelve

Aram clasped Kanza from behind, unable to let her go for even a moment as she handed back the Pride of Zohayd jewelry to the royal guards at the door.

He had to keep touching her to make himself believe this was all real. That she was his wife now. That they were in their home.

Their home.

The fact that it was in Zohayd made it even more unbelievable.

He'd thought he'd lost Zohayd forever. But she'd given it back to him, as she'd given him everything else. Though she'd never loved Zohayd as he loved it, she'd consented to make it her home again.

After seeing her among her family, he now realized why Zohayd had never held fond memories for her. But he was determined to set things right and would put those people in their place. They'd never impact her in any way again.

Now he hoped he could make her see Zohayd as he saw it.

But at any sign of discomfort, they'd leave. He just wanted

her happy, wanted her to have everything. Starting with him and his whole life.

She closed the door then turned and wrapped herself around him. "I just can never predict you."

He tasted her lips, her appreciation. "I hope this keeps me interesting."

Her lips clung to his as she kneaded his buttocks playfully, sensuously. He still couldn't believe, couldn't get enough of how uninhibited she was with him sexually. It was as if the moment he'd touched her she'd let him in all the way, no barriers.

"Don't you dare get more interesting or I'll expire."

"You let me know the level of 'interesting' I can keep that's optimum for your health."

"You're perfect now. You'll always be perfect." She squeezed him tighter. "Thank you, *ya habibi*. For the gift of your song. And every other incredible thing you did and are."

His lips explored her face, loving her so much it was an exquisite pain. "I had to give you a wedding to remember."

"As long as it had you, it would have been the best memory, as everything you are a part of is. *And* it would have been the best possible earthly event. But that…that was divine." Her eyes adored him, devoured him. "Have I told you lately just how out of my mind in love with you I am?"

His heart thundered, unable to wait anymore. He needed union with her. Now.

His hands shook as he undid her dress, slid it off her shoulders. "Last time was ten minutes ago. Too long. Tell me again. *Show* me. You haven't shown me in *three* damn days."

She tore back at his clothes. "Thought you'd never ask."

He shoved off the dress that he'd had ten dressmakers work on day and night, telling himself he couldn't savor her beauty now. He had to lose himself in her, claim her heart, body and soul.

The beast inside him was writhing. This. This flesh. This spirit. This tempest of a woman. Her. It demanded her. And it wouldn't have her slow or gentle. Their lifelong pact had to be sealed in flesh, forged in the fires of urgency and ferociousness. And she wanted that, too. Her eyes were engulfing him whole, her breathing as erratic as his, her hands as rabid as she rid him of his shackles.

He pressed her to the door, crashed his lips down on hers. Her cry tore through him when their mouths collided. He could only grind his lips, his all, against hers, no finesse, no restraint. The need to ram into her, ride her, spill himself inside her, drove him. Incessant groans of profound suffering filled his head, his and hers. He was in agony. Her flesh buzzed its equal torment beneath his burning hands.

He raised her thighs around his hips, growled as her moist heat singed his erection. His fingers dug into her buttocks as he freed himself, pushed her panties out of the way, and her breasts heaved, her hardened nipples branding his raw flesh where she'd torn his shirt off.

Her swollen lips quivered in her taut-with-need face. "Aram…fill me…"

The next moment, he did. He drove up into her, incoherent, roaring, invading her, overstretching her scorching honey. Her scream pierced his soul as she consumed him back, wrung him, razed him.

He rested his forehead against hers, completely immersed in her depths, loved and taken and accepted whole, overwhelmed, transported. He listened to her delirium, watching her through hooded eyes as she arched her graceful back, giving him her all, taking his. Blind, out of his mind and in her power—in her love—he lifted her, filled his starving mouth and hands with her flesh, with the music of her hunger. He withdrew all the way then thrust back, fierce and full, riding her wild cry. It took no more than that. One thrust finished her. And him. Her satin screams echoed his roars as he jetted his essence inside her. Her convulsions spiked with the first splash of his seed against her womb. Her heart hammered under his, both spiraling out of control as the devastating pleasure went on and on and on and the paroxysm of release destroyed the world around them.

Then it was another life. Their new life together, and they were merged as one, rocking together, riding the aftershocks, sharing the descent.

Then, as she always did, she both surprised and delighted him. "That was one hell of an inauguration at the very entrance of our new home. Who needs breaking a bottle across the threshold when you can shatter your bride with pleasure?"

Squeezing her tighter, he looked down at her, his heart soaring at the total satisfaction in her eyes. "I am one for better alternatives."

"That was the *best*. You redefine mind-blowing with every performance. I'm not even sure my head is still in place."

Chuckling, proud and grateful that he could satisfy her that fully, he gathered his sated bride into his arms and strode through the still-foreign terrain of their new home.

Reaching their bedroom suite, he laid her down on the twelve-foot four-poster bed draped in bedcovers the color of her flesh and sheets the color of her hair. She nestled into him and went still, soaking in the fusion of their souls and flesh.

Thankfulness seeped out in a long sigh. "One of the incredible things about your size is that I can bundle you all up and contain you."

She burrowed her face into his chest. "Not fair. I want to contain you, too."

Tightening his arms around her, he pledged, "You have. You do."

* * *

"It is such a relief to be back home in Zohayd."

Kanza looked up from her laptop as Johara waddled toward her, just about to pop.

Johara and her family had returned to Zohayd since her wedding to Aram two months ago. Their stay in New York *had* only been on Aram's account. The moment he'd come to Zohayd, they'd run home.

She smiled at her friend and now new sister-in-law. "I would have never agreed before, but with Aram, Zohayd has become the home it never was to me."

Johara, looking exhausted just crossing their new base of operations, plopped down beside her on the couch. "We knew you'd end up together."

Kanza's smile widened. "Then you knew something I didn't. I had no idea, or even hope, for the longest time."

"Yeah." Johara nodded absently, leafing through the latest status report. "When the situation revolves around you, it's hard to have a clear enough head to see the potential. But Shaheen and I knew you'd be perfect for each other and gave you a little shove."

Her smile faltered. "You did? When was that?"

Johara raised her head, unfocused. Then she blinked. "Oh, the night I sent you to look for that file."

A suspicion mushroomed then solidified into conviction within the same heartbeat. "There was no file, was there?"

Johara gave her a sheepish look. "Nope. I just had to get you both in one place."

Unease stirred as the incident that had changed her life was rewritten. "You sent him to look for the nonexistent file, too, so he'd stumble on me. You set us up."

Johara waved dismissively. "Oh, I just had you meet."

The unease tightened. "Did Aram realize what you did?"

"I'm sure he did when he found you there on his same mission."

So why had he given her different reasons when she'd asked him point-blank what he'd been doing there?

But... "He could have just thought you asked me to do the same thing. He had no reason to think you were setting us up."

"Of course he did. Shaheen had suggested you to him only a couple of weeks before."

"*Suggested* me...how?"

"How do you think? As the most suitable bride for him, of course." Johara's grin became triumphant. "Acting on my suggestion, I might add. And it turns out I was even more right than I knew. You and Aram are beyond perfect."

So their meeting hadn't been a coincidence.

But... "Why should Aram have considered your suggestion? It isn't as if he was looking for a bride."

Johara looked at her as if she asked the strangest things. "Because we showed him what a perfect all-around package you are for him—being you...*and* being Zohaydan. We told him if you married, you'd have each other, he'd have Zohayd back, I'd have my brother back, my parents their son and Shaheen his best friend."

Kanza didn't know how she'd functioned after Johara's blithe revelations.

She didn't remember how she'd walked out of the office or how she'd arrived home. Home. Hers and Aram's. Up until two hours ago, she'd been secure, certain it was. Now...now...

"*Kanzi.*"

He was here. Usually she'd either run to greet him or she'd already be at the door waiting for him.

This time she remained frozen where she'd fallen on the bed, dreading his approach. For what if when he did, when she asked the inevitable questions, nothing would be the same again?

She felt him enter their bedroom, heard the rustle of his

clothes as he took them off. He always came home starving for her, made love to her before anything else, both always gasping for assuagement that first time. Then they settled to a leisurely evening of being best friends and patient, inventive and very, very demanding lovers.

At least, that was what she'd believed.

If everything hadn't started as she'd thought, if his motivations hadn't been as pure as she'd believed them to be, how accurate was her perception of what they shared now?

The bed dipped under his weight, rolling her over to him. He completed the motion, coming half over her as soon as her eyes met his. He'd taken off his jacket and shirt, and he now loomed over her, sculpted by virility gods and unbending discipline and stamina, so hungry and impatient. And her heart almost splintered with doubt and insecurity.

Was it even possible this god among men could truly want her to that extent?

His lips devoured her sob of despair as he rid her of her clothes, sought her flesh and pleasure triggers, cupped the breasts and core that were swollen and aching with the need for him that not even impending heartbreak could diminish.

"Kanza...*habibati...wahashteeni...kam wahashteeni.*"

Her heart convulsed at hearing the ragged emotion in his voice as he called her his love, told her how much he'd missed her. When it had only been hours since he'd left her side.

He slid her pants off her legs, and they fell apart for him. He rose to free his erection, and as she felt it slap against her belly, hot and thick and heavy, everything inside her fell apart, needing his invasion, his affirmation.

Holding her head down to the mattress by a trembling grip in her hair, feeding her his tongue, rumbling his torment inside her, he bathed himself in her body's begging for his, then plunged into her.

That familiar expansion of her tissues at his potency's advance was as always at first unbearable. Then he withdrew and thrust back, giving her more of him, and it got better, then again and again until it was unbearable to have him withdraw, to have him stop. He didn't stop, breaching her to her womb, over and over, until he was slamming inside her with the exact force and speed and depth that would...would...

Then she was shrieking, bucking beneath him with a sledgehammer of an orgasm, the force of it wrenching her around him for every spark of pleasure her body was capable of, wringing him of every drop of his seed and satisfaction.

Before he collapsed on top of her in the enervation of satiation, he as usual twisted around to his back, taking her sprawling on top of him.

Instead of slowing down, her heart hurtled faster until it was rattling her whole frame. It seemed it transmitted to Aram as he slid out of their merging, turned her carefully to her back and rose above her, his face gripped with worry.

"God, what is it, Kanza? Your heart is beating so hard."

And it would stop if she didn't ask. It might shrivel up if she did and got the answers she dreaded.

She had no choice. She had to know.

"Why didn't you tell me that Johara and Shaheen nominated me as a bride for you?"

Thirteen

Kanza's question fell on Aram like an ax.

His first instinct was to deny that he knew what she was talking about. The next second, he almost groaned.

Why had he panicked like that? How could he even consider lying? It was clear Johara or Shaheen or both had told her, but why, he'd never know. But though it wasn't his favorite topic or memory, his reluctance to mention it had resulted in this awkward moment. But that was all it was. He'd pay for his omission with some tongue-lashings, and then she'd laugh off his failure to provide full disclosure about this subject as he did everything else, and that would be that.

He caressed her between the perfect orbs of her breasts, worry still squeezing his own heart at the hammering that wasn't subsiding beneath his palm. "I should have told you."

He waited with bated breath, anticipating the dawning of devilry, the launch of a session of stripping sarcasm.

Nothing came but a vacant, "Yes. You should have."

When that remained all she said and that heart beneath his palm slowed down to a sluggish rhythm, he rushed to qualify his moronically deficient answer. "There was nothing to tell, really. Shaheen made the suggestion a couple of weeks before I met you. I told him to forget it, and that was that."

Another intractable moment of blankness passed before she said, "But Johara set us up that first night. And you must have realized she had. Why didn't you say something then? Or later? When you started telling me everything?"

All through the past months, unease about this omission had niggled at him. He'd started to tell her many times, only for some vague…dread to hold him back.

"I just feared it might upset you."

"Why should it have, if it was nothing? It's not that I think I'm entitled to know everything that ever happened in your life, but this concerned me. I had a right to know."

He felt his skull starting to tighten around his brain. "With the exception of this one thing, I *did* tell you everything in my life. And it was because this concerned you that I chose not to mention it. Their nomination, as well-meaning as it was, was just…unworthy of you."

"But you did act on that nomination. It was why you considered me."

His skull tightened another notch. "No. *No.* I didn't even consider Shaheen's proposition. Okay, I did, for about two minutes. But that was before I saw you that night. If I thought about it again afterward, it was to marvel at how wrong Shaheen was when he thought you'd agree to marry me based on my potential benefits. There's no reason to be upset over this, *ya kanzi.* Johara and Shaheen's matchmaking had nothing to do with us or the soul-deep friendship and love that grew between us."

"Would you have considered me to start with if not for *my* potential benefits?"

"You had none!"

"Ah, but I do. Johara listed them. Stemming from being me and being Zohaydan, as she put it."

"Why the hell would she tell you something like that?

Those pregnancy hormones have been scrambling her brain of late."

"She was celebrating the fact that it all came together so well for all of us, especially you."

"I don't care what she or anyone else thinks. I care about nothing but you. You *know* that, Kanza."

She suddenly let go of his gaze, slipped out of his hold. He watched her with a burgeoning sense of helplessness as she got off the bed, then put on her clothes slowly and unsteadily.

He rose, too, as if from ten rounds with a heavyweight champion, stuffing himself back into his pants, feeling as if he'd been hurled from the sublime heights of their explosively passionate interlude to the bottom of an abyss.

Suddenly she spoke, in that voice that was hers but no longer hers. Expressionless, empty. Dead. "I was unable to rationalize the way you sought me out in the beginning. It was why I was so terrified of letting you close. I needed a logical explanation, and logic said I was nowhere in your league—nothing that could suit or appeal to you."

"You're *everything* that—"

Her subdued voice drowned the desperation of his interjection. "But I was dying to let you get close, so I pounced on Johara's claims that you needed a best friend, then did everything to explain to myself how I qualified as that to you. But her new revelations make much more sense why you were with me, why you married me."

"I was with you because you're everything I could want. I married you because I love you and can't live without you."

"You do appear to love me now."

"*Appear?* Damn it, Kanza, how can you even say this?"

"I can because no matter how much you showed me you loved me, I always wondered *how* you do. *What* I have that the thousands of women who pursued you don't." He again tried to protest the total insanity of her words when lashing pain gripped her face, silencing him more effectively than a skewer in his gut. "When I couldn't find a reason why, I thought you were responding to the intensity of my emotions for you. I thought it was my desire that ignited yours. I did know you needed a home and I thought you found it in me. But your home has always been Zohayd. You just needed someone to help you go home and to have the family and set down the roots you yearned for your entire life."

Unable to bear one more word, he swooped down on her, crushed her to him, stormed her face with kisses, scolding her all the while. "Every word you just said is total madness, do you hear me? You are everything I never dreamed to find, everything I *despaired* I'd never find. I've loved you from that first moment you turned and smacked me upside the head with your sarcasm, then proceeded to reignite my will to exist, then taught me the meaning of being alive."

He cradled her face in his hands, made her look at him. "*B'Ellahi, ya hayati,* if I ever needed your unconditional belief, it's now. My life depends on it, *ya habibati.* I beg you. Tell me you believe me."

Her reddened eyes wavered, then squeezed in consent.

Relief was so brutal his vision dimmed. He tightened his grip on her, reiterating his love.

Then she was pushing away, and alarm crashed back.

Her lips quivered on a smile as she squirmed out of his arms. "I'm just going to the bathroom."

He clung to her. "I'm coming with you."

"It's not that kind of bathroom visit."

"Then call me as soon as it is. There's these new incense and bath salts that I want to try, and a new massage oil."

Her eyes gentled, though they didn't heat as always, as she took another step away. "I'll just take a quick shower."

"Then I'll join you in that. I'll…"

Suddenly the bell rang. And rang.

Since they'd sent the servants away for the night as usual, so they'd have the house and grounds all to themselves, there was no one to answer the door. A door no one ever came to, anyway. So who could this be?

Cursing under his breath as Kanza slipped away, he ran to the door, prepared to blast whoever it was off the face of the earth.

He wrenched the door open, and frustration evaporated in a blast of anxiety when he found Shaheen on his doorstep half carrying an ashen-faced Johara.

He rushed them inside. "God, come in."

Shaheen lowered Johara onto the couch, remained bent over her as Aram came down beside her, each massaging a hand.

"What's wrong? Is she going into labor?"

"No, she's just worried sick," Shaheen said, looking almost sick himself.

Johara clung feebly to the shirt he hadn't buttoned up. "I talked with Kanza earlier, and I think I put my foot in it when I told her how we proposed her to you."

"You *think?*"

At his exclamation, Shaheen glared at him, an urgent head toss saying he wanted a word away from Johara.

Gritting his teeth, he kissed Johara's hot cheek. "Don't worry, sweetheart. It was nothing serious," he lied. "She just skewered me for never mentioning it, and that was it. Now rest, please. Do you need me to get you anything?"

She shook her head, clung to him as he started to rise. "Is it really okay? She's okay?"

He nodded, caressed her head then moved away when she closed her eyes on a sigh of relief.

He joined Shaheen out of her earshot. "God, Shaheen, you shouldn't be letting her around people nowadays. She unwittingly had Kanza on the verge of a breakdown."

Shaheen squeezed his eyes. "*Ya Ullah*... I'm sorry, Aram. Her pregnancy is taking a harder toll on her this time, and I'm scared witless. Her pressure is all over the place and she loses focus so easily. She said she was celebrating how

well everything has turned out for you two and only remembered when she came home that Kanza didn't know
how things started." He winced. "Then she kept working
herself up, recalling how subdued Kanza became during
the conversation, the amount of questions she'd asked her,
and she became convinced she'd made a terrible mistake."

"She did. God, Shaheen, Kanza kept putting two and two
together and getting fives and tens and hundreds. But right
before you came she'd calmed down at last."

Hope surged in his friend's eyes. "Then everything is
going to be fine?"

He thought her spiraling doubts had been arrested, but
he was still rattled.

He just nodded to end this conversation. He needed to get
back to Kanza, close that door where he'd gotten a glimpse
of hell once and for all.

Shaheen's face relaxed. "Phew. What a close call, eh?
Now that that's settled, please tell me when are you going
to take my job off my hands? In the past five months since
I offered you the minister of economy job, juggling it with
everything else—" he tossed a worried gesture in Johara's
direction "—has become untenable. I really need you on
it right away."

"So this is why you *have* to become Zohaydan."

Kanza's muffled voice startled Aram so much he stag-
gered around. He found her a dozen feet away at the
entrance to their private quarters. Her look of pained realization felt like a bullet through his heart.

Her gaze left his, darting around restlessly as if chasing
chilling deductions. "Not just to make Zohayd your home,
but you need to be Zohaydan to take on such a vital position. But as only members of the ruling house have ever
held it, you have to become royalty, through a royal wife."

"Kanza…"

"Kanza…"

Both he and Shaheen started to talk at once.

Her subdued voice droned on, silencing them both more effectively than if she'd shouted. "Since there are no high-ranking princesses available, you had to choose from lower-ranking ones. And in those, I was your only viable possibility. The spinster who never got a proposal, who'd have no expectations, make no demands and pose no challenge or danger. I was your only safe, convenient choice."

He pounced on her, trembling with anxiety and dismay, squeezed her shoulders, trying to jog her out of her surrender to macabre projections. "No, Kanza, hell, *no*. You were the most challenging, *in*convenient person I've ever had the incredible fortune to find."

She raised that blank gaze to his. "But you didn't find me, Aram. You were pushed in my direction. And as a businessman, you gauged me as your best option. Now I know what you meant when you said I 'work best.' For I do. I'm the best possible piece that worked to make everything fall into place without resistance or potential for trouble."

He could swear he could see his sanity deserting him in thick, black fumes. "How can you think, let alone say, *any* of this? After all we've shared?"

Ignoring him, she looked over at Shaheen. "Didn't you rationalize proposing me to him with everything I just said?"

He swung around to order Shaheen to shut up. Every time he or Johara opened their mouths they made things worse.

But Shaheen was already answering her. "What I said was along those lines, but not at all—"

"Why didn't you all just tell me?" Kanza's butchered cry not only silenced Shaheen but stopped Aram's heart. And that was before her agonized gaze turned on him. "I would have given you the marriage of convenience you needed if just for Johara and Shaheen's sake, for Zohayd's. I would have recognized that you'd make the best minister of economy possible, would have done what I could to make it hap-

pen without asking for anything more. But now…now that
you made me hope for more, made me believe I had more—
all of you—I can't go back…and I can't go on."

"Kanza."

His roar did nothing to slow her dash back to the bedroom. It only woke Johara up with a cry of alarm.

Reading the situation at a glance, Johara struggled up
off the couch, gasping, "I'll talk to her."

Unable to hold back anymore, dread racking him, he
shouted, *"No.* You've talked enough for a lifetime, Johara.
I was getting through to her, and you came here to *help* me
some more and spoiled everything."

Shaheen's hand gripped his arm tight, admonishing him
for talking to his sister this way for any reason, and in her
condition. "Aram, get hold of yourself—"

He turned on him. "I *begged* you never to interfere between me and Kanza. Now she might never listen to me,
never believe me again. So *please,* just leave. Leave me to
try to salvage what I can of my wife's heart and her faith
in me. Let me try to save what I can of our marriage, and
our very lives."

Forgetting them as he turned away, he rushed into the
bedroom. He came to a jarring halt when he found Kanza
standing by the bed where they'd lost themselves in each
other's arms so recently, looking smaller than he'd ever
seen her, sobs racking her, tears pouring in sheets down
her suffering face.

He flew to her side, tried to snatch her into his arms. Her
feeble resistance, the tears that fell on his hands, corroded
through to his soul.

Shaking as hard as she was, he tried to hold the hands
that warded him off, moist agony filling his own eyes. "Oh,
God, don't, Kanza…don't push me away, I beg you."

She shook like a leaf in his arms, sobs fracturing her
words. "With everything in me…I do…I *do* want you to
have everything you deserve. I was the happiest person

on earth when I thought that I was a big part of what you need…to thrive, to be happy…."

"You are *everything* I need."

She shook her head, pushed against him again. "But I'll always wonder…always doubt. Every second from now on, I'll look at you and remember every moment we had together and…see it all differently with what I know now. It will…abort my spontaneity, my fantasies…twist my every thought…poison my every breath. *And I can't live like this.*"

Even in prison, during those endless, hopeless nights when he'd thought he'd be maimed or murdered, he'd never known terror.

But now…seeing and hearing Kanza's faith, in him—in herself—bleed out, he knew it.

Dark, drowning, devastating.

And he groveled. "No, I beg you, Kanza. I beg you, please…don't say it. Don't say it…."

She went still in his arms as if she'd been shot.

That ultimate display of defeat sundered his heart.

Her next words sentenced him to death.

"The moment you get your Zohaydan citizenship and become minister, let me go, Aram."

Fourteen

It was as harsh a test of character and stamina as Kanza had always heard it was.

But being in the presence of Amjad Aal Shalaan in Kanza's current condition was an even greater ordeal than she'd imagined.

She'd come to ask him as her distant cousin, but mainly as the king of Zohayd, to expedite proclaiming Aram a Zohaydan subject and appointing him to the position of minister.

After the storm of misery had racked her this past week, inescapable questions had forced their way from the depths of despair.

Could she leave Aram knowing that no matter what he stood to gain from their marriage, he did love her? Could she punish him and herself with a life apart because his love wasn't identical to hers, because of the difference in their circumstances?

Almost everyone thought she had far more to gain from their marriage than he did, especially with news spreading of the minister's position. Her family had explicitly expressed their belief that marrying him would raise her to undreamed-of status and wealth.

But she expected him to believe she cared nothing about those enormous material gains, to know for certain that they were only circumstantial. She would have married him had he been destitute. She would continue to love him, come what may. So how could she not believe him when he said the same about his own projected gains? Could she impose a separation on both of them because her ego had been injured and her confidence shaken?

No. She couldn't.

Even if she'd never be as certain as she'd been before the revelations, she would heal and relegate her doubts to the background, where they meant nothing compared to truly paramount matters.

Once she had reached that conclusion, she'd approached a devastated Aram and tried everything to persuade him that he must go ahead with his plans, to persuade him that she'd overreacted and was taking everything she'd said back.

He'd insisted he'd *never* had plans, didn't want anything but her and would never lift a finger to even save his life if it meant losing her faith and security in the purity of his love.

So here she was, taking matters into her own hands.

She was getting him what he needed, what he was now forgoing to prove himself to her.

Not that she seemed to be doing a good job of championing his cause.

That cunning, convoluted Amjad had been keeping her talking for the past half hour. It seemed he didn't buy the story that she wished Aram to be Zohaydan as soon as possible for the job's sake...that Shaheen needed Aram to take over before Johara gave birth.

He probed her with those legendary eyes of his, confirmed her suspicion. "So, Kanza, what's your *real* rush? Why do you want your husband to become Zohaydan so immediately? He can assume Shaheen's responsibilities without any official move. I'd prefer it, to see if my younger brother wants to hand his closest friend the kingdom's fate as a consolation prize for the 'lost years,' or if he is really the best man for the job."

"He is that, without any doubt."

Those eyes that were as vividly emerald as Aram's were azure flashed their mockery. "And of course, that's not the biased opinion of a woman whose head-over-heels display during her wedding caused my eyes to roll so far back in my skull it took weeks to get them back into their original position?"

"No, *ya maolai*." It was a struggle to call him "my lord," when all she wanted to do was chew him out and make him stop tormenting her. "It's the very objective opinion of a professional in Aram's field. While there's no denying that you, Shaheen and your father have been able to achieve great things running the ministry, I believe with the unique combination of his passion for the job and for Zohayd, and with the magnitude of his specific abilities and experience, Aram would surpass your combined efforts tenfold."

Amjad's eyebrows shot up into the hair that rained across his forehead. "Now, *that's* a testimony. I might be needing your ability to sell unsellable goods quite soon."

"As reputedly the most effective king Zohayd has ever known, I hear you've achieved that by employing only the best people where they'd do the most good. I trust you wouldn't let your feelings for Aram, whatever they are, interfere with the decision to make use of him where he is best suited."

He spread his palm over his chest in mock suffering. "Ah, my feelings for Aram. Did he tell you how he broke my heart?"

You, too? she almost scoffed.

Not that Aram had broken hers. It was she who'd churned herself out with her insecurities.

But that big, bored regal feline would keep swatting her until she coughed up an answer he liked.

She tried a new one. "I'm pregnant."

And she was.

She'd found out two days after Johara's revelations. She hadn't told Aram.

"I want Aram to be Zohaydan before our baby comes."

Amjad raised one eyebrow. "Okay. Good reason. But again, what's the rush? Looking at you, I'd say you have around seven months to go. And you seem to want this done last week."

"I need Aram settled into his new job and his schedule sorted out with big chunks of time for me and the baby."

"Okay. Another good reason. Want to add a better one?"

"I haven't told Aram he's going to be a father yet. I wish him to be Zohaydan before I do to make the announcement even more memorable."

His bedeviling inched to the next level. "You have this all figured out, haven't you?"

"Nothing to figure out when you're telling the truth."

Those eyes said "liar." Out loud he said, "You're tenacious and wily, and you're probably making Aram walk a tightrope to keep in your favor...."

"Like Queen Maram does with you, you mean?"

He threw his head back on a guffaw. "I like you. But even more than that, you must be keeping that pretty, pretty full-of-himself Aram in line. I like *that*."

"Are we still talking about Aram, *ya maolai?*"

His cruelly handsome face blazed with challenge and enjoyment. "And she can keep calling me *ya maolai* with a straight face, right after she as much as said, 'I'd put you over my knee, you entitled brat, if I possibly could.'"

Even though he didn't seem offended in the least by the subtext of her ill-advised retort, the worry that she might end up spoiling Aram's chances was brakes enough.

"I thought no such thing, *ya maolai*."

He hooted. "Such a fantastic liar. And that gets you extra

points. Now let's see if you can get a gold star. Tell me the real reason you're here, Kanza."

Nothing less would suffice for this mercilessly shrewd man who had taken one of the most internally unstable kingdoms in the region, brought it to heel and was now leading it to unprecedented prosperity.

So she gave him the truth. "Because I love Aram. So much it's a constant pain if I can't give him everything he needs. And he *needs* a home. He needs *Zohayd*. It's part of his soul. It *is* his home. But until it is that for real, he'll continue to feel homeless, as he's felt for far too long. I don't want him to feel like that one second longer."

Amjad narrowed his eyes. He was still waiting. He knew there was just a bit more to the truth, damn him.

And she threw it in. "I didn't want to expose his vulnerability to you of all people, to disadvantage him in this rivalry you seem to have going."

His lips twisted. "You don't consider this rivalry would be moot and he'd be in a subordinate position once he becomes a minister in my cabinet, in a kingdom where I'm king?"

"No. On a public, professional level, Aram would always hold his own. No one's superior office, which has nothing to do with skill or worth, would disadvantage him. But I was reluctant to hand you such intimately personal power over him. I do now only because I trust you won't abuse it."

It seemed as if he gave her a soul and psyche scan, making sure he'd mined them for every last secret he'd been after.

Seemingly satisfied that he had, Amjad flashed her a grin. "Good girl. That took real guts. Putting the man you love at my mercy. And helluva insight, too. Because I am now bound by that honor pact you just forced on me to never abuse my power over your beloved, I'm definitely going to be making use of this acumen and power of persuasion of yours soon. And as your gold star, you get your wish."

Her heart boomed with relief.

He went on. "Just promise you will not be too good to Aram. You'd be doing him a favor exercising some...*severe* love. Otherwise his head will keep mushrooming, when it's already so big it's in danger of breaking off his neck."

She rose, gave him a tiny bow. "I will consult with Queen Maram about the best methods of limiting the cranial expansion of pretty, pretty full-of-themselves paragons, *ya maolai*."

His laugh boomed.

She could hear him still laughing until she got out of hearing range. The moment she was, all fight went out of her.

This had been harder than she'd thought it would be.

But she'd done it. She'd gotten Aram the last things he needed. Now to convince him that it wouldn't mean losing her.

For though she was no longer secure in the absoluteness of his need for her, and only her, she'd already decided that anything with him would always remain everything she needed.

Amjad did far better than she'd expected.

The morning after her audience with him, he sent her a royal decree. It proclaimed that in only six hours, a ceremony would be held at the royal palace to pronounce her husband Zohaydan. And to appoint him as the new minister of economy.

She flew to Aram's home office and found him just sitting on the couch, vision turned inward.

The sharp, ragged intake of breath as she came down on his lap told her he'd been so lost in his dark reverie he hadn't noticed her entrance. Then as she straddled him, the flare of vulnerability, of entreaty in his eyes, made eversimmering tears almost burst free again.

Ya Ullah, how she loved him. And she'd starved for him.

She hadn't touched him since that night, unable to add passion to the volatile mix. He hadn't tried to persuade her again. Not because he didn't want to. She knew he did. He'd gone instantly hard between her legs now, his arousal buffeting her in waves. He'd been letting her guide him into what she'd allow, what she'd withstand.

She'd show him that for as long as he wanted her, she was his forever. That he was her everything.

She held his beloved head in her hands, moans of anguish spilling from her lips as they pressed hot, desperate kisses to his eyes, needing to take away the hurt in them and transfer it into herself. He groaned with every press, long and suffering, and remorse for the pain she'd caused him during her surrender to insecurity came pouring out.

"I'm sorry, Aram. Believe me, please. I *didn't* mean what I said. It was my insecurities talking."

He threw his head back on the couch, his glorious hair fanning to frame his haggard face. "*I'm* sorry. And you had every right to react as you did."

She pressed her lips to his, stopping him from taking responsibility. She wanted this behind them. "No, I didn't. And you have nothing to be sorry about."

His whole face twisted. "I just am. So cripplingly sorry that you felt pain on my account, no matter how it happened."

She kissed him again and again. "Don't be. It's okay."

"No, it's not. I can't bear your uncertainty, *ya habibati*. I can't breathe, I can't *be*...if I don't have your belief and serenity. I'd die if I lost you."

"I'm never going anywhere. I was being stupid, okay? Now quit worrying. You have more important things to worry about than my insecurities."

"I worry about nothing but what you think and feel, *ya kanzi*. Nothing else is important. Nothing else even matters."

"Then you have nothing to worry about. Since only

you…only us, like *this*…matters to me, too." Her hands feverishly roved over him, undoing his shirt, his pants. She rained bites and suckles over his formidable shoulders and torso, releasing his daunting erection. A week of desolation without him, knowing that his seed had taken root inside her, made the ache for him uncontrollable, the hunger unstoppable.

But it was clear he wouldn't take, wouldn't urge. He'd sit there and let her do what she wanted to him, show him what she needed…take all she wanted. And she couldn't wait.

She shrugged off her jacket, swept her blouse over her head, snapped off her bra and bunched up her skirt. She rose to her knees to offer him her breasts, to scale his length. He devoured her like a starving man, reiterating her name, his love.

Her core flowed as she pushed aside her panties then sank down on him in one stroke. Her back arched at the shock of his invasion. Sensations shredded her. *Aram.* Claiming her back, taking her home. Her only home.

She rose and fell over him, their mouths mating to the same rhythm of their bodies. He forged deeper and deeper with every plunge, each a more intense bolt of stimulation. She'd wanted it to last, but her body was already hurtling toward completion, every inch of him igniting the chain reaction that would consume her.

As always, he felt her distress and instinctively took over, taking her in his large palms, lifting her, thrusting her on that homestretch to oblivion until the coil of need broke, lashing through her in desperate surges of excruciating pleasure.

"Aram, *habibi,* come with me…."

He let go at her command, splashing her walls with his essence. And she cried out her love, her adoration, again and again. *"Ahebbak, ya hayati, aashagak."*

Aram looked up at Kanza as she cried out and writhed the last of her pleasure all over him, wrung every drop of his from depths he'd never known existed before collapsing over him, shuddering and keening her satisfaction.

She'd taken her sentence back, had again expunged his record, giving him the blessing of continuing as if nothing had happened. She'd called him her love and life again. She'd made soul-scorching love to him.

So why wasn't he feeling secure that this storm was over?

She was stirring, her smile dawning as she let him know she wanted to lie down.

Maneuvering so she was lying comfortably on her side on the couch, he got her the jacket she reached for. She fished an envelope from its pocket. At its sight, his heart fisted.

He recognized the seal. The king of Zohayd's. He was certain what this was.

With a radiant smile, she foisted it on him. And sure enough, it was what he'd expected. She'd gone and gotten him everything that just a week ago she'd thought he'd married her to get.

And she'd made love to him before presenting it to him to reassure him that accepting this wouldn't jeopardize their relationship. She was giving him everything she believed he needed. Zohayd as his home. The job that would be the culmination of his life's work, putting him on par with the ruling family.

He again tried to correct her assumptions about his needs. "I need only you, *ya kanzi*...."

"How many times will I tell you I'm okay now? I just showed you how okay I was."

"But we still need to talk."

She kissed him one last time before sitting up. "And we will. As much as you'd like. After the ceremony, okay? Just forget about everything else now."

Could *she* forget it, or would she just live with it? When she'd said before that she couldn't?

He feared *that* might be the truth. That she was just giving in to her love, her need for him, but even more, his love and need for her. But in her heart, she'd never regain her total faith in him, her absolute security in his love.

"Let's get you ready," she said as she pulled him to his feet. "This is the most important day of your life."

"It certainly isn't. That day is every day with you."

She grinned and he saw his old Kanza. "Second most important, then. Still pretty important if you ask me. C'mon, Shaheen said he'd send you the job's 'trimmings.'"

He'd always known she was one in a million, that he'd beaten impossible odds finding her. But what she was doing now, the extent to which she loved him, showed him how impossibly blessed he was.

And he was going to be worthy of her miracle.

Aram glanced around the ceremony hall.

It looked sedate and official, totally different than it had during his and Kanza's fairy-tale wedding. The hundreds present today were also dressed according to the gravity of the situation. This was the first time in the past six hundred years that a foreigner had been introduced into the royal house and had taken on one of the kingdom's highest offices.

As Amjad walked into the hall with his four brothers behind him, Aram stole a look back at Kanza. His heart swelled as she met his eyes, expectant, emotional, proud.

What had he done so right he'd deserved to find her? An angel wouldn't deserve her.

But he would. He'd do everything and anything to be worthy of her love.

Amjad now stood before his throne, with his brothers flanking him on both sides. Shaheen was to his right. He met Aram's eyes, his brimming with pride, pleasure, excitement and more than a little relief.

Aram came to stand before the royal brothers, in front

of Amjad, who wasn't making any effort to appear solemn, meeting his eyes with his signature irreverence.

Giving back as good as he got, he repeated the citizenship oath. But as he kneeled to have Amjad touch his head with the king's sword while reciting the subject proclamation, Amjad gave him what appeared to be an accidental whack on the head—intentionally, he was certain.

Aram rose, murmuring to Amjad that it was about time they did something about their long-standing annoyance with each other. Amjad whimsically told him he wished he could oblige him. But he'd promised Kanza he'd share his lunch with him in the playground from now on.

Pondering that Kanza had smoothed his path even with Amjad, he accepted the citizenship breastpin.

Yawning theatrically, Amjad went through the ritual of proclaiming him the minister of economy, pretending to nod off with the boredom of its length. Then it was the minister's breastpin's turn to join the other on Aram's chest. This time, Amjad made sure he pricked him.

Everyone in the hall rose to their feet, letting loose a storm of applause and cheers. He turned to salute them, caught Kanza's smile and tearful eyes across the distance. Then he turned back to the king.

In utmost tranquility, holding Amjad's goading gaze, he unfastened the breastpins one by one, then, holding them out in the two feet between them, he let them drop to the ground.

The applause that had faltered as he'd taken the breastpins off came to an abrupt halt. The moment the pins clanged on the ground, the silence fractured on a storm of collective gasps.

Aram watched as Amjad shrewdly transferred his gaze from Kanza's shocked face back to his.

Then that wolf of a man drawled, "So did my baby brother not explain the ritual to you? Or are you taking off your sharp objects to tackle me to the ground here and now?"

"I'll tackle you in the boardroom, Amjad. And I know exactly what casting the symbols of citizenship and status to the ground means. That I renounce both, irrevocably."

Amjad suddenly slapped him on the shoulder, grinning widely. "What do you know? You're not a stick-in-the-mud like your best friend. If you're as interesting as this act of madness suggests you are, I might swipe you from him."

"Since you did this for me to please Kanza, you're not unsalvageable yourself, after all, Amjad. Maybe I'll squeeze you in, when I'm not busy belonging to Kanza."

"Since I'm also busy belonging to Maram, we'll probably work a reasonable schedule. Say, an hour a year?"

Suddenly liking the guy, he grinned at him. "You're on."

As he turned around, Shaheen was all over him, and Harres, Haidar and Jalal immediately followed suit, scolding, disbelieving, furious.

He just smiled, squeezed Shaheen's shoulder then walked back among the stunned spectators and came to kneel at Kanza's feet. Looking as if she'd turned to stone, she gaped down at him, eyes turbid and uncomprehending.

He took her hands, pulled her to his embrace. "The only privileges I'd ever seek are your love and trust and certainty. Would you bestow them on me again, whole, pure and absolute? I can't and won't live without them, *ya kanzi*."

And she exploded into action, grabbing him and dragging him behind her among the now-milling crowd.

"Undo this!"

Amjad turned at her imperative order, smiling sardonically. "No can do. Seems this Aram of yours *is* too much like me, poor girl. He's as crazy as I am."

She stamped her foot in frustration. "You *can* undo this. You're the king."

Amjad tsked. "And undo *his* grand gesture? Don't think so."

"So you can undo it!" she exclaimed.

Amjad shook his head. "Sorry, little cousin. Too many pesky witnesses and tribal laws. Your man knew exactly what he was doing and that it cannot be undone. But let me tell you, it makes him worthy of you. That took guts, and also shows he knows exactly what works for him, what's worthy. *You.* So just enjoy your pretty, pretty full-of-himself guy's efforts to worship you."

She looked between him and Amjad in complete and utter shock. "But…what will Shaheen do when Johara gives birth? What about Zohayd…"

"The only world that would collapse without your Aram is yours. And I guess that's why he's doing this. To make it—" Amjad winked at her "—impregnable."

As she continued to argue and plead, Aram swept her up in his arms and strode out of the palace, taking her back home.

Her protests kept coming even after he'd taken her home and made love to her twice.

He rose on his elbow, gathered her to him. "I'll work the job as if I'd taken the position, so I won't leave Shaheen in the lurch. All that'll be missing is the title, which I care nothing about. I want the work itself, the achievement. But contrary to what Shaheen said, I don't need to be always in Zohayd or need to belong here. I already belong. With you, to you."

She wound herself around him, inundating him with her love, which, to his eternal relief, was once again unmarred by uncertainty and fiercer than ever before. "You didn't have to do it. I would have gotten over the last traces of in-security in a few weeks tops."

"I wouldn't leave you suffering uncertainty for a few minutes. You are more than my home, *ya kanzi.* You're my haven. You contain me whole, you ward off my own demons and anything else the world could throw at me. I haven't lost a thing, and I have gained everything. I *have* everything. Because I have you."

She threw herself at him again before pulling back to look at him with shyness spreading over that face that was his whole world.

"And you're going to have more of me. Literally. And in seven months I'll give you a replica of you."

He keeled over her. As she shrieked in alarm, he laughed, loud and unfettered, then kissed her breathless, mingling their tears.

A baby. There was no end to her blessings.

After yet another storm of rapture passed, he said, "I want a replica of *you*."

"Sorry, buddy, it'll be your replica. In Zohayd they say the baby looks like the parent who is loved more. Uh-uh-uh…" She silenced him as he protested. "I've loved you longer, so you can't do a thing about it. So there."

"I trust this applies only to the first baby. The second one doesn't follow those rules. Second one, your replica."

"But I want them all disgustingly pretty like you!"

He pounced on her, and soon the laughter turned to passion, then to delirium, frenzy and finally pervasive peace.

And through it all, he gave thanks for this unparalleled treasure, this hurricane who'd uprooted him from his seclusion and tossed him into the haven of her unconditional love.

* * * * *

CONVENIENT BRIDE
FOR THE KING

KELLY HUNTER

CHAPTER ONE

PRINCESS MORIANA OF ARUN wasn't an unreasonable woman. She had patience aplenty and was willing to give anyone the benefit of the doubt at least once. Maybe even twice. But when she knew for a fact she was being passed around like a Christmas cracker no one wanted to pull, all bets were off.

Her brother Augustus had said he wasn't available to speak with her this morning. People to see, kingdom to rule.

Nothing to do with avoiding her until she regained her equilibrium after yesterday's spectacularly public jilting...the *coward*.

So what if Casimir of Byzenmaach no longer wanted to marry her? It wasn't as if it had ever been Casimir's idea in the first place, and it certainly hadn't been hers. When you were the progeny of kings it was commonplace for a politically expedient marriage to be arranged for you. And yet...inexplicably... Casimir's defection after such a long courtship had gutted her. He'd made her feel small and insignificant, unwanted and alone, and, above all, not good enough. All her hard work, the endless social politics, the restraint that guided her every move, had been for what?

Nothing.

Absolutely nothing.

Arun's royal palace was an austere one, mainly because Moriana's forefathers had planned it that way. Stern, grey and never quite warm enough, it invited application to duty over frivolous timewasting. It chose function over beauty, no matter how much beauty she found to hang on its walls. It favoured formal cloistered gardens for tidy minds.

Her brother had taken residence in the southern wing of the palace in the gloomiest rooms of them all, and not for the first time did Moriana wonder why. Her brother's executive secretary—an elderly courtier who'd been in service to the House of Arun since before she was born—looked up as she approached, his expression smooth and unruffled.

'Princess, what a pleasant surprise.'

She figured her appearance was neither pleasant nor a surprise, but she let the man have his social graces. 'Is he in?'

'He's taking an important call.'

'But he is in,' she countered and kept right on walking towards her brother's closed door. 'Wonderful.'

The older man sighed and pressed a button on the intercom as she swept past. He didn't actually *speak* into the intercom, mind. Moriana was pretty sure he had a secret code button set up just for her—doubtless announcing that Moriana the Red was incoming.

Her brother looked up when she walked in, told whoever he had on the phone that he'd call them back, and put the phone down.

Damn but it was cold in here. It didn't help that the spring just past had been a brutal one and summer had been slow to arrive. 'Why is it like an ice box in here?'

she asked. 'Have we no heating you can turn on? No warmer rooms you could rule from?'

'Or you could wear warmer clothes,' her brother suggested, but there was nothing wrong with her attire. Her fine wool dress was boat-necked, long-sleeved and fell to just above her knees. Stockings added another layer to her legs. She was wearing knee-high leather boots. Had she added a coat she'd be ready for a trip to the Antarctic.

'It is a perfectly pleasant day outside,' she countered. 'Why do you choose the coldest rooms we have to call your own?'

'If I had better rooms, more people would be tempted to visit me and I'd never get any work done.' His eyes were almost black and framed by thick black lashes, just like her own. His smile was indulgent as he sat back and steepled his hands—maybe his whole *I'm in charge of the universe* pose worked on some, but she'd grown up with him and knew what Augustus had looked like as a six-year-old with chickenpox and as a teenager with his first hangover. She knew the sound of his laughter and the shape of his sorrows. He could wear his kingly authority in public and she would bow to him but here in private, when it was just the two of them, he was nothing more than a slightly irritating older brother. 'What can I do for you?' he asked.

'Have you seen this?' She held up a thick sheet of cream-coloured vellum.

'Depends,' he said.

She slammed the offending letter down on the ebony desk in front of him. Letters generally didn't slam down on anything but this one had the weight of her hand behind it. 'Theo sent me a proposal.'

'Okay,' he said cautiously, still looking at her rather than the letter.

'A *marriage* proposal.'

Her brother's lips twitched.

'Don't you dare,' she warned.

'Well, it stands to reason he would,' said Augustus. 'You're available, he's under increasing pressure to produce an heir and secure the throne, and politically it's an opportunistic match.'

'We loathe each other. There is no earthly reason why Theo would want to spend an evening with me, let alone eternity.'

'I have a theory about that—'

'Don't start.'

'It goes something like this. He pulled your pigtail when you were children, you gave him a black eye and you've been fierce opponents ever since. If you actually spent some time with the man you'd discover he's not half as bad as you think he is. He's well-travelled, well-read, surprisingly intelligent and a consummate negotiator. All things you admire.'

'A consummate negotiator? Are you serious? Theo's marriage proposal is a *form* letter. He filled my name in at the top and his at the bottom.'

'And he has a sense of humour,' Augustus said.

'Says who?'

'Everyone except for you.'

'Doesn't that tell you something?'

'Yes.'

Oh, it was *on*.

She pulled up a chair, a hard unwelcoming one because that was all there was to be had in this farce of a room. She sat. He sighed. She crossed her legs, etiquette be damned. Two seconds later she uncrossed her legs, rearranged her skirt over her knees and sat ram-rod-straight as she stared him down. 'Did you arrange this?' Because she wouldn't put it past him. He and their three neighbouring monarchs were close. They plotted together on a regular basis.

'Me? No.'

'Did Casimir?' He of the broken matrimonial intentions and newly discovered offspring.

'I doubt it. What with burying his father and planning a coronation, the instant fatherhood and his current wooing of the child's mother... I'm pretty sure he has his hands full.'

Moriana drummed her fingers on his ugly wooden desk, partly because it gave her time to digest her brother's words and partly because she knew it annoyed him. 'Then whose mad idea was it?'

He eyed her offending fingers for a moment before casually pulling open his desk drawer and pulling out a long wooden ruler. He held it up, as if gauging its reach, before bringing the tip to rest gently in his palm. 'Stop torturing my desk.'

'Or you'll beat me? Please,' she scoffed. Nonetheless, she stopped with the drumming and brought the offending hand in front of her to examine her nails. No damage at all. Maybe she'd paint her nails black later, to match the desk and her mood. Maybe her rebellion could start small. 'You haven't answered my question. Whose idea was it?'

'I'm assuming it was Theo's.'

She looked up to find Augustus eyeing her steadily, as if he knew something she didn't.

'It's not an insult, Moriana; it's an honour. You were born and raised for the kind of position Theo's offering.

You could make a difference to his leadership and to the stability of the region.'

'No.' She cut him off fast. 'You can't guilt me into this. I am *through* with being the good princess who does what she's told, the one who serves and serves and *serves,* without any thought to my own needs. I'm going to Cannes to party up a scandal. There will be reckless-ness. Orgies with dissolute film stars.'

'When?' Augustus did not sound alarmed.

'Soon.' He didn't *look* alarmed either, and he should have. 'You don't think I'll do it. You think I'm a humour-less prude who wouldn't know fun times if they rained down on me. Well, they're about to. I want the passion of a lover's touch. I want a man to look at me with lust. Dam-mit, for once in my life I want to do something that pleases *me*!' She'd had enough. 'All those things I've been taught to place value on? My reputation, my sense of duty to king and country, my virginity? I'm getting rid of them.'

'Okay, let's not be hasty.'

'Hasty?' Princesses didn't screech. Moriana dropped her voice an octave and gave it some gravel instead. 'I could have had the stable boy when I was eighteen. He was beautiful, carefree and rode like a demon. At twenty-two I could have had a sheikh worth billions. He only had to look at me to make me melt. A year later I met a musician with hands I could only dream of. I would have gladly taken him to my bed but I *didn't*. Would you like me to continue?'

'*Please* don't.'

'Casimir's not a virgin,' she continued grimly. '*He* got a nineteen-year-old pregnant when he was twenty-three! You know what I was doing at twenty-three? Tak-ing dancing lessons so that I could feel the touch of someone's hand.'

'I thought they were fencing lessons.'

'Same thing. Maybe I wanted to feel a little prick.' All these years she'd denied herself all manner of pleasures others took for granted. 'I have *waited*. No romance, no lovers, no children for Moriana of Arun. Only duty. And for what? So that today I could wake up and be vilified in the press for being too cool, too stern and too focused on fundraising and furthering my education to have time for any man? I mean, no wonder Casimir of Byzenmaach went looking for someone else, right?'

Augustus winced. 'No one's saying that.'

'Have you even read today's newspapers?'

'No one *here* is saying that,' he amended.

'What did I do wrong, Augustus? I was promised to an indifferent boy when I was eight years old. Now I'm getting a form letter marriage proposal from a playboy king whose dislike for me is legendary. And you say I should feel honoured?' Her voice cracked. 'Why do you sell me off so *easily*? Am I really that worthless?'

She straightened her shoulders, smoothed her hands over the skirt of her dress and made sure the hem sat in a straight stern line. She hated losing her composure, hated feeling needy and greedy and hard to love. She was wired to please others. Trained to it since birth.

But this...expecting her to fall all over herself to comply with Theo's request... 'Theo's uncle is making waves again and questioning Theo's fitness to rule. I do read the reports that come in.' She read every last one of them. 'I understand Liesendaach's need for stability and a secure future and that we in Arun would rather deal with Theo than with his uncle. But I am *not* the solution to his need for a quickie marriage.'

'Actually, you're an excellent solution.' Augustus was watching her carefully. 'You've been looking forward to having a family for years. Theo needs an heir. You could be pregnant within a year.'

'Don't.' Yes, she wanted children. She'd foolishly once thought she'd be married with several children by now.

'You and Theo have goals that align. I'm merely stating the obvious.'

Moriana wrapped her arms around her waist and stared at the toes of her boots. The boots were a shade darker than the purple of her dress. The pearls around her neck matched the pearls in her ears. She was a picture-perfect princess who was falling apart inside. 'Maybe I don't want children any more. Maybe keeping royal children safe and happy and feeling loved is an impossible task.'

'Our parents seemed to manage it well enough.'

'Oh, really?' She knew she should hold her tongue. She didn't, and all her years of trying and failing to please people bubbled to the fore. 'Do you think I feel loved? By whom?' She choked on a laugh. 'You, who would just as soon trade me into yet another loveless marriage in return for regional stability? Casimir, who never wanted me in the first place and was simply too gutless to say so? Theo, with his form letter marriage proposal and endless parade of mistresses? Do you really think I've basked in the glow of unconditional parental love and approval for the past twenty-eight years? Heaven help me, Augustus. What *planet* are you living on? Not one of you even remembers I exist unless I can *do* something for you.'

She felt stupid. Stupid for putting her life on hold for a decade and never once calling into question that childhood betrothal. She could have asked for a time frame from Casimir. She could have pressed for a solid commitment. She could have said no to many things and got over trying to please people who didn't give a damn about her. She gestured towards Theo's offending letter. 'He doesn't even *pretend* to offer love or attraction. Not even mild affection.'

'Is that what you want?'

'Yes! I want to be with someone who cares for me. Why is that so hard to understand?'

'Maybe he does.'

'What?'

'Theo. Maybe he cares for you.'

'You don't seriously expect me to believe that.' Moriana looked at him in amazement. 'You do. Oh. You must think I'm really stupid.'

'It's a theory.'

'Would you like me to disprove it for you?' Because she had years and years of dealing with Theo to call on. 'I can count on one hand the times I've felt that man's support. The first was at our mother's funeral when he caught me as I stumbled on the steps of the church. He made me sit before I fell. He brought me water and sat with me in silence and kept his hatred of women wearing black to himself. The second and final time he was supportive of me was at a regional water summit when a drunk delegate put his hand on my backside. Theo told him he'd break it if it wasn't removed.'

'I like it,' said her brother with a faint smile.

'You would.'

'He knows where you are in a room full of people,' Augustus said next. 'He always knows. He can describe whatever it is you're wearing.'

'So he's observant.'

'It's more than that.'

'I disagree. Maybe he's wanted me a time or two,

I'll give him that. But only for sport, and only because he couldn't have me.' She plucked the form letter from the desk and folded it so that the offending words were hidden. 'No, Augustus. It's a smart offer. Theo's a smart man. I can see exactly what kind of political gain is in it for him. But there's nothing in it for me. Nothing I want.'

'I hear you,' Augustus replied quietly.

'Good.' She sent her brother a tight smile. 'Maybe I'll send a form letter refusal. *Dear Applicant, After careful consideration I regret to inform you that your proposal has been unsuccessful. Better luck next time.*'

'That would be inviting him to try again. This is Theo, remember?'

'You're right.' Moriana reconsidered her words. *'Better luck elsewhere?'*

'Yes.' Her brother smiled but his eyes remained clouded with concern. 'Moriana—'

'Don't,' she snapped. 'Don't you try and guilt me into doing this.'

'I'm not. You're free to choose. Free to be. Free to discover who and what makes you happy.'

'Good. Good chat. I should bare my soul to you more often.'

Augustus shuddered.

Moriana rounded her brother's imposing desk and kissed the top of his head, mainly because she knew such a blatant display of affection would irritate him. 'I'm sorry,' she whispered. 'I like what Theo's doing for his country. I applaud the progress and stability he's bringing to the region and I want it to continue. There's plenty to admire about him these days, and if I thought he actually liked me or that there was any chance he could meet my needs I'd marry him and make the most of it. I don't need to be swept off my feet. But this time I *do* want attention and affection and fidelity in return for my service. Love even, heaven forbid. And that's not Theo's wheelhouse.'

Augustus, reigning King of Arun and brother to Moriana the Red, watched as his sister turned on her boot heel and headed for the door.

'Moriana.' It was easier to talk to her retreating form than say it to her face. 'I do love you, you know. I want you to be happy.'

Her step faltered, but she didn't look back as she closed the door behind her.

Augustus, worst brother in the world, put his hands to his face and breathed deeply before reaching for the phone on his desk.

He didn't know, he couldn't be sure if Theo had stayed on the line or not, but still…the option to do so had been there.

Mistake.

He picked up the phone and listened for a moment but there was only silence. 'You still there?' he asked finally.

'Yes.'

Damn. 'I wish you hadn't heard that.'

'She's magnificent.' A thousand miles away, King Theodosius of Liesendaach let out a breath and ran a hand through his short-cropped hair. He had the fair hair and blue-grey eyes of his forefathers, the build of a warrior and no woman had ever refused him. Until now. He didn't know whether to be insulted or to applaud. 'The stable boy? Really?'

'I wish *I* hadn't heard that.' Augustus sounded weary. 'What the hell are you doing, sending her a form letter marriage proposal? I thought you wanted her cooperation.'

'I do want her co-operation. I will confess, I wasn't expecting quite that much *no* in response.'

'You thought she'd fall all over the offer.'

'I thought she'd at least consider it.'

'She did.' Augustus's tone was dry—very dry. 'When's the petition for your removal from the throne being tabled?'

'Week after next, assuming my uncle gets the support he needs. He's close.' The petition was based on a clause in Liesendaach's constitution that enabled a monarch who had no intention of marrying and producing an heir to be removed from the throne. The clause hadn't been enforced in over three hundred years.

'You need a plan B,' said Augustus.

'I have a plan B. It involves talking to your sister in person.'

'You heard her. She's not interested.'

'Stable boy,' Theo grated. 'Dissolute film star. Would you rather she took up with them?'

'Why are you any more worthy? A damn *form letter*, Theo.' Augustus appeared to be working up to a snit of his own. 'Couldn't you have at least shown up? I thought you cared for her. I honestly thought you cared for her more than you ever let on, otherwise I would have never encouraged this.'

'I do care for her.' She was everything a future queen of Liesendaach should be. Poised, competent, politically aware and beautiful. Very, *very* beautiful. He'd dragged his heels for years when it came to providing Liesendaach with a queen.

And now Moriana, Princess of Arun, was free.

Her anger at her current situation had nothing on Theo's when he thought of how much *time* they'd wasted. '*Your sister* put herself on hold for a man who didn't want her, and you—first as her brother, and then as her King—did nothing to either expedite or dissolve that commitment. All those years she spent sidelined and waiting. All her hard-won self-confidence dashed by polite indifference. Do you care for her? Has Casimir *ever* given a damn? Because from where I sit, neither of you could have cared for her any *less*. I may not love her the way she wants to be loved. Frankly, I don't love anyone like that and never have. But at least I notice her *existence*.'

Silence from the King of Arun.

'You miscalculated with the form letter,' Augustus said finally.

'So it would seem,' Theo gritted out.

'I advise you to let her cool down before you initiate any further contact.'

'No. Why do you never let your sister run hot?' Even as a child he'd hated seeing Moriana's fiery spirit squashed beneath the weight of royal expectations. And, later, it was one of the reasons he fought with her so much. Not the only one—sexual frustration had also played its part. But when he and Moriana clashed, her fire stayed lit. He *liked* that.

'I need to see her.' Theo ran a hand through his already untidy hair. 'I'm not asking you to speak with her on my behalf. I've already heard you do exactly that and, by the way, thanks for nothing. What kind of diplomat are you? Yes, I'm being pressured to marry and produce heirs. That's not an argument I would have led with.'

'I didn't lead with it. I mentioned it in passing. I also sang your praises and pushed harder than I should have on your behalf. You're welcome.'

'I can give her what she wants. Affection, attention, even fidelity.'

Not love, but you couldn't have everything.

'That's your assessment. It's not hers.'

'I need to speak with her.'

'No,' said Augustus. 'You need to grovel.'

CHAPTER TWO

PUBLIC FLAYING OR NOT, Moriana's charity commitments continued throughout the day and into the evening. She'd put together a charity antique art auction for the children's hospital months ago and the event was due to start at six p.m. in one of the palace function rooms that had been set up for the occasion. The auctioneers had been in residence all day, setting up the display items. Palace staff were on duty to take care of the catering, security was in place and there was no more work to be done beyond turning up, giving a speech and subtly persuading some of the region's wealthiest inhabitants to part with some of their excess money. Moriana was good at hosting such events. Her mother had taught her well.

Not that Moriana had ever managed to live up to those exacting standards when her mother was alive. It had taken years of dogged, determined practice to even reach her current level of competence.

The principality of Arun wasn't the wealthiest principality in the region. That honour went to Byzenmaach, ruled by Casimir, her former intended. It also wasn't the prettiest. Theo's Liesendaach was far prettier, embellished by centuries of rulers who'd built civic buildings and public spaces beyond compare. No, Arun's claim to fame lay in its healthcare and education systems, and this was due in no small measure to her ceaseless work in those areas, and her mother's and grandmother's attention before that. Rigidly repressed the women of the royal house of Arun might be but they knew how to champion the needs of their people.

Tonight would be an ordeal. The press had not been kind to her today and she'd tried to put that behind her and carry on as usual. The main problem being that *no one else* was carrying on as usual. Even Aury, her unflappable lady-in-waiting, had been casting anxious glances in Moriana's direction all day.

Moriana's favourite treat, lemon tart with a burnt sugar top, had been waiting for her at morning tea, courtesy of the palace kitchens. A vase full of fat pink peonies had been sitting on her sideboard by lunchtime. She'd caught one of her publicity aides mid-rant on the phone—he'd been threatening to revoke someone's palace press pass if they ran a certain headline, and he'd flushed when he'd seen her but he'd kept right on making threats until he'd got his way.

There'd been a certain lack of newspapers in the palace this morning, which meant that Moriana had had to go online to read them.

She should have stayed away.

There was this game she and her lady-in-waiting often made out of the news of the day. While Aury styled Moriana's hair for whatever function was on that evening, they'd shoot headlines back and forth. On a normal day it encouraged analysis and discussion.

On a normal day the headlines wouldn't be proclaiming Moriana the most undesirable princess on the planet.

'Too Cold to Wed,' Moriana said as Aury reached for the pins that would secure Moriana's braid into an elegant roll at the base of her head.

'No,' said Aury, pointing a stern hairbrush in the direction of Moriana's reflection. 'I'm not doing this today and neither are you. I stopped reading them so I wouldn't choke on my breakfast, and you should have stopped reading them too.'

'Jilted Ice Princess Contemplates Nunnery,' Moriana continued.

'I'm not coming with you to the nunnery. They don't care what hair looks like there, the heathens,' said Aury, pushing a hairpin into place. 'Okay, no, I will give you a headline. *Byzenmaach Mourns as the Curse Strikes Again.'*

'Curse?' Moriana had missed that one. 'What curse?'

'Apparently you refused to marry King Casimir in an attempt to avoid the same fate as his mother. Namely, being physically, mentally and verbally abused by your husband for years before taking a lover, giving birth to your lover's child, seeing both killed by your husband and then committing suicide.'

'Ouch.' Moriana caught her lady-in-waiting's gaze in the mirror. 'What paper was that?'

'A regional one from Byzenmaach's northern border. The *Mountain Chronicle.'*

'Vultures.' Never mind that she'd accidentally overheard her parents discussing a remarkably similar scenario involving Casimir's parents. She'd never repeated the conversation to anyone but Augustus and she never would. 'Casimir doesn't deserve that one.'

'Byzenmaach Monarch Faces Backlash over Secret Lover and Child,' said Aury next.

'That one I like. Serves him right. Do we have the run sheet for the auction tonight?'

'It's right here. And the guest list.'

Moriana scanned through the paperwork Aury

handed her. 'Augustus is attending now and bringing a guest? He didn't say anything about it to me this morning.'

Not that she'd given him a chance to say anything much. Still.

'Word came through from his office this afternoon. Also, Lord and Lady Curtis send their apologies. Their granddaughter had a baby this afternoon.'

'Have we sent our congratulations?'

'We have.'

'Tell the auctioneer to put my reserve on the baby bear spoon set. They can have it as a gift.' Arun might not be the wealthiest or the prettiest kingdom in the region but its people did not go unattended.

'I put the silver gown out for tonight, along with your grandmother's diamonds. I also took the liberty of laying out the blood-red gown you love but never wear and the pearl choker and earrings from the royal collection. The silver gown is a perfectly appropriate choice, don't get me wrong, but I for one am hoping the Ice Princess might feel like making a statement tonight.'

'And you think a red gown and a to-hell-with-you-all attitude will do this?'

'It beats looking whipped.'

'The red gown it is,' Moriana murmured. The Ice Princess was overdue for a thaw. 'Now all I need is a wholly inappropriate date to go with it.' She took a deep breath and let it out slowly. 'Actually, no. I'm not so merciless as to drag anyone else into this mess. I'll go alone.'

'You'll not be alone for long,' Aury predicted. 'Opportunists will flock to you.'

'It's already started.'

'Anyone you like?'

'No.' Moriana ignored the sudden image of a harshly

hewn face and glittering grey eyes. 'Well, Theo. Who I've never actually tried to like. It never seemed worth the effort.'

Aury stopped fussing with Moriana's hair in favour of looking stunned. 'Theodosius of Liesendaach is courting you now?'

'I wouldn't call it courting.' Moriana thought back to the form letter and scowled. 'Trust me, neither would anyone else.'

'Yes, but *really*?'

'Aury, your tongue is hanging out.'

'Uh huh. Have you *seen* that man naked?'

'Oh, yes. God bless the paparazzi. *Everyone* has seen that man naked.'

'And what a treat it was.'

Okay, so he was well endowed. And reputedly very skilled in the bedroom. Women did not complain of him. Old lovers stayed disconcertingly friendly with him.

'You'd take me to Liesendaach with you, right?' asked Aury as she started in on Moriana's hair again, securing the roll with pearl-tipped pins and leaving front sections of hair loose to be styled into soft curls. 'I can start packing any time. Say the word. I am there for you. Of course, I am also here for you.' Aury sighed heavily.

'You should have pursued a career in drama,' Moriana said. 'Arun's not so bad. A little austere at times. A little grey around the edges. And at the centre. But there's beauty here too, if you know where to look.'

'I know where to look.' Aury sighed afresh. 'And clearly so does Theodosius of Liesendaach. Be careful with that one.'

'I can handle Theo.'

Aury looked uncommonly troubled, her dark eyes wary and her lips tilted towards a frown. 'He strikes me as a man who gets what he wants. What if he decides he wants you?'

'He doesn't. Theo's been reliably antagonistic towards me since childhood. And when he's not prodding me with a pointy stick he's totally indifferent to my presence. He's just…going through the motions. Being a casual opportunist. If I turn him down he'll go away.'

Aury sighed again and Moriana could feel a lecture coming on. Aury had several years on Moriana, not enough to make her a mother figure, but more than enough to fulfil the role of older, wiser sister. It was a role she took seriously.

'My lady, as one woman to another… Okay, as one slightly more experienced woman to another…please don't be taken in by Theodosius of Liesendaach's apparent indifference to events and people that surround him. That man is like a hawk in a granary. He's watching, he's listening and he knows what he wants from any given situation. More to the point, he knows what *everyone else* wants from any given situation.'

'He doesn't know what I want.'

'Want to bet?' Aury sounded uncommonly serious. 'Yes, he's charming, he's playful, he's extremely good at acting as if he couldn't care less. But what else do we know of him? Think about it. We know that for the first fifteen years of his life he never expected to be King. We know that for ten years after the death of his parents and brother he watched and waited his turn while his uncle bled Liesendaach dry as Regent. *The young Crown Prince is indifferent to our plight*, the people said. *He's bad blood, too busy pleasing himself to care about the rape of our country*, they said. *We can't look to him to save us. He will not bring an end to this*. That's what his uncle thought. It's what everyone thought. It's what he wanted them to think.'

Aury reached for another pin. 'Do you remember the day Theodosius of Liesendaach turned twenty-five and took the throne? I do. Because from that day forward he systematically destroyed his uncle and squashed every last parasite. He targeted their every weakness, he knew exactly where to strike, and he has fought relentlessly to bring his country back to prosperity. That's not indifference. That's patience, planning, ruthless execution and fortitude. He was *never* indifferent to his country's plight. I don't trust that man's *indifference* one little bit.'

'Point taken.'

'I hope so.' Aury finished with Moriana's hair and pulled the make-up trolley closer. She rifled through the lipstick drawer and held up a blood-red semi-gloss for inspection. 'What else are we thinking?'

'I'm thinking smoky eyes and lipstick one shade lighter. It's a charity auction, not a nightclub.'

'Boring,' said Aury.

'Baby steps.' Moriana had already chosen a dress she wasn't entirely comfortable with.

Aury found a lighter shade of lipstick and held it up for inspection. 'What about this one?'

'Yes.' Aury rarely steered her wrong. 'And Aury?'

'Yes, milady?'

'I'll be careful.'

Augustus was a deceitful, manipulative son of Satan, Moriana decided when he stepped into the auction room later that evening with his *guest* in tow. It wasn't a woman. Oh, no. Her brother hadn't done anything so lacklustre as bringing a suitable date with him to the event. Instead, he'd brought a neighbouring monarch along for the ride. Theo, to be more precise. He of the hawkish grace, immaculate dinner suit and form letter marriage proposal.

Theo and Augustus had been thick as thieves as children. They'd grown apart in their teens when Theo had flung himself headlong into reckless debauchery after the death of his family. Augustus had only followed him so far before their father, the then monarch of Arun, had reined him in. Theo had experienced no such constraints. Lately though…now that Theo bore the full brunt of the Liesendaach Crown… Moriana didn't quite know what kind of relationship Theo and her brother had. They'd been working together on a regional water plan. They trusted each other's judgement in such matters. They still didn't socialise together.

Much.

That they were socialising now, the same day she'd refused Theo's offer, spoke volumes for Augustus's support of the man.

So much for blood being thicker than brotherhood.

She turned away fast when she caught her brother's gaze because this betrayal, on top of Casimir's rejection, on top of Theo's demeaning form letter, almost brought her to her knees. So much for men and all their fine promises. You couldn't trust any of them.

The chief press advisor for the palace appeared at her side, his eyes sharp but his smile in place. 'Your Highness, you look pale. May I get you anything?'

'How about a brand-new day?' she suggested quietly. 'This one's rotten, from the core out.'

'Tomorrow will be a better day,' he said.

'Promises.' Her voice was light but her heart was heavy.

'I promise we're doing our best to shine the brightest light we can on everything you do for us, milady. The entire team is on it. No one dismisses our princess lightly. No one has earned that right.'

'Thank you, Giles.' She blinked back rapid tears and looked away. 'I appreciate your support.'

And then two more people joined them. One was Theo and the other one was Augustus. Years of burying her feelings held her in good stead as she plastered a smile on her face and set about greeting them.

'Your Majesties,' she said, curtseying to them, and something of her hurt must have shown on her face as she rose because Augustus frowned and started to say something. Whatever it was, she didn't want to hear it. 'What a surprise.'

'A pleasant one, I hope,' said Theo as he took her gloved hand and lifted it to his lips.

'Oh, we all live in hope,' she offered. 'I live in hope that one day the people I hold dear will have my back, but that day's not here yet.'

'Yes, it is; you just can't see it,' Theo countered. 'I'm here, welcome or not, with the ulterior motive of being seen with you in public.'

'Indeed, I can see the headlines now. *Ice Princess Falls for Playboy King. Liesendaach Gives It a Week.*'

'Perhaps.' Theo didn't discount it. 'Or I can give your publicity officer here a quote about how much respect I have for you as a person and as a representative of the royal family of Arun. I can mention that it's no hardship whatsoever to continue to offer you my friendship, admiration and support. I can add that I'm not at all dismayed that you're now free of your ridiculous childhood betrothal to the new King of Byzenmaach. And we can see how that goes down.'

The press advisor melted away with a nod in Theo's direction. Theo and her brother stayed put.

'Damage control, Moriana. Look it up,' Theo said curtly.

'Well, I guess you'd know all about that.'

'I do.' But he didn't defend his wild past or the chaos he occasionally still stirred. He never did. Theodosius of Liesendaach didn't answer to anyone.

A small—very tiny—part of her respected that.

'So,' she said. 'Welcome to my annual Children's Hospital Charity Auction. Have you seen the catalogue?'

'I have not.'

'I'll have one sent over.' She nodded towards some nearby display cases. 'By all means, look around. You might see something you like.'

'You won't accompany me?'

'No, I'm working.' He'd dressed immaculately, as usual. No one wore a suit quite the way Theo did. He was broad-shouldered and slim-hipped. Tall enough to look down on almost everyone in the room. His cropped blond hair was nothing remarkable and his face was clean-shaven. It wasn't a pretty face. A little too stern and altogether too craggy. Lips that knifed towards cruel when he was in a bad mood. His eyes were his best feature by far. She might as well give the devil his due. They were icy blue-grey and often coolly amused. They were amused now.

'I have other duties to attend and people to greet,' she continued bluntly. 'How fortunate Augustus is here to take care of you. What a good friend.'

'Indeed he is.' Theo's gaze had yet to leave hers. 'I like it when you wear red. The colour suits you and so do the pearls. My compliments to your wardrobe mistress.'

'I'll be sure to let her know. I mean, it's not as if I

could ever be in charge of my own clothing choices, right? Who knows what I'd come up with?' There was something different about Theo tonight. Something fierce and implacable and hungry. She bared her teeth right back at him. 'Any other underhand compliments you'd like to shower me with before I take my leave?'

Augustus winced. 'Moria—'

'No!' She cut him off. 'You don't get to diminish me either. All your fine talk this morning of supporting my decisions, of letting me be. I believed you. Yet here we are.'

'Your brother's not at fault,' Theo said smoothly. 'Moriana, we need to talk.'

'About your proposal? My reply is in the mail, seeing as that's your preferred method of communication. Seeing as you're here, I dare say I can give you the highlights. I refuse. It's not you, it's me. Or maybe it is you and all those other women I'd have to live up to, I don't know. Either way, my answer's no. I am done listening to the two-faced, self-serving babble of kings. Now, if you'll both excuse me.'

'Go. Greet your guests. We can talk after you're done here. I'll wait,' said Theo the Magnanimous. 'I'm good at waiting.'

Moriana laughed. She couldn't help it. 'Theo, you may have waited for your crown but you've never waited on a woman in your life.'

She was close enough to see his jaw clench. Close enough to see hot temper flare in those eyes that ran more towards grey tonight than blue. 'Oh, Princess. Always so *wrong.*'

It wasn't easy to turn away from the challenge in his gaze but she did it, more mindful than ever of Aury's warning. This wasn't the boy she remembered from

childhood or the teenager who'd poked and prodded at
her until she'd snapped back. This was the man who'd
watched and waited for ten long years before rising and
taking his country back. This was the hawk in the granary.

And maybe, just maybe, she was the mouse.

Fifteen minutes later, after personally greeting all the
guests in attendance and seeing that they were well lu-
bricated, Moriana looked for Theo again. Not that she
had to look hard. She always knew where Theo was in
a room, just as she always tracked where her security
detail was, and where her brother was. It was an awareness that would have made a seasoned soldier proud and
she'd been trained for it since birth.

*Know your exits. Know where your support is. Know
where your loved ones are at any given moment.* Theo
wasn't a loved one but he'd always been included in that
equation for he'd been a treasured child of royalty too.
The last of his line and therefore important.

Casimir, her former intended, had also been the last
of his line and she'd always tracked his whereabouts too,
whenever they'd been at functions together. She'd misplaced Casimir on occasion—no one was perfect. She'd
misplaced him on several occasions.

Many occasions.

Moving on.

Theo didn't look up from the display he was brows-
ing as she made her way to his side. He didn't look up
even as he began to speak. 'You're good at this,' he said.

'Thank you.' She wanted to believe he could pay
her a genuine compliment, not that he ever had before.
'I've been hosting this particular fundraiser for the past
seven years and I have it down to a fine art, pardon the

pun. Collecting the auction items, curating the guest list, knowing what people want and what they'll pay to have it. Knowing who else they might want to see socially. People say I have a knack for fundraising, as if I simply fling things together at the last minute and hope for the best, but I don't. I put a lot of work into making sure these evenings flow like water and do what they're meant to do.'

'I don't doubt it,' he said, finally turning his gaze on her. 'Hence the compliment.' He tilted his head a fraction. 'You're an exceptional ambassador for your people and you'd have been an exceptional asset to Casimir as queen consort. It's Byzenmaach's loss.'

He wasn't the first person to say that to her tonight and he probably wouldn't be the last. 'I doubt Casimir's feeling any loss.' She didn't like how thready she sounded. As if she'd been stretched too thin for far too long.

'He hurt you.' Three simple words that cracked her wide open.

'Don't. Theo, please. Leave it alone. It's done.'

She turned away, suddenly wanting to get away from the sedate auction room and the gossip and the expectations that came with being a Princess of Arun. Perfect composure, always. Unrivalled social graces. A memory trained to remember names and faces. She had a welcome speech to give in fifteen minutes. Who would give it if she walked out?

He stopped her before she'd taken a step. The subtle shift of his body and the force of his silent appraisal blocked her retreat. 'You're not coping,' he said quietly. 'Tell me what you need.'

She didn't know why his softly spoken words hurt so much, but they did. 'Damn you, Theo. Don't do this to me. Don't be attentive all of a sudden because you want something from me. Do what you usually do. Fight. Snarl. Be you. Give me something I know how to respond to.'

He stilled, his face a granite mask, and she had the sudden, inexplicable feeling she'd just dealt him a brutal blow. And then his gaze cut away from her face and he took a deep breath and when he looked at her again he wore a fierce and reckless smile she knew all too well. 'I'll fight you mentally, physically, whatever you need, until we both bleed,' he promised, his voice a vicious caress. 'Just as soon as you stop *breaking* in front of me. I know your family trained you to hide weakness better than this. It's what you do. It's all you do. So do it.'

Yes. This was what she needed from him, and to hell with why. No one said she was the most well-balanced princess in the universe.

Thread by thread she pulled herself together, drawing on the anger she sensed in him to bolster her own. *Build a wall—any wall.* Anger, righteous indignation, icy disdain, attention to duty, whatever it took to keep the volcano of feelings in check.

'Have you seen the Vermeer?' she asked finally, when she had herself mostly back under control. 'I thought of you when it first came in. It would round out Liesendaach's Dutch collection.'

He studied her for what felt like hours, before nodding, as if she'd do, and then held out his arm for her to claim. 'All right, Princess. Persuade me.'

Moriana carved out the time to show Theo the most interesting pieces in the auction. She made her speech and the auction began. And by the end of the evening a great deal of money had been raised for the new children's hospital wing and Theo had almost purchased the Vermeer for a truly staggering sum. In the end the painting had gone to a gallery and Moriana dearly hoped they needed a tax write-down soon because they clearly hadn't done their sums. That or they *really* wanted to support the children's hospital.

'I thought you'd lost your mind,' she said when only a handful of guests remained and he came to congratulate her on the evening's success. 'Not even you could justify that amount of money for a lesser Vermeer.'

'But for you I tried.'

His smile reminded her of young boys and frog ponds and sultry, still evenings, back when Theo's parents had still been alive. Augustus had always caught his frogs with quick efficiency and, once examined, had let them go. Theo, on the other hand, had revelled in the chase. He'd been far more interested in which way they jumped and where they might try to hide than in actually catching them. To this day, Moriana didn't know what that said about either Theo or her brother.

'Are you ready for that drink yet?' he asked.

'What drink?'

'The one we're going to have tonight, when you graciously reconsider my proposal.'

'Oh, *that* drink. We're not having that drink any time soon. You're getting a form letter rejection in the post, remember?'

'You wouldn't.'

'I did. You'll receive it tomorrow, unless you're still here. I assume Augustus has offered you palace hospitality?'

Theo inclined his head.

Of course. 'Then perhaps you should find him. I'm about to retire for the evening.'

'You said you'd give me five minutes of your time.'

'I said nothing of the sort. And yet here I am. Giving you my time.' If she'd worn a watch she'd have glanced at it.

'I gave you a fight when you needed one earlier.' Since when had his voice been able to lick at her like flames? 'I didn't want to, but I did. Here's what I want in return. One kiss. Here or in private. Put your hands on me, just once. You have my permission. I'll even keep mine to myself. And if you don't like touching and kissing me I'll withdraw my pursuit at once. Does that not sound fair and honest? Am I being unjust?'

Gone was the teasing menace of her childhood and the reckless philanderer of her youth. In their place stood a man in pursuit, confident and dangerous.

He'd been waiting for her when she'd finished her speech, approval in his eyes and a glass of champagne in hand that he handed to *her*. Faultlessly attentive. Silently supportive.

Tell me what you need.

A fight. A snarl. Barbed compliments. His attention. Something other than rejection to focus on.

'One drink. One kiss,' he murmured. 'Do you need to collect a coat of some sort? Because I'm ready to leave.'

'Why would I leave with you? Why would I indulge you in this?'

'Because I have something you want. Several somethings.'

'No, you don't. If you had anything I wanted, I'd be giving your proposal all due consideration.'

'Position.' His eyes never left her face.

'Yawn.' She was Princess of Arun.

'Passion. You've never felt it but you want it, nonetheless.'

'Maybe.' She was honest enough to concede his point. 'But you're not the only man to inspire passion in a woman. Plenty do. I can find passion without you.'

His eyes flashed silver.

'Temper, *temper*,' she said.

'Commitment,' he offered next.

'We all exercise that. I'm already committed to various causes, not to mention my country and my family. Some would say I'm blindly overcommitted to many things and receive little in return, and they're probably right. Commitment is overrated.'

His eyes never left her face. 'Commitment to you.'

CHAPTER THREE

HE WAS GOOD at this. Aury had warned her. He knew exactly what to offer in order to make her heart thump with painful hope and longing.

'Let's talk about this somewhere without the avid audience,' he muttered.

She glanced beyond him discreetly, only to realise he was right. Those who had yet to leave seemed to have no intention of doing so with her and Theo putting on a show right in front of their eyes. Even Augustus was staring at them, his eyes full of clear warning.

Don't make a spectacle of yourself. Remember your place.

Don't embarrass me.

Don't make me regret that we're related.

'Five minutes,' she said to Theo, as she nodded minutely at her brother—*message received*—and headed for the door.

Moriana lived in a wing of the royal palace. She'd furnished it to her taste, raided the palace's art collection until she was satisfied with the result and had purchased whatever pieces she felt were missing. Augustus could complain about her spending—and he did—but her ledger was in the black.

In the space of five years she'd tripled the value of

the royal art collection and outlaid only a fraction of that cost. She wheeled and dealed, had an eye for a bargain and the sensibilities of a curator. And, of course, she had the throne of Arun behind her.

She had dual degrees in politics and fine arts. Connections the world over. She was the ambassador for a dozen different charities and she took those roles seriously. She was educated, accomplished and blessed with favourable looks, or so she'd been told. She was in a position to make a difference.

And nervous. Dear heaven, she was nervous as Theo prowled around her sitting room, staring at her furnishings and possessions as if they held secrets he wanted to know.

'You wanted a drink?' she asked.

'If you're having one.' He put his hands in his trouser pockets and continued to study the sculpture on a small side table. 'It's fake,' he said of the copied Rodin.

'I know. But it's a good copy and it's still very beautiful.' She'd paid a pittance for it. 'How do you know it's a fake?' Not many would. Not without examining it thoroughly, and he hadn't.

'Because my father gifted the real one to my mother on their tenth wedding anniversary.'

Oh, well. There you go. 'I have Scotch.'

'Perfect.'

She poured him a serve and then doubled it because it wouldn't do to have her serve be twice the size of his.

He was standing by the fireplace and she crossed the room with all the grace she could muster and handed him the drink.

'I like this room,' he said. 'It's more comfortable than I thought it would be.'

'I use it,' she said simply, and tried not to look at his

lips but they were impossible to ignore now that he'd put the idea of kissing into her head. 'I like jewel colours and textured fabrics. I like comfortable furniture.'

'Your taste is exquisite.' He sipped his drink. 'Does Augustus know you serve his special Scotch?'

'Does he need to know?' she countered. 'Because, frankly, he's slightly precious about it.' She took a sip of hers. 'You sent me a form letter proposal.'

'I had it specially made just for you.'

'Now you're making fun of me.'

'Not really. The scions of the House of Liesendaach always put their marriage proposals in writing. It's the rule.'

Byzenmaach didn't have such a rule and neither did Arun. Her and Casimir's engagement had been more of a verbal agreement between their parents than anything she'd signed up for. Maybe there was some small merit to Theo's form letter after all.

'A marriage proposal is usually accompanied by a ring,' she said. There'd never been one of those between her and Casimir either.

Theo slipped his hand into his trouser pocket and pulled out a small wooden box.

'Oh, for heaven's sake. I suppose you had that especially made for me too,' she said.

'Yes.'

He was the best liar she knew. And she'd been surrounded by courtiers and politicians since birth.

'What?' He looked anything but innocent. He was inviting her to enjoy the joke, but she couldn't.

She turned away.

'I'm putting it on your mantelpiece so you can think about it.'

'I've thought about it.' She'd thought of little else all

day. 'I've decided I'd rather pursue a different kind of life. I'm going to take half a dozen lovers, one for every day of the week, and I'll rest on Sundays,' she continued. 'I'm going to throw debauched parties and seduce the unwary. I'll use you as my role model.'

'You don't want to do that.'

'Oh, but I do. Purity is a construct of my own inhibitions. It's time to let those inhibitions go.'

He smiled tightly. 'As much as I agree that you should definitely explore your sensual side, I'm not a fan of your proposed method of doing so. May I suggest choosing one person to take you on that journey? More specifically, me. We could aim for one new sensory experience a day. I could teach you everything I know. Assuming you enjoy our kiss and agree to marry me.'

'I've yet to agree to kiss you at all, let alone all the rest. What if I enjoy the kiss and refuse to marry you? What if I ask you to teach me everything you know regardless? Would you do it?'

'No.'

'Why not?'

'Yawn.' He stared into his drink and then drained it in one long swallow before setting the delicately cut crystal tumbler on the mantel next to the ring box. 'It's not what I want and it's definitely not what I need. I meant what I said about commitment. I'm prepared to pay close attention to your wants and needs and see that they're met.'

She wanted to believe him, even if she couldn't quite bring herself to. 'And you expect the same from me.'

'Face it, Moriana, you've spent a lifetime making sure other people's needs are met. It's ingrained in you.'

He made her sound like a particularly comfortable leather chair. 'That's about to change. I'm on a *Moriana First* kick.'

'It's about time.' He smiled faintly. 'I happen to believe a person can be both kind to themselves and committed to the people they care about. But first things first. What is it you think I can't give you?'

Where did she begin? 'You've never been exclusive with a woman before.' Understatement.

'I've never asked one to marry me either, yet here I am.' He met her gaze, and there it was again, something hard and implacable and patient in his eyes. 'I happen to think we'd make a good team. There's fire between us; there always has been. We rub each other the wrong way. We could also rub each other the right way—so much so that there'd be no room for other lovers. That's what I believe. I'm attracted to you. I may have missed that point in the form letter.'

'You did.'

'I'm making it now.'

He was. 'Theo, you're attracted to a lot of people. You've proven that quite spectacularly over the years. Kissing me and enjoying it would prove nothing.'

'You're wrong. A kiss could prove extremely informative for us both.' He smiled that charming smile. 'Come on, Moriana. You have nothing to lose and only experience to gain. Don't you want experience?'

'Yes, but I'd rather have it without strings.'

'No strings.' She'd never seen him so obliging.

'There's an engagement ring on my mantelpiece,' she said drily.

'That's a measure of my sincerity, not a string.'

'We get this wrong, you go away,' she said firmly.

'You have my word.'

It sounded so deliciously reasonable. He was offering up his warm, willing and very attractive body for experimentation and, for all her fine talk of acquiring a legion of lovers, she didn't have the faintest idea how to actually go about getting even *one* lover in place. Men did not approach her. They never had and she had no idea if they ever would. One kiss. She could probably learn something. 'So…how do you want to do this? The kissing.'

'You tell me. However makes you comfortable.'

He was laughing at her; the little crinkle at the corner of his eyes gave it away.

'Maybe if you sat.' She waved her hand at a number of sofa and armchair options.

He unbuttoned his jacket—nothing a gentleman wouldn't do before being seated. And then he made an utter production of taking it off completely and draping it over the back of a chair. He made an even bigger production of rolling up his sleeves, his blunt nails and long fingers making deft work of it. His royal signet ring stayed on and so did his watch. He'd probably been a stripper in a former life.

'Well?' he said when he'd settled in the middle of a crimson sofa, legs wide and eyes hooded. 'What next?'

'You said I could touch you as well as kiss you.' She didn't stammer, but it was close.

'You can.'

'Right. Good. So.' She didn't move. Instead she sipped at her drink for courage, only she sipped a little too deeply and almost choked on the fire in her throat.

To his credit, he let her flounder for a full minute before breaking the silence. 'Put the drink down and come closer. It's hard to touch and kiss someone from such a distance.'

Distance. Yes. Was she really going to do this?

'What do you have to lose?' he murmured, and the answer was nothing.

Absolutely nothing.

She set her drink next to his little ring box and his empty glass and turned her back on them. She crossed to the sofa he'd claimed as his own and sank to her knees between his wide open legs, pleased when his breath faltered and his lashes fluttered closed. Was he nervous? Why would he be nervous? He wasn't the virgin here and, frankly, she was nervous enough for both of them.

She didn't even know where to look. At his shoes? The subtle sheen of his very expensive suit? His legs to either side of her? Anywhere but the not so subtle bulge in his pants. Then there was the not so small matter of where to put her hands. On his shoulders? His waist? Where? He looked altogether unsettled. 'Is this okay?'

He ran a hand over his face. 'Yes. Continue.'

Yes. Continue. Let's just seduce the playboy king with her untried self because *of course* he'd find her tentative floundering attractive. 'I don't—'

'Touch me.'

'Where?'

'Anywhere.'

'I thought you were supposed to be patient.'

'I am patient. I have the patience of a *saint*.'

'Hardly.' She put her hand on his leg, just above the knee, and felt his muscles shift. Even through the fine fabric of his suit she could feel the warmth of him. Cautiously, she circled her thumb over the inseam and slid her hand an inch or so up his leg. She'd never been this close to a man before. She'd never been invited to touch and explore.

He felt good.

She placed her other hand above his other knee and braced herself as she leaned forward, stopping just before her lips hit the juncture between skin and the snowy white collar of his shirt. She closed her eyes and let her other senses take hold. 'You smell good,' she murmured. 'What is it?'

'Soap,' he rasped, his hands now clawing at the velvet upholstery before he deliberately let out a ragged breath, tilted his head back and closed his eyes.

She drew away slightly to study his face, the frown between his eyes and rigid cord of his neck. 'Did you close your eyes so you can pretend I'm someone else?'

He opened his eyes specifically to glare at her. 'I swear on my mother's grave, Moriana, you're the most infuriating woman I know. I'm thinking of you. Get used to it.'

She could get very used to it. She moved her hands up his thighs until her fingers brushed the crease where hips met legs, her eyes widening as he gave a tiny rolling grind of his hips in response. 'You seem very…ah… responsive.'

'Yes.' A harsh rumble of a word, nothing more.

'Are you always like this?'

He had no answer for her.

She rolled her fingers, he rolled his hips, and that proved a powerful incentive to become even bolder in her exploration. It hadn't escaped her notice that Theo's eyes being closed allowed her to look wherever she wanted to look without being caught. He'd never know. And if he didn't know, how could he possibly reproach her for it?

She looked to his crotch, fascinated by the size and shape of him beneath the fine cloth. She flexed her fingers and dug into firm flesh, just a little, just below where she truly ached to touch, and he sucked in a breath but kept his eyes closed.

'Touch wherever you want,' he whispered harshly. 'I'm not going to judge.'

She traced her hands over his hips to his waist, up and over his powerful chest and the lines of his neck, she looked her fill until she reached his lips. He was biting his lower one and she didn't want that, so she touched her fingers to the spot and smoothed out the crush. His chest heaved and a broken sound escaped his lips as he turned his face towards her touch, eyes still closed, and he was beautiful in his abandon.

Was this sex? This utter acquiescence to someone else's touch?

She cradled his jaw and felt the prickles from invisible whiskers against her palm. She dragged her thumb across the seam of his lips, inordinately pleased when he parted them for her. She wanted to kiss him and keep touching him in equal measure and didn't know if she had the co-ordination for both.

She started with her lips to the underside of his jaw, close to his ear. It seemed safer than starting with a kiss to his lips and if she dragged her lips across his skin it would hardly count as a kiss at all, merely a warm-up.

'That wasn't a kiss,' she murmured against his skin. 'I'm working my way up to your lips.'

His tongue against her thumb was her only reply so she kept right on exploring, opening her own mouth and employing her tongue to learn the taste of his skin and find the pulse point in his neck, there, right there, fast and strong, and she sucked, just a little, and he groaned and the world burned that little bit hotter because of it.

She went up and over the cleft of his jaw, emboldened, but that wasn't her only area of exploration. She was working on two fronts here as she traced the long, thick length of his erection with unsteady, barely-there fingers.

She let her fingertips dance lightly over the crown and finally, finally pressed her lips against his.

One kiss, just one, because this was Theo and she believed him when he said he wouldn't judge her, and that if she didn't like it he would leave. She felt strangely safe with him.

She wanted to make the most of the opportunity he was offering.

His lips were warm and softer than she would have believed possible. He didn't invade; he let her take her time and adjust the pressure to her liking before moving forward. The tiniest tilt of her head allowed for a better fit overall. The lessening of pressure allowed her to tentatively touch her tongue to his upper lip, and the taste, oh, it was deep and dark and hinted of Scotch and flavours she wanted more of. Further exploration with her tongue was followed by the shifting of his body beneath her hand so that she cupped him more firmly, and maybe she was supposed to stroke and kiss and breathe all at once, and she probably could if the heat coursing through her body wasn't quite so overwhelming.

His tongue had come to play with hers, softly teasing, and she couldn't help her whimper or the way she wordlessly begged him to teach her more.

The sweetly subtle grind of his erection into her hand became a demanding roll.

He had no problem whatsoever co-ordinating mouth and body in a clear attempt to drive her out of her mind with lust.

It was one kiss and it blew her mind, and she couldn't breathe and she couldn't stop.

Even as he pulled his lips away from hers she ached for more.

'Breathe,' he whispered and she did, and then dropped

her head to his shoulder to hide the fact that she was already utterly undone.

'Right,' she murmured, more to herself than anyone else. 'One kiss. All done.'

She looked down and there was her hand, still laying claim to his privates. She snatched it away and he huffed out a laugh.

'Right,' he murmured.

'You said I could touch.'

'And I'd never deny it. Pour me another drink before I forget my promise *not* to touch you back.'

She pushed off him and up as gracefully as circumstances would allow. She turned her back and closed her eyes, trying not to imagine exactly how good sitting in his lap and rubbing against him might feel.

She cleared her throat. She poured the Scotch and by the time she turned back around he was standing in front of the fireplace again, his features an impassive mask.

'Did you enjoy the kiss?' he asked.

'Yes.'

'Did you enjoy putting your hands on me?'

She nodded. 'It was extremely educational, thank you.'

He took the drink from her outstretched hand. 'Are you wet for me?'

She sipped her own drink and dropped her gaze. 'Yes.'

'Marry me,' he said next.

Theo watched as Moriana crossed her hands around her tiny waist and turned away from him. Her back was ramrod-straight and her bearing regal. All those dancing or fencing lessons or whatever they were had clearly paid off. She looked at the ring box for a very long time but made no move to touch it. And then she turned back to face him.

He honestly thought she'd say yes. Between persuasive argument, the strength of that kiss and the benefits to both Arun and Liesendaach, he thought he had her.

And then she spoke.

'I'm flattered by your offer.'

It wasn't a yes.

'I'm surprised by your chivalry and more than a little stunned by my response to your...your *that*, although maybe I shouldn't be,' she continued quietly. 'You're clearly very experienced and I'm a dry river bed that's never seen rain. I would soak up as much of *that* as you'd give me. And then you'd grow bored and move on.' She shook her head, her gaze steady and shuttered. 'That wouldn't end well for either of us.'

'Why would I grow bored and move on?'

'You always do.'

'Doesn't mean I always will.'

'And then there's your family history to consider. Your marital role models, so to speak.'

Theo scowled. His parents' marriage had been... complicated. The joint state funerals for his mother, brother and father had been even more complicated. Seven of his father's mistresses had turned up for the show. Three of them had offered to comfort a fifteen-year-old Theo before the night was through. 'My parents are long dead,' he said flatly. 'Let them rest. Leave them out of this.'

'No. Your father wasn't exactly one for marital fidelity. I need to know if you want the same kind of marital relationship for us that your parents had.'

'I am not my father.'

'Nor am I your mother. She was a tolerant, pragmatic

woman who was willing to turn a blind eye to your father's many dalliances in exchange for a title and a great deal of power. I already have titles and enough power to satisfy me and I'm no longer feeling either tolerant or pragmatic. Do you really want to marry a woman who'd rather cut out her husband's eyes than have him look elsewhere for sexual pleasure?'

Bloodthirsty. He liked it. 'I'd rather keep my sight.'

'Pick a different wife and you can keep your mistresses *and* your sight.'

'Or I could be faithful to you. I don't do love, Moriana. You know it and I know it, but if you help me out in this…if you wear my ring I *will* be faithful to you. Think of it as part of our negotiation. You need it and I'm willing to accommodate it in return for your service. This isn't an area of potential conflict. Move on. Say yes.'

But she didn't say yes.

'What now?' he grated. He didn't have time for this.

'That kiss we shared, was it normal?' she asked tentatively.

He didn't know what she meant.

She sent him a look, half-pleading, half-troubled. 'I don't have the experience to know if it was good, bad or mediocre. You do.'

'It was good.' Blindingly good. 'Surely you've kissed Casimir before?'

'Not like that.' She looked away.

'Someone else?'

She shook her head.

'*Anyone* else?'

'No.'

'It was good.' Never had he cursed a woman's inexperience as much as he did in that moment. Her eyes widened as he stalked towards her. 'What would you have me do to convince you? Another kiss, perhaps? A better one?'

She didn't say no.

He wasn't patient with her the way he was before. He didn't bury his desire to touch and to take. Instead he wrapped one hand around her neck, wrapped his other arm around her waist and hauled her against him.

Her sudden rigidity shouldn't have thrilled him the way it did. Her gasp as he plundered her lips shouldn't have made him stake his claim the way he did. She opened for him, melted against him and let him own the kiss in the same way he wanted to own her.

At the age of ten, the betrothal arrangement between Moriana, Princess of Arun, and Casimir, then Crown Prince of Byzenmaach, had been nothing but an amusement to tease them with.

At fourteen, their arrangement had been like a thorn in Theo's paw. He'd known what the stirring in his trousers meant by then. Known full well he wanted her with an intensity that never waned, no matter what he did. *Pick at her, scowl at her, argue with her and, by all that was holy, don't touch her.* That had been his motto for more years than he could count.

At fifteen, his father had seen where Theo's gaze had led and told him in no uncertain terms that Moriana of Arun was off-limits. Liesendaach needed to maintain cordial relationships with bordering kingdoms far more than Theo needed to seduce a pretty princess.

At fifteen, he'd done his father's bidding.

At fifteen, his parents and brother had died and ripped Theo's heart straight out of his chest. There'd been no room for love after that. When he chased women, he'd been chasing only one thing: sweet oblivion. They'd meant nothing to him.

Standing here at thirty, he still chased sweet oblivion. The open, loving part of him had broken long ago, and no one had ever come close to fixing it—least of all him. But he could give the woman in his arms some of the things she wanted. Good things. A good life. All she had to do was let him.

He heard a groan and realised belatedly that it had come from him, but she answered with another and that was all he needed to keep going. She tasted of warm spirits and untrained passion and it shouldn't have lit a fire in him the way it did. The slide of their lips and the tangle of tongues turned to outward stillness as she learned his taste and he learned hers.

She was slender to the touch, long-legged and gently curved, and he pressed her into his hardness because to do otherwise would be sacrilege. She had both hands on his chest and he wanted her to do more. He could teach her everything she wanted to know about passion.

But not until he got what he wanted.

Theo eased out of the kiss and took his sweet time letting her go, making sure his hand stayed on her waist in case she needed steadying. She wasn't the one with a clearly visible erection but she did have a fine flush running from cheek to chest, her lips looked plump and crushed and her eyes were satisfyingly glazed.

She looked…awakened. It was an extremely good look on her.

'Our bed would not be a cold one, Princess.' Theo stepped back and reached for his jacket. 'The weight of the crown is heavy enough without adding infidelity and a spurned queen to the mix. I would not look elsewhere if I had you. We *are* sexually compatible. Save yourself the trouble of years of casual sex and take my word for it.' He let his gaze drift from her face to glance at the little wooden box on the mantelpiece. 'You know what I want.' Time to leave her be before he opted for plan C—which was to take her back into his arms and have her pregnant by morning. 'Think about it.'

CHAPTER FOUR

MORIANA SLEPT BADLY. Maybe it was because Theo's words and his kisses were on a replay loop in her brain. Maybe it was because Theo's marriage proposal was still on the table and his ring box was still unopened on her mantelpiece. Maybe it was because she was so sexually frustrated that nothing was going to fix the ache in her tonight. Whatever the reason, sleep proved elusive and there was no other option but to get out of bed, fix a post-midnight snack of banana, blueberries and unsweetened yoghurt and take it through to her sitting room. The same sitting room she'd entertained Theo in.

The room with the ring in it.

If he had commissioned the ring especially for her—and she didn't believe that for a minute, but if he had—what would he choose? Something traditional like a solitaire diamond? Something ostentatious like a coloured stone surrounded by diamonds and big enough to picnic on? Something square-cut and colourless? She wouldn't put it past him.

And there was the box, sitting oh-so-innocently on the mantel, just waiting for her to open it and find out.

She retrieved it from the ledge and set it on the side table beside her chair. There it sat until she'd finished her snack and then she picked up the box and ran her fingers across its seam. The box was beautiful in its own right—a walnut burl, polished to a dull sheen, with a maker's mark she didn't recognise. A clover leaf or some such. Pretty.

Theo of Liesendaach had offered for her, and it wasn't a joke. He'd promised to be faithful to her. He'd offered kisses that made her melt.

He'd even made her forget the debacle with Casimir and the morning's Ice Princess headlines.

Words of love had been noticeably missing from his offer—at least he'd been honest about that—but he had done something good for her this evening. He'd made her feel wanted.

Oh, she still resented his form letter proposal. She still thought marriage to him would be a volatile, love-less endeavour, but there would be benefits she hadn't previously considered.

Like him. Naked and willing.

Taking a deep breath, she closed her eyes and opened the ring box. On the count of three she opened her eyes and looked.

He'd chosen an oval, brilliant cut diamond, flanked on either side by a triangular cluster of tiny dove-grey pearls. The stones were set in a white-gold filigree almost too delicate to be believed. She'd seen some beautiful diamonds in her time, and this one was flaw-less. Not too big and unwieldy for her finger, not too small as to be overlooked. The grey pearls reminded her of her homeland, and as for the whimsical, playful design…that element put her in mind of Liesendaach. She slipped it on.

It fitted.

'Bastard,' she murmured with half-fond exasperation,

because it really did seem as if he'd chosen it with her in mind. And then her smile faded as anxiety crept back in.

How—in the space of two kisses—had he managed to make her feel so alive? He'd been so responsive, so free with his body and secure in his sexuality, so *open*. No one had ever given themselves over to her so freely and it had been better than any aphrodisiac.

He'd said it was good and she'd believed him.

There were reasons for this marriage that she could understand. A political merger, yes. Stabilisation for a region. A smart, politically aware queen could lighten her husband's load considerably. It didn't matter how hard Moriana had worked to get there, she *was* a smart and politically aware player these days. An asset to any monarch. She knew this.

She'd been worried about Theo's sexual experience and her lack of it but, after that kiss and Theo's parting words, she wasn't nearly as worried as she had been. Call it attraction, pheromones or alchemy, their kisses had been explosive.

Moriana knew she had self-esteem issues. Her utter fear of never measuring up had turned her from a curious child with a too-hot temper into a humourless, duty-bound over-thinker with an unhealthy attention to detail. A woman who thought of failure first and for whom success had always been hard won.

And then there had been Theo, telling her to touch him and that he wasn't going to judge her curiosity or her inexperience and find her wanting, and hadn't *that* been a revelation. Touching him, wanting him, enjoying him—everything had been so *effortless*.

She smirked, and then snorted inelegantly as she pictured her mother at the dining table, damning Moriana with faint praise for whatever task her daughter had tried and failed to do that day. Disguising her disappointment behind impeccable manners as she told Moriana yet again that one day she would find her true calling, something she would be instinctively good at.

Not fencing or dancing or music or drawing. Not horse riding or shooting or politics or fundraising or running a castle or making a social function an event to be remembered. She'd never been good at any of those to begin with.

But kissing Theo, she'd been good at that.

Moriana ran her hand across the sofa cushion, smoothing the velvet first one way and then digging her nails in to rough it up on the back stroke.

He'd been sitting right where she sat now, taking up more space than any one man had a right to, and she closed her eyes and wondered if she could still scent his arousal in the air. Maybe not. Maybe it was long gone.

Maybe he was right this minute taking care of his needs somewhere in the palace, and he'd damn well better be alone, his legs spread wide and his hand pressing down, just as hers was snaking down towards her panties, pushing aside the layers of silk and cotton, dipping into warmth. Maybe he had no shame whatsoever when it came to pleasing himself while remembering every shudder and every breath he'd given to her this evening.

Why *should* there be shame in this?

Her fingers moved quickly and her body grew taut. She'd always known what her body could do in this regard, how lost she could get. She'd never before thought of her inherent sensuality as a strength, but Theo had it too and tonight he'd shown her how he wielded his, succumbed to it, even as he owned it, until it was more than just a strength.

It was a gift.

* * *

The headlines the following morning were still not kind to Princess Moriana of Arun. She'd found the newspapers in their usual place in the breakfast room and had mistakenly thought that their presence heralded other more appealing news than her love life or lack of it.

Not so.

Out of Her League one paper proclaimed, with a picture of her and Theo from last night beneath the headline. The photographer had caught them as they'd been discussing the merits of the Vermeer. Theo looked sharp-eyed and handsome, the edges of his lips tilted towards a smile but not quite getting there as he studied the painting. She'd been looking at Theo and the photographer had captured her from behind. There was something vulnerable about the lines of her shoulders and neck and the curve of her cheek. From the position of their bodies, it was obvious her attention had been on Theo rather than the painting. Her hand had been resting on his sleeve, and instead of it looking like a courtesy on his part it looked like a desperate plea for attention on hers.

Great. Just great. She tossed the paper aside and picked up the next one.

The Fall and Fall of Arun's Perfect Princess this one said, and the photo must have been taken when she first saw Theo and her brother stepping into the auction room last night because she looked gutted. It was there in her eyes, in the twist of her lips. One single moment of despair at her brother's betrayal and they'd caught it; of course they had. Her mother would have been horrified by such a vulgar display of emotion. Moriana didn't much care for it herself. Not in public. Masks should

never slip in public. All that ever did was invite preda-
tors to circle.

The article went on to criticise her dress, her shoes
and her too-slender frame, and suggest she needed professional help in order to cope with her rejection. Arun's
relationship with Byzenmaach was now strained, they
said. Trust between the two kingdoms had been shattered and she *knew* that wasn't true, only there it was
in black and white.

And then Theo walked into the breakfast room and
drew her attention away from the hateful words.

He wore his customary dark grey trousers and white
dress shirt but he'd done away with the tie and undone
the first two buttons on his shirt.

'You're still here,' she said, and he nodded agreeably.

'I still need a wife.'

Half-dressed and unashamedly comfortable in his
skin, he leaned over her shoulder and plucked a paper
from the pile she'd already looked at before settling into
the chair next to hers to read it.

'Two-timing Princess,' he read aloud. 'Go you.'

'Read on,' she muttered. *'You're* a ruthless despoiler
of all that is pure and good in this world.'

'Of course I am. How is this even news?' He put that
paper down and picked up another and was smirking
two minutes later. 'Don't let anyone ever tell you those
shoes you wore last night were a bad fashion choice.
The shoes were good.'

The shoes had been vintage Jimmy Choo. Damn right
they were good. 'You're reading the one about how I was
dressed for seduction last night in a desperate attempt
to end civilisation as we know it and finally get lucky?'

'I am. You should dress for boar-hunting one evening.
Knee-high leather boots, armguards, stiffened leather cor-

set, breeches and a forest-green coat that sweeps the floor and hides your weapons. See what they make of that.'

He was even better than Aury at mocking press articles. He truly didn't seem to give a damn what was printed about them.

'Doesn't it bother you? All these stories?'

'No.' His voice turned hard and implacable. 'And it shouldn't bother you. The only reason the press are on you now is because you've never been at the centre of any scandal before and they're hungry for more. Strangely enough, now is the perfect time to reinvent yourself in the eyes of your public—assuming that's something you want to do. Or you could mock them. Tell them you're pregnant with triplets and don't know who the father is. Make Casimir's day. *Four* royal bastards for the new King of Byzenmaach.'

'Oh, you cruel man.'

'Made you smile though, didn't it?'

She couldn't deny it.

Finally he turned his attention away from the newspapers. She could pinpoint the moment he truly looked at her, because her body lit up like sunrise.

'Good morning,' he murmured. 'Nice dress.'

She'd worn one of her favourite casual dresses from the same section of her wardrobe where the red gown usually hung. It was part of her 'love it but where can I wear it?' collection. It was lemon yellow, strapless, snug around the bodice and flared gently from the waist to finish a couple of inches above her knees. She'd kept her jewellery modest. Two rings for her fingers—neither of them *his* ring—a pair of diamond studs for her ears, and that was it. Her sandals were the easy on and off kind and she'd caught her hair back in a messy ponytail that spoke of lazy weekend sleep-ins.

'Yeah, well. Maybe I'm out to seduce you.'

'A for Effort,' he murmured. 'That dress is a weapon. You need to be photographed in it looking all tumbled and content. With me.' He picked up the pile of still un-read papers and dumped them on the ground between their two chairs.

'I hadn't finished with those yet.'

'They were making you unhappy. Why read them?' He reached for a croissant and the blackberry jam. 'I need you to be more resilient in the face of bad press. I honestly thought you were.'

She wasn't. Not at all. 'And it bothers you that I'm not?'

'It bothers me a lot.' For the first time this morning he sounded deadly serious. 'Liesendaach's court can be hard to navigate. My uncle's legacy of corruption still lingers, and every time I think I've stamped it out, it comes back. I don't trust my politicians or my advisors. I barely trust my palace staff. You *will* get bad press if you marry me. You *will* get people trying to befriend you and use you in the hope that you can influence me on their behalf. I can't protect you from either of those things, so I need to know in advance that they won't break you. I need you to know that some days it's going to feel as if the world is out to get you and no one has your back.'

'You're not exactly selling your marriage proposal this morning, are you?'

'Not yet. I'm mainly mentioning the fine print. But I will be selling it. Soon.' He shot her a quick glance. 'Just as soon as I think you're up for an onslaught.'

'Maybe after my next cup of coffee,' she murmured.

He reached for the coffee pot and offered to top her up but she shook her head so he filled his own cup. 'How did you sleep?'

'Poorly. Your ring is lovely, by the way. I lasted until almost two a.m. before looking at it.'

'Well done.' He smiled wryly. 'I notice you don't have it on.'

'Don't push. I'm considering your proposal. Yesterday, I wasn't even doing that.'

'Yesterday, you thought me indifferent to you. Now you know I'm not.'

'Which means you now get a hearing. It doesn't mean we're ready for marriage. Why the rush?'

'Well, we could always wait for old age.' He was annoyed and doing little to hide it.

'There's something you're not telling me.' She'd been around him long enough to know that this relentless pushing wasn't usually his style. 'You're too urgent. You're pushing too hard for this to happen and making mistakes in your approach. It's not like you.'

A muscle flickered in his jaw.

Something was very definitely up. 'Spill,' she murmured. 'I know you're under pressure to marry. Liesendaach wants a queen and you need an heir. But I didn't think you were under this much pressure.'

'My uncle is petitioning for my dismissal,' Theo said finally. 'He can't get me on fiscal incompetence or general negligence. I do my job and I do it well. But there's a loophole that allows a monarch of Liesendaach to be replaced if they haven't married and produced an heir by the time they turn thirty. We didn't even know it was there until my uncle found it and raised it. I turned thirty last month. I can challenge the clause at a judicial level, no problem. Buy myself some time. But the best way to address the petition is for me to secure a fiancée and schedule a wedding as soon as possible. When Casimir let you down I saw a solution I could live with. Meaning you.'

'And here I was beginning to think you had a crush on me all these years and simply couldn't wait to claim me now that I was free.'

'That too. I should have led with that.'

'I wouldn't have believed you.' Moriana definitely needed more coffee this morning.

Theo sighed and started slathering jam on his croissant. 'There's no talking to you this morning, is there?'

'Not before the caffeine hits my bloodstream. So who will you marry if you don't marry me? A Cordova twin?' The Cordova twins had made a splash last year, when they'd taken turns dating him. One twin one week, the other twin the next. It had gone on for months. Theo either hadn't cared or hadn't noticed.

'You're picking a fight that's not there.'

'And here I thought I was identifying an alternative solution to your problem.'

His eyes flashed silver and his lips thinned. 'You're a better one.'

'I know.' There was no point pretending the Cordova women were better options when it came to political connections. 'But you have to look at your offer from my point of view too. For the first time in my life I'm free to do what I please. I want to cut loose and have some fun. I want some romance.' She gave a helpless little shrug. 'I know what your offer means. I know the work involved. There's a lifetime of it, and I'm not sure it's what I want.'

'Yet you were all set to marry Casimir.' His voice had cooled. 'You wanted it once.'

She had. She'd looked forward to it. So what made Theo's offer so disturbingly different?

Breakfast continued in silence until finally she could stand the silence no more. 'I spoke to Casimir this morning.'

Theo looked up from his breakfast but made no comment.

'I'm investigating my flaws. I had ten years in which to kiss him properly and I didn't. Nor did he ever push for more. We spoke about that.'

Theo raised his eyebrow. 'Did he tell you he was celibate? Blind? Hormonally challenged?'

'No, but thank you for the suggestions for my own utter apathy.'

'You weren't apathetic last night.'

Maybe that was what was different about this offer of marriage. Casimir had never really hurt her with his indifference because Moriana had been similarly indifferent right back. But Theo—she wasn't indifferent to him, and never had been. He could wind her up at whim and leave her reeling, without any effort whatsoever. And that was a dangerous position for a queen to be in.

'Casimir mentioned that—for him—chemistry with another person starts well before the kissing,' she began hesitantly. 'He said there's an awareness between two people, a connection that can't be faked. He said that good kisses, spectacular kisses, were as much about letting someone into your head as they were a physical thing. He said kissing random strangers and expecting to see fireworks was a stupid idea.'

'Remind me to send him a fruit basket,' said Theo.

'I told him you'd offered for me. He laughed.'

'A fruit basket minus the strawberries.'

'Why did he laugh?'

'I'm not a mind-reader, Moriana. You'd have to ask him.'

She had.

Casimir had mumbled something about everything falling into place. He'd wished her every happiness, told her she'd be happier with Theo than she ever would have been with him, and she'd cut the call shortly thereafter. It was that or start wailing at her former intended for being an arrogant moron.

'He did give me one nice compliment,' she offered wryly. 'He's going to miss our political conversations. He said I have great depth of knowledge and an impressive ability to influence decisions. His and beyond. I'm a political muse. Go me.'

Theo's gaze grew carefully shuttered. 'The unseen hand.'

'A guiding hand,' she corrected.

'I don't need one.'

'You've never had one.' But she was one, with intimate knowledge of how deals were done across four kingdoms.

Theo said nothing.

'You offer physical intimacy with such a sure hand,' she murmured. 'But would you ever seek my counsel?'

'I'd…think about it,' he said with a twist of his lips that suggested discomfort. 'I find it difficult to trust people. Anyone.'

'And you would include me with the masses? Don't you want to be able to trust your wife?'

'When it comes to trusting people, it's not really about what I want. It's about what I'm prepared to lose.'

'Wow. You really are alone. In your head and in your heart.' She couldn't quite comprehend how a king who trusted no one could function in office. 'Aren't you lonely?'

'No.'

'So *the main duty* of a queen towards her king—that of offering full and frank emotional, political, social and *well-being* support to the man behind the throne—you don't want it.'

He said nothing.

Moriana sat back in her chair, still stunned. 'Seriously, Theo, you don't need me. Just pick anyone.'

He didn't like that, she could tell. But she didn't much care for the position he was offering either.

'I mean it,' she said. 'I am not trained to sit at your side and do nothing. I need your trust in order to function as your queen. Without it, I'm worse than useless. And I will *not* be rendered useless this time around.'

'Come to Liesendaach for the week,' he offered abruptly. 'And I'll try and give you what you want.'

'Not want. Need. This one's a deal-breaker,' she finished quietly.

'Trust takes time,' he snapped, and, yes, she'd give him that.

'I have time. You might not, but if you want my co-operation I suggest you make time. I can deal with a marriage minus the love. I've been prepared for that for a long time. But I'm telling you plain, I will not become your queen until I have your absolute trust.'

'Is that your final position?'

She nodded.

'Then I'll try. There can be political discussion and getting to know each other and a great deal of kissing and touching and fun. You might like it more than you think.'

'Perhaps. Okay, here's the deal. I *need* your trust. But I *want* more sexual expertise. I'd like to prioritise both, this coming week in Liesendaach. Can we do that?'

It was as if her question flipped a switch in him. His uncertainty bled away, leaving a confident, sharp-eyed negotiator in its wake. 'I'll do you a deal,' he murmured.

She stopped ripping her pastry into ever smaller pieces and brushed her fingers against each other to rid them of crumbs before reaching for her napkin and squeezing. 'I'm listening.'

'I'm prepared to offer you a minimum of one new sexual experience each and every day of your stay,' he continued. 'As an offer of good faith I'll even throw in a lesson here and now at the breakfast table. But if at any time during our lessons you climax for me…from that point onwards you wear my ring.'

'No deal.' She didn't trust her body to remain sufficiently restrained during these lessons. He'd have her seeing stars so fast she'd be wearing his ring by lunchtime.

'Okay, I'll do you a new deal. What if you were able to stop me with a word at any point during a lesson? Climax averted, so to speak. Everyone backs off to allow for breathing space. We could even think of it as an exercise in trust-building. No commitment or ring-wearing required. Easy.'

'It doesn't sound that easy.'

His eyes gleamed. 'Some lessons *are* harder than others. You did say you wanted to learn. Also, it'll be fun. You said you wanted that too. I'm merely attempting to provide some for you.'

'Good of you.'

'I know.'

The room temperature jacked up a notch as their gazes clashed and she contemplated just how badly wrong this week could go. 'You're offering me a week full of fun, sex education, political discourse and trust-building exercises? What about romance?' She'd bet he wouldn't offer that.

'The offer includes romance. You'd be a fool not to see if I can deliver.'

Even if he didn't deliver, she'd quite like to see him *try*.

And they said she didn't have a sense of humour.

'Agreed,' she murmured. 'Let's go to Liesendaach for a week.'

He sat back, pushed his meal aside. 'First lesson starts now. You might want to lock the doors.'

Even as she dropped her napkin across her plate and headed for the double doors that would take her from the room, Moriana still didn't know whether she would lock the doors or not.

Theo was playing her, she knew that much.

But maybe, just maybe, she wanted to be played with.

She closed the doors and locked them, and then did the same to the doors on the other side of the room. She stood there, with her eyes closed and her back to him for a moment, trying to find her equilibrium but it was gone.

He thought her innocent, and in a physical sense she was. She'd never been touched, she'd never had sex. But she was twenty-eight years old and there was no cap on her imagination. In her imagination, she'd had any number of sexual experiences. She knew exactly what kind of things he might teach her. She could describe them in great detail.

And, oh, how she wanted to see if the reality lived up to her imagination.

'Come here.' Even his voice could seduce her when he wanted it to.

She took a deep breath, opened her eyes and turned. He was right where she'd left him. She walked towards him, feigning a confidence she didn't have.

He smiled.

He'd pushed away from the table and sat sprawled in his chair and he indicated the cleared space where his meal had once been. 'Sit on the table.'

He could have her for breakfast.

She half leant, half sat, hands curling around the table edge, and all the time he watched her like a hawk. She could feel the weight of his gaze and the assessment behind it as he sized her up and planned his approach.

'Your dress has a zip at the back. Undo it.' The purr was back in his voice and so was the edge of command.

'Why should I?' She was embarrassed to undress for him here in broad daylight. It smacked of her owning her actions when maybe, just maybe, she wanted to be led. 'You have hands.' They were very nice hands. Large and strong-looking, with short nails and an appealing ruggedness about them.

'And I'll use them. Right now I'm more interested in watching you undress for me. You blush so beautifully.'

Well, he would know. He could make her blush with a glance, and if that didn't work all he had to do was use his words. Haltingly, she fumbled behind her back and slid the zip down to her waist. The bodice of her dress had boning and would stay up unless pushed.

He raised an aristocratic eyebrow.

She pushed the top part down and folded her arms around her waist for protection. Moments later she unfolded her arms again, dropped them to her sides and curled her hands over the table edge in a desperate bid to at least *appear* a little more casually confident than she was.

She still had a bra on. It was white, strapless and covered almost as much as the dress had.

His eyes grew intent and he reached out to draw a path from her collarbone to the very top of her bra, tracking the shape of it with his fingertips as it fell away under her arms. 'This too.'

Her nipples pebbled at his words and he rewarded them by stroking his thumb gently across one of them, back and forth, back and forth, causing the tug of want in her belly to pull tight. She reached behind her for the hook and the bra fell away—he helped it fall away.

'Your breasts are perfect.' He sounded almost angry.

They were a little on the small side, as far as she was concerned, and right now they were aching for more than just the flick of his thumb, but the appropriate response to a compliment, sincere or not, had been drummed into her since birth. 'Thank you.'

Heat stole into her cheeks and across her chest and she looked away from his fierce, bright gaze. The wall was right there, suitably dressed with a painting. Nothing abnormal about that wall. The only abnormal thing in this room was her. And maybe Theo. Or maybe sitting half naked atop the breakfast table *was* normal in his world. 'What next?'

He moved, and she closed her eyes and when she felt his lips on her they weren't where she'd expected him to put them. He'd placed them just below her left ear and she shivered when his tongue came out to trace a delicate circle.

'Promises,' she muttered and she could feel his smile on her skin.

'Patience.' He placed his hands either side of hers and continued to kiss a leisurely path across to her lips, where he proceeded to tease and tempt and never give her any actual substance.

'I hate you,' she muttered next.

'You shouldn't. I'm giving you my best.'

He went lower, with his hair brushing her neck as he

kissed her collarbone and the swell of her upper breast, and *now* they were getting somewhere. Her nipples had been tightly furled since she'd unzipped her dress and now they were throbbing and desperate for attention. She pushed up against him, not begging, but hoping, and he responded by drawing that tiny circle with the tip of his tongue again and then pulling back to blow on the skin he'd just licked.

Heat pooled low in her stomach and made her gasp. Dear heaven, he was good at this.

He kissed her some more, lighting a fire beneath her skin, and then finally he closed his mouth around her nipple and sucked.

'Oh.' She kept her legs tightly closed and rode out the thrumming clench of pleasure his actions had caused.

A lick for her other breast now, and then he obliged by closing his mouth over it and suckling hard. There. That. The fierce pull of want and the heady coil of desire. She moaned her pleasure, and he grazed her with his teeth. And then his lips were on hers again only this time he was claiming her, devouring her, and she melted into that too. She went where he led, mindless and willing, and when he pulled back and studied her again with glittering grey eyes she obligingly caught up on her breathing.

'Nice,' she whispered raggedly. 'Good lesson.'

'There's more.'

She wasn't at all sure she was ready for more.

'Raise your skirt,' he ordered gruffly.

'I—' There was a whole world of imagination waiting for her in that region. 'What's the lesson?'

'The lesson is that compliance has its rewards.'

She met his darkly mocking smile with a level stare.

At least she hoped that was what her face was doing. She'd rather *not* look like a startled fawn.

'Of course, if you don't comply you'll never know,' he murmured.

He knew he had her; she could see it in his eyes. He knew exactly how badly she wanted to know. Not just to imagine her sexual encounters but to *know* what one felt like.

With as much shamelessness as she could muster, she put her hands on the skirt of her frock and slid it slowly up her thighs, up and up until he could see her underwear. She'd worn white panties today, with tiny black polka dots, and they were pretty but nothing special. Not skimpy, not lacy, just normal. She wondered whether he would ask her to take them off.

'Good.' She could barely hear his low rumble. 'Now put your hands back on the table and lean back a little.'

The skirt stayed up, her head stayed low and her hands went back on the table as she waited for his next move.

His hands finally settled either side of her thighs, the heat of his body engulfing her as he set his lips to that place where her pulse beat frantically in her neck.

'You drive me mad, Moriana. You always have. You think you're so flawed.'

His next kiss landed on her shoulder and she shuddered her surrender. The kiss after that touched the outer curve of her breast and avoided her nipple, but not for long. He left no part of her breasts and belly uncovered as he worked his way down to her panties, and by the time he got there she was a flushed and writhing mess.

'I tend to think you're rather perfect,' he murmured as his breath ghosted over her underwear. He pushed them aside a little and licked. She'd heard about this.

Hell, she'd *dreamed* of it. But not in the broad light of day, and not in the breakfast room.

Slowly, hesitantly, she slid her hand down over the front of her panties, putting a barrier between herself and him. She didn't know if she wanted him to continue his exploration or not. On the one hand, there was embarrassment. On the other hand, her fingers found the damp, swollen groove, even over her panties, and her eyes closed on an involuntary shudder.

'What are you doing?' he rasped, looking up at her with a glittering warning in his eyes.

'Helping.'

'Hands on the table, Moriana. I don't need any *help*.'

And then his hands were high on her thighs, gently parting her legs. Moments later something soft and warm and moist found her hard little nub through already moist panties, and she thought it was his finger but both his hands were well and truly accounted for, wrapped around her thighs as they were, and his hair was tickling her inner thigh and, yes, indeed, that right there was his tongue.

It was even more spectacular than she'd imagined.

Heat flooded through her and she didn't know whether to scramble away or stay right where she was. There was another option, of course, and that was to give him as much room as possible so he could keep right on doing what he was doing.

Option three won.

'Hold on,' he muttered, and then he was pushing her legs wide apart and her panties aside and then his mouth was on her, kissing and kissing and flicking and sucking and *kissing*. It was too much. It was not enough. Her hand raked its way through his hair before she could even think to hold back, and *there*, right there, as she whimpered and began climbing through clouds.

Not yet.

Not. Yet.

Up and up and up.

'Stop!'

He stopped. He kept his word, his chest rising and his shoulders granite-hard as he pulled back and rested his forehead on her knee, his hands still curved high on each thigh, holding her open, keeping her in place. One more stroke was all it would take to topple her. She closed her eyes and pushed his hands away. Closed her legs and bit down on a whimper, because even the clench of her thighs had almost been enough to send her soaring.

'What do you want?'

He sounded ragged, almost as desperate as she'd been, and she laughed weakly and pressed the heel of her palm down over her centre to try and stave off completion and wasn't that a mistake. She was too close to climax.

'Oh, no…' she whimpered. 'No— Stop…stop… stop…'

He wasn't even touching her and she was toast, soaring, and cursing, and toppling over onto her side on the table as she rode out the waves breaking inside her body.

Control. She didn't have it. Another tremor racked her. 'That was—that.' She was vastly surprised she still had the power of speech. 'Phew! That was *close*.'

He barked out a laugh and she gathered her courage and continued with the deception.

'Yeah.' She pushed her cheek into the cool wooden table and tried not to drool through her smile as she cracked one eye open the better to see his response. 'Really close. You almost had me there.'

'Princess, I *got* you there. You came. I win.'

'No. I didn't come.' Lies, all lies, as another wave rode her hard. She fought the lassitude that followed in its wake by pushing up off the table and into a sitting position, hands either side of her and her legs pressed tightly together. She had a fair idea what she looked like, but she'd see to herself in a minute. She was far more interested in what Theo looked like, and he didn't disappoint. His eyes glittered fiercely and his colour was high, as if he was either mightily aroused or mightily annoyed. It was hard to say which sentiment rode him harder. His lips were moist, his jaw tight. His crotch was…well. It was reassuring to know she hadn't been the only one enjoying the lesson.

'You came.' He sounded so utterly confident.

'No, I *almost* came.' She looked for her bra and found it at the far end of the table. She wrapped it around her and fastened it quickly. The reapplication of her dress took longer, mainly because it was all askew and tangled around her waist. She figured her legs would probably hold her but she kept one hand to the table just in case, as she stood up and tried to get dressed. Panties—they were already on and damper than a wet cloth. Bra—on. Dress—

'Turn around and let me help,' he muttered.

So she turned around and he zipped her up and then smoothed her dress down over her curves. 'You came,' he murmured in her ear. 'You know it. And I'd trust you a whole lot more if you admitted it.'

Damn. She couldn't look at him. She didn't want to uphold her end of the bargain. 'I can't.'

'Hard, isn't it? Knowing when and who to trust,' he offered silkily.

She stepped away to reclaim her shoes. 'Time will tell.'

'I'll give you a pass this time because that's what you seem to need but, I promise you, your body's not that hard to read.' His words licked at her. 'You're headily responsive, Moriana, but I do know what I'm doing. This time I *wanted* you to come for me. Next time I'm going to keep you on the edge of satisfaction until you're begging for release.'

He was better at these games than she was. 'That sounds…'

'Cruel?' he asked. 'Depraved? Torturous?'

'Kind of perfect.' She smoothed back her hair and wondered how she was going to explain her current state of dishevelment to her lady-in-waiting. Maybe she could set Aury to packing for Liesendaach by way of distraction.

'So,' she began, and if she was a little throaty, a little breathless, it couldn't be helped. Having Theo's warmth at her back and his words in her ear did that to her. 'I'm coming to Liesendaach for a week, and at this point I won't be wearing your ring. Any social functions I should know about?'

He hadn't given up when it came to seducing her into marrying him. The glittering promise in his eyes told her he was just getting started. She was flustered, still reeling from the negotiating and the kissing and the not so simple act of resisting him.

The trust issues between them were a little bit heartbreaking.

'One State Dinner on Friday, four luncheons, bring riding gear if riding's something you like to do, and you're going to need at least half a dozen breakfast out-

fits similar to the one you have on. We'll be breakfasting together every morning. Think of it as lesson time.'

'And in the evening? What do you do of an evening?'

'Usually I work.'

'Oh.' She was ever so slightly disappointed. 'I'll bring
some of my work too. You don't mind?'

'I don't mind. Or we could occasionally meet for a
nightcap.'

'We could.'

He was laughing at her, not outwardly, but she could
still sense his amusement. She was like putty after only
one of his lessons. Totally malleable and greedy for more
of his attention, never mind that he'd just given her more
than she could handle.

'When would you like to leave?' Thankfully she
could still manage to ask a sensible question.

'Whenever you're ready.'

Still so *amenable*. She was looking forward to this
week. 'I can be ready within the hour if you'd like to
leave this morning? My lady-in-waiting can follow later
this afternoon with a suitable wardrobe and my work.'

'Let's do that.'

'Theo.' He was a king in need of a queen, a ruler with
a genuine predicament and she respected that he was
trying to solve his problem. 'I'm not going to meekly
say yes to marriage after a week with you on your best
behaviour. You might be wasting your time.'

'I'm not wasting my time. I know you'll give me a
fair trial, and that you'll be looking at ways to make this
work for you and everyone else around you. You won't be
able to help yourself.' He held her gaze and she couldn't
read the look in his eyes. 'It's what you do.'

CHAPTER FIVE

THE ROYAL PALACE of Liesendaach was exactly as Theo had left it. Grey slate roofs, creamy sandstone walls arranged in a U-shape around a huge central courtyard that could fit a small army. Six hundred and eighty-five white-sashed windows graced the building. The front half of the palace was surrounded by immaculately kept lawns and the back half of the palace grounds was a series of garden rooms, radiating outwards like the spokes of a wheel.

The palace employed fourteen full-time gardeners and many more seasonal workers, and every spring and autumn he opened the gardens to the public and allowed tours and special events to take place there. It was an incredible waste of water, according to some, but Theo's gardeners knew better than to be wasteful with the precious resource. They were forever experimenting with hardy plant varieties and watering regimes. The forest that bordered the gardens on three sides kept the worst of the hot drying winds away in summertime and took the edge off the icy north winds in winter. Theo's ancestors had known what they were doing when they'd kept the forest in place centuries ago. Naysayers could kiss his royal brass before he let anyone dismiss the gardens as frivolous.

They more than paid their way.

Moriana had been to the palace before, but not lately. Theo signalled to the helicopter's pilot to loop around the building to give her a bird's eye view.

The palace of her birth was starkly grey and forbidding, and beautiful in its own way. This place probably looked like a blowsy showgirl in comparison, but he wanted her to like it.

'The beauty here is not just for beauty's sake,' he said, leaning over her shoulder to look out of the window at the orchard. 'A lot of botanical research takes place here, education for schoolchildren, animal husbandry and breeding programmes, patronage of the arts—'

'Theo,' she interrupted gently. 'I know. Liesendaach's royal palace is and should always remain both functional and beautiful. You've no need to defend it. Not to me.'

'Do you have any idea how you might split your allegiance between Liesendaach and Arun?'

She turned to look him in the eye and her smile was bittersweet. 'You need to read the *Princess Handbook*,' she said. 'If I take your name my loyalty will be to Liesendaach.'

'But how would you feel about that?'

'Given the caning I'm getting in Arun's papers at the moment, I'd feel quite vengefully good about it. On a more practical note, it might just give my brother the incentive to take a wife.' She turned back to look out of the helicopter window. 'Your country has been without a queen for almost two decades. For me that means no recent shoes to step into, no impossible expectations. There's just me and what I might make of the role, and that's liberating in a way. I'm not scared.' Her lips twisted. 'I've been well trained. Byzenmaach would have given me that fresh start too.'

He didn't like the reminder of Byzenmaach and her future there up until a few days ago. A couple of kisses and a tiny taste of her and already he was feeling a possessiveness he'd never felt before. 'Byzenmaach's loss.'

'Indeed.'

They landed, both of them well used to getting in and out of helicopters. Theo had been hoping to make a quiet entrance but his Head of Household Staff had other ideas. Samantha Sterne stood waiting for them at the entrance closest to the helipad and one look at her ultra-serene demeanour promised a storm of rare intensity. The calmer she appeared, the worse the problem was.

'Sam,' he said. 'Meet Princess Moriana of Arun, my guest for the week. You got my message about readying the Queen's chambers?'

Moriana might not be wearing his ring but he could make it clear in a multitude of ways that she was no ordinary guest.

'Yes, Your Majesty.' Sam turned and curtseyed to Moriana. 'My apologies, Your Highness. The maids are finishing up now. The suite is clean but hasn't been in use for some time. I wanted it aired, fresh flowers brought in, new linens...'

'And he gave you fifteen minutes' notice?'

Sam smiled slightly at Moriana's dry words. 'Something like that, Your Highness.'

'Sam, is it?'

'Yes, Your Highness. Head of Household Staff.'

'Ma'am is fine.'

'Yes, ma'am.' Sam nodded, but didn't move on. 'Your Majesty.' She turned back towards Theo and there it was, the surface calm that spoke of a major problem. 'Your cousin arrived this morning, requesting an audience with you. When you weren't here he insisted on waiting, no matter how long it took. I put him in his old suite. George is currently seeing to his needs.'

'I'll take care of it.' Cousin Benedict had called the royal palace home during the years his father—Theo's uncle—had been Regent. He'd never shown any outward desire for the throne, preferring a playboy lifestyle to one of service, but he was a troublemaker at heart and a sly one at that. Family on the one hand; one laughing breath away from stabbing Theo in the back on the other. Benedict hadn't actively sought his company in years.

Sam nodded and took her leave, her stiletto heels clicking rapidly across the polished marble floor. Theo turned to see Moriana watch the other woman go, her expression assessing.

'She's very young to be your Head of Staff,' said Moriana finally.

'The old one was loyal to my uncle. This one's not.' That wasn't the line of thought he was expecting. His mind was still on Benedict.

'She's very pretty.'

'She's very competent.'

'I hope so. There are people I'll want to bring with me to Liesendaach if we do go ahead with a union.'

'Your Head of Household Staff?' he asked drily.

'No, Augustus would kill me. I'm merely pointing out that some staffing changes and additions will be inevitable. I like things done a certain way and I'm not shy about making it happen. Don't worry,' she murmured. 'If Samantha Sterne is as competent as she is pretty, she won't be going anywhere. What's up with Benedict?'

'You mean besides the usual? It's hard to say.'

'You were close to him for a while, weren't you?'

'If by *close* you mean that after my parents died he and I set about creating as much havoc as we could, then yes, we were close. I grew up. He grew petulant. And now would be a very good time to slip my ring on your finger if you wanted to. For your protection. Not that I'm harping on, but I don't trust my cousin not to skewer you when you're not looking. It's his specialty.'

'And how exactly is wearing your ring going to protect me from that? Because I would have thought it painted a target on my back. Unless competing with you for something you've laid claim to is something your cousin *never* does.'

He and Benedict had often made a game out of competing for women; he couldn't deny it. 'It'd still make me feel better.'

'Ownership usually does.'

Ouch.

'Ring or no ring, I can handle cousin Benedict,' she said with a smile. 'Shall we see what he wants?'

Benedict could wait. 'Let me show you to your rooms and then *I'll* see what he wants.'

'Of course, Your Majesty.'

He wasn't nervous about showing her his home. He wasn't suddenly sweating, hoping she'd like her quarters, and the artwork, and the gardens, and the people. He wasn't.

It was just warm in here.

Moriana knew Theo's palace was beautiful. She'd been there before, in its ballrooms and Theo's living quarters when he was growing up. But she'd never been in his mother's rooms before and she hadn't quite realised how stunning the incoming light from a wall full of windows would be, or how magnificent the second storey view out over the gardens would be. The floor of the Queen's chambers consisted of polished wooden parquetry in a floral design and the ceiling was high and domed. Someone, at some point, had fallen in love with chandeliers, and they caught the sunlight and scattered it.

'There are other suites to choose from.' Theo was watching her, waiting for her reaction. She walked towards the windows to stare out, not wanting to drool.

'This'll do.'

'I can bring in some grey stone. Make you feel more at home.'

She turned in a circle, feasting her eyes on absolutely everything. 'Don't you dare.' Okay, maybe she could be seen to drool a little bit.

And there was Theo, hands in his trouser pockets and his back to the wall, standing just inside the door. Watching her. 'Where are your rooms?'

'The other side of the hall, with windows facing east. I get the sunrise, you get the sunset.'

'But do you have chandeliers?' she said.

'You want to see my rooms?'

She did.

His suite was situated on the other side of the long hallway. There were more windows. Lots of tans and blues, hidden lights rather than chandeliers and the pick of the artwork. She eyed the Botticelli painting over his decorative fireplace with frank interest and heard a faint growl from somewhere behind her.

'You can't have it,' he murmured. 'You want to look at it, you can come here.'

'But *would* I look at it if I came here? That's the question.' If it came to a competition as to whether she'd be more likely to study Theo or that painting, Theo would win. She still hadn't forgotten what he'd taught her this morning at the breakfast table. She wondered what he could teach her in a living room with soft surfaces all around them.

'I could be persuaded to have more than one lesson per day,' she said, eyeing the nearby sofa.

'I need to preserve my strength.' He looked darkly amused.

'Ah, well. Tomorrow morning, then.' She didn't linger during her tour of his rooms. It felt a little like trespassing, for all that he seemed to have no problem with her being there. He kept to the corners of his rooms as well, whereas she was currently standing in the middle of a parquetry circle that was itself probably the dead centre of the room. She let him escort her back to her quarters, where he obligingly made way for two chambermaids, one carrying a vase, the other with her arms full of blooming roses that left a fragrant trail in their wake, but he didn't make to follow her inside. 'I'll leave you to settle in,' he said. 'If you want anything changed or moved, call Sam.'

Moriana nodded. 'Give your cousin my regards. Will I see him at dinner?'

'On Friday at the State Dinner, yes. He's on the guest list.'

'So you do still socialise with him on occasion?'

'It's unavoidable.'

'But you won't be inviting him to stay on, now that he's here?' She couldn't fathom Theo's relationship with his cousin.

'No. He won't be staying on.'

'Because I'm here?'

'That's one of the reasons, yes.'

'Benedict has always been courteous to me,' she said.

'I'm sure he has. You are sister to a king. You were betrothed to a crown prince. You outrank him. Besides, why make enemies when you can charm someone instead?'

That was one way of looking at it. 'How come *you* never embraced that philosophy around me?'

'You were annoying.' He smiled as he said it, and for a moment she felt the heat of his laser-like focus. 'If Benedict stays, my attention will be split. I'd rather concentrate on you alone.'

'Very charming,' she murmured. And she quite enjoyed the view as she watched him go.

Theo didn't have to go looking for his cousin. Five minutes after stepping into his office, Benedict found him. Benedict was two years older than Theo, two inches shorter and as vain as any peacock. He appeared in the doorway to Theo's office, wearing a sneer Theo strongly hoped wasn't hereditary. Benedict had introduced a teenage Theo to Europe's fleshpots and vices, and back then Theo had needed no encouragement to make the most of them. Still finding his way after the death of his parents and older brother, he'd found a willing companion in Benedict.

But Benedict, for all his easy grace and charm, had a viciousness and immorality about him that couldn't be ignored. Theo had started pulling back from their exploits. Benedict hadn't liked that.

It had gone steadily downhill from there.

'You could say hello and offer me a drink,' Benedict said.

'I assumed you'd already helped yourself,' Theo replied, turning his attention momentarily from the other man to finish an email response to his secretary. 'What do you want?'

'The palace requested my presence at dinner on Friday so here I am.'

'You're early.'

'Quite. Had I known you were returning with a guest I may not have made myself quite so at home. On the other hand I get to watch you try to impress the lovely Princess of Arun. That could be fun.'

'Benedict, you specifically asked to see me and I was given to understand that you thought the matter important enough to wait for my return. What do you want?'

'A couple of things. First, the petition for you to marry and reproduce or get off the throne is being abandoned. I never supported it, by the way. It would put me in line for the throne and, suffice to say, I have even less desire for a wife and children than you do.' Benedict's smile turned sly. 'Does Moriana know she's the chosen one? Will you promise her your all? Faithful at last? I'd like to see that.'

'Perhaps you will.' Indifference was important when dealing with Benedict. Admitting weakness or desire was tantamount to handing him a sword to skewer you with.

'I'll tell Father you're courting with intent. He'll be thrilled.'

'I'm sure he will. Are you ever going to tell me why you're here? Run out of money? Still can't choose between the Cordova twins and their younger brother?'

'It's almost as if you know me.'

'I have work to do.' Theo reached for a pile of reports and dropped his gaze to the topmost.

'Father's dying.' Benedict's words came tightly furled, like little bullets that Theo hadn't seen coming until they hit. 'He found out two weeks ago that he has cancer and it's too advanced to treat. He's riddled with it. That's why he's dropping the petition—he can't follow through and take the Crown and I have no desire to. He's in hospital in France. I know you're not given to mercy, but he wants to come home.'

Theo sat back in his chair, reports forgotten, and gave Benedict his full attention. 'Your father's exile was self-imposed. He doesn't need my permission to return to Liesendaach.'

'He wants to come here. He wants to die in his childhood home.'

'No. That's not happening.' Dying or not, Constantine of Liesendaach was a dangerous adversary who'd never once stopped looking for ways to tear Theo down.

'It's not as if he wants the royal suite,' snapped Benedict. 'He's barely lucid. I'll provide the medical care and pick up the cost. All he wants is a room.'

'Then take him home with you.' Benedict had a townhouse in the city, provided by and paid for by the Crown. It wasn't a palace but it sure as hell wasn't a hovel.

Theo could see it now—an endless stream of visiting dignitaries and schemers coming to pay their last respects. People who hadn't graced the palace doors for years. Let Benedict deal with them; Theo would have none of it.

'What are you so afraid of?' Benedict taunted. 'You won. He lost. The world turns. So my father wasn't cut out to be King. Few are. He ruined the economy, so say some. He made too many deals in his own interest, so say others, and maybe they're right. He also raised you, fed and clothed you and never limited your education. He didn't *stop* you from doing anything. You wanted him gone; he *went*.'

'That's one version of his Regency,' Theo said acerbically. 'Would you like to hear mine?'

'*Yes.* I would. Because maybe then I could under-stand why you turned on us like a rabid dog the minute you took the Crown!'

Theo watched as his cousin turned away, his face red and his lips set in an ugly twist.

'I knew this for a fool's errand,' Benedict said into the deepening silence.

'Then why come?'

'Because he's my father. It's his dying wish to return to the place he calls home, and maybe, just maybe, he will find peace here.' Benedict leaned against the door frame, crossed his arms and employed a passable gimlet stare. 'He knows you think he orchestrated your family's death, even if he doesn't know who fed you the idea. He said to tell you that if he had done, you'd have been on that helicopter too.'

'I was supposed to be. Instead, I was skiving off with you. Horse racing, wasn't it? Your sure-fire winner you simply had to see race?'

'Lucky for you. Or would you rather have been on that flight?' Benedict smiled but it didn't reach his eyes. 'We were family once. I cared about you. Looked after you.'

Saved you.

To this day, Theo still didn't know if Benedict had acted in complete ignorance when he'd prevented Theo from getting on that flight, or whether he'd known what his father was up to and simply hadn't been able to stom-ach losing Theo. Whatever the reason, Theo had lived. His parents and brother had not.

And Benedict had ceased to be Theo's confidant.

'Leave the numbers for the doctors.'

'And what?' said Benedict. 'You'll monitor the sit-uation? I left those numbers with your secretary two weeks ago, one week ago, and again yesterday. *Three times* I asked you to call me. Good thing I remember where you live.'

'I didn't receive any of those messages.'

'Then fire your secretary.'

'Was there anything else?' He'd had enough of this conversation.

'Yes. I won't be joining you and all the other righteous souls for dinner this week, or any other week in the foreseeable future. I would have let your staff know…if I thought the message would ever reach you. Don't set a place for me. Don't expect me to play the royal prince once my father is gone. I'm done.'

'You'll lose your title and your allowance.'

Benedict spread his arms wide. 'At least I'll be my own man. My position in this family is untenable. I've tried to get through to you. I can't. Nor am I willing to do what my father wants me to do. Time to move on.'

'I'll let my staff know.' Theo didn't want to feel sick to his stomach. There was no use wishing for a different outcome. 'By the way, Moriana knows you're here. She sends her regards.'

Benedict laughed. 'Poor little pedigree princess, always so proper. First Casimir and now you. I feel sorry for her. Maybe I should ask her if she wants to run away with me. She'd probably be better off.'

'I wouldn't advise it.'

'Then tell her I hope she enjoys her stay and regret that I must take my leave before renewing our acquaintance. There. Aren't we all so civil and grown-up?' Benedict bowed, a mocking salute. 'See you at the funeral. *Cousin.*'

He turned and made his exit, his long, angry stride echoing down the corridor.

Theo closed his eyes and banged his head softly against the padded headrest of the chair.

Of all the confrontations he'd ever had, dealing with Benedict had always been the hardest. He *wanted* to trust the man. They'd been close as children. Similar in age, similar in temperament, royals but not the heir apparent. Less had been expected of them and they'd lived up to that expectation and beyond.

Benedict *had* looked after him at times.

And sometimes, when his back was to the wall and the vultures were gathering, Theo still wanted Benedict at his side.

Theo was still sitting in his chair half an hour later. He'd done no work. Hadn't even glanced at the reports on his desk other than to leaf through them in search of a memo saying Benedict had called. If the information was buried in there somewhere, he hadn't yet found it. And then his deputy Head of Security knocked on the door frame. He'd asked the man to monitor Benedict's departure from the palace. Discreetly, of course.

'Has he gone?' he asked, and the older man nodded.

'Not before he found the visiting Princess and had a few words with her.'

'Was he civil?'

'Exceedingly, sire. The Prince told the Princess she was looking divine and said something to the effect that her broken engagement must be agreeing with her. She laughed and asked after his health and they talked a little about a painting they'd both bid for at auction but neither of them had won. He asked how long she was staying and she said a week. He bid her a pleasant stay, told her to make sure she saw the artwork in the southeast drawing room and then left.'

'Did I ask for a rundown on their conversation?'

'No, sire. My recount is probably wholly unimportant.'

'Wrong.' The information was extremely important. Benedict hadn't told Moriana about the petition being buried. He hadn't caused trouble. And that was unusual. 'Thank you. It's useful knowledge.'

The man nodded. 'I'm also here because you'd best be telling me what you want done regarding security for the Princess. Because she's just stationed the three men I put on her too far away to be of use and she didn't bring any security personnel of her own.'

'They'll be arriving this afternoon.' Augustus had insisted.

Theo picked up his desk phone and searched his mind for the internal number for the Queen's chambers. He thought it was zero zero two, but he couldn't be sure. It had been so long since he'd used it.

She picked up, and her voice was warm and relaxed as she said, 'Hello.' His Princess was in a far better mood than he was. Hopefully she'd stay that way when he overruled her security arrangements.

'You need to know what is and isn't going to happen, security-wise,' he told her curtly. 'There's a briefing in ten minutes. My security team will show you to my office.'

'Actually, I've just ordered tea brought to the most romantic little sitting room I've ever seen,' she said, the laughter in her voice a startling contrast to the encounter he'd recently had with his cousin. 'There's a huge vase of fragrant roses on the table, the sun is streaming in through the open windows and the breeze is sending the gauze curtains flying. I can smell the forest and I've just discovered a pair of armless white leather recliners which are either sunbeds or massage beds. Regardless, I'm currently lying on a cloud and your chances of getting me off it any time soon are…ooh, *nil*. More to the point, if this security discussion is about me and my needs I want it to happen here, in these quarters, so I can see for myself what you're proposing. I want you to walk me through it.'

Her words made sense, more was the pity. 'Be ready in five minutes,' he grated.

'I'll order more tea,' she said smoothly, and hung up on him.

His security deputy stood there, still largely oblivious to the force of nature Theo was about to unleash on their world. 'We're going to her.'

He was a good man, his security guard. Well trained. Because all he did was nod.

Theo's mood did not improve as Moriana negotiated her security requirements. He overrode most of her requests, acceded to two of them, and wore her contemplative stare in silence once the security team was back in place.

'Seems like overkill,' she said.

'My team is experienced. They'll only step in when needed.' He couldn't joke about security measures and he would never, ever downgrade them. 'I don't take risks. I do need to sleep at night, and I won't if I'm worried about the safety of the people under this roof. I can protect you, Moriana. But you need to let me.'

He wasn't negotiating.

Finally, she spread her arms wide. 'Okay.'

But he still didn't relax.

'Bear with me while I try and figure out what pitched your mood blacker than tar,' she said as she headed for the sunroom she seemed to like so much. 'Augustus gets like this. It's not always my doing but I'm not ruling it out. More tea?'

'No, thank you.'

'What did Benedict want?'

'Too much.' The words were out of his mouth before he could call them back. Then again, wasn't he supposed to be sharing his life with her? Trusting her with the complications of his court?

'So either you refused him and you're brooding about it or you agreed to do something you don't want to do,' she said. 'Which is it?'

'Do you think me cold?' he asked instead of answering her question.

'No.'

'Do you think me ruthless? Calculating?'

'Yes. Both. Show me a good ruler who isn't.'

'My uncle's dying,' he said.

Her eyebrows rose.

'He wants to spend his last days here at the palace.'

'Ah,' she murmured. 'And the petition for your removal? What's happening there?'

'Benedict says it's been abandoned.'

'Interesting. Do you believe him?'

Theo couldn't sit still beneath her carefully assessing gaze. He stood and crossed to the window but he could still feel her eyes on him like an itch between his shoulders. 'I don't know.'

'How long does your uncle have left?'

He didn't know that either, but apparently he had the doctor's contact details somewhere to hand. 'Got a phone?'

She disappeared through the doorway and came back moments later and handed it to him. It was gold-plated and disguised as a set of balance scales. He looked at the phone, looked back at her.

'If there's a less absurd phone around here, I've yet to find it,' she said. 'Why do you think I always sound so thoroughly cheerful when I answer it?'

Two minutes later, Theo had the contact details he needed. Two minutes after that he was speaking to his uncle's head physician in France. When he put the phone down ten minutes later he was armed with the knowledge that Benedict hadn't been exaggerating Constantine of Liesendaach's illness. The doctor had given Constantine days to live. Already, he was slipping in and out of consciousness as his body's organs began to fail. Constantine had refused life support assistance and Benedict had told the medical staff to honour the request. Palliative care only for the former Regent.

'We're talking days,' he said. 'Assuming he doesn't die in transit.'

'Okay. Now we know.' Her calm poise steadied him. 'Will you grant him a state funeral?'

'No.' He couldn't stomach giving that honour to a murderer. 'There can still be enough pomp to satisfy the burial of a former Prince Regent without gazetting it as such.'

'Do you seek my opinion on the matter?' she asked.

'Yes.' Why not? There was something grounding about the sheer practicality of her questions so far.

'Okay, here goes. You neutralised the man ten years ago but didn't exile him. Either before he dies or after, you're going to have to bring him home. You're going to have to try and make sense of his life and actions and then you're going to speak in public of human frailty, temptation and forgiveness, whether you mean those words or not. Do it now. Get it done. Show your people—and him—a strong king's mercy.'

She hadn't moved from the sofa but her words drew him away from the window and back around, such was her command of his attention. She sipped her tea, an island of serenity, and it dawned on him that she was extremely good at being someone's muse.

'Your uncle is no threat to you now. Benedict, bless him, is in the same boat as you in that he has no wife or heirs. Benedict won't challenge you. He *can't* challenge you. The throne is yours.'

She was good at this. 'I still need a queen.'

'And now you can take your time and search properly and find one who suits your needs.'

She was *right there in front of him*. How could she be so clear-eyed when it came to dealing with his uncle and cousin and not know she was the perfect candidate?

'How often does Augustus seek your counsel?' he asked.

'Almost daily, why?'

'You're good at it.'

She smiled wryly. 'I grew up listening to my father speak freely of state concerns at dinner each night. Not major concerns, nothing classified to begin with, but even as children we always had one topic of state to discuss, alongside the regular conversation about our days. He'd ask our opinions. Make us defend our positions. Showed us how to respectfully discuss problems and the fixing of them. They were lessons in statecraft.'

'And how old were you when you started this?'

'I hardly recall when it started, only that it was an everyday occurrence. My father always paid attention to my mother's voice. He relied on her for support and to bring fresh perspective to the table. When she died, so too did much of my father's enthusiasm for his role. It's one of the reasons he abdicated early, even if not the only one.'

She put down her teacup. 'I'm scaring you, aren't I? You're not used to dealing with women who expect a great deal of intellectual intimacy from their nearest and dearest.'

He wasn't used to dealing with *anyone* who expected intellectual intimacy from him.

'I did warn you,' she said.

'You did.' And, God, he wanted more of it. He ruled alone; he always had. But this…this effortless back and forward, argument and counterargument, not for argument's sake but with the clear aim of lifting a burden… He would have more of this.

'You're looking a little wild-eyed,' she said.

He'd just realised what he'd been missing all these years.

She rose and came to stand beside him, looking out over the gardens, following his lead and dropping the subject. 'What's that?' she asked, pointing towards a tiny cottage on the edge of the forest.

'It used to be my mother's painting studio. These days the gardeners use it as their headquarters.'

'Will you walk me there? Through the gardens?'

'Now?'

She nodded.

'You'll need a hat. And a shawl for your shoulders. Possibly an umbrella.'

She looked at him as if he amused her.

'What?' he said. 'It's a long way. You're fair-skinned. You'll burn.'

'I have dark hair, dark eyes, olive skin and when I encounter the sun I tan. Also, you're starting to sound like my mother.'

Her mother had been a tyrant.

'You do realise,' he murmured, 'that mothers are, on occasion, right?'

By the time they reached the outer doors of the palace there was a woman's sun hat, an umbrella and a gauzy cotton scarf waiting for them. Moriana sighed. Theo smiled. Heaven knows where his household staff had sourced them from.

First the scarf—Theo draped it around her neck and made a production of rearranging it several times until it completely covered her bare shoulders. Clearly he was more adept at taking a woman's clothes off than helping one put clothes on.

The hat came next. Then he offered her his aviator sunglasses. 'We should take water,' he said.

'It's a walk in the garden, not a mountain trek. Why are you being so…'

'…attentive?' he offered.

'I was going to say *weird*. I've been in gardens with you a dozen times over. Never before have you offered me a hat.'

'It wasn't my place. Ask me how often I wanted to offer you a hat. You wore one once. It was bright green, floppy-brimmed and had a red band with purple polka dots. You had your hair in a long plait that went half-way down your back and your hair ribbon matched your hat band.'

'I remember that hat,' she said. 'I don't remember the day you speak of.'

'Your brother dared you to fetch us some wine from the kitchens but you told him you already had two strikes against you and he'd have to get it himself because three strikes a day was your limit and you still had to get through your dance lesson.'

'Do you remember what my strikes were?'

'Apparently you'd chosen the wrong shoes for the right dress and embarrassed your mother in front of her friends. That was strike one. Strike two happened at lunch because you'd forgotten the name of someone's pet spaniel.'

'Oh.' One of *those* days. 'Good call when it came to me not stealing the wine, I guess.' Moriana drew the scarf more tightly around her shoulders. Criticism had shaped her days as a child. It had been constructive criticism, of course. But it had also been relentless and demoralising, and she'd crawled into bed and cried herself to sleep more nights than she cared to remember, convinced she was an utter failure at life, the universe and everything. 'I used to take criticism too much to heart. I still do.'

'But you're working on it. *Moriana First*, remember?' His smile was warm and his eyes more blue than grey today. 'I'd never seen you looking prettier, that day, mismatched shoes and all. Naturally I had to steal the wine myself and pull your hair when I returned. Heaven forbid you didn't notice my reappearance.'

'I remember now. You then proceeded to ignore me for the rest of your visit.'

'I was fourteen. You were the prettiest thing I'd ever seen. Your hat made me want to sneak beneath it and kiss you and the wine made me almost brave enough to do it. But you were already spoken for and I was still a good boy back then. Kissing you would have sparked an international incident involving parents. My father would have handed me my ass. Naturally, I ignored you for the rest of my visit.'

His words were sweet. His eyes were shielded by long, sweeping lashes several shades darker than his hair.

'And why are you telling me this now?'

'Because confession is good for the soul.' He slid her a smile that held more than a hint of the boy he'd once been. 'I still wish I'd done it.'

And then he ducked his head beneath the brim of her hat and kissed her swiftly on the cheek.

What was that for? She didn't say the words but her eyes must have spoken for her.

'You said you wanted romance,' he said.

'You can stop courting me now. You're free and clear, remember?'

'I know.' He shoved his hands in his pockets and fixed his gaze on the horizon, giving her a clear view of his strongly hewn profile. 'But maybe I want to court you anyway.'

CHAPTER SIX

LIESENDAACH WAS A treasure trove of loveliness, Moriana decided later that afternoon as she and Aury investigated the Queen's wardrobe facilities more thoroughly. Theo had retreated to his office for the afternoon and exploration had beckoned in his absence. Theo's mother's clothes had been removed, but the three empty rooms devoted to clothes storage, hat and shoe space and a cupboard-sized jewellery safe spoke of a woman who'd loved to dress up and had spared no expense when it came to indulging that passion.

'If I remember correctly, the late Queen of Liesendaach used to collect clothes,' said Aury. 'Period clothes. Centuries-old gowns once worn by the aristocracy. Venetian masks, Russian uniforms, everything. Want to go looking for them?'

One of the two security guards standing just within her line of sight coughed and Aury rolled her eyes before turning to look at him.

'You wanted to say something?' Aury asked the guard.

'Yes, ma'am. There's a costume collection on the third floor, right above us.'

'I didn't know this place had a third floor,' said Moriana.

'Storage only. There are no windows, Your Highness. But that's where you'll find the costume collection. There's a staircase up to it from the door on your far left. The one that looks like a regular cupboard door.'

'I love secret staircases. Makes me feel right at home,' said Aury, with a flirtatious glance in the guard's direction. 'What's your name, soldier?'

'Aury,' Moriana chided, with a glance that spoke of not seducing Theo's security force within five minutes of their arrival.

'But everything's so *pretty* here,' Aury said with another coquettish glance in the direction of the unwary. Come to think of it, the poor man appeared quite aware and looked to be holding up just fine. And yes. He was very pretty—in a rugged, manly kind of way. Fair-haired and light-eyed, like so many of Liesendaach's people, he was also large of frame and lean when it came to bodyweight.

'What's your name, soldier?' Moriana repeated Aury's question.

'Henry, milady.'

'Good sturdy name,' Aury said. 'We should keep him. He knows where things are.'

'Uh-huh.' Moriana opened the door he'd spoken of. Sure enough, a spiral staircase beckoned, up, up and up towards darkness.

'I'll need to call it in and go on ahead if you want to take a look.' This from Henry again, all security-wise and conscientious.

'Let's do it.'

Two minutes later Henry led the charge up the stairs. Aury let him get all of two steps ahead before she started ogling the man's backside with a pleased little sigh. 'After you,' Moriana told her lady-in-waiting drily.

'*Thank* you, milady.'

'You're incorrigible.' But Aury's obvious enjoyment of her surroundings fuelled her own. Nothing like a fairy tale castle to explore to pass the time.

They eventually reached the third floor. Henry switched on lights as he went and when they reached the top of the stairs he crossed to a bank of old-fashioned switches and flicked them on, one after another. The place lit up, one tennis-court-sized section at a time, to reveal row upon row of gowns and costumes stretching into forever.

'There's a ledger,' Henry said, pointing towards a long side table. 'I believe the costumes are organised by period and then colour.'

'Henry, what's with the superior knowledge of the costumes?' asked Aury.

'My mother was seamstress to the late Queen,' said handsome Henry. 'I spent a lot of days up here as a child.'

'Were you ever a centurion?' Aury wanted to know. 'A Knight Templar?'

Henry smiled but neither denied nor confirmed his tendency towards dress-ups as a child.

'What does your mother do now?' Moriana asked.

'She works as a palace chambermaid, Your Highness.'

Handy. 'I don't suppose she's working *now* and would like to join us up here?'

'Imagine what we could do with these,' said Aury.

'Charity exhibitions, loans to museums…' Moriana was thoroughly on board with investigating ways of making sure these costumes were *seen*.

'Liesendaach's little big book of heavenly dresses,' said Aury. 'For charity, of course.'

Aury flipped open the ledger and started scanning the index. 'Oh, my lord. Royal wedding gowns!'

'We could be here a while.' There wasn't a lot that was going to compete with a collection of royal wedding gowns through the ages.

'Henry, I'm forward. It's a terrible flaw, I know,' Moriana began, and Aury snickered and handsome Henry blushed. 'But I think it's time we met your mother.'

Theo found them two hours later. He'd spent the afternoon on the phone to various medical specialists, including his uncle's physician yet again. He'd organised transport. He'd spoken to Benedict. No way was he bringing his uncle home without Benedict accompanying the man and staying on until Constantine's death.

Benedict probably had whiplash from Theo's change of heart, but he hadn't said no. Instead, he'd offered subdued thanks, asked for the lower west wing to be placed at their disposal, and promised not to linger once his father passed on.

Theo had a knot in his stomach at the prospect of all three of them being under the one roof again, and a burning need for Moriana's company. Not to talk it out, the way he'd done earlier. This time he was looking solely for a distraction.

She didn't disappoint.

There she sat, a tiny general in butter yellow, wholly surrounded by clothes in every colour imaginable, and attended by two chambermaids, her lady-in-waiting, his Head of Household Staff and two royal guards.

'Theo!' Moriana coloured prettily when she saw him. 'How long have we been up here? We were just...er... planning an exhibition for your...er...'

'Consideration,' Sam murmured helpfully.

'Yes, indeed. For your consideration.' Moriana smiled.

'And the benefit to me would be…?'

'Immense,' she said. 'Think of the children.'

'I'd like four,' he said silkily, and watched her expression grow wary. 'Walk with me. Please. There's something I'd like to discuss.'

'Of course,' she murmured and, with a nod for those surrounding her, she followed him along the narrow walkway with costumes on either side.

'What is it?' she asked as they began their descent down the spiral steps towards the second floor.

'The press know you're here.'

'How?'

'How do they know anything? On the one hand, my reputation precedes me. On the other hand, you're you, freshly jilted and vulnerable, and they know I was at your charity auction last night. They can smell a story and they've already been in contact with my press secretary for a statement. I'm willing to let them speculate as to what I'm doing with you. What are you willing to do?'

'No comment?' She nibbled on her lower lip and he was hard pressed not to bend his head and join her. 'I think "no comment". I'm through with thinking the press will treat me well any time soon, and you've never thought of them as allies.'

Worked for him.

'Do you really want four children?' she asked.

'Why not?' The only number he didn't want was two. The heir and the spare.

He'd been the spare, forever in the shadow cast by his brother's bright light, and he'd never liked the dynamic.

'Do you want children?' He remembered her reply to Augustus.

'Would you still offer for me if I didn't?' She slid him a rueful glance. 'Don't answer that. Rhetorical question. I know full well you need heirs.'

'But do you want children?' he pressed.

'Yes,' she said quietly. 'And there's no medical reason why I can't have them. I'm still fertile.'

'Do you remember that conversation? The one at your place when we were younger?' All the children of neighbouring monarchs had been there. All the young crown princes—him, Augustus, Casimir and Valentine—along with Moriana and Valentine's sister. Moriana had been subject to a fertility test in the days beforehand and had ranted long and loud about women's rights and invasion of privacy. And then Valentine and his sister had revealed they too had been tested for fertility and a host of other genetic flaws. Casimir had then bleakly revealed he'd been subject to not one but two DNA paternity tests.

There'd been a question on everyone's lips after that, and it had nothing to do with fertility.

It had been Valentine who'd finally caved and asked if Casimir was his father's son.

The answer had been a sullen, scowling, 'Yes.'

'I still remember that conversation,' he murmured.

'So do I,' said Moriana. 'Is it wrong for me to breathe a sigh of relief now that Casimir's poisonous father is dead? Is it wrong for me to think that you'll have less to worry about once your uncle has passed, and that I really like the shape of this new world order? Because I do like it. It makes me feel hopeful for the future—and the future of any children I might have.'

'*We* might have.'

'So you're still courting me,' she said. 'I thought now your marriage problem has been solved we might go back to being adversaries.'

'I still need a wife. Liesendaach still needs a Queen and an heir. And I'm doing my very best to be open and trusting with you and, believe me, it doesn't come easy.' Damn right he was still courting her. 'I'm asking questions. I'm sharing my thoughts. I brought a personal problem to you earlier. Marriage may not be something I need quite so urgently, but it's still something I want. See? This is me—sharing and caring.'

'I…see,' she said dubiously. 'Well, then…good job.'

'And there you go again. Lying to me,' he said darkly. 'What *else* can I improve on?'

'I…' She spread her hands somewhat helplessly. 'Theo, I appreciate your efforts and the confidences you've shared with me today. Truly.'

'But you're still not taking my proposal seriously.'

'I am now.'

She looked at him uncertainly and he wished he could rid her of her insecurities.

'I'd even throw in your favourite wedding gown from upstairs.'

'They're all quite exquisite.'

But she didn't say yes.

'I wonder what Casimir's going to do about his daughter,' she said suddenly.

'Where did that come from?' Moriana was hard on his ego at times; he'd give her that. Moments ago he'd been offering up his innards for her perusal. Now she was talking about her former fiancé's daughter.

'I'm thinking about a king's need for an heir—you started it. Then I thought of Casimir. He'll claim his daughter—he told me as much—but she's still illegitimate. She'll never rule.'

'Did he say he was going to marry the mother?'

'No. He spoke of her only briefly, to say that everything was up in the air. But I get the feeling he cares for her more than he's letting on. More than he let on to me, at any rate.'

'You care for him.' Theo had never liked that thought.

'Yes, although perhaps never as romantically as I should have. I feel for Casimir. For over twenty years I thought I was to marry him. He has a six-year-old daughter he never knew he had. He may be considering taking a commoner—a foreigner—for a wife. He's burying his father, who he had a difficult relationship with. And now he's a king. I wouldn't want to be him.'

Moriana was well rid of him. 'His transition to the throne is assured.'

'Do you think he'll have an easier time of taking up the reins than you did?'

'He's older, wiser, and there's no other royal alternative waiting in the wings. The throne is his.'

'Will you help him? Counsel him?'

'If he asks for my counsel, yes.'

'Why did you never ask for help when you first took the throne?'

Always with the difficult questions. 'Help from whom? Byzenmaach? Casimir's father supported my uncle as Regent; there was no help for me there. Thallasia stayed neutral until Valentine took the throne. Only then could I look there for support and by then I was through the worst of it. Your father was the only one to ever offer the hand of friendship and even then I didn't take it because I didn't trust him. I didn't trust anyone.'

'We know. It was one of those round-table conversations we had about you. My father thought you a wastrel, initially. In his defence, you had gone out of your way to give that impression.'

Theo smirked. 'I was hiding in plain sight.'

'But then you neutralised your uncle and began to undo the damage done and within six months my father was your biggest fan.' She slanted him a glance. 'Would it surprise you to know that another reason my brother took the throne early was so that *you* would have a regional ally you might trust?' Theo stopped walking. Moriana continued her stroll along the corridor before finally looking over her shoulder. 'Do keep up.'

He had no words. His day had been full of too many surprises already. 'Who *are* you?'

'I'm Moriana of Arun, sister to a King, daughter to a King, and potentially your future Queen.'

'I need a drink.'

'I concur. How about you walk me to a bar?'

He turned her around and walked her to his rooms instead. They were closer and there was a bar in there. It wasn't fully stocked, but all his favourites were present and hers could be delivered.

'Is now a good time to let you know that if we marry I'll be wanting full access to Liesendaach's education, healthcare and arts portfolios, and I wish to be kept apprised of the regional water resources plans?' she asked.

'Tomorrow would be a better time to hit me with that,' he muttered. 'I'm surprised Augustus is willing to let you go, what with all you do.'

'Needs must.' They'd reached his rooms and he stepped back to let Moriana enter before him. 'Although, in the interest of full disclosure, there is the small matter of my overdrawn bank account,' she said dulcetly. 'He's not particularly happy about that.'

'What did you buy?' Augustus had never mentioned his sister being a frivolous spender. He was more likely to gripe about her inability to stop buying and selling major artworks.

'A tapestry. It was one of ours from long ago. My great-grandfather sold it and seven others like it. Together they told a story of love, war and an abandoned child who grew to be a great warrior and mistakenly fell in love with his mother, at which point he put a sword through her heart and then fell on his own. Sword, that is.'

'Happy. I can see why you had to have it back.'

'Yes, well, unfortunately, the original set was split between several buyers. My grandmother bought the first one back; my mother recovered three more. Augustus found one. I found two more. The last remaining seller knew their tapestry would complete the set and priced accordingly. I paid up and Augustus froze my spending account until June next year.'

She sounded amused rather than put out. 'Quite a good time for me to consider marriage, all things considered. I *will* have a spending account as your Queen, right?'

'Yes, but you'll have to answer for it.'

'I always do.' She crossed the room to look out of his window. 'You keep horses here.'

'We breed horses here. Warhorses for Liesendaach's mounted guard regiment.'

Moriana hummed her approval. '*Very* nice.'

She was biting back a smile and he crossed to her side and looked out. His stable master was supervising the unloading of horses from a livestock transport truck into the courtyard below. Three big greys and a tiny black Shetland stallion were being introduced to several stable hands.

'Is there anything here that's not pretty?' she asked, and he remembered an overheard conversation about stable boys and lustful thoughts.

'You'd best be looking at my horses, Princess, and not my stable hands. And I suggest you avoid entirely the company of royal horsemen stationed here.'

Moriana's smile turned positively beatific. 'You have a company of royal horsemen stationed here? How did I not know this? I need to tell Augustus.'

She wanted to torture Augustus with visions of her sleeping her way through Liesendaach's mounted regiment, most likely. The problem was, Theo couldn't admit to overhearing that conversation between her and her brother because then all hell would break loose. He didn't want all hell to break loose right now. He wanted to relax and regain some small sense of control and maybe, just maybe, get her to look at him the way she'd looked at him last night and then again this morning.

'Have you ever just wanted a day to be over?' he asked.

'You mean how I felt most of yesterday and the day before?'

'Point.'

'Are you thinking about your uncle?'

'And Benedict. And you. And the future and what to make of it.' And trust and how to build it with this woman.

'No wonder you need a drink. Weighty topics all.'

And connected all, for together they did—or would— make up his family unit.

Moriana turned, her back to the window now, as she stood before him. At least her attention was no longer being diverted by his horsemen. 'Of course you don't have mindless sexual conquests to distract yourself with any more. What a shame.'

'Moriana, I'm going to strangle you soon,' he warned.

A mischievous smile lit her face. 'Are you ready to teach lesson two? I'm ready for lesson two.'

'Breath play? I doubt it.'

She blinked.

He smiled. 'Was that not what you meant?'

'I…er…no. Definitely not what I meant. Baby steps, Theo. It's only lesson two.'

'A lesson that isn't scheduled until tomorrow.'

She sighed. 'Guess I'll have to keep looking at all the pretty horses…and their handlers.'

On the other hand, it wasn't as if he had anything better to do. He could use a little distraction. And there was something to be said for physical release as a means of easing tension.

'Would you like to keep looking at my stable hands?' he murmured. 'Because hands on the windowsill if you would.'

'Oh, no. No.' She quickly put distance between her and the window, before turning to keep him in sight. 'I know what "hands on flat surfaces" involves. We covered that lesson this morning, and we are not doing it again in front of a window with your men looking on. That's lesson eight hundred and sixty-five *thousand*. Not to mention a very bad idea.'

'Or you could sit on the bed.'

One moment she was railing at him, eyes wide. The next minute she was perched on the end of his bed, arms crossed in front of her.

'I have a request,' she said.

He expected nothing less.

'I'd like you naked this time,' she said.

'As you wish.' Theo smiled, the focus firmly back on him as he stalked towards the bed. 'Perhaps you could undress me.'

Moriana tucked her hands a little higher beneath her arms. 'I didn't expect these lessons to require quite so much initiation on my part.'

'Live and learn. You could start with my buttons if my belt's too intimidating.'

'I refuse to be intimidated. I can do this. I want to do this.'

'That's the spirit.'

She started with his belt buckle, her touch deft and light. By the time she had his fly undone he was hard beneath the brush of her hands and he was the one unbuttoning his shirt, because bravery should be rewarded.

She leaned in and closed her eyes and set her cheek to the skin just above the low ride of his underwear, and when she turned her head the better to taste skin he clenched his hands into fists instead of sliding them through her hair and guiding her actions. If the last lesson had been about Moriana surrendering control of her body to him, he wanted this lesson to be about her taking control and keeping it, exploring it. And for that he had to ease off on his.

He shouldered his shirt to the floor and she looked up as if he was offering the finest of feasts after a lifetime of starvation. He wished she had more experience but he wasn't ever going to let her get it from anyone else. She'd had her chances and hadn't taken them.

She took her time when it came to getting his trousers off. He took his time laying her on the bed and stretching out beside her. She liked looking at him, when he wasn't distracting her with kisses, deep and drugging. She liked touching him and he encouraged it.

'What's the lesson?' she asked again, so he named one.

'Rubbing,' he whispered. 'Rocking.' Until they drove each other mad. 'No penetration.' He hadn't done this since his teens. 'Easy.'

He wrapped his arm around her waist and hauled her on top of him, knees to either side of his hips, and if that wasn't giving her full control he didn't know what would.

'Should I take my clothes off?'

'Your call.' Her dress was soft and her panties felt like silk against his erection. Hot wet silk.

The panties came off and her dress stayed on as she positioned herself over him again, and slowly settled against him.

'I like feeling you against me,' she murmured against his lips and he closed his eyes and tried to think of anything but the feel of warm wet womanhood against him. Slowly she began to rock against him, her hands either side of his head. 'Like this?'

'Yes.' Sliding his hands beneath her dress, up and over the globes of her buttocks, the better to position her for maximum drag over sensitive areas.

She was slick enough for both of them and for the most part he let her find her way, only sliding his hand around to rest his thumb against her once or twice to begin with until she arched up to a sitting position, grabbed his hand by the wrist and held it there.

She closed her eyes and her trembling increased as he used every trick he'd ever learned to make it good for her.

'Do you close your eyes the better to imagine someone else?' he grated, because he could be cruel and tender in equal measure and because she'd said the same to him.

'Put it in,' she whimpered. 'Theo, please. Fill me. Put it in.'

'Not until we're married.'

'Since when has this been one of your conditions for bedding a woman?' Disbelief coloured her voice but her body still moved and so did his.

'Since you.' He rolled her over and wrapped her legs around him and added his weight and a sinuous roll to the negotiations; it had been years since he'd been this close to coming with such minor stimulation, but this was Moriana and her abandon had always fuelled his. 'I will put my mouth on you and my hands, do this all day long, take you to the edge and make you wait, but you only get me in you when you're mine.' Which begged the question... How long did it really take to arrange a royal wedding? Because the restraint was killing him.

'I hate you.' But her hands were in his hair and she was drawing his head down into a kiss so hot and desperate that the groan he heard was his.

'You want me.'

'Yes,' she sobbed. 'Theo, I'm—'

Coming, and so was he, all over her stomach, messing her up, painting her his.

She was too responsive. 'You came again, I don't care what you say. I win.'

She laughed a little helplessly.

'You know, simultaneous satisfaction is quite a feat. Very rare.'

'Is it? I wouldn't know.'

'It's rare.'

She studied his face, her eyes searching and solemn. 'You're still courting me.'

'Yes, and I fully intend to win you. How much plainer do I have to make it?'

'I have a temper,' she said next.

'Pent-up passion has to go somewhere.'

'I have high standards. I'm hard on myself and on others. I'll be hard on you if you fail me.'

'I'd expect nothing less. If I think you're being too hard on either yourself or others I'll call you on it. We'll argue and your passion will go somewhere.'

'I can be a workaholic.'

'Liesendaach needs a lot of work.'

'You're not the slightest bit self-conscious about lying here naked, are you?'

'Should I be?'

She sighed and shook her head. 'No. Your body is flawless.' She dropped her gaze below his waist. 'And very well proportioned. I never realised that shamelessness could be quite so enticing.'

He was comfortable in his skin. She, on the other hand, still had her dress on. 'I would see you comfortable in your skin before we're through,' he told her. 'Especially in private.'

'More lessons.' The curve of her lips was captivating and always had been.

'Yes, many more lessons, starting now. Take your dress off.'

'But…aren't we done for now?'

'I promised to keep you strung out on the edge of release for hours,' he reminded her silkily. 'I need to keep my word.' She had a very sensitive neck. It responded well to lips and tongue and the faintest graze of his teeth.

'I think you're overestimating my resistance to your touch,' she murmured as she arched beneath him.

Twenty minutes later and after two orgasms, ripped from her body in rapid succession, Princess Moriana of Arun told him to stop.

'Have I persuaded you to marry me yet?'

'Not yet,' she murmured with a thoroughly satisfied smile. 'But full points for trying.'

CHAPTER SEVEN

MORIANA CRACKED ONE eye open to the sound of cutlery landing on a table. She was in Theo's room, in Theo's bed, wholly naked, but the man himself wasn't there. Instead, a chambermaid was busy setting a dinner table in the room next door. Moriana could see bits of her every now and again through the half-closed door and the reflection on the window. It was dark outside and dark in the room she'd been sleeping in. The adjoining room looked as if it was lit by candlelight.

Perhaps it was.

She'd been schooled, she remembered that much. She remembered Theo playing her body the way a master violinist played a foreign instrument. Paying attention, learning what worked and what didn't, down to the tiniest detail, and adjusting his attentions accordingly. He'd played her to perfection. He'd known what she wanted before she did and kept her waiting.

He still hadn't bedded her fully.

And now she was in a strange room with no clothes to wear other than stained ones, and no idea what to do next. The maid finished her preparations and slipped from view and Moriana took the opportunity to escape into the bathroom. A shower later, she entered his dressing room and took one of his shirts from its hanger and put it on. It was of the softest cotton and fell to the tops of her thighs. She found her panties and put them on too.

She tried not to think about what she looked like but there were mirrors on three walls and in the end it was inevitable that she would meet her reflection. Make-up gone and hair untended, she barely recognised herself. In her eyes was an awareness of pleasure. On her skin were faint marks left by the press of strong hands and a hot, sucking mouth. Theo hadn't treated her like a princess. He'd treated her like a woman fully capable of pleasing herself and, in doing so, pleasing him.

She took a blue two-tone tie from his collection and used it as a hairband, and now she looked all carefree and confident.

Looked, not felt. Because she'd never felt quite so laden with doubt.

She'd only ever repressed the more passionate side of her nature and here she was feeding it, and Theo was nothing if not encouraging. With him at her side she was slowly eroding the self-control she'd fought for all her life—the control her family valued above all else.

'You're screwed,' she told the woman in the mirror, and then turned her back on her and there stood Theo. Watching. The hawk in the granary.

'Not yet,' he said, and straightened as she approached. 'What is it you think I can't give you?' His eyes were sharp, more grey than blue in this light.

'There doesn't appear to be anything you can't deliver.'

He was still watching her so she sent him a smile to back up her words.

'Don't do that,' he said.

'Do what?'

'Retreat behind your mask of cool politeness. It

doesn't work when you're wearing nothing but my shirt.' His gaze slid to her face. 'And my favourite tie.'

'Is it really your favourite tie?'

'It is now.' She needed to get used to Theo's lazy compliments and the intensity of his gaze. 'Dinner's ready. It's the romance portion of the evening. I added candles.'

He turned away and she followed him into the adjoining room. 'So I see.' The room was bathed in soft light and shadows and the table was set for two. A nearby balcony door stood open and she could smell the scent of the forest and feel the lingering heat of the day in the air.

'I love it here.' It wasn't like the palace she'd grown up in, heavy on grey stone and small, defensible windows. This palace had been built for openness and sensual delight and showing off its beauty. It made her feel wide open to possibilities in a way that her home palace never had.

Or maybe it was the man currently pulling her dining chair out for her who was doing that.

His loose weave shirt was a dove-grey colour and unstarched. His trousers were khakis and he hadn't got around to putting on shoes.

'I got your meal preferences from the Lady Aury and took the liberty of sending them to my kitchen staff,' he said. 'We have our own regional specialities, of course, and tonight I thought we could try a mix of both your preferences and mine. See how well they mesh. The serving staff will come to the door. We can take it from there.'

A soft ping of a bell prevented her from answering. Theo went to the door and came back with a trolley laden with dome-covered dishes. There were scallops, fish stew or soup of some sort, duck salad with a pomegranate dressing—one of her favourites—and there was Mediterranean salad, heavy on the olives—which was perhaps a favourite of his. There was baked bread and lots of it.

'Fish stew and sourdough. Messy but worth it,' he said.

She took the bowl of stew he handed her and passed him the bread basket in return. 'Do you dine in here often?' she asked.

'More often than I should,' he answered. 'There's a family dining room, of course. It hasn't been used for years. Not since my uncle's rule.'

'Where did your family dine? You know—before.'

Before the helicopter crash that had cost them their lives. 'My mother used to enjoy dining on the west terrace on warm summer nights. In winter there was a modest dining room with a large fireplace that we used a lot. I don't use either any more. Too many ghosts and there are so many other rooms to choose from.'

'Do you ever get lonely here?'

'There are people everywhere,' he said by way of an answer and, yes, they were his people but they weren't family or loved ones; they were employees. He'd lost two families, she realised. One in a terrible accident and the other when he'd taken the throne and stripped his uncle of power. No wonder he kept to himself and found it hard to contemplate having loved ones he could rely on.

'I took your advice. Benedict and my uncle will be arriving tomorrow or the next day, depending on my uncle's condition,' he said. 'It may not be fun. I'm considering sending you home until it's done.'

Moriana put her fork down and her hands in her lap. Hands were revealing. And she was suddenly nervous. The food she'd been enjoying suddenly sat heavy in her stomach. She didn't have the right clothes on for a farewell speech. More to the point, she'd only just got here and didn't want to go. They'd been making progress, of a sort. Working each other out, learning each other's strengths and weaknesses, and she wanted that to continue because it was challenging and fun and the sex was flat-out fantastic, and did he really expect her to get a taste of that and then just *leave*? Because that was inhumane.

'Of course.' She couldn't look at him.

And then she did look at him, and it wasn't just lust she felt. She also had the strong desire to comfort him and be with him so he didn't have to go through this alone. 'Unless, of course, you think I might be of use to you here. I could stay if you thought that. I've been through the death of a family member before. I know how it goes and what to do. Of course, so do you.'

'I'm trying to spare you, not push you away.' His voice was soft and deep and utterly compelling. 'Would you rather stay?'

'If you—'

'No,' he said gently. '*Moriana First*, remember? You're turning over a new leaf. What do *you* want to do?'

'I want to stay and be of use,' she said, and meant it. She wanted to be with him, stand by him.

'And would you like the lessons and the romance and my awkward moments of oversharing to continue?' he asked, and there was no more denying that he was turning her into a believer of all things Theo.

'Yes.' She nodded, and reached for more bread so she wouldn't reach for him. 'Yes, I would.'

Benedict and his father arrived the following morning. They were put in the west wing, out of the way, no visitors allowed, and Moriana stayed out of their way. Benedict did not dine with them—she didn't see him for two days—but on the morning of the third day he ventured into the garden and when he saw her he headed her way.

He looked haggard and sleep-deprived, but the reason for it was obvious. His father was dying. Theo was ignoring him. This family was a fractured one, and she didn't know what to make of it.

'You were right about the artwork here,' she said when he reached her. 'It really is extraordinary.'

'I know. My ancestors have done us proud. This place. These gardens.' He smiled faintly and looked around. 'There's nothing quite like them.'

'How's your father?'

'Asleep. That's the easy word for what he's doing. Better than unconscious or comatose. The journey here knocked him around, but he knew he was home. He recognised it.'

'Does your father ask for anyone?'

'No.'

'Has Theo seen him yet?'

'No.' Benedict smiled grimly. 'I doubt that's going to happen.'

'Have *you* caught up with Theo yet?'

'Briefly.' Benedict shoved his hands in his pockets as they started walking and she fell into step beside him. 'Not that there was a lot of catching up involved. We haven't been close for years.'

'I heard that.'

'Theo wasn't always like he is now,' said Benedict. 'He was more open as a child. More inclined to let people in. Then his family died, and that dimmed him a lot but he was still accessible. Still him. It was a couple of months after his twenty-third birthday that everything changed between him and me—between him and everyone—and it was like a wall went up overnight and it was twenty feet high and made of obsidian and there was no way to scale it.'

Moriana said nothing.

'God knows I'm not without flaws,' Benedict muttered. 'But they'd never bothered him before. These days I like to think I've got a better handle on those flaws.'

'Do you care for him?' she asked quietly.

'I used to. He was like a brother to me. Now he's a stranger and I'm here under sufferance. Once my father is dead and buried I'll choose a new life and walk away from this one. It's time.'

She'd voiced a similar sentiment only days ago. The circumstances were different but the dream to simply walk away from a life of royal duty was a vivid one at times. Hard to say how it would work in reality. No one she knew had ever been bold enough or weary enough to try.

'You're his closest blood relative. Second in line to the throne. He could use your support.'

Benedict snorted softly. 'Theo doesn't want my support. I've already offered it too many times to count. By the way, this State Dinner tomorrow night that I can no longer avoid—I'm bringing a date. One of the Cordova twins.'

She narrowed her gaze and shot him a sideways glance. 'Why would you do that? To make Theo uncomfortable or to make me uncomfortable?'

'Two birds, one stone,' he said, and then shrugged as if in half-hearted apology. 'Would you believe it wasn't my idea? I owe the Cordovas a favour. They called it in.' Benedict held her gaze. 'Don't be jealous, Moriana. Theo's Theo. He has history with half a dozen women who'll be there tomorrow night, none of whom he ever wanted for his Queen. That list only ever had your name on it. You win. You both win.'

'He…had a list?'

'He had a wish. Why is this news to you? My cousin has never been able to take his eyes off you, even as a kid. He's yours. He always has been.'

'But…'

'Let me guess. His marriage proposal was framed as pure politics.'

'His marriage proposal was a form letter with my name filled in at the top and his signature at the bottom.'

Benedict laughed long and hard.

Moriana glared, until a reluctant tug lifted her lips. 'I hate humour. I'm a serious soul and why can't people just *tell me things*?' she muttered, and set Benedict off all over again.

'Seriously, go easy on my date,' Benedict said when finally he caught his breath. 'You're hard to compete with.'

'You mean I'm the perfect Ice Princess? Because, you've probably been too preoccupied to read the papers but that particular image is swiftly becoming tarnished. This morning I'm apparently intent on blackmailing Theo into marrying me by being pregnant with his triplets.'

Benedict's gaze skidded to her flat stomach. 'Congratulations?'

'Oh, shut it. It's pure fabrication.'

'You don't say.' And then he was grinning again. 'Tomorrow you should tell them they're mine.'

'Tomorrow I'll probably be brawling in public with a Cordova twin. I don't share well.' She chewed on her lip. 'You might want to forewarn her that I'm not feeling merciful.'

'If I do that her twin will want to come along as backup. Not to mention their brother.'

'I'll see to it that two more places are set for you and your friends. I may as well deal with them all at once.'

'You're fearless.'

'So I'm told.'

'Also slightly scary.'

'Spread that thought,' she said encouragingly.

They walked some more in companionable silence, and then Benedict spoke again. 'Moriana, a favour, if you please. If you do mean to invite all the Cordovas to dinner, seat Enrique next to me—as my partner. Because he is. In every sense.'

Oh. 'Oh, I see.' No wonder Benedict didn't want the throne. The fight required to accommodate his partner of choice would be enormous. 'Does Theo know?'

'He knows I enjoy both men and women, yes. I doubt he knows that I've finally made my choice. It's been made for years. Hidden for years.'

Oh, again. 'Does your father know?'

'No.'

'And yet you still want the Cordova brother at your side tomorrow night rather than wait until your father's dead? Why?'

'Because I'm burning bridges. I've no wish to be King and this is the strongest message I can send to those who might be inclined to rally around me after my father's death. Because Enrique thinks I'm ashamed of him and I'm sick of being that man. I don't care any more what anyone thinks. I love Enrique. I can't imagine my life without him in it. End of story.'

'Well, in that case, an invitation for Enrique and his

sisters can be with them this afternoon,' she murmured. 'I'm game if you're sure.'

'I'm sure.'

'You realise you should be having this conversation with Theo rather than me?' she asked him.

'I can't talk to a wall.' He turned on a smile that nearly blew Moriana away with its wattage. 'I've decided I like you, Princess. You're easy to talk to, you're smart and I suspect you're very kind. You're also very beautiful. Theo chose well for Liesendaach.' He stopped in front of her, heels together, and reached for her hand before bowing low and brushing her knuckles with his lips. 'A favour for me; now it's my turn to do a favour for you. Never forget—no matter who comes at you from Theo's past and tries to make you doubt him—never forget that he chose you. He even seems willing to change his ways for you.'

'You don't know that,' she said raggedly, no matter how much she suddenly longed to believe it. 'You don't know him any more.'

'I have my sources. Besides, I still have eyes. He still watches you as if there's no one but you in the room. He's watching you now.'

She looked around the garden and back towards the palace, where the guards stood stationed. Theo stood with them, hands in the pockets of his trousers. 'How long has he been there?'

'A few minutes, maybe a few more,' Benedict answered obligingly. 'I don't think he likes you walking with me. Hence the kiss.'

'What are you, five years old? How is annoying him going to help your cause?'

'It won't. But it does amuse me. Shall I walk you back to him?'

'Only if you're going to play nice.'

'Ah, well.' Benedict's amusement hadn't dimmed. 'I was heading to the stables anyway. Your Highness.' He bowed again. 'The pleasure was all mine.'

'You're a rogue.'

'Runs in the blood.'

'You realise I'll more than likely relay our conversation to Theo, word for word.'

'I never would have guessed.'

Benedict smiled as he walked away and she knew that look, even if she'd never seen it on this particular face before.

Do try and keep up, Moriana. You're my conduit to my cousin.

That was the point.

'What did he want?' asked Theo when she joined him. His eyes were flinty and his jaw was hard, and if he thought she was going to be their messenger girl he could think again.

'He wanted to talk to you. Apparently I'm the next best thing. The Cordovas are coming to the State Dinner tomorrow night. All of them, and it's going to be interesting.' She snaked her hand around his neck, with every intention of drawing his lips down towards hers. 'Are you angry with him for waylaying me?'

'Yes.'

'Are you angry with me for letting myself be waylaid?'

His lips stopped mere centimetres from her own. 'Yes.'

'Scared I'll like him?'

Theo's lips tightened. 'He can be charming.'

'I like you more.' She closed the distance between

their lips, not caring who saw them. She closed her eyes and stroked the seam of his lips until he opened for her. He was as ravenously hungry for her as she was for him and the thought soothed her soul even as it inflamed her senses. His arm was a steel band around her waist, the hardness between his legs all the encouragement she needed to continue.

And then one of the nearby guards cleared his throat. 'Photographers,' he said, and Theo's palm cupped her face protectively as he eased them out of the inferno of their kiss.

'Sorry,' she whispered, her confidence evaporating as he escorted her inside.

'Don't be. Think of the headlines. There'll be a love triangle. That or Benedict and I will be sharing you. Either way, you can expect a stern talking-to from your brother. So can I, for that matter.'

Moriana sighed. 'Welcome to my world.'

'I like your world, Princess. And I sure as hell like having you in mine. Don't overthink it.'

And he kissed her again to make sure she wouldn't.

The papers the following morning did not disappoint. *Claimed*, one headline ran, with a trio of pictures directly below it. Theo and Moriana just before that kiss, lips close and tension in every line of their bodies. Then the kiss itself, and it made her hot just to look at because it was a kiss better kept for the bedroom. Her family would despair of her. The third picture had Theo in full protective mode, his hand on her face and her head turned towards his shoulder as he glared at whoever had taken the picture. Mine, mine and *mine* that glare said.

That one she liked.

'Oh, message *received*,' Aury said when she saw the

headline and the pictures. 'That man is going to peel the skin off the flesh of anyone who tries to hurt you. It's even better than the picture of him butt naked. Your future king just bared his soul for you, and he did it for all to see.'

'What do you see?' Moriana snatched the paper back from the other woman. 'What soul?'

'It's there in every line of his body. His focus, the *want* in that kiss, the protection. Oh, this one's going on the fridge.'

'What fridge?' Moriana still couldn't see past her own surrender. 'What soul?'

'That man is totally committed. I knew it!' Aury was beaming. 'This isn't *just* the royal wedding of a generation...this is a love match.'

'Wait! What wedding? No! I'm not in love. I barely know the man. This is a...a sex match, if we ever get around to having sex. And it's convenient.'

'To have a husband who is head over heels in love with you, yes, it's very convenient.' Aury was practically dancing around the room. 'Henry, did you see this?'

'Yes, ma'am.'

'Henry, how many times do I have to tell you to call me Aury?'

Henry smiled with his eyes but his face remained impassive. 'Ma'am, I'm on duty. There are protocols.'

'But we *can* still solicit your opinion on the headlines, yes? It's a matter of state and safety and stuff.' Aury waved her hand in the air, possibly to encapsulate all the stuff she wasn't saying.

'The King knows what he's doing, ma'am.'

'See?' Aury whirled back around to face Moriana. 'Henry thinks Theo's in love.'

'That wasn't what he said.' Moriana did a little hand

waving of her own. 'I need new guards. And I definitely need a new lady-in-waiting.'

'You're right. I'm not waiting any more,' Aury declared. 'You're done. Gone. Claimed by a man who will move heaven and earth for you. It's my turn now.' She glanced at Henry from beneath her lashes.

'Henry,' said Moriana. 'Run.'

'Sorry, Your Highness, but I can't.' Henry looked anything but sorry. 'I'm on duty.'

'Do you want her back?' Theo asked Augustus, neighbouring King and brother of one Moriana of Arun. 'Because she's been here four days and I've lost control of my palace staff, my press coverage and the plot,' said Theo into the phone. He was staring down at the paper and wondering if Moriana was going to speak to him any time soon. *Claimed!* was the headline, and then there were pictures. And the pictures were revealing. Theo wanted to find a hole in the ground and bury himself in it.

Some things were meant to be common knowledge. His dangerous growing infatuation with Moriana was not one of them.

'She's a Combat General in a sundress,' he moaned.

'And you've *claimed* her,' Augustus said smugly. 'Enjoy.'

'You're looking at exactly the same paper as I am, aren't you?'

'When can I post the banns?' How could Augustus sound even more smug?

'I'm working on it. She's invited the Cordova twins and their brother to dinner, at Benedict's request. I'm taking it as a declaration of war on my past.'

'Reasonable call.'

'I don't often ask for advice,' Theo began.

'You've never asked for advice,' Augustus said drily.

'What should I do?'

'Why, Theo, you sit back and enjoy the tempest that is Moriana proving a point. You have to remember, *you wanted to let her run hot!*'

'You're saying this is my fault?'

'I'm saying you wanted it; you've got it.'

'She sent my dying uncle a book of prayer and a book about war.'

'Very subtle. You've already neutralised him. She's simply making sure he sees no avenue of counter attack through her. I imagine that's what inviting the Cordovas will be about too. Moriana's not one for extended torture. She'll give them a hearing, try to get them to reveal their hand, and if she doesn't like what's in it she'll cut them off at the wrist. Your role in this endeavour is to watch and learn what it's like to have my sister in your corner when enemies are present. Should you be foolish enough to reminisce with either of the delectable Cordova twins, you will lose your balls.'

Theo snorted.

'This is Moriana unleashed, remember? What could possibly go wrong?' said Augustus, with the blithe disregard of a man who knew he'd be elsewhere that evening. 'By the way, I'll be sending Moriana's dowry to you by the usual method. Meaning three hundred matched black cavalry horses and their riders will escort the dowry from my palace to yours—in full ceremonial garb.'

'I—what dowry?'

'Didn't she mention it? It's quite considerable. Paintings, linens, jewels, a regiment or two. It'll take the cavalry just under a month to get to you and I suspect Moriana will want to ride with them part of the way.

They should aim to reach your palace one week before the wedding, unless the Liesendaach cavalry decides to meet them at your border. You've met us at the border before, by the way, some three hundred years ago when Princess Gerta of Arun married Liesendaach's good King Regulus. If that happens it may take them all a little longer to reach you on account of all the jousting and swordfights that will likely take place along the way. I've been reading up on royal wedding protocol.'

'You're telling me you want *six hundred* steeds and riders prancing through *my* countryside for two weeks. Guarding *linen*?'

'And you thought Arunians were stern and resoundingly frugal.' Augustus was enjoying this. Theo was mildly horrified to find his reckoning of Augustus's character all wrong. 'Theo, I've already had six meetings with my highest advisors on how to honour Moriana properly should she ever decide to marry you. We will be parting with one of our most revered national treasures. If I had elephants I'd be sending them.'

'Elephants?'

'And now you're repeating my words. My work here is done. Good luck at dinner. Remember, do not take your eyes from the prize. Not that you ever do.'

'You're enjoying this too much.'

'I am'. And there's more, and it needs to be said. If ever you want my advice regarding your beloved future wife, just call. I have the experience to help you through. Soon-to-be brother, I am here for you.'

Theo hung up on him.

Never again would he call Augustus of Arun for advice. Never, *ever* again.

CHAPTER EIGHT

MORIANA PREPARED FOR Liesendaach's State Dinner with the same kind of care she gave to any new social situation. She dug into the history of those attending, noted their interests and successes and their relationships to each other, memorised names, and dug deeper into anyone she thought might pose a problem. The information file on the people attending this dinner was already three hundred pages long, not including the staff, for she would have her eyes on them too, looking for areas of improvement.

Aury was on deck to guide her clothing choices and so too was the sixty-four-year-old former seamstress to Theo's mother and mother to bodyguard Henry. Of late, Letitia Hale had been a chambermaid and palace function assistant, which was, to Moriana's way of thinking, a regrettable waste of palace resources that she would see rectified. Letitia had a lifetime of service to call on and the inside knowledge Moriana needed when it came to what palace guests would be wearing.

Wise Owl Counsel, Aury called her. 'We need her,' she said, and Moriana agreed.

Henry just called her Mother.

'This evening I need to outshine the Cordova twins

and every other woman Theo has ever bedded,' Moriana told them.

'An admirable goal; I'm all for it,' said Aury. 'But we don't have half your jewellery here. Intimidation by necklace is going to be difficult.'

'Let's start with the gown. What did I bring?'

'Forest-green, floor-length and backless?' Aury disappeared into the dressing room and returned moments later with the garment. It was another one from Moriana's love-it-but-never-wear-it collection.

'Did you bring *anything* I normally wear?'

'Ah…'

'What *did* you bring?'

'The silver gown that makes you look like a fairy tale villain. Your favourite black gown—always a winner. The beaded amber with the ivory chiffon.'

'Can we see that last one?' said Letitia. 'Please?'

Aury brought it forward.

'Yes,' said Letitia. 'That one. The dining room is decorated in ivory with amber and silver accents. The tables are polished walnut, the floors a shade darker; the tableware has blue accents. The gown will play to all of those colours. Plus, the beading on that dress is magnificent.'

It was and there was no denying it. The strapless bodice was beaded, the fall of the chiffon skirt inspired. Back in Arun she'd have felt overdressed but it was the type of gown this palace called for. Elegant yet showy too, no apologies. Moriana had never worn it before, had never had to choose jewellery to match. Aury had not been remiss when it came to packing jewellery to go with the gown. The coffers of Arun didn't *have* any jewellery to match this one.

'The amber beaded gown it is,' she said. 'What jewellery *did* we bring? And if we brought sapphires let's ignore them. I'd rather not match the tableware.'

'Why did we not pack rubies?' said Aury, decidedly upset. 'I don't think we have time to—'

'Aury,' Moriana said gently, 'don't worry about it. We don't have anything that fits this dress. You know it as well as I do. There's no shame in it. Besides, I have it on good authority that I'm intimidating enough, even without the jewels.'

'Well, this is true,' said Aury, slightly mollified.

'Liesendaach has Crown Jewels to match the gown,' said Letitia and promptly blushed. 'It was my job to know what jewels were available to the late Queen. I often designed dresses around them. I wasn't only a seamstress.' The Honourable Letitia looked to Aury. 'What the Lady Aury is to you—that was my role.'

Confidante. Friend. Moriana vowed, then and there, to make this woman an integral part of her world, should she ever reside here permanently. Gifts like Letitia should never be shelved.

'You could always ask His Majesty for access to Liesendaach's jewellery vault,' said Aury boldly. 'Nothing ventured.'

'I could.' Moriana chewed on her lower lip. On the other hand, she'd already been imposing her will all over the place and it seemed somewhat presumptuous to be calling on Liesendaach's treasures. 'Okay, calling for a vote from all present, and no exceptions, Henry, or your mother will find out. Do I ask Theo to let me at Liesendaach's Crown Jewels? If yes, say aye.'

'Aye,' said Aury swiftly, still holding up the amber and ivory beaded gown as her gaze drifted to some point behind Moriana. 'Oh, hello, Your Majesty.'

'Lady Aury,' said a dry voice from the doorway, and

there stood Theo. He wasn't dressed for dinner yet, but he was wearing a suit nonetheless and it fitted him to perfection. 'What do you need?'

'Rubies,' said Aury.

At the same time Letitia said, 'The South Sea Collection.'

'Both,' said Aury, ever the opportunist.

Moriana turned. Theo smiled.

'Your brother is wanting three hundred of my mounted guards to be put at your disposal for a month should you ever decide to marry me, and I said yes,' he said by way of hello. 'Do you seriously think I'll object to you requesting old jewellery that's there for the wearing? One of these actions involves prostrating myself before my cavalry and begging their forgiveness. The other involves walking down to the vault and opening a drawer.'

'I adore pragmatic kings,' said Aury. 'Truly, they're in a league of their own.'

Moriana agreed but she had other angles to pursue. There was a lot to unpack in his offhand comment. 'What do I want three hundred of your mounted guards for?'

'Your wedding procession. Apparently.'

'You've spoken to Augustus?' He must have done. 'Did you know that royal Arunian dowries used to be delivered on the backs of elephants?'

'So I've heard.'

Moriana smiled. Aury looked utterly angelic, as was her wont. Letitia looked vaguely interested, in a serene, grandmotherly fashion that belied her sharp mind, and the guards at the door never moved a muscle—facial muscles included.

'Elephants in procession,' she murmured. 'Think about it. There are lesser evils.'

'Whatever you want from Liesendaach's vaults by way of jewellery you can have,' he countered. 'Anything rubies and the South Sea Collection. What else?'

'That's it.'

Letitia nodded. Aury nodded. Henry observed.

'I'm cultivating a new image that involves less austerity and more…something,' Moriana explained.

'*Something* being a whole lot more in-your-face fairy tale beauty,' added Aury.

'I can't wait.'

Hopefully he could. 'Is there a battle room where we gather beforehand to discuss strategy?'

'Not until now,' Theo murmured. 'But stateroom six should serve the purpose. Anything else you need?'

'The name of every person in attendance tonight that you've ever been intimate with.' The words were out of her mouth before she could call them back.

Theo looked as calm as ever, even if it felt as if everyone else in the room had taken a breath and held it.

'That's not a list you need to worry about,' he said.

His opinion, not hers. Forewarned was forearmed. 'Shall I simply assume everyone between twenty and fifty is a possibility, then?'

'You can assume it won't be a problem.' His voice carried a cool warning. 'Leave us,' he told everyone else in the room, and they left and Moriana held his gaze defiantly. She shouldn't have asked for the list in front of his people or hers. Chances were she shouldn't have asked for it at all, but she wanted to be as prepared as she could for the evening ahead, and that included being prepared for smiling barbs from the women Theo had bedded and then spurned.

He strode lazily over to where she sat at her dressing table and took up the space Aury usually occupied, facing her and a little to the right.

'Want to tell me what's wrong?' he asked quietly.

'Nerves.' Enough to make her hands shake when they weren't folded in her lap. Enough to make her drop her gaze. New court, new people, new...*hope* that this thing between her and Theo was going to work out fine. 'Fear of making mistakes tonight. Fear of letting people down.'

'You won't.'

'I just did, when I asked for the list in front of everyone. But I'm not jealous, not...really. I always do this. I like to be prepared.' She gestured towards the sheaf of papers on the dressing table in front of her. It had the name and head shot of every person attending the dinner on it, along with a brief rundown on their interests, family lives and political affiliations.

He picked it up and scanned the first page and the next.

'I have it almost memorised. A couple more hours should do it.'

'You do this for every event you attend?' His eyes were sharp, his expression non-committal.

'I used to.' Her mother had insisted. 'I don't need to be quite as diligent at home any more. I remember them all. I haven't made a mistake in years. I don't want to make mistakes here either.'

He frowned. 'I don't expect you to remember the name and occupation of everyone at dinner tonight. There will be over two hundred people there. No one expects that of you.'

'Which will make it all the better when I do.'

'Are you having fun?' he asked abruptly.

'What?'

'Is this fun for you?'

Not exactly. She'd woken up feeling anxious, had barely touched her breakfast, been blissfully distracted by Theo's daily lesson, and then had reverted straight back to a state of anxiety the moment he'd left.

She had work to do. She still did. 'I don't understand,' she said, and wanted to squirm beneath his fiercely intent gaze. 'It doesn't have to be fun. This is my job. This is what I do.'

'Not today,' he said. 'I have to look at yearling horses this morning. My horse-breeding specialist has brought them in for selection. You can come too. Help us choose.'

'Theo, I don't have time for this.' She put out her hand and he took it, but only to pull her from the chair and coax her to lean into him.

'Humour me.' He could make her melt when his voice was pitched just so. 'I'll have you back in time to dress.'

Which was how she found herself far from the castle, on the other side of the forest, driving alongside a high stone wall that seemed to stretch for miles. Theo drove them through an elaborate set of wrought iron gates and finally the stables came into view.

It was a huge three-sided structure with an arena in the middle as big as a soccer field. She'd seen similar in Arun—where the mounted regiments were based— but never had she seen climbing roses frame the stable stalls the way they did here.

Theo raised his hand in greeting to a woman on the other side of the arena. The woman lifted her hand in return and started walking towards them, and the closer she got the more familiar she seemed.

She had a perfect face and eyes so deeply violet

they looked painted, and she was dressed for riding. The woman was from Moriana's mother's era, and she greeted Theo like an old beloved friend.

'Belle,' he said, 'this is Moriana. Belle is in charge of the horse breeding programme that supplies Liesend-aach's mounted guard.'

The name clued Moriana in, even though she'd never met Belle in person. This was Theo's father's legendary mistress—the circus performer he'd always kept close, no matter what.

'Ah. You know my name.' Belle's smile turned wry. 'Many don't in this day and age but I had a feeling you might. I like to think I was the late King's favourite mistress, but he never did say and I never did ask. And you, of course, are the Arunian Princess. I remember a very young Theo getting positively indignant about you from time to time. Apparently your mother never taught you how to handle boys of his ilk. Trust me, a smile and a compliment would have made him your slave.'

'I would have liked to know that,' Moriana said.

'It's never too late. Come, let me show you the year-lings before I let them out into the arena. Benedict has already been by to make his choices.'

Theo eyed the older woman sharply. 'They're not his choices to make.'

'And yet I value his opinion and so should you,' Belle admonished. 'No one has a better eye for temperament than your cousin—not even you.'

'So tell me what else you look for in the yearlings you choose?' asked Moriana hurriedly, hoping to prevent argument.

'Let me show you instead,' said Belle, gesturing them towards the nearest stall.

It wasn't difficult to feign interest in the horses on

show. They were big grey warmbloods with hundreds of years' worth of breeding behind them, many of them destined to serve in Theo's mounted regiment. There was a gelding with one white leg and Belle hurriedly went on to explain that, aside from colour, the horse had perfect form and his leadership qualities amongst the other yearlings were well established. The horse was unshakeable, Belle said. 'He does everything in his power to compensate for not being the perfect colour.'

'You know we don't take marked horses.'

'Make an exception,' Belle said, but Theo did not reply.

'If you don't keep him, I will,' Belle said next. 'Or Benedict will. He has a soft spot for imperfection, that boy. Here he is now.' She looked beyond them and Moriana turned too, just in time to see Benedict leading a saddled black horse in through the double doors at one end of the stable complex. 'That's Satan,' said Belle. 'I brought his grandsire with me when I left the circus, and he's a menace to ride. Too smart for his own good. Benedict always takes him out when he visits. I get the impression they both enjoy the challenge.'

Benedict had seen them and nodded in their direction. Theo's expression hardened.

'He won't come to you, if that's what you're worried about,' said Belle drily. 'Even as a boy he knew better than to abandon a freshly ridden horse in my stables.'

True enough, Benedict handed the saddle off to a groom and haltered the horse himself before leading it to the wash area. But he looked back at Theo and beckoned him over with the tiniest tilt of his head.

'Have you asked after his father yet today?'

'The physicians keep me updated.'

'Physicians don't know politics,' said Belle. 'Perhaps you should see what he wants.'

'Did he know I was going to be here?'

'He's here every morning, Theodosius, from around five a.m. onwards, and I put him to work. Just like when he was a boy.'

With a curt, 'Excuse me,' Theo headed towards his cousin.

'Shall we continue our rounds?' Belle asked Moriana and, without waiting for a reply, made her way to the next stall. This one was a filly, proud and fully grey.

'I've never seen Theo so easily led,' Moriana said finally, polite conversation be damned. 'How did you do that?'

'It helps that I've known both those boys since their teens. They were inseparable once.'

'Do you know why that changed?'

'I have my suspicions.'

'A woman?'

Belle snorted. 'They never fought over women—there were always so many to choose from—and for Benedict, men and women both. No. I fear the rift was caused by something far less mundane.'

'Can it be mended?'

'I try to help.' Belle smiled. 'Perhaps you will try too. Now, *this* filly has an interesting bloodline...'

Theo didn't wait until Benedict had finished hosing down the horse before speaking. *Get in, get out, keep it short.* Those were his rules when dealing with Benedict. 'You have something to say?'

Benedict nodded, not even sparing him a glance as he turned the hose off and picked up a nearby scraper. 'You're not going to like it.'

No surprises there.

'My father filed the petition for your dismissal early this morning. He says he has the numbers and he doesn't care that I've no intention of challenging you for the position and that there is no other option from our bloodline. He's simply in it for the chaos now. It's his parting gift to you.'

'He has to know I'll fight it.'

'I'm sure he does.'

'And that I'll win.'

'You usually do.' Benedict began stripping water from the horse's back. He rode them hard, as a rule, but never beyond what a horse would willingly take and the care he took of his ride afterwards would have done an Olympic athlete proud. 'You could announce your engagement to Moriana and bury the petition within a day.'

He could. That had been his intention all along and he'd made no secret of it. And yet... *Moriana First.* 'Not happening,' he grated.

'Why not? It's the perfect solution. You've always been hard for her.'

'Because I've already asked and she didn't accept.'

Wicked amusement danced across Benedict's face. '*You* couldn't get the girl? Oh, that's beautiful.'

Never give Benedict ammunition. Why could Theo never remember that? 'If I applied pressure to Moriana now and appealed to her sense of duty and the need for ongoing regional stability, I *would* get the girl. But I'm not going to do it. For the first time in her life Moriana has a chance to make up her own mind about what she wants to do and who she wants to be, going forward. I'm not going to take that away from her.'

'You're getting soft.'

It wasn't a compliment. 'You want to know what Moriana was up in her rooms doing just now? She was memorising tonight's guest list. She has dossiers of information on every guest invited. And she was miserable. Near frantic with worry that she wouldn't perform to expectations. That's not the life I want for her. She deserves more. She has to believe she can find happiness here, and I'll wait on her answer for eternity if I have to. I will not put time pressure on this decision. My court, my people, they can all *wait* on her answer.'

'And if her answer is no?'

Benedict sounded strangely subdued and now Theo was the one who needed to be doing something with his hands. He picked up a towel and began to rub the horse dry. 'If it's no, only then will I consider other options. Because she's it for me.' It was easier to say it to the side of a horse than it was to say it to a person. 'She always has been.'

Voices carried here. Belle had to know it, for she'd shepherded Moriana into a stall to examine a foaling mare. They were out of sight but plenty close enough to overhear the conversation between Theo and Benedict. And now the older woman was leaning against a stable wall, scuffing patterns in the sawdust with her boot, listening, as Moriana was listening, and Theo was putting his crown on the line. Declaring his allegiance not to his country first but to Moriana's happiness.

And then Belle's gaze met hers. 'I've only ever loved one man,' Belle said quietly. 'I gave up my world for him and I loved him as hard as I could—whenever he wanted, wherever he wanted—and he took, and he took, and he *took*. I've always told myself a King can never afford to put a woman first, but he can. And some do.'

And then Belle moved forward and her hand snaked

out to catch a tiny hoof that had appeared beneath the mare's tail. 'Aha. This foal is breech. I thought as much.' She smiled conspiratorially. 'Do you want to see what those two boys can do when they work together?' And in a louder voice that was bound to carry, 'Theo! Benedict! We need a hand. Or two.'

CHAPTER NINE

Moriana dressed for the evening with uncommon care. Some of Liesendaach's Crown Jewels had been delivered to her room in her absence, and Aury and Letitia fussed and compared and had a glorious time and Moriana let them. The list of names she hadn't finished memorising sat to one side of her dressing table. A little wooden box sat on the other side, and she knew exactly what was in it, even if Aury didn't. She'd put it there herself as a reminder of a decision that needed to be made. A decision Theo had not asked her to revisit but he *needed* her to revisit it nonetheless.

She thought he might have said something about the petition on their way back from the stables, but he hadn't. He'd talked of the new foal instead—a little colt that he and Benedict had delivered with ease.

When they reached the palace entrance he'd excused himself from her company. He had a little business to attend to before the dinner, he'd said. And kept her clueless as to the nature of it.

The amber gown with the beaded bodice won them all over once she had it on, and the diamonds and pearls of the South Sea Collection complemented it beautifully. First the earrings and then the necklace. There was a bracelet too, but she waved it away. 'I think the white gloves instead,' she said. The ones that went up and over her elbows. She could take them off at some point. And then...

She reached for the little wooden box and snapped it open, her decision made.

And then Theo would have his answer.

She slid it onto her wedding ring finger and Aury gasped. 'Is that...?'

'Yes.'

'Congratulations, Your Highness,' said Letitia.

'When did this *happen*?' asked Aury.

'He asked me before we came here. I've been trying to decide what to do ever since. And now I have.'

'But...are you sure?' Aury's eyes were dark with concern. 'I mean, I know the two of you get on better than you used to, but if you're going to obsess over all of his past conquests, I mean, that's not a habit you want to get into if you want to stay healthy.'

'I know,' she murmured. 'I'm over it.' *She's it for me. She always has been. She has to believe she can find happiness here.*

The sex, the fun, all the attention Theo had paid to her needs these past few days had come together in one blinding moment of clarity. He cared for her. He was willing to put her needs before the needs of the Crown and his own best interests.

Theo might not call that love, but it was close enough.

She wanted this.

She wanted him.

Duty and passion—and a little bit of trust and that thing they weren't calling *love*—had made the decision easy. She *wanted* to stand beside this man, proudly and for ever.

And love him.

'Wish me luck,' she said as she pulled the glove on over the ring and began to work her fingers into it. 'He doesn't know my answer yet.'

Aury snorted. 'You're going to slay him.'

'One can only hope.' She worked the other glove on, took a deep breath and reached for the royal blue sash that proclaimed her a Princess of Arun. Aury helped her slip it on and fastened it with a clasp that proclaimed the highest honours a King could bestow. When she straightened again her posture was perfect.

'You will not fail me,' she told the regal woman staring back at her from the mirror. 'You are a Princess of Arun and a future Queen of Liesendaach. You've got this.'

Aury nodded, her expression grave. The lady-in-waiting had heard it all before, the pep talks that masked Moriana's screaming insecurity every time she had to perform in public.

'Milady, Your Highness—' Letitia looked to the floor, her fingers twisting together with either hesitation or anxiety '—on behalf of myself and…and others—all the people you've taken the time to get to know this week, so many of whose names you already know—we are so very proud to serve you. We are grateful for your care.' She raised her eyes. 'We will not fail you either.'

She never forgot a name. Theo watched in outright awe as Moriana worked the room. He'd seen her in action before but that was on her turf, with dignitaries she'd grown up with. That she could so easily converse here was a testament to ruthless discipline and hours of preparation.

She favoured no one, except perhaps Benedict, who

she'd shared a few words with towards the beginning of the evening.

Theo's uncle was unwell, unable to make the dinner and receiving no visitors. Theo had already uttered that line more times than he cared to remember. He wondered cynically if he hadn't been playing into his uncle's hands by not allowing him visitors. Would so many from his court support the petition to dethrone Theo if they knew Constantine of Liesendaach was dying?

They must know, some of them. And they were behind the petition regardless.

Theo had been in a foul mood ever since his conversation with Benedict and not even saving the little colt had shifted it. Did his court really want him gone or were they simply trying to mobilise him towards marriage? He knew what they wanted.

He'd never thought dragging his feet on the issue could cost him the Crown.

He'd put a security detail on Benedict the minute he'd returned to the palace. He wanted to know who Benedict spoke to, who he phoned, what was said.

Benedict hadn't gone to see his father before dinner. He'd called the Cordova house and spoken to the brother, a curt conversation that hadn't gone well, according to the security team. He'd dressed for dinner. Taken two whiskies and paced his sitting room until it was time to attend.

Theo wished he knew how to trust his cousin the way he'd trusted him as a child.

Had Benedict been complicit in his father's plans?

If only he *knew*.

Theo watched his cousin move assuredly between one group of people and the next, and wondered exactly when the thought had taken hold that Benedict had to have known about his father's plans.

Shortly after Theo had obtained proof of his uncle's actions, he figured grimly. He'd re-examined every move the people around him had ever made, and Benedict hadn't made the cut.

Moriana and her brother had, and so had Casimir. Valentine and his sister—the royal children of Thallasia—had made the grade. No one older had—there'd been too much doubt.

'What's he done?' asked a voice from beside him, and there stood Theo's Head of Household Staff, a picture of elegance and efficiency in black trousers, black shirt and buttoned blazer.

'Who?'

Sam sent him one of those looks that told him she was aware of his avoidance tactic but she didn't call him on it outright.

'Why are you here?' She usually left the running of state dinners to the functions team.

'Her Highness wanted things done a certain way tonight. I'm making sure it happens.' Sam looked unruffled.

Theo eyed her warily. 'Is that a problem?' he asked.

'No problem. Quite frankly, it's an honour. This is me wanting to make a good impression on a woman who can teach me, and possibly everyone else around here, how best to run a royal household.'

He nodded, his attention already returning to his cousin. Moriana was with Benedict again; she'd sought him out and the conversation they were having looked to be a private one, their dark heads bent towards one another, familiar enough to be close in each other's space. Any closer and tomorrow's press would have them eloping.

The press was fascinated by the newly emerging Moriana—the one who'd always moved through the spotlight with seeming effortlessness. Her dress made her look every inch the Princess she was and the Liesendaach jewels had not gone unnoticed. Her long white gloves were driving him mad. All he wanted to do was take her some place private and peel them off, and why stop there?

Theo watched as Benedict smiled unhappily and Moriana touched her hand to his forearm in comfort as she started to speak again.

And then she pulled back and began to peel her gloves off. Why the hell was she doing that? So she could touch Benedict with her bare hands?

Theo's feet were moving before his brain had even made sense of it. All he knew was that the time for watching from afar was over and that Benedict needed to step away from Moriana right about *now*.

They looked up as he approached, Benedict's gaze widening and then turning assessing.

And then Theo looked down at Moriana's bare arms and hands. Only they weren't quite bare because she was wearing his engagement ring.

Happiness licked through him, fierce and complete. Moriana was his. *To have and to hold*, and he'd never wanted anything more than he wanted this. His world narrowed to a point, sharp and bright, as he lifted her hand and put the ring to his lips, and then his lips to hers. 'Are you sure?' he asked, rough and gruff against her lips.

'I'm sure,' she whispered, and put her beringed hand to his cheek. 'I want this.'

'For yourself.' He had to be sure.

'You're very persuasive.'

'Can someone please spare me?' said Benedict. 'I don't want to be sick. The stains, they never come out of the sashes.'

Moriana blushed and dropped her hand. Theo glared at Benedict. 'I'm sorry—are we boring you?'

'Yes,' said Benedict. 'A thousand times *yes*.'

Never give Benedict a tree branch to club you with. Because he would.

'Benedict, there you are!'

Theo turned to scowl at whoever dared interrupt them and there stood Angelique Cordova, wearing a red gown and a serene smile. *Perfect*. That was all they needed. But she was Benedict's date, and Benedict stepped back to allow more room in the circle for her.

'I gather you got Enrique's message?' Angelique said next.

'Yes.' Benedict smiled bleakly, but then he rallied and gave her a kiss on the cheek. 'Thank you for coming.'

'Someone had to support you, darling. We couldn't *all* leave you hanging. We're family.'

'How so?' asked Theo.

'Family of the heart,' she said next. 'Bear with my brother, Benedict. He's frightened for you as well as himself. He thinks now is not the time and I happen to agree with him.' She glanced up, as if only now noticing Moriana, and dropped into an elegant curtsey.

Benedict sighed, and waved his hand in a languid parody of an introduction. 'Your Highness, Princess Moriana of Arun, and so on and so forth, may I present my lovely companion for this evening, the utterly fearless Angelique Cordova, one of the brightest lights of my life. Or, at the very least, a matchstick in the darkness.'

'Pig,' she said and turned towards Moriana and curt-seyed again. 'A pleasure to meet you, Your Highness. I've heard so much about you.'

'Tell her you have so much in common,' Benedict prompted his date maliciously.

'Be a boor then,' Angelique replied smoothly. 'I intend to do no such thing.'

'I'm happy to finally meet you, Ms Cordova.' Moriana had rallied in the face of the interruption and was every inch the regal princess. 'I hear we have a lot in common.'

Theo blinked. Benedict crowed a laugh. Angelique looked momentarily startled but recovered quickly.

'Only in that I gave the world countless opportunities to tease Theo for his utter inability to tell two women apart. Of course, that then backfired because men will be men, and I'm now known as a woman not memorable enough to require close attention. I truly wish we'd never pulled that foolish stunt, but the world still turns, no?'

'Indeed it does,' Moriana murmured.

'May I offer my congratulations on your engagement?' the woman said next.

'You're the first to congratulate us,' said Moriana lightly. 'Thank you.'

'Please, let me be the second to offer my congratulations,' said Benedict. 'Assuming, of course, that Theo doesn't mess it up by assuming you don't really mean it.'

'But I do really mean it,' said Moriana.

'Good for you. Tell him often.'

And then Sam was between them, drawing Theo's attention with a glance. 'Your Majesty, my apology for interrupting but your uncle's physicians are requesting a word with both you and Prince Benedict. Now.'

That couldn't be good. 'Where are they?'

'In your uncle's room, Your Majesty.'

'Go,' said Moriana. 'I can hold the fort here until your return. I suspect Ms Cordova and I can amuse ourselves and doubtless find more shared interests in your absence.'

The mind boggled. Theo wanted not to think about it. Ever.

'Yes, that's not going to set tongues wagging at all,' murmured Angelique Cordova, heavy on the caution. 'Are you sure?'

'I don't think tomorrow is going to be a slow news day,' Moriana said and pressed a kiss first to Theo's cheek before turning to Benedict and doing the same. 'Go.'

'Scary woman,' said Benedict when they were halfway along the west wing corridor. There were guards to the rear and more up ahead but otherwise they were alone.

'Which one?'

'Yours. I waver between being totally intimidated by her one minute and wanting to bask in her attention the next.'

'Stay away from her.' Of all the emotions seething inside him, this one was foremost.

Benedict frowned and glanced Theo's way. 'I'm not a threat to you where she's concerned.'

'I know better than to believe you.'

'Then you're a fool.'

Benedict subsided into silence and Theo was glad of it. They walked the rest of the wing in silence until they reached the suite of rooms that currently housed Benedict's father. Two security guards stood sentry; one of them opened the door for them and Theo stood back to let Benedict through first—and that *was* a first. Benedict's startled glance and hesitation in stepping forward confirmed it.

'He's not my dying father,' Theo said and waved his cousin forward. It was a callous move rather than an act of respect and Benedict knew it.

'You're a monster,' Benedict muttered.

An insecure, needy, untrusting one, yes.

Theo let Benedict ask most of the questions as they spoke first to the physicians and then entered the bedroom where Constantine of Liesendaach lay. They'd taken away all life support machinery and the man lay in bed, his eyes closed and the shallow rise and fall of his chest the only indication that he still lived. *Not long now*, the physicians had said. *Tonight*. The shadow of death was in the room.

Benedict sat beside his father and took his hand, but when the old man's eyes slitted open they focused on Theo, not Benedict.

'I knew you'd come,' said Constantine, his voice no more than a rasping protest against a throat too close to seizing. 'You want to confront me before I die.'

'Maybe I do. Maybe it's time.' Theo had kept the knowledge so close that sometimes he'd felt as if it was strangling him. But it was family business and if Constantine wanted to air it, family would bear witness. 'I know you killed my family,' he told the dying man. 'I've had proof of it for years and I don't care for your denial and I sure as hell don't care to hear your confession. You did it. I know it. I know why, and I only have one question left. Did Benedict know of your plans?'

The cadaverous old man wet his shrunken lips with his tongue, tried to speak and then started to laugh before any words formed. 'That keep you awake…at night…boy?'

'Yes.' It was no lie, and there was no ignoring Benedict's pale and frozen face.

'Father, what—?'

Benedict stopped speaking when his father started coughing but it wasn't so much coughing as it was cracked and rattling laughter. 'My weak, pathetic…son. Think I don't know…about your sodomy…or your plans to renounce your family? No loss. No loss.'

Benedict recoiled from that serpent's tongue but Theo moved in; his need to know the truth was riding him hard. 'I'm talking to you, old man. Did Benedict know of your plans?'

'Weak…like his mother. Soft…'

'Answer me!'

His uncle's eyes gleamed with pure malice. 'Don't think I…will.'

But Theo wasn't looking at his uncle any more; his attention was solely for his cousin and the blank, uncomprehending shock in Benedict's eyes as he stared at Theo. Theo pushed away from his chair, toppling it as he stood.

'Did you know? Is that why you saved me?' This time Theo's question was for Benedict.

'Is that what you think? You truly believe me capable of saving you and letting the rest of your family fall? What for, Theo? To what purpose? Because I'm my father's son? Does it sound to you as if I enjoy his approval?' Benedict looked shattered, lost in memories maybe, or mired in his father's cruel contempt. '*This* is what you've been punishing me for all these years?'

Benedict stepped back, and then again, still facing them both. As if he didn't dare turn his back on either of them. And then he drew himself up. 'Father, I've never been the son you wanted. I've always known it. I used to crave your approval, more than anything. I don't any more. I have value—maybe not to you or to the King, but to some, and I am content.' Benedict turned to Theo next. 'I renounce you.' Benedict's voice shook. 'I absolve you of all dealings with me, going forward. We are not kin. I have no King. Now, get out of my sight while my father dies, and then I will get out of yours.'

It was no small matter, renouncing one's family. It was a testament to how badly Theo had handled things here tonight. He'd left cool intellect at the door, already emotionally engaged and disinclined to give Benedict the benefit of the doubt. He'd let the old man get to him while simultaneously trying to analyse Benedict's reaction, and now the old man was laughing, and Benedict was broken and Theo was responsible. 'Do you need— would you like anyone else with you? I can bring Angelique.'

'Unfortunately, she's not the Cordova for me.' Benedict crossed to the sideboard and poured a full tumbler of Scotch.

'Her brother then. I can get him here.'

'Why? So you can display your tolerance for our kind?'

'So you're not alone,' Theo said doggedly.

'Too late.' Benedict scowled. 'He won't come.'

'Then I'll stay.' He held his cousin's bitter gaze.

'You just want to hear your family's murderer draw his last breath.'

'I would see that chapter of my life closed and a new one opened, yes,' Theo admitted. 'Benedict, I'm sorry I ever doubted you.'

'Yeah, well.' Benedict drained his drink in one hit and opted to pour another. 'Your loss.'

Constantine of Liesendaach, former Prince Regent and father to Benedict, died during the main course of Moriana's first State Dinner in Liesendaach. Both Theo and Benedict were absent when the meal was served and rumours had already started to spread as to why. Some said they were in conflict over Moriana's favouring of Benedict earlier in the evening. Others declared Angelique Cordova the bone over which they fought. Moriana withstood the mutterings until the main course had been cleared away and then stood and held up her hand for silence.

Two hundred people quietened and stared at her with varying degrees of tolerance. Her introduction to Liesendaach society wasn't exactly going to plan but there was nothing she could do except stand tall and bear their regard.

She was a Princess of Arun and the future Queen of Liesendaach, assuming Theo didn't want his ring back. And she would damn well command their attention if she wanted it.

'Many of you here tonight have offered congratulations on my engagement to your King, and I welcome it,' she said. 'All of you are no doubt wondering where my fiancé is right now. You might be thinking what could possibly lure him from my side? Is Moriana of Arun being jilted? *Again.*'

A titter of nervous laughter ran the length of the room.

'Exactly,' she said drily, and lowered her hand now that she had their attention. 'Former Prince Regent, Constantine of Liesendaach, died ten minutes ago. Prince Benedict and the King attended him, and won't be returning to dine with you this evening. Dessert will be served directly, after which we'll bring the evening to an early conclusion. I look forward to meeting you all again under easier circumstances and I thank you for your understanding.'

She didn't expect applause and she didn't get it. Her appetite for sweets was non-existent. For the first time in her life, she walked out of a function and didn't care if she was doing right or wrong. She caught the Cordova twin's eye on the way to the door and gestured for her to join her. Benedict had brought her here. Moriana would not abandon her.

'What now?' asked the other woman once they were clear of the dining room. But Moriana's confidence had run out.

'We go and find them.' Although, given the way tonight was running, they'd probably stumble straight into whatever it was that Benedict and Theo needed to sort out between themselves.

'I need to call my brother,' said the other woman. 'He'll want to know.'

'Brothers are like that.' Augustus too could do with an update. 'Do you need privacy? I'm sure there are rooms available.'

'Here is fine, Your Highness.'

She could like Angelique Cordova, given the chance. 'See if you can get your brother here. I'll see to it that he has security clearance.'

'I'll try, Your Highness, but, with all due respect, it may be better if I simply find Benedict and take him home. My brother will be waiting.'

Moriana nodded and turned to walk away.

'Your Highness, thank you for your patronage this evening. It was more than I expected.'

It was more than Moriana had expected to give the Cordova twin, truth be told, but she didn't regret it. 'My mother used to tell me to face my fears rather than let them grow. And I did fear you, just a little, as a woman who might have held Theo's heart.'

Angelique Cordova smiled ruefully. 'I never even came close, and neither did my sister.'

'Tell your sister I'd like to meet her too. Perhaps we could all go riding one day. Tell me, do you ride?'

'Since infancy, Your Highness. My father breeds horses in Spain. They're quite famous.' Angelique Cordova paused. 'But then, you already knew that.'

'I did. Still. There's a forest here I've yet to explore and an entire regiment of mounted guards with nothing to do but tend horses. I'm sure some of them could be persuaded to accompany us.'

'That would definitely be a pretty ride.'

Aury was going to like this woman too.

Angelique Cordova took her leave, pulling a phone from her evening bag and retreating to the far corner of the ballroom foyer for privacy.

As for finding Theo and Benedict, Sam was heading her way and would probably know. 'Where are they?'

'Benedict went to his rooms and the King is in the Lower West Library. Past the Rafael, two doors down on the left. Neither of them are in fine spirits.'

That was hardly a surprise. 'You'll see to it that the guests take their leave?'

'Leave it with us.'

'Thank you, Sam. The meal was delicious and the service was prompt and unobtrusive. Let the kitchen know I'm pleased.'

'Yes, ma'am.'

'And have some food sent to Theo. He hasn't eaten yet.'

'Yes, ma'am. Shall I organise a meal for the Prince as well?'

'No. Just take Angelique Cordova to him once she finishes her call.'

Moriana found Theo in a room that reminded her less of a library and more of her father's den. Dark leather and wood dominated a setting scattered with low reading lamps, deep wingback chairs and a wall full of books with ancient spines. There was a bottle of whisky on the table at Theo's side and one crystal tumbler. He watched her come in but said nothing. He didn't smile.

'I'm guessing it was a rough finish,' she said, approaching cautiously. She didn't know this Theo, the one with the burning eyes and the coiled tension. Her teasing suitor was gone and in his place stood a man with a gleam in his eye that said, *Don't push me—stay back.*

She never had learned how to back away from a situation she didn't know how to deal with. She'd only ever learned how to push on and muddle through.

Theo didn't answer her so she filled his silence with words. 'The dinner is winding up. I announced that your uncle had died and you wouldn't be returning. I hope I didn't overstep.'

'Do you ever? You're the perfect princess. What more could a man want?'

Something else, judging by the sneer on his face, and she should have retreated then and there and left him to his grieving. The ring on her finger had never felt heavier. She hadn't even *warned* him she would be wearing it. 'May I stay and have a drink with you?' she asked.

'Help yourself.'

She did and eyed him pensively while she sipped. 'Did you and Benedict clear up your differences?'

'No.' Theo drained the rest of his drink.

'Is it because Liesendaach's royal family can't accommodate his relationship preferences?'

'Benedict can bed whoever he wants.' Theo's lips curled. 'As long as it's not you.'

'Where did *that* come from? You know I will never encourage Benedict to see me as romantically available. I mean…how can you not know that? I'm wearing your ring. What have I *ever* done to make you or anyone else think I'll not honour my promises?'

'Nothing.' He put his drink down and slumped forward in his chair, elbows to knees and hands clasped loosely together. He fingered the royal signet ring on his middle finger, looking for all the world like a penitent boy. 'I trust you. I do. I was just…jealous earlier, when you put your hand on his arm.'

'It was an act of comfort. His partner refused to attend the dinner. He was upset.'

'He was playing you.'

'No, Theo. He wasn't. Benedict is at his most vicious when he's upset. How can you not know that? It's all he ever is around you. And as for you… You never give him the benefit of the doubt. Why is that? What did he do to you?'

Theo ducked his head and ran his hand through his hair. 'Trust, right? I need to trust you with my secrets and my failings, even the worst of them. Even the ones you'll think less of me for. Especially them. For years I've held Benedict partly responsible for something he knew nothing about. I should have trusted him. I didn't.'

Trust wasn't his strong suit. He knew it. Everyone knew it.

'You could ask for your cousin's forgiveness,' she suggested.

Theo snorted. 'Yeah, that'll fix it.'

'It might.'

'You know *nothing*, Moriana! Why are we even talking about this?'

'Because you're upset and I want to help you!' Her temper rose to match his. 'It may have escaped your notice but it hasn't escaped mine that I still don't know what the hell you're talking about. Why do you limit yourself and not share a problem? Why do you limit *me*?'

'You're not limited!' *Here* was the fiery boy she remembered from childhood. The one who fought and scrapped and roared. 'Whatever you want to do, *you do*. My palace is open to you for reorganisation, my regiments mobilised at your request, education and health reports sit on your desk. Every time you want me to put my hands on you, *I do*. There is nothing I wouldn't do for you!'

'Except confide in me.'

'*I do confide in you*. I just did! The details are irrelevant. My uncle is dead and I will not grieve for him. Benedict is gone, and I don't blame him and I can't fix it. Enough! I bend for you, I do. Come on, Moriana, *please*. You need to bend too.'

She looked away rather than continuing to burn beneath the fierceness of his gaze. His cousin was gone, his uncle was dead and she was making things worse.

'I'm sorry; you're right. I came in here to see if there was anything you needed me to do. I didn't come here to push or to argue with you, and you never asked for my company in the first place, and I have no experience with grief other than when my mother passed and I remember when you made me sit at her funeral and gave me a glass of water and it was just what I needed and right now I want to give you just what you need and I'm not, and I'm sorry, and I'm babbling and I need to stop right now and leave you be.' She dug her nails into her palm and tried to find her lost composure. It was definitely time for her to leave. 'I apologise. I'll try to do better next time.'

She set her glass down and headed for the door, her back ramrod-straight and her heart thundering. She'd screwed up. Talked too much. Made things worse, not better. *Stop, Moriana. Don't panic. Breathe.*

He hadn't made her take the damn ring off. Not yet, at any rate.

She had her hand on the brass doorknob and another breath of air in her lungs when his palm snaked out to slam against the door and keep it shut. She hadn't heard him move, she'd been too busy berating herself, but she felt his arms come around her and saw his other hand land on the other side of the door, trapping her between his big body and smooth oak.

'Stay.' His breath warmed her cheek. 'Please. I know I'm not good company, just… I don't want to be alone.'

It wasn't the same as *I want you to stay because you're the only one for me* but she stilled her hand on the doorknob nonetheless. *Stay. Concentrate on the request and leave his reasoning the hell alone.*

'Stay,' he said again, and she closed her eyes as he pressed his lips to her neck. 'Sit with me, read with me, curse me. Just don't leave.'

She pressed her forehead to the door and let her body melt into his. 'I don't want to. I'm trying to be what you need.'

She turned and brought her lips to his, to offer comfort and a way for him to forget, and he took to the kiss like a dying man to water. There was no finesse, no les-

son here, only need and heat and Moriana was powerless in the face of it.

He picked her up and carried her to the overstuffed
leather daybed, all without releasing her mouth. She
ended up stretched out beneath him, her fingers at his
collar and tie and then his jacket as she slid it from
his shoulders, but her dress stayed on and her jewellery
stayed on and her hair stayed up.

She raised her hands to one earring and began to
take it off, but he shook his head and clenched his jaw.

'Leave them on.'

'I can't.' She had one earring out before he'd even
sat up. 'The jewellery's too valuable to lie on and the
gown is heavier than it looks. I want them gone.' She
took the other earring out and held them in one hand as
she fumbled with the clasp on the necklace. It was too
complicated, never meant for the wearer alone to take
off, and certainly not in a hurry. 'Please.' She captured
his mouth again with hers, soft and crushed where he
was hard and demanding. Willing. And he was still willing too, was he not? 'I don't want the worry of them.'

She needed him to know that there was a woman beneath the perfect princess image.

'Turn around.'

'One of my favourite phrases. Who knew?' she said
raggedly but she turned around so he could remove the
necklace. The zip was to the side of the gown but he
found it without prompting and she held her breath as he
slid it down her side and over her hip. She let the dress
fall to the floor and there was no bra to bother with,
only panties and high heeled shoes, and she slipped out
of those too, before he could say *leave them on*.

She wanted nakedness and skin on skin and nothing
between them but sweat and sweet promises.

'Still every inch a princess,' he offered when she turned around to face him, but he stepped in closer and slid his hand up and around the nape of her neck. 'It's in the curve of your neck.' His hand slid around to the front and his thumb tilted her head until she raised her eyes to his. 'And the tilt of your jaw. It's in your heart.' Fingertips slid back down her throat and over her curves until he flattened his palm just below her breast. 'My heart now.'

Because it was.

Another kiss. A ragged sigh.

He reached for his cufflinks and then for his belt and shortly thereafter he too stood naked and proud, pinning her with his hungry gaze. She was ready for whatever came next. Mindless pleasure and the losing of self. She could help him there.

He drew her down onto the leather daybed, on his back with her half draped over him. He ran his hand from neck to flank and then urged her leg up and over his exquisitely hard body, opening her up but not boxing her in, pressing against her but not pushing in.

'That's it,' he murmured into her mouth but she was through with being schooled by him.

She dragged her lips from his and started again at his shoulder, tasting his skin until she reached his pebbled nipple. She closed her mouth over him and sucked, darkly pleased when his breath left his body with a whoosh and his head dropped back on the bed.

Moriana rubbed her cheek against his skin as his body bowed towards her, releasing the tight little nub in favour of settling herself across him more fully. He let her wriggle until she'd found the most comfortable place to sit, and it was like the rubbing lesson all over again, with her finding friction against the silken hardness of his erection. She looked down towards where they weren't quite joined as intimately as she wanted them to be and swallowed hard at the sight. There was so *much* of him still visible, and how it was *ever* going to fit was still a mystery to her at this point.

She wasn't scared, but she could admit to being ever so slightly daunted.

He'd been over every inch of her body with lips and hands but he'd always pulled back from truly claiming her. She'd thought he was waiting until after the wedding, part of his royal need for legitimate heirs, but now she wondered if he hadn't simply been letting her get used to the idea of something that size going places no man had ever been.

'Are you sure about this?' There was no judgement in his quiet question.

'I want to. You want to forget, right? This is how you do it.'

'I won't forget this,' he said, his eyes darkening. 'We need to get you ready.'

'I'm ready.'

'Not quite. You're still capable of thought.'

Five minutes later, that was no longer a problem. He'd used his fingers to tease and tempt and stretch and a wave of pleasure hovered just out of reach. Skin on skin, one hand soothing as the other inflamed, he murmured nonsense words of encouragement as she took him in hand and lined him up until she felt the wide, wet press of him against her opening. Her gaze met his and his eyelashes fluttered as she gained an inch. She bit her lip, because there was no way this didn't hurt, but he'd never been wrong about pleasure yet and if she could just get *past* this first bit she'd be fine.

She willed herself to relax and gained another inch

that felt like a mile and lost her breath somewhere along the way. No more, surely, except he was less than half-way in and she was stuck. 'I—help?'

He took control, hands that had been quietly stroking and coaxing, turning firm as he cupped her buttocks and slid her off him, not all the way but enough that she could breathe.

'Circle your hips.' Big hands guided her way and slickness returned and this time when she slid back down on him she ventured further. This time he helped by drawing back before she did, his palm coming to cover her belly and his thumb gently pressing down on her sensitive flesh. 'Better?'

They were going to be here all night.

'You're thinking again,' he rumbled.

'Patience isn't one of my gifts.'

His eyes warmed. 'I have enough for both of us.'

He pulled out as he rolled her beneath him and slid down her body, proceeding to turn her into a mind-less, writhing wreck again. This time when he rose back up and entered her it was easier. Slowly, inexorably, he worked his way in and somewhere along the way he stopped being so careful and she stopped worrying about pain versus pleasure, because the pleasure was back and it was constant.

She tilted her hips and he groaned and she thought he might have been seated to the hilt, but then he wrapped his hand beneath one of her knees and brought her leg up and thrust, and *now* he was all the way in and it was tight, and breathtakingly good.

For her, at any rate.

It was more intimate than anything she'd ever experi-enced with him. His previous lessons in sexual exploration had been fun, heady and all too often overwhelming. This was soul-stealing.

She would have more of it.

She drew him closer, sipped delicately at his lips and then licked within. He'd never been more beautiful to her than he was at this moment, his tightly controlled movements bound only by his will.

'Please,' she whispered, because surely he needed more than this. His focus had never wavered from his quest to make this good for her, not once. When did he get to let go and feel? 'I'm really, *really* ready.'

His lips quirked above hers. 'What would you have me do?'

'Move.'

The man could follow direction when he wanted to. He raised himself to his knees, still inside her, one hand to her hip and the other to her nub, and he moved. Every stroke sent a tremor through her, every slide and every breath wound her tighter as he coaxed her to a rhythm she somehow already knew. Sensation piled in on her—it was too much, too good, and she wasn't a quiet lover, she discovered, but neither was Theo. The flush on his cheekbones had spread down his neck and across his chest, a sheen of sweat made his skin glow, and there was nothing she wanted more than to see him come undone.

'Tell me what you need.' His voice was hoarse but his eyes spoke true. He meant it.

'Give me all of you.' They were thoughtless words but true. He stilled above her and then with a groan that choked out like a sob he let go of his restraint.

It took him less than half a dozen savage thrusts before she felt her body clamp around him. She tightened unbearably as the rest of her scattered to the four winds.

There was no thought beyond this, and him, and when he followed moments later she could have sworn she could feel him spilling into her, claiming and being claimed in equal measure.

'This. I need this, whatever this is,' she whispered against his shoulder and his arms tightened around her. 'Let me love you.'

CHAPTER TEN

MORIANA WAS SILENT in the aftermath, but it wasn't the comfortable, sated silence a man could fall asleep in. This silence was prickly, tense, and for the first time in forever Theo wondered if he'd done wrong by a woman sexually. Had he been too reckless, too forceful, too greedy? Or all of those things? Because with Moriana involved all bets were off. Smoothness deserted him and neediness ruled.

Self-control fled when passion crept in.

He could barely believe she was his.

She'd curled into his side, her cheek to his shoulder and her hair a rampant tumble of curls. Her limbs were curled around his and the evidence of their joining lay wet between them both.

'You okay?' he asked gruffly, when what he wanted to ask was, *Was I good enough for you? Do you still want me the way you did before? Have you changed your mind about all this?*

He tightened his arm around her and ran his fingers over the knuckles of the hand she'd placed on his chest, which led him to the ring she wore, the one he'd chosen for his Queen. It was about time he admitted to himself that Moriana had always been there in the back of his mind. Practically perfect. Unobtainable. Already taken.

And claimed now, by him.

He turned, ever so slightly, and pressed a kiss into her hair. 'Have I rendered you speechless?'

'No, just sated. And thinking.'

'Thinking what?'

'That making love to you was more than I ever imagined. And I imagined a lot.'

He could stand to hear a little more. He brushed his fingers over her ring, loving that she'd chosen to wear it. 'When did you decide?'

'Oh.' Her fingers curled into themselves a little but he wasn't having it; he wanted their fingers entwined and now they were. 'Well. Today some time, around about the time you delivered that foal, or a little bit before then. After letting me at the Crown Jewels but before the dinner. And then the petition to remove you because you weren't married got resurrected and I figured—'

'You figured *what*?'

'I figured now would be a good time to tell you I was ready,' she said.

He pulled away. Not hard but enough for him to see her face. Such a beautiful face. The one that now haunted his dreams.

'You knew the petition had landed.'

'I—'

He could see the truth in her eyes.

'I knew,' she said.

'Get up.' True rage had always settled on him cold rather than hot. 'Get dressed. I don't need you to marry me because it's your royal duty to shore up my reign.'

'I'm not.'

'Get up! Get dressed. And *get out*. Do you think I want you to do this because duty compels you to? Moriana the perfect, Moriana the good. For God's sake, for once in your life *do what you want!*'

'I did! I am! And if you can't see that you're blind. I love you, Theo. Wholly and without caveats, but no. You can't have that. I'd get too close.' She picked up his trousers and threw them at him. '*You* get out. You're the one who can't stand being here with me like this. Give you a reason, any reason, to mistrust a person and you're there, filling in the blanks. You did it with Benedict. You're doing it with me. So get out and take your conspiracies with you and leave me alone.'

He got up. He put his trousers on and reached for his shirt. 'Moriana—'

'Get out! You don't *see* what other people want you to see. You couldn't accept love if someone laid it at your feet. Benedict loves you. I love you, but no. You can't see past your own towering mistrust.'

'Moriana, I—'

'Please go.' She picked up her dress. 'I don't want to talk to you right now. Just go. And in the morning I'll go.' He looked at her, just looked at her, and, to his utmost horror, got to see Moriana, perfect Princess of Arun, break wide open.

'For heaven's sake, Theo, get out,' she screamed. *'Can't you see I'm giving you exactly what you want?'*

He got out.

He went back to his rooms and sent Aury to her, and Sam to her, and food to her. Everything he could think of except himself.

And then he too held his head in his hands and broke.

She should have seen it coming. Moriana stood at a window in the Queen's suite and looked out over the grounds below, bathed in soft morning light. She'd showered already this morning, and twice last night, but her body still ached in places it had never ached before, and her feelings kept slipping to the surface, bringing hot tears she couldn't afford to show. She *had* seen this coming—Theo's inability to let her into his life and share his innermost thoughts and feelings. And then she'd gone and fallen deeply in love with him anyway.

She's it for me.

That was the moment she'd lost all caution. But those words weren't the same as *I'll fight my demons for you.* They weren't *I'll never hurt you.* Quite the opposite, in fact.

Moriana stared down at the ring on her finger, tracing it with unsteady fingers, twisting it round and round. She'd take it off soon and leave it sitting on the dresser in its box. Engaged for less than twenty-four hours. A new record for Moriana of Arun. The illustrious members of the press were going to crucify her and she could barely raise the will to care.

Let them.

'Milady, will you be breakfasting with the King this morning or shall I see to it that breakfast is served here?' said a voice from the far corner of the room, and she turned and there stood Aury in the doorway, still sleepy and dressed in her nightgown. Aury, who'd come for Moriana last night and got her back to the Queen's quarters with a minimum amount of fuss, and who'd then firmly shut everyone else out and earned Moriana's undying gratitude.

And then Aury had left too, with a sympathetic smile and eyes sure with the knowledge that some things were best worked through alone.

Breakfast. Right. She'd never felt less hungry but it was the principle of the matter. Hearts got given and sometimes those holding them didn't know how to keep them safe, and the sun still rose.

'I'll be having breakfast here, please, Aury. Just some fruit and coffee.'

'No bacon?' Aury shot her a pleading look. 'Bacon on sourdough, with the heritage tomatoes and mushrooms from the gardens. Not that I'm mourning the impending loss of such bounty. At all.'

'All right, that too. And the yoghurt and the passionfruit and the black sapote.'

'Oh, *yes*,' said Aury. 'And about that outfit you're wearing... It's perfect. Very sensual. Very confident.'

'Good.' Because she wasn't inclined to take it off. The sundress was another from her never-worn-before collection, bright orange and red silks and chiffons, unapologetically fitted to make the most of her curves, and she'd pulled her hair into an untamed ponytail and secured it with a white silk scarf. 'It's the new me.' Moriana liked being confident in her sensuality, a virgin no more. 'I guess I have Theo to thank for that.'

'Or we could call him an emotionally stunted imbecile and not thank him at all,' offered Aury. 'Just a thought.'

But Moriana shook her head and turned back to the view out of the window and the weak sun on her face. 'Let's not. Theo's taught me a lot this week, and a lot of it was good.' He'd encouraged her to think more of herself and she couldn't regret that. He'd shown her how to embrace her sensuality and make a man fall apart in her arms and she'd never regret that. He'd stolen her heart, and that was unfortunate given that he didn't seem to want it, but at least now she knew love in all its passionate, painful brightness.

And she refused to regret that.

Only the wearing of the ring had been a mistake, and that was easily fixed. All she had to do was take it off.

Word came with breakfast that Theo's helicopter would be at her disposal from nine a.m. onwards. Aury received the message in silence and Moriana acknowledged it with a cool nod. Only when Moriana bade the guards to leave the room and shut the door behind them did her brittle façade drop. She'd been hoping Theo would come for her this morning, ask to see her, maybe even be contrite when it came to their harsh words spoken last night. She wanted him to fight for her love. He was a fighter, was he not? A master strategist who knew what everyone else at the table wanted?

She guessed not.

She took the ring off and set it on the table and Aury looked at it and sighed. 'So that's it?'

Moriana nodded, not trusting herself to speak.

'You could talk to him,' Aury suggested carefully.

'I have talked.' And loved, and given him her all and discovered herself stronger for it. 'Marriages are built on trust and Theo trusts no one. I'm worth more than he's offering and I don't want to compromise.'

'Good for you.' But Aury looked as miserable and uncertain as Moriana felt. 'His loss.'

A knock on the door drew their attention—and Moriana's hope—but it was only the newspapers for the day and she sent them away unread.

'I've grown,' she told the uncharacteristically silent Aury.

'I'll say.'

'For the better, I hope.'

'Definitely for the better.' Aury smiled and it was small but genuine. 'So, this foreign palace for a week was adequate but ultimately unsatisfying.' She waved her hand dismissively at the chandeliers and the light streaming in through gauze-curtained windows. 'We can do far better than this. Perhaps somewhere with more sunshine and fewer kings.'

'I think perhaps the south of France.' Moriana could get behind that. 'Sun, fun and healing.'

'Please let there also be retail therapy,' added Aury.

'There can be. I'll sell a painting.'

'We could go there directly.' Aury never complained of rapid changes in plans; she embraced them. 'It would take one phone call to get the villa up and running.'

'Do it.' Maybe there could even be hedonism and debauchery and falling in love all over again with someone new.

Doubtful, but still... Better than thinking she was going there to mourn the loss of a future that would have been a perfect fit.

Had Theo loved her.

'Pack light for us both and have Sam send the rest back to Arun.' There was no point staying where she wasn't wanted. 'We leave at half nine.' Long enough to pen thank you notes for the staff who had attended her so well during her stay. Long enough to draw up a plan for exhibiting those heritage gowns and to hand it over to Letitia, who might see it done.

'Good plan,' said Aury. 'Consider it done. Would you like me to call Arun and let them know?'

'Yes, but I don't want to talk to anyone.' She couldn't deal with speaking to either Augustus or her father right now. She had no strength left for flippant defences or breezy reassurances. 'If Augustus wants to talk, he can call Theo. Tell them I'm busy seducing the unwary and I'll call once we get to France and I have a spare moment.'

'You do realise your brother will have a fit when he learns the engagement is off?' Aury warned.

'His choice.' Moriana tried to shrug off her guilt at disappointing her family and almost succeeded. 'I tried to fit in here and didn't succeed. I hurt, I bleed, I make mistakes and love unwisely. No one's perfect and I'm through with trying to be. I'm me. And they can take me or leave me.'

Theo handed Moriana into the helicopter and tried not to let his terror show. This past week had been more intense than he ever could have imagined. Laughter and luxury, anguish and self-loathing, argument and unbearable intimacy—he'd been bombarded by emotion, and he still hadn't told Moriana how much she meant to him.

Oh, he'd shown it in a thousand wordless ways but Moriana didn't speak the language he'd perfected back when there was no one to talk to and no one he could trust and the only way to show favour was by deed. He could have trusted Benedict, had he known then what he knew now, but he hadn't, and that was a stain on his conscience that was destined to spread. He trusted Moriana more than he'd ever trusted anyone, and he loved her beyond measure, but he couldn't find the words, and here he was putting her into a helicopter similar to the one that had taken his family and all he could think was *Never again*. He couldn't go through that again.

They'd travelled from palace to palace by helicopter to get here but that was different. He'd been going with her then. He wasn't the one on the ground about to look skyward.

'Don't go.'

She either hadn't heard him above the noise of the rotor blades or she didn't understand. He leaned closer, caught her arm and figured he must look like a madman. 'Go by car, by train, by damn horse—anything but this. My family died like this and my uncle arranged it. Don't leave in a helicopter. I can't stand it. I can't lose you too.'

He saw her eyes, dark and startled. And then she was out of the helicopter and tilting forward as she strode towards the castle, turning when within safe distance to draw a line across her throat for anyone watching. *This flight wasn't happening, cut the engine, stand down, at ease.*

He'd never felt less at ease.

He strode from the courtyard, Moriana silent at his side, keeping pace with him but only just. They passed Sam, who stood at the doorway but she chose not to make eye contact and neither did any of his security detail. Good call. What could he tell them that they didn't already know? The Princess wasn't leaving as arranged.

He kept his silence as they walked to his rooms. Moriana kept her confusion to herself, faltering only when they were away from prying ears and eyes and he'd shut the door behind them.

When he turned back around she stood by the fireplace, hands clasped in front of her and her stance so regal and assured that he knew she was quailing inside.

'What was that?'

That was him, trying to make things right with her, only it was entirely possible that he needed to do some more explaining. 'I didn't want you to go. Not like that.'

'Your office organised that flight. *You* authorised it.' Her voice held a hint of disbelief.

'I know. I changed my mind. I had a flashback to the day my family died and… I may have lost faith in helicopter travel. A little.'

There was no objection from her there.

'Your uncle did what?' she asked tentatively.

Theo pocketed his hands and nodded. It was now or never, and never wasn't an option with this woman. 'The day my family died I was meant to be on that helicopter too. The trip had been planned as a family outing, but I was wilder then and not always inclined to obey my parents. Benedict had turned up and talked me into going to the races with him. Fortune had favoured me—that's what they said. I had a bad case of survivor guilt—that's what Benedict said. It wasn't until years later that the information came to light that the helicopter had been tampered with and my uncle was behind it. He wanted the throne. He'd have kept it if not for me.'

'And do you think this helicopter has been tampered with too?'

'No. Nothing like that.' He'd been standing there, watching her leave, and fear had snaked into him and squeezed. 'But all of a sudden I couldn't stand to watch you leave in one. My uncle's gone. Benedict's gone. I've only just claimed you and you were leaving too. I couldn't let you.'

He wanted her to talk now, to gently guide him, to be his muse but she stayed silent.

'I always assumed that Benedict had known of his father's plans and had...saved me...or something. I realised yesterday that Benedict knew nothing. He just wanted someone to go to the races with. When Benedict realised what his father had done, and that I'd thought him complicit, he disavowed us both. Who could blame him? But it made me realise that I should have trusted him. I could have talked to him more, not kept everything to myself. That's not a mistake I want to make with you. I trust you. I need you to know what I think of you.'

'Go on,' she said warily, looking for all the world as

if she expected him to list a dozen faults in minute detail, but that wasn't where he was going with this at all.

'You think I don't know how to love you but I do,' he began. 'You don't know whether I enjoyed this past week or not but it's the best week I've ever had, and as for the sex…the sex is incandescent. I don't get lost in it the way I used to but that's only because there's never a moment when I can't see you and feel you and want you. That connection to you means everything to me. I want you at my side more than ever and I've wanted *that* since I was fourteen years old.' He took a deep breath and ploughed on. 'I love you and never want to lose you the way I've lost so many others, and sometimes that's going to mean that I haul you off a helicopter for no good reason other than I'm scared.'

'You love me?'

'So much. And I would spend my life trying to make you happy and proud of me, and maybe sometimes you'd have to poke and prod before I let you into my thoughts, but I'd do it. For you I'd do it. For us. And I know I've never asked properly, but I'm asking it of you now. Please will you marry me?'

She ventured forward, tentatively at first, but by the time she reached for his tie and wound it around her fist and reeled him in she was smiling. 'I'm going to hold you to the sharing part, and the loving part. And the having fun. And there should definitely be more lessons. Yes, I'll marry you,' she said, and kissed him and it felt like coming home.

'I'll drive you to Arun later,' he promised. 'Or we'll both go by helicopter. Okay?'

'I'm a little busy here.' Unbuttoning his shirt, yes. Why wasn't he *helping* with that? 'We should travel to Arun tomorrow.'

'We *should*.' She'd discovered his belt buckle and his rapidly rising appreciation.

'I have a form letter to write today,' she continued as she took him in hand. '*I, Moriana, the almost Perfect, take you, Theo, the mostly Magnificent*—this is where you write your name—*to have and to hold and never let go. Know that when you place your trust in me I will never let you down or give you cause to doubt my allegiance. You're mine and I'm yours and with you at my side I feel invincible.*' She smiled and he was powerless to stop himself pressing his lips to that generous curve. 'That should worry you.'

'It doesn't,' he murmured, with a kiss for the dimple at the corner of that smile.

'I'll make you proud.'

'You always do.' She didn't know her own worth but he had a lifetime in which to convince her of it. 'You make me strong.'

'You've always been that.'

'Not always.' Sometimes he'd been lost. 'I've never been surer of anyone. I've never been more prepared to make a spectacle of myself in pursuit of you. I love you.'

She lifted her hand to his cheek and brought her forehead to his. 'I love you too.'

CHAPTER ELEVEN

MORIANA LOOKED IN the gilt-edged mirror and a royal bride stared back at her. The gown glowed with a faint ivory sheen, the bodice and waist crafted to fit and the skirt flaring gently to flow like water when she walked. Her tiara glittered with centuries-old Arunian diamonds and her veil was currently pushed back to show her face. Today was the day and although Letitia fussed and Aury sighed, Moriana had never missed her mother more.

It was four weeks to the day since Theo had buried his uncle, with full State Honours. Three weeks and six days since Theo and Benedict had settled their differences by getting royally drunk after the funeral and facing off against each other in the palace vegetable garden, wielding antique swords and shields that neither of them could lift and wearing helmets that rendered them blinder than they already were.

They'd been aided in their reconciliation efforts by their capable and significantly less inebriated seconds, namely one Princess Moriana of Arun, who stood for the King, and commoner Enrique Cordova, who stood for Prince Benedict. Moriana liked Enrique—he balanced Benedict's acerbic wit and volatile disposition with dry good humour and unshakeable calm.

Theo had knighted Enrique just prior to the duel, although to what Order was anyone's guess. No one remembered the finer points.

What Moriana did remember was Benedict and Theo stretched out on the ground staring at the sky and ragged words dredged from somewhere deep within both of them.

Words like, 'I still love him, even though I hate him for what he did.'

Words like, 'You could stay on. You and your Knight.'

By morning Theo had a best man and Benedict had his cousin back. In the past weeks they'd reconnected and Liesendaach had loudly rejoiced that the rift that had come between the two cousins these past years had been mended.

Long live antique swords, alcohol and forgiveness.

If Theo had Benedict at his side today, Moriana had Aury—who would not stop nervously double-guessing the stylists and dressers until forced to desist by the ever-wise Letitia. The older woman took control, and by the time they were ready to leave for the cathedral both bride and bridesmaid looked their absolute best.

The spectacle that greeted them as they stepped from the palace and headed for the closed bridal carriage made the breath catch in her throat. She'd grown used to having a mounted guard these past three weeks as she'd journeyed from Arun's palace to Liesendaach's. She and three hundred of Arun's finest black warhorses had been met at the border of the two countries by three hundred of Liesendaach's matching greys—and then all six hundred mounted guards had accompanied her the rest of the way, with the big greys leading the way and the black steeds protecting the rear.

A circus had nothing on the last three weeks of travel. On the jousting and melee demonstrations the horsemen put on each evening for the gathering crowds. On the way Theo often turned up at the end of the day and rode with her for the last hour so that when they stopped he could help her from her horse and lavish her with a meal provided by a local hotelier or innkeeper.

Today, though, the mounted guards had opted for a different formation. The six steeds pulling the carriage were all black, but the rest of the guards had formed in groups of four. Grey, black, black, grey—two countries entwined and stronger for it.

She had all of this and at the end of the day she would have a man who worshipped her body and kept her warm and looked at her as if she hung the moon.

It was two hours to the cathedral, with the horses moving at a fast walk. They'd debated taking a car instead but Moriana had insisted that tradition be upheld. They had water in the carriage and biscuits that would leave no stain if dropped on clothes. They had a computer and could watch the procession on the news, and wasn't that a surreal experience? Watching an aerial view of the crowds lining the streets, and the horses and her father and brother at the head of the guard coming into view, being talked about in glowing terms, and then seeing the carriage come into view and knowing she was *in* the carriage.

She watched as various guests made their way into the cathedral. Watched as Theo and Benedict arrived by Bentley and smiled and joked as they strode up the steps, only for the cathedral to then swallow them too.

The press were being more than kind to Moriana today—it seemed she could do no wrong. From her choice of wedding gown, courtesy of the coffers of Liesendaach's costume collection, to the clear happiness of King Theodosius—every wedding choice she'd made had been celebrated and embraced.

The old Moriana would have revelled in the honeymoon period with the press. The new Moriana had been too damn *happy* to give it more than a passing thought.

And then it was time to touch up her make-up and bring the veil down over her face, and to take her bouquet of white roses from their storage place and let Aury alight before her to pave the way for Moriana's appearance.

With her father on one side and her brother on the other, she stepped out of the carriage and into first her father's arms and then her brother's.

'Do you feel loved yet?' Augustus asked drily, because as far as he was concerned the past three weeks had been one long, loving, expensive farewell. 'Or would you like even more adulation?'

'You can tell me I'd make our mother proud of me today and that you're going to miss me like crazy,' she suggested, and blinked back sudden tears when her ultra-reserved brother did exactly that.

The veil brushed her face as Aury made last-minute adjustments to its fall. Finally the flowers, veil, the train of her gown, *everything* was perfect as Moriana started up the stairs on her father's arm. They stopped at the cathedral doors and waited for the signal to continue.

Moriana had practised for this moment. In the flesh and in her head, more times than she could count. But nothing had prepared her for the roar of the crowd and the butterflies in her heart as the bishop appeared and beckoned them inside.

'Are you ready?' asked her father quietly.

'I love him.'

'Then you're ready.'

She didn't remember how she walked up that aisle, only that the choir sounded like angels and the ceiling soared and light shone down on everyone from behind stained glass windows and not for a moment did she falter. Theo was waiting for her, Theo was there, in full black military uniform, weighed down with military braid, medals and insignias. He was every inch the royal figurehead, and then he turned to her and smiled and it was wicked and ever so slightly sweet, and *there* was the man she wanted to spend the rest of her life with.

She remembered very little of kneeling and taking her vows. She did remember the ring sliding onto her finger and sliding a similar ring onto Theo's finger and she definitely remembered the lifting of her veil and the wonder in Theo's eyes as he kissed her.

'You're mine now.' His hands trembled in hers and she was grateful for that tiny show of frailty, just for her. It matched her own.

'I really am. For the rest of our lives.'

'I love you,' he whispered as they turned to face the congregation and beyond. 'And I'm yours.'

* * * * *

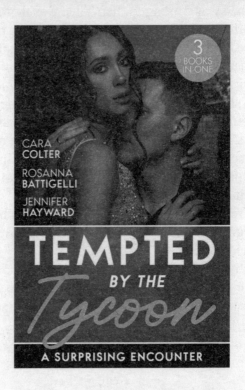

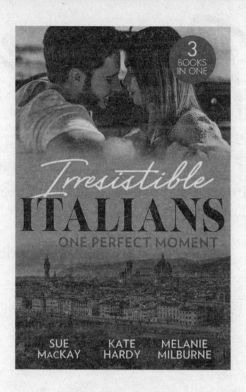

LET'S TALK

Romance

For exclusive extracts, competitions
and special offers, find us online:

f facebook.com/millsandboon

🐦 @MillsandBoon

📷 @MillsandBoonUK

♪ @MillsandBoonUK

Get in touch on 01413 063 232

For all the latest titles coming soon, visit
millsandboon.co.uk/nextmonth

MILLS & BOON

THE HEART OF ROMANCE

A ROMANCE FOR EVERY READER

MODERN
Prepare to be swept off your feet by sophisticated, sexy and seductive heroes, in some of the world's most glamourous and romantic locations, where power and passion collide.

HISTORICAL
Escape with historical heroes from time gone by. Whether your passion is for wicked Regency Rakes, muscled Vikings or rugged Highlanders, awaken the romance of the past.

MEDICAL
Set your pulse racing with dedicated, delectable doctors in the high-pressure world of medicine, where emotions run high and passion, comfort and love are the best medicine.

True Love
Celebrate true love with tender stories of heartfelt romance, from the rush of falling in love to the joy a new baby can bring, and a focus on the emotional heart of a relationship.

Desire
Indulge in secrets and scandal, intense drama and sizzling hot action with heroes who have it all: wealth, status, good looks…everything but the right woman.

HEROES
The excitement of a gripping thriller, with intense romance at its heart. Resourceful, true-to-life women and strong, fearless men face danger and desire - a killer combination!

To see which titles are coming soon, please visit

millsandboon.co.uk/nextmonth

JOIN US ON SOCIAL MEDIA!

Stay up to date with our latest releases, author news and gossip, special offers and discounts, and all the behind-the-scenes action from Mills & Boon...

 @millsandboon

 @millsandboonuk

 facebook.com/millsandboon

 @millsandboonuk

It might just be true love...